Afraid

D0318117

About the author

Mandasue Heller was born in Cheshire and moved to Manchester in 1982. There, she found the inspiration for her novels: she spent ten years living in the infamous Hulme Crescents and has sung in cabaret and rock groups, seventies soul cover bands and blues jam bands. She still lives in the Manchester area with her musician partner.

MANDASUE HELLER

Afraid

HODDER

First published in 2015 by Hodder & Stoughton
An Hachette UK company

First published in paperback in 2015 by Hodder & Stoughton

1

A CIP catalogue record for this title
is available from the British Library

ISBN 978 1 444 76955 5

Typeset in Plantin Light by Palimpsest Book Production Limited,
Falkirk, Stirlingshire

Printed and bound by Clays Ltd, St Ives plc

Hodder & Stoughton policy is to use papers that are natural,
renewable and recyclable products and made from wood
grown in sustainable forests. The logging and manufacturing
processes are expected to conform to the environmental
regulations of the country of origin.

Hodder & Stoughton Ltd
Carmelite House
50 Victoria Embankment
London EC4Y 0DZ
www.hodder.co.uk

This book is dedicated to my precious mum,
Jean; my children, Michael, Andrew, and
Azzura; my grandchildren, Marissa,
Lariah, and Antonio; and, of course,
my man, Win. You are the flames
that leap in my heart, and
I love you all dearly.

As always, much love to my and Win's families: Ava, Amber, Martin, Jade, Reece, Kyro, Diaz, Auntie Doreen, Pete, Lorna, Cliff, Chris, Glen, Joseph, Mavis, Nats, Dan, Lauren, Toni, Valerie, Jascinth, Donna and their children.

Love and thanks to my ace agent, Sheila Crowley; and to everyone at Hodder, especially Carolyn Caughey, who is so much more than a brilliant editor; Nick Austin, and Cat Ledger.

And love to dear friends: Norman, Betty and Ronnie, Kimberley, Liz, Katy and John, Rowetta, Jac and Brian Capron, Ann Mitchell, Angela Lonsdale, Hilary Devey, Martina and Wayne Brookes.

Big thanks to Jennifer for the Social Services advice. Thanks also to the buyers, readers, libraries, and my FB & T friends.

And, lastly, a special mention to the Crescents crew, especially those lost but never forgotten: Jaynie, Karen, Ray, Dino, Carole – to name but a few.

Live fully, love deeply, and laugh often, my friends. We get one shot, and this is it.

PROLOGUE

'Oscar, come!'

Bob Wilks shielded his eyes with his hand and peered down the muddy bank to the litter-strewn path which verged the stream below. He had taken his dog for its usual early-morning walk through the woods but it had decided to go exploring and, while Bob could still hear it snuffling around, he could no longer see it.

He glanced at his watch. It was almost eight a.m. His wife would soon be awake, and he needed to be home before she took it into her head to try to go to the toilet on her own again. The last time, she had slipped and fractured her elbow. Bob still felt guilty, despite everyone insisting that it wasn't his fault.

'Oscar!' he called again. 'Come on, boy, we've got to go.'

The dog was making little whining noises now. Afraid that the dozy creature might have got itself entangled in something, Bob carefully made his way down the bank. He slid the last few feet, and just about managed to stay upright as he landed on the narrow strip of ground at the water's edge.

The dog's head was buried in the grass a couple of hundred yards away, its tail sticking up in the air. It was foraging, and Bob hoped it wasn't worrying a rabbit or some other small creature. He knew it was nature, but he hated seeing animals in distress and he really didn't have the time to rescue it *or* put it out of its misery.

'Leave it,' he ordered as he approached. 'Let's go.'

The dog wagged its tail at the sound of his voice but carried on digging and whining. Bob pushed the long grass aside and saw an ancient sewage-outlet pipe, the mouth of which was stacked with debris that had gathered there over the years. Guessing that Oscar had probably chased a rat into the pipe and was trying to go after it, Bob gripped the dog's collar and tried to tug him away. But, just as he was about to clip the lead on, something caught his eye that caused him to freeze for a second.

Sure that he had imagined what he'd glimpsed, Bob reached into his inside pocket for his key-ring torch. He leaned forward and directed the faint beam at the heap of tin cans and bottles that were snagged behind a mangled bicycle wheel. As his vision sharpened, a sickly taste flooded his mouth. He tried to tell himself that it was an animal that had crawled into the pipe and died, but no animal he'd ever seen had long blonde hair like that.

'Oh dear lord!' Legs almost giving way with shock, Bob staggered back onto the path. 'Oscar!' he barked when the dog seized the opportunity to go back to its digging. '*Stop that!*'

The dog obeyed and Bob quickly clipped its lead on. Then, hands shaking wildly, he fumbled his mobile phone out of his pocket.

'Police!' he blurted out when his call was answered. 'I've found a body. I th-think it's a young girl.'

I

Skye Benson pulled her pillow down around her ears to block out the sound of her parents arguing in the living room below. It didn't work. No matter how hard she pressed, she could still hear every word.

When the sound of smashing glass filtered up through the floorboards, followed by several loud bangs, she sat up and checked the time on her small bedside clock. Almost two a.m. Were they *crazy*? Their landlord had already threatened to evict them if they disturbed the neighbours in the early hours again. Luckily, the old man who lived to their right was in hospital, so he couldn't grass them up again; and the students on their left were always too stoned to care. But if the fight got any louder the whole street would soon be up.

Skye lay back down and pulled her quilt right up over her head, whispering '*Stop it, stop it, stop it*' over and over, as if the mantra would actually have an effect. There was no way she was going down there after what had happened the last time. She had been hit in the face by a flying ashtray, and they had asked so many questions at the hospital that she'd been terrified they were going to lock her mum and dad up for life. And her parents had obviously thought the same, because they had both acted really sorry when she got home. Her mum had fussed over her all the next day, fetching her drinks and dinner in bed; and on his way home from work her dad had bought some magazines for her to read in bed, along with a big bag of mixed sweets. Treats like those were rare in their house, so Skye had relished it while it lasted. But the small scar on her cheek was a permanent reminder of the pain and fear she'd felt that night, so she had never made the mistake of interfering again.

Her mum was screaming now, and Skye squeezed her eyes shut. When she could no longer stand the smell of her own damp breath she pushed the quilt off her face, rolled over and slid her laptop out from under the bed. It belonged to the school, and every kid in her year had been loaned one some months earlier as part of the new headmaster's stupid plan to drag them into the modern world. He'd thought that getting the pupils to do their homework online would eradicate the 'forgot it, sir . . . dog ate it, miss' excuses, and get the kids interested in learning. But it hadn't worked out too well so far. Sammy Green and Matthew Fletcher had claimed that theirs had been stolen, but Skye knew they had sold them to a guy in the pub on their estate. And most of the other kids just used them to faff about on Facebook and Twitter, or to watch porn.

They hadn't had internet access in Skye's house since her mum, during one of her scarier episodes, had declared it the Devil's tool to trap souls and had closed their account, so Skye hadn't been particularly excited about having a laptop. She certainly hadn't bothered doing any stupid homework on it. Then, one day, she'd been messing about with it in her room and had accidentally discovered that the students next door hadn't password-protected their WiFi. She'd been secretly logging on via their signal ever since; she just had to be super careful to cover her tracks after a session, because her mum would totally hit the roof if she ever found out.

She covered the laptop with her quilt now, and signed into Facebook. As she'd expected, given the time, her best friend Hayley wasn't online, so she switched to her *WhisperBox* account instead. She and Hayley had found this site after they had been caught slagging off some girls from school on Facebook and had got into a massive fight, and they used it whenever they wanted to gossip, safe in the knowledge that no one who knew them would ever suss that it was them behind the screen-names BlueBabe and Sugarplum.

Skye usually only went on this site in the evening, when it was mainly girls online, chatting about boys, make-up and music; but it seemed to be mostly boys right now, and their talk of football and sex both bored and disgusted her.

About to log out again, she hesitated when her *Whisper* button started to flash, indicating that someone wanted to talk to her in a private side-room. She clicked into it and smiled when she saw that it was *QTPye*: a girl she and Hayley had met in the open room a few months earlier.

Hey BlueBabe, QTPye's message read. *Surprised to see you on here so late. Where's Sugarplum?*

Probably in bed, Skye replied. *She wasn't well today so she didn't come to school.*

What's up with her?

Think she's got a cold.

Another one?

Yeah, I know, typed Skye, a twinge of guilt causing her to chew on her lip as she added, *Feel dead sorry for her sometimes.* In truth, she actually thought that Hayley put these colds on for sympathy, because she was always moaning that she didn't feel well, and had stayed off school three times this term already. Skye didn't believe that anyone could catch so many colds, but she didn't blame Hayley for trying it on, and she'd probably do the same if she thought she could get away with it. But her mum wasn't as soft as Hayley's, so she had no chance. She'd have to be dying before her mum would believe that she was too ill to go to school. And even then, her mum would probably bring her schoolwork in to the hospital and force her to do it on her deathbed.

Still, whether or not Hayley was lying, she was her best mate, and Skye wasn't about to betray her by dissing her to QTPye.

Oh well, hope she gets better soon, QTPye typed now. *What you up to?*

Can't sleep, Skye told her, glad that the subject had been changed.

S'up? Folks at it again?

Yep.

Leave them to it, babes. Not worth the hassle.

I know. Just pisses me off.

Tell me about it, QTPye sympathised. *Mine have been going at it all day as well. Wish they'd grow up and get a life instead of wrecking mine, selfish bastards.*

Horrible, isn't it?

The pits! But at least we've got each other, and you know you can talk to me about anything, don't you?

Yeah, I know, Skye replied gratefully. *It's great having someone who understands what I'm going through.*

I'm always here for you, babes, you know that.

Skye smiled when she read that. Like herself and Hayley, QTPye was fourteen, and had the same taste in music and boys. Hayley wasn't so keen on her, but Skye suspected she was just jealous that they got on so well and was scared that they'd get too close and push her out. She didn't want to upset Hayley, but she liked the other girl and didn't see why she should have to stop being friends with her. Anyway, QTPye's parents were also going through a rough patch, so she understood Skye in a way that Hayley, whose own parents were happy, never would.

About to type a reply now, Skye hesitated when she heard footsteps on the stairs. When, seconds later, a floorboard on the landing outside her door creaked, she quickly closed the laptop lid and pretended to be asleep in case her mum or dad looked in on her. They didn't, and she listened as which-ever one of them it was went into their own room. Drawers were opened and closed, and then the footsteps thundered back down the stairs, followed by the sound of the front door slamming shut.

Skye raised herself up on her elbow and eased the curtain aside in time to see her dad walk out onto the pavement below. A car's headlights flashed in the darkness at the other end of the road, and when he walked quickly towards it she guessed that he must have ordered a taxi to take him to his mate's place. That was what he usually did when things went as far as they had tonight, and she was glad, because at least it meant it was over.

As she watched her dad throw his work-bag onto the back seat of the car, Skye heard her mum sweeping up whatever had been smashed in the living room below. She was sobbing quietly as she did it, but Skye couldn't summon up much sympathy for her right now. She was okay when she took her tablets regularly, but when she forgot, or decided that she was better and didn't need them any more, she turned into a right cow, and Skye kind of understood why her dad ended up snapping. *Any*one would if they were pushed as far as her mum pushed him at times.

Still, it was a relief that her dad had taken to walking out after a fight, instead of waiting for her mum to call the police. Skye hated it when the cops came round, because they always got her out of bed to quiz her about what she'd heard and check if she'd been involved. She always had to lie and say that she had been asleep and had heard nothing, but she was always terrified that she might slip up and drop her parents in it – which was almost as stressful as having to listen to it in the first place.

When the car had driven away, Skye let the curtain drop and reopened the laptop to tell QTPye what was happening. She was disappointed to see that the girl's light had turned red, but she figured it was probably just as well. If she didn't get some sleep, she'd be so tired tomorrow that she would probably doze off in class and get put on report for a week.

Everything will be okay tomorrow, she told herself as she closed the laptop down and slid it back under the bed. *Dad will come home from work and act as if nothing's happened, and Mum will start taking her pills again, and then everything will go back to normal.*

Until the next time.

Annoyed with herself for allowing the unwelcome thought to creep in, Skye flopped down in the bed and dragged her quilt back up over her head.

2

The house was silent when Skye went downstairs the next morning, and she guessed that her mum had probably drunk herself to sleep after her dad had left, and wouldn't surface again until later in the afternoon. Glad that she'd already put on her shoes when she heard glass crunch underfoot as she walked into the living room, she shook her head in disgust when she saw that the mirror above the fireplace had been smashed. The frame was hanging askew on the wall, and the shattered glass was sitting in a pile beside the fireplace, but tiny shards still littered the carpet so she tiptoed through them and went into the kitchen.

There was yet more evidence of the fight in there. Pieces of smashed cups and plates were scattered around the ledges and floor, the kettle was in the sink, and the fridge door was dented as if it had been punched. Depressed by the sight of it, and annoyed with her parents for wrecking what little was left of their home, Skye decided not to bother checking if there was anything for breakfast and, grabbing her schoolbag, headed angrily out.

Three girls were standing beside the entrance to the path at the rear of the school when Skye rounded the corner a short time later. A cloud of smoke was hovering in the air above their heads from the cigarette they were sharing, and she could hear them laughing at some younger kids who they were taking the piss out of. She pulled the hood of her jacket up over her head and scuttled past, hoping that they would be too preoccupied to notice her. But she hadn't taken two steps down the path when a painful blow landed between her shoulder blades.

'Where do you think you're going, you scruffy bitch?' Janet Hampson stepped in front of her and gave her a vicious shove in the chest.

'School,' Skye muttered, her gaze flicking nervously between each of the three girls. They were in the year above her, and they were the hardest girls in the school so everyone was scared of them.

'Where's my money?' Janet demanded, a nasty glint in her eye.

'Wh-what money?' asked Skye, conscious that a crowd was beginning to form behind them.

'*My* money!' Janet seized her by the throat and shoved her up against the hedge that bordered the pathway. 'You think you can walk this way without asking my permission or paying a toll?'

'I don't know what you mean,' Skye spluttered, wincing as the girl's fake nails dug into her neck.

'I *own* this path,' Janet informed her. 'And no one gets to come this way without my say-so.'

Tears of humiliation flooding her eyes when she heard laughter from the crowd, Skye said, 'I'm sorry, I didn't know. I'll go the other way.'

'Too late,' said Janet, enjoying herself too much to let her victim go just like that. 'You've trespassed, so now you'll have to pay a fine. It's a tenner. Pay up.'

'I haven't got any money,' Skye whimpered, hating herself for being so weak.

'Oh dear,' Janet drawled nastily. 'Well, you'll have to pay some other way, then, won't you?'

'Can I give it to you tomorrow?' Skye pleaded, terrified that she was about to get her head kicked in.

'Nah, I want it now,' Janet replied coldly. Then, her lips twisting with spite as an idea came to her, she said, 'Take your skirt off.'

'What? *No*!' Skye's cheeks turned scarlet as she clocked some boys grinning in anticipation.

'You fuckin' what?' Janet bared her teeth and dug her nails in deeper. 'You daring to disobey me, you little slag?'

Sickened by the smell of stale tobacco on Janet's breath, and terrified that her windpipe would snap if the girl squeezed any harder, Skye felt as if she was about to faint.

'What's going on down there?' a voice suddenly boomed from the school end of the path. 'Get yourselves inside immediately. Anyone who's late for registration will be on detention for a week!'

It was the headmaster, Mr Talbot, and even Janet – as tough as she liked to think she was – didn't have the guts to ignore his command, because she immediately let go of Skye.

'One word and you're dead,' she hissed as she backed away. 'And you'd best have twenty quid for me first thing tomorrow – or else.'

She merged in with the crowd now, and moved off down the path. Mr Talbot clapped his hands to hurry them along.

Over their heads, he spotted Skye disentangling herself from the hedge, and raised his arm. 'You, there!' he called, clicking his fingers at her. 'Come here.'

Skye dipped her head as she approached him, desperate to hide her tears and the marks that Janet's nails had left on her neck, because he'd be bound to guess what had happened if he saw them.

When she reached him, Mr Talbot peered down at her with thinly concealed distaste. This was a deprived area, so a lot of his pupils fell short of his presentation and hygiene expectations. But this girl, with her lank hair, unhealthy pallor, scuffed shoes and grubby uniform, looked particularly unkempt.

'Have you been fighting?' he demanded.

'No, sir.' Skye shook her head. 'I just tripped and fell into the hedge.'

Mr Talbot didn't believe her, but before he could quiz her further the school bell rang and he remembered that he had a meeting to get to. 'Right, in you go.' He waved her on her way. 'And don't run or you'll be going on report.'

Relieved to be off the hook, Skye walked quickly to her form room. If Mr Talbot had pushed for answers, she might have accidentally dropped Janet in it – and that would have been as good as signing her own death warrant. As it was, she still had to get her hands on twenty quid by tomorrow morning or she was in for a kicking at the very least. She had no idea how she was going to manage it, and the worry pressed down on her like a lead weight for the rest of the day.

When the home-time bell rang, she hid in the toilets until she was sure that everyone had left the premises. Then, scared that Janet and her friends might be waiting out back, she left by the front gate. It was the long way home, but at least she'd get there in one piece, and that was all she cared about right now.

Hayley was dozing, but she forced herself to wake up when she heard that Skye had come to visit.

'Ten minutes,' Kathy Simms cautioned as she waved her daughter's friend into the bedroom. 'The doctor said she needs to rest.'

Skye nodded and smiled politely, but the smile slipped as soon as the door closed, and she felt a twinge of envy nibble at her stomach as she gazed around. Her own room was decorated with shabby mismatched furniture that belonged to their landlord; the dresser drawers were dodgy, the wallpaper was ripped and showed patches of damp in every corner, and her lumpy mattress had probably been slept on by a thousand people before her. In contrast, Hayley's room was every princess's dream; from the silky pink wallpaper and pretty white furniture, to the comfortable-looking bed with its plump pillows and thick duvet. But it was the small flat-screen TV sitting on the chest of drawers facing the bed that really irked Skye. They didn't even have a TV as good as that in the living room at their house, never mind one all for herself in her bedroom.

Hayley was peering up at Skye from the bed. 'Are you okay?' she asked when she saw the look on her face.

'What?' Skye shook herself out of it and turned around. She immediately felt guilty for having thought that Hayley was putting her illness on when she saw how pale she was, and how dark the rings around her eyes. 'Sorry,' she apologised, perching on the edge of the bed. 'It's been a crap day. But never mind me, how are you? You look terrible.'

'Wow, thanks.' Hayley gave a weak smile and pushed herself up on her pillows. 'I'm so sick of these chest infections. It's like I only have to look at someone blowing their nose and I catch another one.'

'What's the doctor said?'

'The usual.' Hayley shrugged. 'Rest, drink loads of water,

and take my antibiotics. Anyway, I don't want to talk about that. What's up with you?'

'Had a run-in with Janet Hampson and her bulldogs,' Skye told her. 'The bitch jumped me this morning and said I had to pay to go down the path.'

'Cheeky cow!' Hayley was indignant. 'What did you do?'

'Told her to piss off,' Skye lied. Then, rolling her eyes, she admitted, 'Nothing I *could* do, was there? I stood no chance against the three of them.' She looked down at her feet now, and chewed on her lip for a moment before saying, 'Can you lend us twenty quid?'

'*Twenty?*' Hayley's eyebrows shot up. 'That's a bit much, isn't it? What do you need it for?'

'Nothing, it doesn't matter,' Skye said miserably. 'I shouldn't have asked.'

Hayley frowned when Skye's shoulders slumped. She'd never seen her as low as this, and Skye had never asked to borrow money before. Concerned, she said, 'What's wrong, hon?'

'Nothing,' Skye lied.

'There clearly is,' Hayley persisted. 'And you know you can tell me anything, don't you?'

Skye sniffed softly and gave a wan smile. 'That's what QTPye said last night when I told her my mum and dad were at it again. Doesn't change anything, though, does it? Talking, I mean.'

'Depends *who* you're talking to,' said Hayley, battling resentment at the thought of Skye chatting to *that* girl without her again. She knew it was unreasonable; that she had no right to expect Skye not to be friends with anyone else. But she couldn't help it. She was supposed to be Skye's best friend, and they were only supposed to tell each other their secrets, no one else.

Skye sighed and shook her head. 'Nah, it doesn't make any difference; nothing ever changes.' She stood up now and forced a smile. 'I'd best go before your mum kicks me out.'

'Wait a minute,' Hayley said decisively. 'Pass me my piggy bank.'

'No, it's okay.' Skye backed towards the door. 'It's my problem, I'll sort it.'

'If you walk out, I swear to God I'll never talk to you again,' Hayley warned.

Skye couldn't help but grin when she saw the stern expression on Hayley's face. 'Don't look at me like that,' she teased. 'You look like Mrs McCready.'

'Well, if you did as you were told instead of arguing all the time I wouldn't have to tell you off,' Hayley retorted mock-sternly. Then, softening, she said, 'Look, Skye, you're my best mate and I want to help you, so just pass me the damn piggy bank. Or do I have to get it myself?'

'Don't you dare,' Skye hissed, glancing at the door. 'Your mum'll kill me if she thinks I made you get out of bed.'

'Get it, then.'

Skye did as she'd been told and lifted the heavy piggy bank off the shelf. Sure from the weight that it must be crammed with copper coins, her eyes widened when Hayley pulled the little plastic stopper out and, sticking two fingers inside, extracted a folded wad of notes.

'Here.' Hayley peeled off a twenty and held it out. 'You don't have to tell me what it's for if you don't want to.'

'It's for Janet,' Skye admitted, gratefully taking it and slipping it into her bra. 'She said I had to give it to her first thing, or else. I'll pay you back as soon as I can – cross my heart.'

'Don't worry about it,' said Hayley, a resigned edge to her

voice as she added, 'I won't be spending it anytime soon stuck in here, will I?'

Skye frowned as she gazed down at her friend. 'No, but you'll be better soon. You're always getting colds, you; you'll fight it off in no time. Better had,' she added, smiling now. 'I'm getting fed up of walking to school on my own.'

Hayley smiled back, and gave a weak salute. 'Okay, boss, I'll do my best.' Then, remembering something, she rolled over and reached into her bedside drawer. 'Here.' She took out a tiny square wrapped in tissue paper. 'This is for you.'

'What is it?' Skye asked.

'It's your birthday on Monday,' Hayley reminded her. 'I was going to give it to you on the way to school, but it looks like I'm going to be off for another week, so I thought you'd best have it now.'

'You didn't have to get me anything,' Skye murmured, touched that she'd remembered.

'Open it,' Hayley ordered, eager to see her reaction. 'It's only little, but I thought of you as soon as I saw it.'

Skye carefully unwrapped the tissue, and gasped when a delicate silver chain with a tiny angel hanging from it fell out onto her lap. 'Oh, it's gorgeous,' she exclaimed, picking it up.

'It's your guardian angel.' Hayley beamed. 'Anytime you feel low, just touch her and make a wish and she'll put everything right.'

'That's lovely,' Skye said, unhooking the catch. 'Here, put it on for me.'

Hayley reached up and fastened the necklace around Skye's throat, and then watched as she went over to the dressing table to take a look in the mirror.

'I love it,' Skye murmured, gazing at it. 'It's the best present *ever*.'

The door opened just then, and Kathy walked in carrying a bottle and a spoon. 'Sorry, you'll have to go now,' she said to Skye. 'Hayley needs her medicine.'

'I was just going,' Skye told her. 'Thanks for letting me see her. Can I come again tomorrow?'

'We'll see.'

'I gave her the necklace,' Hayley said. 'Suits her, doesn't it?'

Kathy nodded and smiled. She hadn't been particularly pleased when Hayley had first struck up a friendship with Skye, because the girl was quite scruffy and seemed a bit rough around the edges. But since she'd learned a little about her home life, she felt sorry for her and was pleased if the necklace had given her a bit of joy.

'Hurry up and get yourself home, pet,' she said softly. 'And no dawdling. It's getting dark out there, and there are some funny people about.'

'I'll be careful,' Skye promised. Then, turning back to the bed, she leaned down and hugged her friend, whispering, 'Thanks, Hayls, you're the best.'

When she stepped out of the house a few seconds later, the cold air hit Skye like a sledgehammer. Teeth already chattering, she zipped up her jacket and shoved her hands deep into her pockets before heading home. There had been a lovely smell of cooking in the air back at Hayley's, and she hoped that her own mum had bothered to make dinner today – and, if so, that it would be something hot, for a change. She didn't mind salad every now and then, but it was all they seemed to have lately, and she didn't see why she should have to eat it just because her mum was on a diet. She wouldn't have minded so much if her mum even needed to lose weight, but she was already too skinny. It was just another symptom of her illness, though: seeing herself as fat, when everyone else saw her as thin; thinking she was hot, when everyone else was freezing. Getting paranoid that everybody was talking about her, when no one had said a word. Crazy.

The house was in darkness when Skye let herself in, and she was disappointed not to smell food. 'Mum?' she called, looping her jacket over the newel post at the bottom of the stairs. 'Are you in?'

When no answer came, she blew on her icy hands and walked down the hall to the living room. Hesitating in the doorway when she saw her mum's silhouetted figure hunched at the far end of the couch, she said, 'I thought you were out. Why are you sitting in the dark?'

'Don't turn the light on, I've got a headache.' Andrea Benson's voice sounded hoarse, as if she'd been crying.

'Has something happened?' Skye asked, immediately concerned. 'Dad hasn't hit you, has he?'

'Stop shouting,' Andrea said sharply. 'You'll wake the baby.'

'What baby?' Skye frowned. 'We haven't got a baby, Mum. It's just me – remember?'

'Oh, you'd like that, wouldn't you?' spat Andrea. 'Just because *you* can't have one, you pretend that *I* haven't got one. But you're fooling no one, Linda Harris. Everyone knows your game.'

Skye's legs began to tremble. Linda was her mum's sister, and the two had fallen out years earlier when Linda had miscarried and accused Andrea of wishing it on her. If her mum now thought that she was Linda and there was a baby in the house, it could only mean that she was having a bad episode.

'Mum, where are your tablets?' Skye asked, taking a tentative step into the room. 'Are they in your handbag? Shall I get them, then make you a nice cup of—'

She stopped talking when her foot hit something soft and heavy, and a rush of dread coursed through her when she looked down and saw the man-shaped figure on the floor.

'Dad?' she gasped. Then, hysteria rising into her throat, she stared at her mum and screamed, 'What have you *done*?'

3

Skye was in shock. She remembered having made the 999 call, but everything had happened so fast after that, it had been just a blur of flashing lights, uniforms, and people running in and out of the house.

The sound of her mum's screams when the police had handcuffed her and thrown her into the back of a van was still echoing in Skye's ears; but it was the sight of her dad lying on the floor that would haunt her for ever. She'd already known there was blood, because her hands and knees were crusted with it from when she'd kneeled down and tried to rouse him. But she hadn't realised how *much* blood until one of the coppers had turned the light on. It had looked like a scene out of a horror film, and she couldn't get the image out of her mind – even now, hours later.

The police had taken her to the station after carting her mum off, and she'd been made to wait there until somebody from Social Services came for her. Huddled in the back seat of the social worker's car now, en route to the emergency foster home where they had arranged for her to spend the night, her heart was breaking. Nobody had told her anything, and she was convinced that her dad was going to die – if he hadn't already; and it was tearing her apart to think that she might never see him again.

Desperate for it to be a bad dream, she kept digging her

nails into her leg in an effort to wake herself. But it was no dream; it was a real living nightmare, and she knew that life was never going to be the same again.

'Almost there,' Val Dunn said, glancing at Skye in the rear-view mirror. 'Are you okay?'

Skye clamped her teeth together and stared angrily out at the dark road. Every time she'd asked about her dad they had said they didn't know anything yet, but she knew they were lying. They must know *some*thing, they just didn't want to tell her because they thought she was a kid. And that really pissed her off, because she was almost fifteen and had a *right* to know what was happening with her own dad. But if they wouldn't talk to her, then she was determined not to talk to them.

Val gazed at the girl for a few more seconds before turning her attention back to the road ahead. It would have been good to know what was going through her mind, but she had clammed up back at the station, so Val could only guess how she must be feeling. She was clearly scared, which was only to be expected under the circumstances because no child enjoyed being lifted from their home and handed over to strangers. She was also angry, Val sensed; frustrated that nobody was giving her the answers she wanted. But the truth was, they simply didn't know anything yet. Skye's father had been in surgery when Val arrived at the station, and the hospital still hadn't reported back by the time she and Skye had left. She would call for an update in the morning and decide what to tell Skye depending on the news, but her priority right now was to get the child settled.

They drove on in silence for a while, and Skye didn't raise her gaze until they began to slow down. She'd known they were some distance away from her home because of how

long it had taken to get here, but when she looked out along
the tree-lined avenue and saw all the big houses she felt sick.
This was rich-people territory, and those who could afford
to live here had to be really old and posh, so they were
bound to look down their noses at her. In a way, she kind
of hoped they did, because if they refused to let her into
their house the social worker would be forced to take her
home. And that was all she wanted right now: to go home,
climb into bed, and pretend that none of this was happening.

When Val pulled onto the drive of a large detached house,
a middle-aged couple came out onto the step. Skye cast a
hooded glance at them from beneath her lashes and hated
them on sight. Some lads she knew from school had spent
time in care, and they had all said the same thing: that foster-
parents were evil bastards who acted nice in front of social
workers but turned nasty as soon as they were gone.

The woman of the couple came over to the car and opened
the back door for Skye as Val climbed out from behind the
wheel.

'Hello, love, I'm Marie. You must be Skye?'

'She's exhausted,' Val explained when Skye climbed out
sulkily without answering. 'Shall we go inside?'

'Of course.' Marie waved for Val to go ahead, and then
placed a hand on Skye's back to guide her in.

Skye recoiled from her touch and stumbled over the step,
desperate to get away from her. Marie had a soft voice and
smelled of washing powder and perfume – like Hayley's mum.
The reminder of home had brought a lump to Skye's throat,
and she swallowed hard to clear it.

The house had looked like a mansion to Skye from the
outside, but it was surprisingly cosy on the inside. The carpets
felt thick and plush underfoot, and the couches in the spacious

living room were big and comfortable-looking. The walls were lined with pictures of smiling children, and she guessed they must be foster-kids who had stayed here, because there were far too many for them to be the couple's own.

'Sit down while I have a quick word with Marie and Dennis,' Val said, gesturing towards the couches. 'We won't be long.'

Skye did as she'd been told and watched, resentfully, as the adults moved to the other end of the room and sat around a dining table. Unable to hear what they were saying, she angrily ground her teeth together. They didn't even know her, so how dare they talk about her as if they knew what was best for her.

After briefing the couple, Val came back to Skye. 'Right, I'm going to leave you to settle in,' she said. 'I've got a few meetings in the morning, but I should be free by lunchtime, so I'll come back as soon as I'm done. Anything you'd like to ask before I go?'

When Skye carried on glaring down at the floor, Val sighed and glanced at her watch. This call-out had dragged on for far longer than she'd anticipated, and she desperately wanted to go home to her own children.

As his wife went to show the social worker out, Dennis Vaughn strolled over to Skye and smiled down at her. 'Val says you haven't eaten yet, so how about I whip up some of my world-famous cheese on toast?'

Skye folded her arms over her stomach when it growled. She was starving and would have loved some cheese on toast, but there was no way she was taking anything from this stranger.

'You're probably too tired to eat,' Dennis said understandingly. 'Come on; I'll show you to your room.'

He walked towards the door and paused there, waiting for

Skye to follow. When she didn't, he said, 'I know this must be tough, and you're probably dying to go home, but everything will look brighter in the morning – I promise. And anything you want while you're here, you only have to ask. Okay?'

Marie came back just then. When she saw how miserable Skye looked, she touched Dennis's arm and whispered, 'Go on up; I'll see to her.'

When he'd gone, she went over to Skye and held out her hand. 'Come on, love, you can't sit here all night. Let's get you up to bed.'

Her voice was so soft and kind that Skye had to bite down hard on her lip to stop herself from bursting into tears. The events of the day were really starting to take their toll on her and, as much as she didn't want to be here, she was too tired to resist the lure of bed.

But she wasn't about to let them think they had won. So, maintaining the frosty expression, she ignored Marie's hand and stood up on her own.

Jeff Benson was struggling. The anaesthetic from his operation was wearing off fast, and he had a banging headache, while his body felt as if it had been trampled by a herd of elephants. The doctor who'd been to check on him a short time ago had told him he was lucky the knife hadn't gone in a couple of millimetres deeper or he'd have been buggered. As it was, he had a nasty wound that would take a while to fully heal, and he'd be on antibiotics for some time to come in order to ward off infection. Yet, for the life of him, he still couldn't remember what had happened.

Snapped from his muddled thoughts by the muffled sound of his mobile phone ringing, Jeff looked around and located it as coming from the pocket of his jacket draped over the back of the visitors' chair. Conscious of the other patients who were sleeping around the dimly lit ward, he gingerly rolled over and tugged the chair closer to the bed. Queasy at the sight of the dried blood and the jagged tear where the knife had entered, he pulled the phone out of his pocket and pushed the jacket aside.

'Where are you?' The voice shot down his ear when he answered. 'I've been trying to get hold of you for hours.'

'I'm in hospital,' Jeff said quietly, pressing the palm of his hand against his throbbing forehead.

'Oh, God, are you okay? I've been hearing all sorts, but I didn't know what to believe. Is it true you were stabbed?'

'Yeah, but I can't really talk right now,' Jeff muttered, desperate to get off the phone before his head exploded. 'Let me call you in the morning.'

'Okay. But are you all right? Is there anything you need?'

'No, I'm fine, but I've got to go. Speak tomorrow, yeah?'

Jeff cut the call and switched the phone off in case it rang again. His memory was starting to come back, and he closed his eyes as he recalled the argument he'd had with Andrea last night. It had been a nasty one, and he'd come really close to retaliating when she'd started throwing stuff at him. But he'd kept his cool and walked out, sure that she would have calmed down by the time he got home from work this afternoon. Unfortunately, she hadn't, and here he was.

A soft touch on his shoulder made him jump, and he squinted up at the nurse who was standing over him.

'Just checking you're awake,' she said quietly.

'Yeah, but I wish I wasn't,' he moaned. 'The doc said he was going to give me something for the pain, but he must have forgot. Don't suppose you could chase it up for me, could you?'

'I'll check his notes and see what I can do,' she promised. Then: 'The police have been waiting to talk to you. Are you up to it, or shall I ask them to come back tomorrow?'

Jeff swallowed deeply and shook his head. 'No, you can send them in. But don't forget the tablets, will you?'

'I'll try not to.' The nurse smiled.

Jeff groaned when two police officers walked up to his bed a couple of minutes later. He'd never met the first one before, but the second, PC Andy Jones, had attended several domestics at his place in the past, and he was one of the cuff-happiest coppers Jeff had ever come across.

'Well, this is a turn-up.' Jones peered down at him with a hint of a smirk on his lips. 'I always knew one of you would end up in hospital, but I never guessed it'd be *her* putting *you* here.'

'What are you talking about?' Jeff stared coldly back at him.

'Oh, here we go,' Jones drawled. '*Jackanory* time.'

'I'm PC Dean,' the second officer introduced himself as he pulled a chair up to the bed. 'We'd like to ask you a few questions, if that's okay?'

'Whatever,' Jeff muttered.

'Can you start by telling us what happened this afternoon?'

'And don't bother telling us it wasn't her,' Jones chipped in. 'She's already confessed.'

Dean shot a hooded look at his colleague, and said, 'We just need to hear your account of what happened, sir – in your own words.'

Jeff's mind whirred. It was a shock to hear that Andrea

had confessed, but if Jones thought that Jeff was about to grass her up then the bastard was in for a long wait.

'My wife's ill,' he said.

'Are you saying that's why she did it?' Dean asked.

'No, I'm saying that'll be why she's confessed. That's if *he*'s telling the truth and she has.' Jeff cast a scathing glance at Jones. 'Wouldn't put it past him to have beaten it out of her, knowing him. If he thinks you're guilty, he'll do anything to make it stick so he can up his arrest rate, him. Hasn't worked out too well so far, though, has it?' He directed this at Jones. 'Still only a plod, after all this time.'

Unfazed, Jones's smirk widened. 'I'm fine where I am, mate; gives me a chance to keep the druggies and dealers in line. *And* the wife-beaters,' he added pointedly.

'Okay, let's just get back to this, shall we?' Dean cut in. 'Are you saying that your wife *didn't* stab you, Mr Benson?'

'Course she didn't,' Jeff lied. 'She wouldn't hurt a fly.'

'Whatever!' Jones scoffed.

'Then can you explain why she would say that she did?' Dean persisted.

'The only reason I can think of is if *he* was the one who questioned her,' said Jeff. ''Cos if he did, he'll have put the fear of God into her.'

'And why would I do that?' Jones drawled.

'Because you get off on it,' Jeff shot back. 'I've been on the receiving end, don't forget; I know how you operate.'

No longer in the mood for playing games, Jones dropped the smirk and looked Jeff square in the eye. 'Look, Benson, we haven't got time for this, so quit the bullshit and let's get real, eh? We *know* she did it. She's admitted it, and she still had the knife in her hand when we got there.'

'So why are you bothering to question me?' Jeff challenged

him. 'Why haven't you charged her already if you're so sure she did it?'

'It doesn't work like that,' Dean interjected. 'There has to be proof; preferably a witness statement. Your daughter was the one who found you and called us, but she arrived home after the incident, so that's why we need *your* account.'

'Okay, fine,' said Jeff, thinking on his feet. 'I got jumped in the alley on my way home from work. I heard them running up behind me, but they got me before I could turn round, so I didn't see who it was. I just know it was a bloke. Maybe more than one, I'm not sure.' He shrugged.

'What a crock!' Jones sneered.

'It's the truth,' Jeff said evenly. 'And I don't give a toss if *you* believe it; that's what happened.'

'So, let's get this right,' said Jones. 'You were coming home from work, and someone jumped you and stabbed you. But they didn't take your wallet, or your phone?' His gaze flicked to the mobile that Jeff had placed on the bedside cabinet. 'They just stabbed you for the hell of it, then legged it. And you *somehow* managed to drag yourself into the house, without losing a single drop of blood along the way?'

'I guess so.' Jeff held his gaze.

'So how come there's a shitload of blood on the carpet in your place?' Jones demanded. 'And how come your missus was covered in it, *and* she was still holding the knife?'

'She must have pulled it out of my back when I went in, then freaked out when she saw the blood,' Jeff lied. 'Like I just told your mate, she's ill, and something like that would tip her over the edge.' He turned back to Dean now, and said, 'I hope she's getting help and you haven't just chucked her in a cell, 'cos that'd kill her. She needs her tablets.'

'She was being assessed by the on-call doctor when we

left the station,' Dean assured him. Then, rising to his feet, he put his notepad back in his pocket. 'I think we'll leave it at that for tonight, sir. We'll need to speak to you again at some point, but if there's anything you want to tell us in the meantime, just give us a call.'

Jeff nodded. 'Thanks, lad; will do.'

Jones stood up and peered down at Jeff with unconcealed disgust. 'You're an idiot,' he said bluntly. 'She nearly killed you, and if you let her get away with it, what's to stop her from finishing the job next time you have a scrap?'

'I've already told you it wasn't her,' Jeff replied coolly.

'And we both know you're lying,' spat Jones. 'What about that kid of yours?' he said then. 'How do you think *she* must have felt finding you like that? The poor girl's so traumatised she hasn't spoken to anyone since we picked her up. And what if it's *her* who cops for it next time? You thought about that?'

Teeth tightly gritted, Jeff said, 'Andrea would never hurt Skye. Just like she didn't do this to me.'

Furious, Jones brought his face down close to Jeff's and hissed, 'You and your missus can carry on kicking the shit out of each other until one of you ends up in the morgue, for all I care. But if anything happens to that girl because you've let her mam get away with this, I'll be blaming you. Are we clear on that?'

'He's threatening me,' Jeff said loudly to Dean.

'Andy, leave it,' Dean ordered, glancing around to see if anyone was listening. 'Let's go.'

Jones backed away from the bed, but he flashed Jeff one last look of disgust before following Dean off the ward.

Jeff flopped back against the pillow when they had gone and closed his eyes. Jones was a cunt, and Jeff hated him with a passion, but he couldn't deny what the man had said. Andrea had almost done for him this time, and there was no telling what might happen if they got into that same situation again and Skye happened to get in the way. His wife was manageable when she took her medication, but she couldn't be trusted to take it as regularly as she was supposed to – and Jeff didn't always see the warning signs before she flipped. And she must have flipped *big* time to have stuck that knife in his back.

He still couldn't let her go down for it, though. She needed help, not punishment. And he was as guilty as she was, in some respects, because he should never have argued with her when he knew she was on the edge. It was just so damn hard not to retaliate when she got in his face. She had a way of getting under his skin like nobody else ever had, and he wasn't saint enough to back down when she provoked him.

Still, the police couldn't charge Andrea if he stuck to his story about being jumped in the alley. Jones didn't believe him, but that was his problem. And Skye couldn't drop them in it, because she hadn't seen anything, so Andrea was in the clear.

But this was the last time Jeff was bailing her out. When she came home, she was going to stay on her tablets no matter what. And the first time she missed one, he was out of there – for good, this time.

4

Skye had fallen asleep as soon as her head hit the pillow. When she woke the next morning, she momentarily forgot what had happened and stretched her arms above her head. But, when she heard the chimes of a doorbell in the hallway below, her eyes popped open and she sat bolt upright and gazed around the unfamiliar room in confusion. A tap at the door a few seconds later, followed by the sight of Marie Vaughn's smiling face, brought everything back in an unwelcome flash.

'Morning, love,' Marie said cheerily. 'Val had a cancellation, so she managed to get here a bit earlier than planned. I washed your things after you fell asleep.' She nodded towards a wicker chair in the corner of the room, upon which, Skye saw from the corner of her eye, her clothes were neatly folded. 'Why don't you go and have a wash, then get dressed and join us in the kitchen? The bathroom is two doors down. I've left a new toothbrush on the sink, and a fresh towel on the rail. Okay?'

Skye didn't answer, so Marie took the hint and retreated from the room. As soon as the door was closed, she jumped out of bed and quickly got dressed.

Val and Marie were talking quietly over a cup of tea at the kitchen table when Skye went downstairs. Dennis was nowhere in sight, but she could hear him moving around in the room above and guessed that he must have decided to leave the women to it.

'Morning.' Val smiled and gestured for her to take a seat. 'How are you feeling today?'

'All right,' Skye muttered, breaking her pledge not to speak to any of them in her desperation to know if there was any news about her dad. 'Have you heard from the hospital yet?'

'Yes, and you'll be pleased to know that your father's operation went very well.'

'Does that mean I can go home now?'

'Not just yet.'

Skye's heart had leapt at the news that her dad was okay, but it plummeted now and tears of despair sprang into her eyes. 'Why not? I don't want to stay here again.'

'You won't have to,' Val told her. 'This was an emergency placement, so I've made arrangements for you to go to a nice children's home until we can find somewhere more permanent.'

'No.' Skye shook her head. 'I want to go home.'

'I'm afraid that's not an option,' said Val. 'We've no idea how long your dad will be in hospital, and your mum's clearly not well enough to look after you.'

'She'll be okay if she gets back on her tablets,' Skye insisted. 'She always gets better really fast when they kick in. Anyway, I'm nearly fifteen; I can look after myself.'

'No, you can't,' Val said firmly. Then, sighing softly, she said, 'Look, I know this isn't what you hoped to hear, but this isn't the first time concerns have been raised about your welfare, and we have a duty to protect you.'

'I don't need protecting.'

'*You* may not think so, but *we* do.'

'You don't even know me.' Skye glowered.

'We've known *of* you for a while,' Val said. 'And we've spoken with your parents several times in the past. Unfortunately,' she went on, trying not to make it sound as if she were criticising the Bensons when, in truth, the couple had done everything in their power to prevent Social Services from gaining entry to their home, 'we weren't able to establish a true picture of the situation on those occasions, so we couldn't make an accurate assessment of your needs. But after what happened last night, it's clear that you're at risk, and we're—'

'You don't know *anything*,' Skye cut in angrily. 'You're just like the police: making things up so you can take me away from my mum and dad. But I love them and they love me, and they won't let you get away with this.'

'I saw your dad this morning, and he agreed to sign you over to us,' Val told her, figuring that there was no use in beating around the bush because the sooner the girl knew the score, the sooner she would be able to come to terms with it. 'It's not that he doesn't love you,' she went on, trying to soften the blow when she saw the raw despair in Skye's eyes. 'He's just being realistic, because he knows he can't cope by himself.'

Skye felt as though she'd been kicked in the stomach. 'You're lying,' she gasped. 'My dad wouldn't do that to me.'

'It won't have been easy for him,' Val said softly. 'But he knows it was the right thing to do. And the children's home is only a temporary measure; just until we find suitable long-term foster-parents to place you with.'

'No!' Skye cried. 'I won't go; you can't make me!'

Marie had stayed quiet while Val was talking, but she placed a hand on Skye's shoulder now and said, 'No one wants to hurt you, my love; we're all just trying to do what's best for you. I think your dad was very brave to admit that he can't cope, and I'm sure your mum will be able to visit when she's better.'

'What do *you* know?' Skye jerked away from her and sprang up from her seat. 'You're just a stupid old woman who steals other people's kids 'cos you can't have your own. And I hate *you*, you fat bitch!' She rounded on Val. 'You don't even know us, so what gives you the right to tell us what to do? I'm going home, and you can't stop me!'

She turned now and rushed towards the door, but was infuriated to find her way blocked by Dennis Vaughn. '*Move!*' she screamed, kicking out at him.

'Calm down,' he ordered, wincing as the toe of her shoe connected with his shin. 'The more you fight, the harder you'll make it for yourself.' He gripped her firmly by the shoulders when she started lashing out with her fists, and said, 'Like it or not, this is the law, and you've got no say in it.'

'Leave me alone!' Skye sobbed, sinking to her knees as the fight drained from her. 'I just want to go *hoooome*!'

An hour later, after a silent journey during which Skye had tried to escape from the back of the car only to find that the safety locks had been activated, Val pulled up at the gates of the children's home. Skye's stomach churned with dread when she gazed out and saw the metal grilles covering the windows, and the razor-wire topping the high wall.

'I know it looks bad,' Val said, shifting in her seat to look back at Skye as she waited for the electronic gate to be opened. 'But it's much nicer on the inside, and there's always lots of fun stuff going on.'

Still reeling from the news that her dad had survived only to turn his back on her when she needed him the most – and convinced that this interfering bitch had *made* him do it – Skye clutched at her angel necklace and desperately prayed that she would wake up to find that it had all been a terrible dream.

When the gates opened, Val drove in and parked beside a broad flight of steps at the top of which four teenage girls were smoking cigarettes.

'Who's on duty?' Val asked them as she released Skye from the car and ushered her up the steps.

'Col and Lucy,' one of the girls replied, eyeing Skye through a cloud of smoke. 'Who's this?'

'Her name's Skye,' said Val. Then, turning to Skye, she gestured to each of the girls in turn, saying, 'And these ladies are Nadine, Simone, Jackie, and . . .' She paused when she reached the last one, and frowned.

'Maz,' the girl grunted.

'And Maz,' said Val. Then, smiling, she said, 'Now you all know each other, I trust you'll help Skye to settle in, because she might be here for some time.'

'You know us, Val.' Nadine flashed a sly glance at Skye. 'We always keep a close eye on the new ones.'

Skye's legs had started to tremble, and she stumbled when Val pushed her on towards the door.

'Don't worry about them,' Val said quietly, catching her by the arm and steering her over the threshold. 'They talk tough, but they're nice once you get to know them.'

Skye glanced back and shuddered when she saw the girls staring in at her. It was the same way that Janet Hampson and her mates stared at the younger kids at school: designed to scare the shit out of them, whilst leaving no doubt that they were perfectly capable of carrying out their unspoken threat if challenged.

As Skye and Val entered the hallway, a door opened at the far end and a tall, thin man walked out. He stopped when he saw them, and drew his head back. 'Have I missed something?'

'I spoke to Ann this morning,' Val told him. 'She said you had a room for me.'

'Nice of her to tell *me*,' he complained. Then, winking at Skye to let her know that he wasn't blaming her, he held out his hand and walked up to her, saying, 'I'm Col. Welcome to Maddison House. Or, as we like to call it, the madhouse.'

'She's a bit upset,' Val explained when Skye shoved her hands into her pockets and stared down at her feet. 'Is Lucy around?' she asked then, glancing at her watch. 'I've got a meeting I need to get to, so I'm going to have to sign Skye over and run.'

'I think she's in the kitchen,' said Col. 'Go and wait in the office while I fetch her.' He turned to Skye now, and smiled. 'Don't look so nervous, Chuck; we run a friendly ship around here.'

In light of the decidedly *un*friendly looks those girls had just given her, Skye doubted that very much, and she struggled not to burst into tears as she followed Val into the office. Everything was spiralling out of control and it was all her fault because, if she hadn't panicked and made that 999 call last night, none of this would be happening. If she'd only taken a bit of time to calm down after she'd found her dad, she was sure she could have patched him up without getting the authorities involved. It happened all the time in films: someone got stabbed, or shot, and their friends poured alcohol over the wounds and bandaged them up, then mopped their brow until the fever broke. Skye could have done that, so why oh *why* had she made that call?

When Col and Lucy joined them a few minutes later, Skye slouched down in her seat and watched as they filled out a pile of paperwork. Itching to get out of there, Val was on her feet as soon as the last form was signed.

'Right, I'll leave you to settle in, Skye. I'll come and see you sometime next week, but if you need to talk to me before that, let Col or Lucy know and they'll get hold of me. And they'll sort you out with some clothes until I've had a chance to collect some of your own things.'

Skye had been staring at the floor the whole time Val had been talking, but she snapped her head up when she heard this. 'You're going to my house? Can I come with you?'

'Sorry.' Val shook her head.

'Why not?'

'Because it would unsettle you,' said Lucy.

A shiver ran down Skye's spine when she caught the coldness in the woman's voice. In contrast to the overweight social worker, Lucy was quite slim and petite, but there was nothing remotely feminine about her, and Skye just knew that she was going to be an absolute bitch.

'Right, I really need to get moving,' Val said, shifting her handbag onto her other shoulder as she headed for the door. She paused there, and looked back at Skye one last time. 'See you next week, and please try to be good.'

As Col went to show Val out, Lucy walked over to a closet in the corner of the room and opened the door, revealing shelves stacked with folded clothes and rows of shoes.

'What size are you?' she asked over her shoulder. When Skye didn't answer, she glanced back and looked her up and down. 'I'd guess a ten, and a five in shoes. If I'm wrong, it's your own fault for not speaking up when you had the chance.'

She selected a pair of pyjamas, a dressing gown, and some slippers from the closet, and then took a toothbrush out of a drawer. She plonked the bundle into Skye's hands and strode towards the door, ordering, 'Come with me.'

Too scared to disobey, Skye got up and followed the woman across the hall and up a flight of stairs to the first floor.

'You've got a room to yourself, for now,' Lucy told her, pushing open a door at the end of the corridor and waving her inside. 'But if anyone else comes in before you're gone, you'll be sharing – and I'd best not hear any moaning about it. Understood?'

Skye nodded and cast a dismayed glance around the tiny room. A set of steel-framed bunk-beds with wafer-thin mattresses was set against one wall, while the facing one was taken up by a chest of drawers and a wardrobe. The walls themselves were painted a depressing shade of green, and the small window was so grimy that it would have been impossible to see out even if the view hadn't been obscured by the metal grille that was fixed across it on the outside. In stark contrast to the comfortable bedroom she'd spent last night in, this one looked – and felt – like a prison cell, and Skye wondered if they were actually going to lock her in.

'These are the house rules.' Lucy pointed out a laminated notice pinned to the back of the door. 'Read them, and try to learn times for breakfast, lunch, dinner, and what-have-you. We have a strict routine here and, if you're late for a sitting, you'll go without. Anything you're not clear on, ask.'

Skye nodded again, and held her breath as the tears she'd been holding in threatened to burst out. When at last Lucy left her alone, she sank down onto the bottom bunk and dropped her face into her hands.

'Boo hoo!' a mocking voice said from the doorway a few minutes later.

Shocked, because she hadn't heard the door being opened again, Skye jerked her head up and was horrified to see the girls from the front steps staring in at her from the corridor.

'What you blubbing for?' Nadine demanded, walking in and opening the dresser drawers to check if there was anything of interest in them.

'Probably missing Mummy and Daddy,' Simone sneered as she followed.

'Fucking crybaby.' Maz kicked Skye's ankle as she squeezed past.

Skye could barely breathe for fear as the last girl came in and closed the door. 'What do you want?' she croaked. 'I haven't got anything.'

'No kidding.' Disappointed to find the drawers empty, Nadine slammed them shut and perched on top of the unit. 'So when's your shit getting here?'

Skye's mouth had gone bone dry, and she eyed the girls nervously. 'I don't know,' she mumbled. 'Val said she'll pick it up when she's got time.'

'What you in for?' Simone demanded.

'Nothing.' Skye's chin wobbled.

'You must have done *some*thing,' Maz said sharply. 'You don't end up in this shithole for nowt.'

Before Skye could answer, Nadine leaned forward and peered at her throat. 'What's that?'

'What?' Skye covered the necklace with her hand.

'That what you're trying to hide,' Nadine said, holding out her hand. 'Pass it here; I want to look at it.'

Skye's stomach churned. She instinctively knew that she would never see her necklace again if she handed it over; but if she refused, she had no doubt that it would be taken from her by force.

The door opened suddenly and Col appeared. He looked at each of the girls in turn before his gaze came to rest on their leader. 'What's this, Nadine? Welcoming committee?'

'Summat like that.' She gave him a sly grin.

'Now why don't I believe you?' He raised an eyebrow. Then, jerking his head, he stepped aside and held the door wide. 'Lunch is ready. Off you go.'

'What we having?' Nadine asked, standing up and straightening her short skirt.

'Smells like fish,' Simone grumbled, pulling a face as she shuffled past Col. 'Makes me heave, that shit.'

'Don't be so ungrateful,' Col scolded. 'There's plenty who'd jump at the chance to eat as well as you lot do.'

'Give 'em our fish, then,' drawled Nadine as she sauntered past him. 'We're going out.'

'No, you're not!' Col called after them as they made their way along the corridor. 'I'd better see you all in the dining room when I come down.'

'Or what?' Nadine called back over her shoulder.

'Why do I bother?' Col shrugged in a gesture of surrender when the girls turned the corner and disappeared from view. Then, turning to Skye, he tilted his head to one side when he saw her tear-stained face, and said, 'Chin up, Chuck; it's honestly not that bad here.'

'Yes, it is.' Skye wiped her nose on the back of her hand. 'I hate it! I want to go home.'

Col walked over and, crouching low to avoid smacking his head on the upper bunk, sat down beside her. 'Everyone feels like this when they first get here,' he said softly, 'but they soon settle in. Take Nadine.' He nodded towards the door. 'She was so scared in her first week we couldn't get her to come out of her room. *Now* look at her; thinks she runs the place. So it can't be that bad, can it? And I bet you lot'll be the best of mates in no time.'

Skye was starting to feel sick. Col didn't know what he was talking about if he thought that Nadine and those other girls were going to let her settle in without a fight. 'I need the toilet,' she said, jumping up and rushing for the door.

'Down the landing, last door on the right,' Col called after her as she darted out. 'Come down for lunch when you're finished.'

Queasy at the thought of trying to stomach food right now, Skye covered her mouth with her hand and ran the rest of the way down the corridor.

Outside just then, Nadine and the other girls had left the grounds and were strolling down the road.

'We'll wait a couple of days,' Nadine was saying. 'Let her think we're not that fussed, then catch her off-guard.'

'Yeah, probably best not to strike too soon,' Simone agreed. 'Col will be watching us like a hawk now he's caught us in her room.'

'He don't scare me,' Nadine scoffed.

'Me neither,' Simone agreed. 'But if he tells Lucy, we're fucked.'

'Whatever,' Nadine said dismissively. Then, clicking her fingers at Jackie who was at the other end of the line, she said, 'Oi, thicko. I thought I told you to get the fags out.'

'There's only three left,' Jackie told her, sliding the pack out of her pocket.

'Looks like you won't be having one till you've bought some more, then, doesn't it?' said Nadine, snatching them from her and passing them out to the others before tossing the box onto the floor. She paused to light hers, and then walked on, saying, 'Right, here's what we're going to do. We're gonna jump her after school on Monday and fuck her up, then tell the nonce and the witch that we rescued her from some other girls, and get ourselves a treat for being heroes.'

'What if she grasses us up?' Simone asked. 'She looks the type, little mardy arse.'

'You said the same about *her*.' Nadine jerked a thumb towards Jackie. 'But she was smart enough to keep her gob shut. And that one will, an' all – if she knows what's good for her.'

As the others walked on, laughing at the memory of the kicking they had given *her* not so very long ago, Jackie shuffled miserably along behind them. She knew exactly what was coming to the new girl – and she didn't envy her one little bit.

Lucy was vacuuming the landing carpet when Skye came out of the toilet a short time later. 'Stop right there,' she ordered, stamping down on the Hoover's off-switch when Skye tried to scuttle past. 'The dining room is *that* way.'

'I'm not hungry,' Skye muttered.

'Are you ill?' Lucy raised an eyebrow. 'Anorexic? Bulimic?'

'No.' Skye shook her head. 'I just—'

'Then do as you're told, and go down for lunch.' Lucy cut her off. 'I've got enough to deal with around here without having to worry about silly girls starving themselves to death.'

Too scared to argue, and sensing that it would be futile to try, Skye did as she'd been told and made her way downstairs.

Ten kids were seated around the table when she walked into the dining room. They had all been chattering loudly but they fell silent when they noticed her, and Skye felt the heat rise to her cheeks when all eyes turned her way. Relieved when they went back to their conversations after a couple of seconds, she skirted around the table and headed for the serving hatch, through which she could see Col and a middle-aged woman moving around in what appeared to be the kitchen.

'Ah, you made it.' Col beamed when he saw Skye. 'Feeling better now?'

'Not really,' she mumbled, feeling sick again as the aroma of the food that was sitting in serving dishes on his side of the hatch reached her. 'Lucy made me come down.'

Already ladling food onto a plate, Col said, 'You'll feel a lot better with something in your stomach.'

When he handed the plate to her, Skye gazed down at the limp-looking piece of fish, a mound of lumpy mashed potato and a pile of garden peas, and swallowed deeply. It looked totally unappetising but she hadn't eaten a thing since yesterday lunchtime, so she supposed she ought to at least try it.

The three older kids had already left the room by the time she carried her plate to the table, and the younger ones got up and wandered out pretty much as soon as she sat down. Glad to be alone, because she'd been self-conscious about eating in front of strangers ever since her mum had told her that she ate like a pig, Skye cut off a tiny piece of the fish – and was surprised to find that it didn't taste half as bad as it looked.

When Col glanced out of the hatch a few minutes later and saw that her plate was almost empty, he said, 'Attagirl! Now, how about some jelly and ice cream for afters?'

Determined not to let him think that he was winning her over, Skye shook her head.

'Oh, well, all the more for me.' Col grinned. 'Last one to finish usually clears up, by the way. But I'll let you off, seeing as it's your first day.'

Skye stood up without answering and headed for the door.

'Going back to your room?' Col asked. 'I'll pop up when I've finished down here; tell you about some of the activities we've got lined up for next week. I'm sure there'll be something we can tempt you with.'

Skye pulled a face and carried on walking. He was one of the most cheerful people she'd ever met, and she had a sneaking suspicion that she might have quite liked him if they had met under different circumstances. But she had no intention of getting involved in any of his stupid activities and she hoped he wasn't going to keep trying to gee her up, because she just wanted to be left alone.

Back in her room, she lay on the bed and stared at the stains on the underside of the mattress above until her eyes drifted shut.

Waking with a start some time later at the sound of raised voices in the corridor outside, Skye crept over to the door and pressed her ear against the wood in time to hear Lucy blast Nadine for having left the grounds without permission.

'I'm getting seriously fed up with your lack of regard for the rules,' the woman was saying. 'I don't know how many times I've warned you, but if you think you can carry on doing as you please without any consequences, you'd best think again.'

'What you gonna do, put me on the naughty step?' Nadine shot back insolently.

'No, I'll make arrangements for you to be moved to a different facility,' said Lucy. 'See how you get along without your little lapdogs egging you on and making you feel like some kind of big shot.'

'Are you calling my mates dogs?' Nadine demanded sarcastically. 'I can get you kicked out for that.'

'Go ahead and report me, then,' Lucy challenged. 'But I can assure you that the only one who'll be leaving is *you*. Now lose the attitude and get yourself down to dinner. And you lot can get moving, too,' she added sharply, obviously talking to Nadine's friends. 'And that goes for anybody else who's still up here,' she yelled then, banging on Skye's door.

Almost jumping out of her skin, Skye hugged herself and waited for a few minutes to make sure that the corridor was clear before reluctantly opening her door. She wasn't hungry, but she had no doubt that Lucy would only come and drag her downstairs if she didn't go of her own accord.

Nadine and the others had already been served and were seated at the table when Skye walked into the dining room. She pretended not to notice them as she made her way to the hatch. She had already been wary of Nadine but she was even more so now, because she figured the girl had to be *really* tough to disobey the rules *and* argue with that battleaxe Lucy.

When she'd been served, Skye carried her plate to the other end of the table and sat with the younger kids. She ate slowly in the hope that Nadine's lot would finish quickly and go about their business. But they had obviously guessed what she was up to and her stomach churned as, one by one, all the other kids left the table, leaving just her and Nadine's crew.

Ten agonising minutes dragged by. But just as Skye was wondering how she was ever going to get out of there in one piece, Lucy popped her head around the door and asked, 'What's taking you girls so long?'

'Keep your hair on,' Nadine drawled, flashing Skye a sly grin as she pushed her chair back and stood up. 'We were just going.'

As Lucy shook her head and went about her business, Simone and Maz followed Nadine's lead and stood up. But when Jackie also went to rise, Nadine shoved her back down, saying, 'Where d'you think you're going? It's your turn to do the dishes.'

'But *she*'s still here.' Jackie nodded towards Skye.

'Who?' Nadine looked around. 'I can't see no one; you must be imagining things.' She slapped Jackie on the back of the head, and then, laughing, linked arms with the others and strolled out.

Skye glanced at Jackie from beneath her lashes, and felt sorry for the girl when she saw that her cheeks were scarlet with embarrassment. She'd already sensed that this one wasn't quite as nasty as the others, and didn't understand why Jackie hung around with them when they were so mean to her.

'Do you want me to help?' she offered when Jackie started gathering the empty plates from around the table.

Jackie shook her head.

'I don't mind,' Skye persisted, hoping that it would break the ice and she'd have someone to talk to while she was here.

'I said *no*,' Jackie hissed, scowling at her as she snatched her plate. 'And don't talk to me again, 'cos I don't want to know you.'

Skye was offended, but she knew when she wasn't wanted so she got up and left Jackie to it. Relieved to see that Nadine and the others weren't waiting for her in the hall, she dashed up the stairs, desperate for the solitude of her room.

5

Skye stayed out of everyone's way for the rest of the weekend, only venturing out of her room when she absolutely had to, to eat or to use the bathroom. Thanks to the uncomfortable mattress and the paper-thin walls through which she could hear everything that was going on in the adjoining rooms, she had barely slept and was exhausted by the time Monday morning came around.

It was Skye's birthday, but she didn't feel the slightest bit excited as she lay there listening to the other kids arguing in the corridor about whose turn it was to use the bathroom. According to Val, her dad knew she was here, but he never remembered her birthday when she was at home so it would be a miracle if he'd sent her a card. And she doubted that anyone here would even know.

Her suspicions were confirmed when Lucy marched into her room a few minutes later without so much as a smile, never mind a Happy Birthday greeting. She pushed herself up onto her elbows when the woman dropped a pile of clothes onto the end of her bed, and asked, 'What's that?'

'Your uniform,' said Lucy, tugging the thin curtains open. 'You'll get a new one when money starts coming through for you, but this will have to do for now.' She turned now, and raised her eyebrows when she saw the look of disgust on Skye's face. 'Problem?'

'It's the wrong colour,' Skye protested. 'We wear red at my school, not green.'

'You'll be going to the local comp with everyone else while you're here,' Lucy told her. 'The minibus takes you in but you all walk back together, so make sure you meet up with the others at the front gate at home-time. And don't be late, or everyone will be grounded for a week,' she warned as she headed back out into the corridor. 'And that won't make you very popular.'

Skye pulled the thin quilt over her head when Lucy had gone and released a silent scream. She hated the bitch with a passion – and hated even more the fact that she was being forced to go to a new school. The thought of seeing her friends again was one of the only things that had kept her going over this weekend, and she had been toying with the idea of skipping out at lunchtime to pay Hayley a quick visit. But that was out of the question now; and she couldn't even call or message her, because they weren't allowed to use phones or the internet here.

'Help me,' she whispered, pressing her angel to her lips. 'I'll do anything, just please, please, *please* get me out of here.'

Skye lay there for a few minutes more, praying for some kind of sign that her plea was about to be answered. Dismayed but not really surprised when nothing happened, she got up reluctantly and, not caring if the clothes she snatched off the pile fitted her, got dressed and made her way downstairs.

Nadine and the others had already claimed the back seat of the minibus when Skye climbed aboard after breakfast, and she could feel them staring at the back of her head when she took a seat up front. Apart from her little run-in with Jackie in the dining room, none of them had spoken directly to her in days, but she suspected they were just biding their time; waiting for an excuse to have another go at her. The tension was unbearable but she forced herself to gaze calmly out of the window, determined not to let Nadine see that she was getting to her.

When the minibus pulled up outside the school gates ten minutes later, Skye's mood took yet another dip. Her old school had been surrounded by houses and greenery, but this place looked as cold and faceless as the home; and the kids who were hanging around outside the gates looked so rough that Skye doubted whether even Janet Hampson would dare to try it on with them.

That first impression carried through into the classroom, where Skye was greeted by dirty looks and whispers from her fellow pupils.

'Who's *that* tramp?' she heard one of them say as she took the seat the teacher had directed her to at the front of the class. 'Dunno,' said another. 'But it best stay away from me, 'cos I can smell it from here; scruffy bastard.'

Skye wanted to shrivel up and die when she heard this. She had stubbornly refused to take a bath since arriving at the home, resentful at being ordered to by Lucy. She also hadn't washed her hair, and the disgusting green jumper made her skin look sallow and unhealthy. But it hadn't even occurred to her that she might smell bad, and the shame at hearing that she did was overwhelming.

The teacher compounded her misery when, after taking the register, she announced that Skye was from the children's home and asked everyone to make her feel welcome – a plea that was guaranteed to have the exact opposite effect, as Skye soon found out. The only ray of light in the whole horrible experience was finding out that she was in the year below

Nadine and the others and so wouldn't have to share any of their classes.

The first four lessons were single sessions, and Skye struggled to navigate her way around the unfamiliar building without help after the two girls she had asked for directions told her to get lost, and the teacher she approached almost bit her head off for wandering around when everybody else was already in class.

The stress of being treated like a leper and having to constantly look over her shoulder in case Nadine caught up with her brought on a headache. It got worse and worse as the afternoon wore on, and by the time her last lesson came around Skye felt so rough that she couldn't concentrate on a word the teacher was saying – which didn't go unnoticed.

'Are you paying attention?' the teacher barked, marching up to Skye's desk and slamming a hand down on it. 'I asked you to tell me the square root of sixteen.'

'I don't know,' Skye mumbled, blushing with humiliation when she heard sniggers from the kids who were sitting behind her.

'What do you mean, you don't know?' The teacher scowled. 'Are you some kind of simpleton?'

The sniggers changed to outright laughter at this, and Skye couldn't take any more.

'Where do you think you're going?' the teacher yelled when the girl jumped up from her seat and rushed towards the door. 'The bell hasn't gone yet. Get back here this instant!'

Skye ignored her and ran out into the corridor and on down to the girls' toilets. But just as she reached out to push the door, it was pulled open from the other side and her heart lurched painfully when she found herself face to face with Jackie. Terrified that Nadine and the others might be right behind, she stepped back and glanced around in search of someone who could help if they tried to do anything.

Jackie felt immediately guilty when she saw the fear in Skye's eyes. She hadn't seen much of her during the weekend and had felt bad about biting her head off when she'd offered to help clear the dishes that day. But she'd had no choice, because Nadine would have made her life hell if she'd thought that Jackie was being nice to the girl. Still, Skye wasn't to know that, and Jackie couldn't help but feel sorry for her now because she clearly wasn't coping very well. It was traumatic to be taken away from your family against your will, and that pain never went away – no matter how many times people told you that it would. But it was so much harder to deal with when you had bitches like Nadine, Simone and Maz to contend with.

Her conscience pricking sharply, Jackie glanced around to make sure that no one was around before jerking her chin up at Skye. 'Come in here a minute.'

Afraid that it might be a set-up, Skye shook her head.

'*Please*,' Jackie hissed. 'I need to tell you something.'

'Tell me now,' Skye said, staying put.

'Not out there. Someone might see us.'

'Promise they're not in there?'

'Honest to God.' Jackie made the sign of the cross on her chest with her finger. Then, flapping her hand to urge Skye to hurry up, she said, 'Come on. I'm dead if they find out I've been talking to you.'

Still nervous, but curious to hear what the other girl had to say, Skye hesitantly followed her into the toilets.

'Nadine's going to jump you on the way home,' Jackie blurted out as soon as the door was shut. 'They've been planning it all weekend. They're gonna get you behind the old factory at the end of the road, then tell Col and Lucy that some girls at school were ganging up on you and they chased them off. They did it to me when I first got here,' she went on, her cheeks reddening at the memory of the humiliation she'd suffered. 'They said they'd cut my face with a Stanley knife if I told on them.'

Skye's legs had turned to jelly, and she leaned back against the door for support. 'Why do you hang around with them if they did that to you?'

'I've got no choice,' Jackie replied miserably. 'My aunt sends me money every month, and Nadine used to take it off me. But then Lucy got suspicious so she started making out like we were mates. And I had to play along and act like I was okay about sharing it with them, or they'd have killed me.'

Skye was still uncertain, and it showed in her eyes. Jackie saw it, and tutted. 'Look, it's up to you if you don't believe me, but just don't say I didn't warn you.'

Shocked when the girl pushed past her and rushed back out into the corridor, Skye stepped out and watched as she ran back to her classroom. *Now* she believed her, and the feeling of dread that had been hanging over her all day intensified a thousand-fold.

Now that she knew what the gang were planning there was no way she was going to meet up with the others at the front gates as Lucy had directed her to. She also couldn't make her own way back to the home, because she had no idea how to get there. And she definitely couldn't ask the teachers for help, because they'd be bound to question Nadine – who would then not only know that Skye had grassed her up but that Jackie had betrayed her, too.

Aware that she had little time to act before school ended, Skye made a snap decision and walked quickly down the corridor in the opposite direction from her classroom. She'd left her blazer hanging over the back of her chair, but she didn't care about that. She just needed to get out of there.

The kids from the home gathered at the front gates after the bell went, but as the minutes ticked by with no sign of the new girl they began to get edgy.

'What if she's sussed what's going down and blabbed?' said Maz.

'She doesn't know anything,' Nadine said with confidence. 'The thick bitch is probably lost. She'll be here in a minute.'

'Well, she'd best get a fuckin' move on,' Maz said, cracking her knuckles as she peered around in search of their prey. 'If I get grounded because of her, she's *really* gonna get it.'

'You can wait your turn.' Nadine grinned slyly. 'I get first dibs. You can have whatever's left.'

'Not a lot, then?' Maz smirked.

While her friends were talking, Simone had been watching Jackie and, suspicious of the way she was jiggling around as if she was nervous about something, she asked, 'What's up with you?'

'Nothing,' Jackie lied, folding her arms.

'You sure about that?' Simone stepped closer and stared down into her eyes. 'You're acting proper shifty, if you ask me. What you shaking for?'

'I'm cold,' Jackie told her, fronting it out.

Nadine noticed them having words and gave them a questioning look. 'What's going on?'

'It's *her*.' Simone nodded at Jackie. 'She's acting weird. I reckon she's warned that bitch off, and that's why she hasn't come out yet.'

'No, I haven't!' Jackie protested, her cheeks blazing with guilt. 'I haven't even seen her since this morning.'

'You'd better not be lying!' Nadine pushed past Simone and shoved Jackie up against the railings. 'You know what'll happen if I find out you've gone behind my back.'

'I haven't said anything, I swear!' cried Jackie. 'Like you said, she doesn't know her way around yet so she's probably just lost.'

Nadine stared down into Jackie's eyes for several long moments. It did seem a bit suspicious that the new girl hadn't turned up yet, and Jackie was decidedly nervous about *some-thing*. But would she really have the guts to betray the gang? Nadine doubted it somehow.

'Right, we're gonna have to leave it for today,' she said. 'But if I find out this is down to you . . .' She left the sentence hanging and gave Jackie a fierce look before walking away.

Jackie cast a worried glance back at the school before following. She had regretted her decision to warn Skye as soon as she'd done it, and had been praying that the girl hadn't gone straight to a teacher to tell on them. If she had, there would be hell to pay when they got back to the home. But the real punishment would come tonight, after lights out.

Skye had no idea where she was going after she'd squeezed her way out through the fence at the back of the school. But she kept her head down and walked quickly on down the road, desperate to put as much distance between herself and Nadine as possible.

The further she went, the more run-down the area became, and her stomach twisted into a huge knot as she passed row after row of scruffy houses and boarded-up shops. Just like the children's home, every building she passed seemed to have razor wire protecting its entry points; and the people who were hanging around on the street corners looked shifty and dangerous.

Half frozen without her jacket, and despairing of ever finding her way out of the area alive, Skye cried out with relief when she spotted a bus up ahead that was bound for the city centre. Remembering that she still had the twenty pounds that she'd borrowed from Hayley stashed in her bra, she slipped her hand inside her shirt and tugged it out as she raced towards the bus stop. She would easily find her way home from town, and then all she had to do was hide until her dad came out of hospital and put everything right.

And he *would* put it right, she was sure, because he loved her and would never have told the social worker that he couldn't look after her. The bitch had either lied about that, or had caught him at a low point and *made* him say it. Either way, he was bound to change his mind once he saw her.

Over an hour later, Skye was glad to be back on familiar territory. It was already dark enough by then that she felt safe to walk the streets without fear of being spotted by anyone she knew. But she kept her head down nevertheless, and scuttled home via a series of short cuts.

A police car was driving slowly towards her when she turned the corner onto her road, and she instinctively ducked behind a wheelie bin and squatted down to watch as the vehicle pulled up outside her house. Two uniformed officers climbed out and one knocked on the front door while the other cupped his hands over his eyes and peered through the living-room window. After getting no answer there they went next door, and Skye strained to hear whatever they were saying to the student who answered. She was too far away to catch their words but it didn't take a genius to guess that she'd been reported as missing when she failed to arrive back at the home with the others.

When the coppers climbed back into the car and drove away a few minutes later, Skye waited to make sure that they didn't come straight back before she slipped out from her hiding place and darted down the back alley.

It was dark in the yard and she had to grope around for the brick under the kitchen window beneath which her dad had stashed a spare key for those times when her mum locked him out. She let herself into the house when she found it, then bolted the door and leaned back against it as an overwhelming sensation of relief settled over her. The air smelled really bad, and she was sure she could hear mice scurrying around. But it was home, and she had never been so happy to be there.

Afraid to switch on the lights in case the police had told the neighbours to keep an eye out for her, Skye tiptoed down the dark hallway and into the living room after a while. The curtains were partially open in there, and the dim beam from the lamp-post across the road highlighted the dark patch of blood on the carpet where her dad had been lying when she'd found him. Her legs wobbled at the sight of it and she staggered back against the couch, knocking her mum's mobile phone which had been sitting on the arm onto the floor.

She reached down for it, but quickly snatched her hand back when her fingertips plunged into something soft and squishy. Terrified that it might be one of her dad's eyes, or a piece of his brain, but unable to keep herself from looking closer, she leaned down and peered at it. As her vision began to sharpen she realised that it was actually a chocolate. There were several more scattered around, and she traced them to an upturned Dairy Milk box. She felt sad when she saw that, because she guessed that her dad must have bought them for her mum as a way of saying sorry for the argument – and the crazy bitch had thanked him by sticking a knife in his back.

Her gaze was drawn back to the blood now, and she shivered, wondering how her dad could possibly have survived losing so much.

Maybe he didn't, a little voice in her head piped up. *Maybe he's dead, and the social worker just told you he was okay to shut you up.*

On the verge of crying again, Skye snatched the phone off the floor and fled to her bedroom. All she wanted to do was climb beneath the quilt and go to sleep, but the police were bound to come back before too long so she needed to find somewhere to hide – somewhere where no one ever would think to look for her.

The attic!

The thought came to her in a flash, and it was perfect. The ceilings in this house were high and there was no ladder up to the attic, so no one would ever dream that she could have climbed up there. She had long ago discovered that she could haul herself up there by standing on the banister rail and holding onto one side of the hatch while throwing her legs up through the gap. Her mum and dad didn't even know she could do that, so she'd be able to stay up there for ages without anyone realising she was even in the house.

As she stood up, her heel clipped the laptop that was sticking out from under her bed and she slid it out and wrapped it in her quilt along with her mum's phone. Then she ran quickly down to the kitchen and grabbed whatever she could find in the cupboards that was edible and didn't need cooking before going back upstairs and hauling her stash up into the attic.

There were no boards on the floor up there: just beams, between which lay wires and sorry-looking strips of glass wool that were so old they were crumbling to dust. Glad that she'd brought the quilt, because it was even colder up there than it was downstairs, Skye wrapped it around herself and perched on a beam with her back to the wall. She could hear the muffled sound of music and laughter filtering through from the students' side and the whistle of the wind creeping through the gaps in the roof where several slates had been dislodged. Glad of the faint sliver of moonlight that was shining through those same gaps, Skye switched the laptop on, and then reached for her mum's phone while she waited for the computer to boot up.

Tears burned her eyes when she pulled up her dad's name, and she bit down hard on her lip to prevent them from spilling over as she stared at it for several long seconds before pressing the *Call* button. Disappointed to hear a recorded message informing her that there was insufficient credit on the phone to make outgoing calls, she sent him a text instead, reading: *Dad, it's me. Ring me if you can see this, I really need to talk to you.*

She waited a few minutes for a reply, but when none came, she sent another, saying, *Please come home, Dad. I'm scared xxx*

Aware that there was nothing more she could do, and praying that her dad would answer soon, Skye turned her attention back to the laptop.

A few streets away, Hayley had just switched her own laptop on. This latest chest infection seemed to be easing, and she'd been looking forward to going back to school next week and

catching up with Skye. But then the police had called round
to ask if she had seen or heard from Skye, and she was unable
to sleep now for worrying about her.

The police hadn't given any details. But news spread like
wildfire around their way, and when her mum had told her
about Skye's mum supposedly stabbing her dad, and Skye
finding him straight after leaving here that day, Hayley felt
guilty that she hadn't thought to ask if Skye could stay for
dinner, or even a sleepover. At least then somebody else
might have found her dad, and Skye wouldn't have had to
go through the trauma of it on her own.

Desperate now to speak to Skye, Hayley logged into
Facebook and checked her messages to see if her friend had
tried to contact her. There were no messages, but when she
went to her newsfeed and saw some of the vile comments
that their so-called friends had posted on their walls about
Skye and the stabbing, she was disgusted. They didn't know
what Skye had been through, and it upset Hayley that they
were slagging off her friend just because her mum was
mentally ill. Hayley was lucky; her parents loved each other
and would never dream of laying their hands on each other in
anger. But Skye's parents were horrible – to each other *and*
to Skye. It sickened Hayley when she heard some of the stuff
that her friend had gone through, but she had long ago
learned to keep her opinions to herself when Skye confided
in her, because Skye could get really, *really* defensive when
it came to anyone criticising her parents.

Sad and worried, Hayley left a message now, telling Skye
that the police were looking for her, and pleading with her
to get in touch. Then, logging out of Facebook, she signed
into *WhisperBox* to do the same.

*   *   *

As Hayley logged out of Facebook, Skye was just logging in. She was touched when she saw Hayley's message, but when she read that the police had been round there she decided not to send a reply, scared that they might have told Hayley to contact her in order to find out where she was hiding. Instead, marking it as unread, she logged out and switched to WhisperBox, only to find that Hayley had left another message there.

I know you must be scared, this one read, *and I'm scared too, 'cos you're my best friend and I love you. Please call me or come round when you get this. My mum and dad will help you, I promise. They'll talk to the police and make sure you get properly looked after until this gets sorted out.*

Skye felt a twinge of resentment when she read this. It was all right for Hayley to sit there in her pretty bedroom promising to help, but if she was half the friend she claimed to be why hadn't she asked her mum and dad if Skye could stay with *them*?

As a wave of self-pity washed over her, Skye was about to log out when her Whisper light started to flash, and she smiled when she saw that it was QTPye.

Hey babes, how's you? the girl asked. *I was worried about you when you went off so sudden last week. Everything okay now?*

Not really, Skye replied, squinting to see the keys in the darkness.

Aw, they're not still at it, are they? Don't they ever stop?

It's way worse this time, Skye typed, the words she had been holding in all weekend pouring out through her fingertips as if someone had pulled an internal plug. *My mum went mental and stabbed my dad.*

OMG!!! You weren't there, were you?

No, I came in just after. I called ambulance, but pigs came as well. They arrested my mum and sent me to a home, but I've legged it, so now they're looking for me. They've been to Hayley's and everything.

Hayley???

Sorry, Sugarplum.

Ah, right. So where are you?

In the attic.

Awww, I bet you're in bits. But you shouldn't have gone home if they're looking for you, babes. That's the first place they'll look.

They've already been, but I've got nowhere else to go, Skye replied, sniffling softly as the tears she'd been holding back began to trickle down her cheeks. *I just want my dad to come home.*

I'm so sorry, babes. Wish I knew you in real life so I could give you a great big hug.

Me too.

An alert suddenly popped up on the laptop's screen, warning Skye that there were just a few minutes of battery life left. Aware that she couldn't risk going back down into the house to find the charger, because somebody might come in and catch her, she quickly typed: *Laptop about to die, so got to go. Don't know when I'll get another chance to talk to you, but thanks for caring, I won't forget it xxxx*

Wait! QTPye wrote back. *Have you got a mobile?*

Only my mum's, Skye replied. *But she's got no credit so I can't ring anyone.*

Me neither, but we can text, suggested QTPye. *Send me the number!*

Panicking, because she didn't know the number off by heart, Skye snatched up her mum's phone and quickly found it. The screen went black at the exact time she pressed 'send' after typing the number, so she laid the laptop on the beam beside her and stared at the phone, praying that her message had got through in time. But when half an hour had passed with no text from QTPye she guessed that she'd been too late and, feeling very sorry for herself, curled into a ball and cried herself to sleep.

6

Jeff Benson was agitated. There was some kind of construction work going on outside the window behind his bed, and this was the second day running that the crew had started at the ungodly hour of eight a.m.

They had been at it for two hours now, and Jeff had a banging headache from the racket that they were making with their hammers and drills. It didn't help that he'd been kept awake half the night by the old man in the bed to his right coughing and spluttering. Although he had felt a bit guilty for fantasising about smothering the old bastard with his pillow when he'd woken this morning, to find the guy's bed had been stripped and had been told by a nurse that the man had passed away in the early hours, and that the noises he'd been making were probably what they called the death rattle.

Still, at least the old man was free now, unlike Jeff, who was going completely stir-crazy. Four days was too long for a man to be lying around on his back like this, so he'd been gutted when the doctor had done his rounds a short time earlier and said that he wanted him to stay for a couple more days at least.

Already pissed off, Jeff's hackles rose when two police officers walked onto the ward and headed straight for his bed. Convinced that they had come to have another crack at getting him to admit that Andrea had stabbed him, he scowled up at them.

'I've already told your mates everything I've got to say, so don't bother asking me the same questions again. My wife is innocent. I was jumped in the alley. End of.'

'We're not here about that,' one of the officers told him. 'This is about your daughter.'

'What about her?' Jeff snapped. 'If she's told you it was her mum who stabbed me, she wasn't even home when it happened, so I suggest you check the facts before you start—'

'She's missing,' the officer interrupted. 'She failed to arrive back at the children's home after school yesterday afternoon, and we're trying to establish where she might have gone. Has she tried to contact you?'

'No.' Jeff sat up and frowned at the man. 'But what's this about a children's home? The social worker said she'd be going to foster-parents – in a proper house, like.'

'That's not really our concern,' said the copper. 'We're just trying to locate Skye, so is there anywhere you can think of where she might have gone?'

'Not really.' Jeff shook his head, and ran a hand through his hair.

'The head at her old school gave us the name of one girl she's friendly with,' the officer told him. 'A Hayley Simms?'

'That rings a bell.' Jeff frowned thoughtfully. 'I think Skye might have brought her round to ours once,' he said, thinking it best not to add that it had only been the once because Andrea had banned the kid from coming again, convinced that she was some kind of spy because she spoke a bit posh. 'Have you talked to her?' he asked.

The cop nodded. 'We did, but she hasn't heard from Skye, and doesn't think she's good enough friends with anyone else to have gone to them for help. That's why we're here: to see if *you* can think of anyone she's likely to have contacted.'

'I don't really know her mates, to be honest,' Jeff admitted. 'I work long hours, and she's usually in her room by the time I get home. Her mum would probably have a better idea about that kind of thing, but I doubt she's in the frame of mind to remember stuff like that just now.'

'Unfortunately not,' the officer affirmed.

'Where is she?' Jeff asked, guessing that they must have already tried to question Andrea. 'I hope you haven't still got her banged up, 'cos, like I told the last lot, she's ill and needs treatment, not locking up.'

'She's in hospital,' the officer told him. 'But if we could get back to Skye . . . Is there a relative she's particularly close to? A grandparent, maybe? Or a favourite aunt or uncle?'

'We're not that kind of family,' Jeff murmured. 'We've had a lot of hassle with them in the past, so we pretty much stick to ourselves. It's less complicated that way.'

'Okay. Well, if you do hear from Skye, please let us know immediately,' said the officer. 'Now she's under the care of Social Services, it would be an offence for anyone who knew her whereabouts to withhold that information.'

'Don't worry, I'd tell you,' Jeff replied. 'She's my kid, and I want what's best for her.'

'Course you do.' The second officer hadn't spoken until now, but his expression contradicted his words – and it wasn't lost on Jeff.

'What's that supposed to mean?' he demanded. 'Me and my missus might have had our troubles, but we've always done our best by Skye, so it's not my fault she's done a runner. It's that social worker you want to be questioning, not me. *She*'s the one who was supposed to be looking after her. And you lot are no better,' he went on angrily. 'You say Skye went missing yesterday, so how come this is the first I've heard of it? I should have been the *first* to know, not the last.'

'Somebody did come to see you yesterday evening,' the first officer informed him. 'But you were sedated, so we couldn't speak to you.'

'Oh,' Jeff muttered, temporarily thrown. 'No one told me. But that still doesn't make it right. And I'm not happy about her being shoved in a home.'

'You'll have to take that up with Social Services,' the man said. 'We'll let you know as soon as we find Skye. But, as I said, if you hear from her in the meantime, please—'

'Ring you,' Jeff cut in. 'Yeah, I know.'

Teeth gritted, he watched now as the coppers made their way off the ward.

'Everything okay, son?'

'Eh?' Jeff snapped his head around at the sound of the voice, and frowned when he saw that it was the man in the bed to his left.

'Just asking if you're okay,' the man said. 'Only that's the third time the bobbies have been to see you in the last two days. You in some kind of trouble?'

Jeff could practically smell the old duffer's curiosity. He opened his mouth to tell him to mind his own business, but quickly changed his mind and clamped it shut again. The way he was feeling right now, he was likely to go too far if he started laying into the man and he couldn't be bothered with the hassle that was bound to cause. Instead, he pushed the sheet off his legs and tugged the curtain around his bed.

A nurse walked over a couple of minutes later and swished

it open again. She frowned when she saw him pulling his trousers on and asked him what he thought he was doing.

'Leaving,' he told her, zipping up his fly and steadying himself on the bed before reaching for his T-shirt.

'You haven't been discharged yet,' she reminded him. 'Doctor Shah wants you to stay for a little while longer.'

'Yeah, well, Doctor Shah's going to be disappointed,' Jeff replied tersely.

'I really wouldn't advise you to leave,' the nurse persisted. 'You're clearly still weak. At least wait until you've spoken to Doctor.'

'What, so he can talk me out of it?' Jeff glanced up at her as he leaned down to retrieve his trainers from under the chair. Then, sighing, he said, 'Sorry, love, I know you're only doing your job, and I really appreciate everything you've done for me while I've been here 'cos you've been brilliant. But my daughter's missing, and I need to go and look for her.'

'I'm sorry,' the nurse apologised. 'I had no idea.'

'I've only just found out myself,' Jeff told her. 'And I'd go crazy lying here not knowing where she is, so you can see why I've got to go, can't you?'

'Of course.' She nodded. 'Just give me a minute to get your discharge papers. And good luck,' she added, patting his arm sympathetically. 'I hope you find her soon.'

'So do I, love.' Jeff smiled sadly. 'So do I.'

Back at the house just then, Skye could hear somebody moving around downstairs. She held her breath when she heard them coming up the stairs, and shuffled deeper into the corner, dragging the quilt with her.

'Front room's clear,' she heard a man say after a minute.

'Back room and bathroom are clear, too,' said another.

'Does it look as if anything's been taken?' a woman asked, and Skye breathed in sharply when she recognised the social worker's voice.

'Hard to tell, the state of this place,' one of the men replied. 'No wonder you lot got called in if this is how they've been living. I wouldn't make my *dog* sleep in those beds, never mind my kids.'

'Unfortunately, some parents aren't as mindful of their children's welfare as the rest of us,' said Val Dunn, her critical words causing Skye to clench her teeth in anger now.

'Well, we've looked everywhere,' the man said. 'She's definitely not here.'

'We haven't checked the attic,' said Val. 'I don't suppose one of you could take a look up there for me, could you?'

Light-headed with fear, Skye bit down on the quilt to keep from crying out and slid lower down into the shadows.

A few seconds later, the hatch was pushed open and a man's silhouetted head appeared. He gazed slowly round for a while, then said, 'Can't see much, but I don't think anyone's up here. I doubt she'd have been able to get up here without a ladder, anyway. I'm six-one, and I'm struggling.'

'Thanks for looking,' said Val, her voice much clearer now. 'But I'll arrange for someone to fetch a ladder over later – just to be on the safe side.'

'No worries.'

When the man withdrew his head and jumped down onto the landing, Skye listened as the three went back down the stairs. She stayed where she was after hearing the front door open and close, scared that it might be a trick and they were standing in the hall waiting for her to come out of hiding. But when several minutes had passed with no sound of movement, she crawled over to the hatch and peeked down.

Relieved to see that the hallway below was empty, she let out a shaky breath and sat back on her heels. That had been too close for comfort, and it was only a matter of time before that bitch social worker came back with a ladder, so there was no way she could stay here now. But where else was she supposed to go? She couldn't go to Hayley's now that she knew her friend's parents intended to hand her over to the police; and there was no way she could risk asking any of the neighbours for help, because they would grass her up as soon as look at her if they thought there might be a reward in it.

As she sat there with her fantasy of hiding in the attic until her dad came home in tatters, Skye heard a beeping sound on the other side of the attic, and her heart skipped a beat when she glanced across and saw a faint glow in the darkness. Realising that a text message had come through to her mum's phone, she scrambled over to it quickly, praying that it would be from her dad.

Hi babes, it's Q, the message read. *Sorry I couldn't get back to you last night, but all hell broke loose over here so I didn't get a chance. Are you okay? I've been worrying about you all night.*

Just nearly got caught, Skye quickly typed back. *Social worker and some men have just been looking for me, and they're coming back in a bit, so I've got to get out of here. Thanks for messaging,* she added. *It's nice to know someone cares.*

Course I care, came the instant reply. *We're mates, and mates stand by each other no matter what.*

Skye was touched to know that she wasn't completely alone in this nightmare. But she still needed to get out of there.

Thanks, that means a lot, she wrote. *But I really need to go now. Where?*

Don't know. Just can't stay here.

There was a pause of a few seconds before QTPye's next message appeared: *You can stay with me, if you want?*

Aw, that's sweet, Skye replied. *But you don't even know me.*

Hey, we're going through the same shit, so I reckon I know you well enough, QTPye reminded her. *You haven't even told Sugarplum half the stuff you've told me, so you obviously trust me.*

Skye felt a bit guilty at the reminder that she'd confided more to this girl than to her best friend in real life. But, like QTPye had just said, she and Skye were going through the same thing, so they had way more in common in that respect.

Course I trust you, she typed now. *But I can't dump this on you, it wouldn't be fair. Anyway, what about your mum and dad?*

What about them? They're so wrapped up in their own shit they don't even notice me *half the time, so they're deffo not going to notice you,* QTPye replied. *You can hide under my bed if they come in. Stay as long as you want.*

Do you mean it? Skye asked.

Wouldn't have offered if I didn't, QTPye assured her. Then: *Look, I'll have to go, 'cos the bell's just rung. I won't be able to get back to you till after school this afternoon. Will you be okay till then?*

Yeah, I'll find somewhere to hide, Skye told her. *And thanks so much for doing this, you don't know how much it means to me.*

Awww, you're welcome babes. Where are you, by the way?

Old Trafford.

Wow, that's freaky! I'm not far from there. Wouldn't it be weird if we actually already know each other? What's your real name?

Skye. Yours?

Jade, but I deffo don't know you, 'cos I'd have remembered a cool name like that. Can't wait to meet you.

Me too.

Right, best let you go before you get nicked, QTPye wrote, bringing Skye down off her cloud with a bump. *Delete our messages on Whisper before you leave. Don't want the coppers tracing us through that, 'cos they'd find you in no time and put you straight on lockdown!!!!*

I'll do it now, Skye replied, terrified at the thought.

Good, and then get out of there! See you later xxx

Skye reached for the laptop to do as she'd been told, but remembered that its battery had died when she tried to turn it on and nothing happened. She bit her lip and gazed at the blank screen. She could take it down to her room and plug it in, but then she would have to find the charger and she didn't really have the time to be searching for anything when the social worker could come back at any time. It would probably be best to leave it up here, she decided. No one ever came up here apart from her, and the social worker would take only a quick look when she came back with the ladder, and then leave when she saw that no one was here.

Convinced that it would be safe up here until her dad came home and she was able to retrieve it, Skye slid the laptop under a layer of glass wool. Then, aware that time was running out, she climbed down quickly from the attic and ran into her room to change into warmer clothes before she left the house by the back door.

Jeff's bus pulled up at the stop on the corner of his road just after Skye had run past with her hood pulled down low. Unaware that he had missed his daughter by mere seconds, he climbed off the bus and walked home, only to remember when he got to the front door that he'd given his key to the social worker so that she could collect some of Skye's stuff.

His back was throbbing by now, and his headache was getting worse, so he wasn't pleased when he went round to the back yard and discovered that the spare key wasn't under the brick where he'd left it. Desperate to sit down with a cup of tea and a smoke, he sifted through the junk until he found a rusty old screwdriver and was able to prise open the window.

After climbing inside, Jeff looked around for the kettle, only to find it in the sink, where it had landed after Andrea had hurled it at him the night before she'd stabbed him. Sighing as he recalled the fight, he filled the kettle and switched it on, then flopped onto a chair to catch his breath.

He gazed around in disgust as he waited for the water to boil. It stank to high Heaven in here, and the filthy floor was littered with shards of broken crockery. Andrea wasn't fond of cleaning at the best of times, and there were days when she wouldn't even get out of bed because of her illness, so the house had never been what anybody would describe as pristine. And Jeff hadn't exactly pulled his weight, either, if he were honest. He tended to leave his stuff where it landed when he got home from work, more concerned about whether or not he could expect dinner than to check if the pots from the night before had been washed. As he viewed it now, through the eyes of the people who had traipsed through here in the last few days, he guessed he could understand why the coppers had treated him like scum back at the hospital. If it hadn't become such a habit to live like this, *he* would probably think that he was scum, too.

A knock at the front door brought him to his feet, and he

wearily made his way into the hall, pulling the kitchen door firmly shut behind him.

'Morning.' Val Dunn smiled up at him when he answered the door. 'I called in at the hospital, but they told me you'd discharged yourself.'

Jeff saw that she was holding his key and, suspecting that she would probably have let herself in if he hadn't been here, he held out his hand.

Val passed it over, and asked, 'May I come in for a minute?'

'If you must,' Jeff muttered, stepping back. This was the third time he'd met her, and she was wearing the same pleated skirt, spotted blouse, granny shoes and scruffy brown coat that he'd seen her in on both previous occasions – which made him wonder if she actually had a life outside of social work, or just lived to stick her nose into other people's business.

Val picked up on his hostility and stayed close to the door when she stepped inside. 'I know you've already been informed about Skye having gone missing,' she said. 'And I came round earlier with a couple of police officers to check if she'd been home. There was no sign of her, but we weren't able to check the attic, so I've arranged for someone to fetch a ladder round later this afternoon – if that's okay?'

'No, it's not,' Jeff snapped. 'I gave you the key so you could get some of her stuff, not to let yourself in whenever you feel like it and snoop around.'

'We only took a quick look,' Val assured him. 'Nothing was touched.'

'That's beside the point,' said Jeff, shoving the key into his back pocket to let her know that she wouldn't be getting her hands on it again. 'You should have asked first. And you can cancel that ladder, 'cos no one's going into my attic except me.'

'That's your prerogative,' Val conceded. 'As long as you let us know if there's any sign that Skye's been here. I'm sure you're aware that it would be an offence to—'

'You can save the lecture.' Jeff cut her short. 'I've already had it off the coppers. And to be honest, I think it's a joke that I'm being treated like I've done something wrong when *I'*m the one who asked for your help in the first place. Which reminds me,' he added accusingly. 'You said you were going to put Skye with foster-parents in a proper house, so how come she ended up getting shoved into a children's home?'

'It's always our intention to rehome children in a family environment,' Val explained. 'Unfortunately, that option wasn't immediately available for Skye. And, given the circumstances, we decided it was best to place her in a more secure facility until the interim protection order was put into place.'

'You what?' Jeff drew his head back and peered down at her through narrowed eyes. 'You never said anything to me about a protection order. This was supposed to be a voluntary arrangement – just till her mum comes home.'

'I'm afraid things have changed since we last spoke,' Val told him. 'Given what happened, and the fact that there's an ongoing police investigation, Skye has been categorised as at risk.'

'*I'*m the one who got stabbed,' Jeff reminded her incredulously. 'So how can you say *she*'s at risk?'

'Because her mother is the suspect, and it happened in the family home.'

'Says who?'

'Mr Benson, I've spoken with the police at length, so I know all I need to know to make an informed decision. And I can assure you that the magistrate wouldn't have granted the order if we hadn't been able to show valid cause.'

'Well, you'd best go back and tell them you got it wrong,' Jeff argued. "Cos, like I've already told the police, I wasn't stabbed in here; I got jumped in the alley.'

'I am aware of what you told the police,' said Val, choosing not to add that they didn't believe a word of it and were waiting until his wife was fit enough to be questioned again before deciding whether or not to press for a prosecution. 'But until a conclusion has been reached, the order stands and Skye remains in our care.'

'Are you for fucking real?' Jeff spluttered. 'She isn't *in* your care, you stupid cow, 'cos you lot are so useless you've *lost* her! How's that protecting her? Go on – explain that to me, 'cos I'm *dying* to know.'

'Calm down, Mr Benson.' Val slipped her hand into her pocket as she spoke, to check that her mobile phone was there in case she needed to call for urgent assistance. 'I appreciate that you're upset, but I have a job to do, and I can't—'

'That just about sums it up, that,' Jeff cut in scathingly. 'It's just a job to you, and if you lose a kid or two along the way, oh well.' He raised his hands in a *so what* gesture.

'It's unfortunate that Skye managed to slip away,' Val said evenly. 'But I assure you that she *will* be found.'

'Yeah, and when she is she'll be coming back *here* where I can keep an eye on her,' Jeff shot back angrily. 'I'm her dad; she's *my* responsibility, not yours. And I don't give a toss what *you*, the police, *or* the magistrates have got to say about that.'

Val decided that it was time to stop beating around the bush, and said bluntly, 'That's not going to happen, Mr Benson. Whether or not your wife is charged, she has mental-health issues, and we'll need to assess how that impacts on

Skye before we can even begin to talk about her being allowed to come home. There's also a documented history of domestic violence that we'd need to look into.'

Infuriated to hear that they had been digging into his private life, Jeff barked, 'That's got absolutely nothing to do with this. It's none of your business what happens between me and my wife.'

'No, but it *is* our business if Skye has been involved.'

'Which she hasn't been, because me and Andrea *never* argue in front of her; she's always in bed.'

'If that's true, then why would you have needed to take Skye to the hospital at midnight last year?' Val gazed coolly up at him. 'According to her records, she had a cut to her cheek that required stitches. How could *that* have happened if she was in bed?'

'She fell out and banged her face on the dresser,' Jeff lied, unable to remember off the top of his head if that was the excuse they had used at the time.

'Really?' Val raised an eyebrow. 'And when her PE teacher reported bruising to her back and arms a few months prior to that, which Skye claimed was the result of falling down the stairs?'

'*I* don't know?' Jeff gave an exasperated shrug. 'Kids have accidents all the time, don't they? I can't be expected to know every little thing that happens to her when I'm at work.'

'And that is *precisely* where the problem lies.' Val pounced. 'You can't be here because you work, so Skye would be left in the care of your wife if we allowed her to come home; a woman who is currently undergoing psychiatric evaluation, suspected of trying to kill you. *That* is why we've got the protection order, and why we intend to retain custody of Skye until we're satisfied that she is no longer at risk.'

Jeff clenched his fists and ground his teeth together. He was trying his damnedest not to fly off the handle, but this bitch was pushing him to the edge. She had obviously been doing her homework and, while he couldn't deny what she'd said, he was furious that everything had gone so far so fast.

'I think you'd better leave,' he said quietly, scared that he might snap and say something he would later regret. 'And don't bother coming back, 'cos you won't be getting in.'

'Okay, I'll go.' Val gave a tiny nod of acceptance. 'But just be aware that I won't need your permission to enter if I have reason to believe that Skye has come home and you're harbouring her. She's a minor who's been identified as being at risk, and the law is fully on my side if I choose to come back.'

'Whatever.' Jeff reached behind her and yanked the door open.

Already angry, his blood began to boil when he spotted his landlord's car pulling up at the kerb. 'What do *you* want?' he asked churlishly when the man climbed out.

'My rent, for starters,' Alan Ford replied, flicking Val an uninterested look when she stepped out from behind Jeff and made her way to her car on the other side of the road. 'Then *you* out of my house.'

'Do one.' Jeff went to close the door, but hesitated when the man pulled an official-looking sheet of paper out of his pocket.

'Court order for eviction,' Ford declared, triumphantly thrusting it under his nose. 'I warned you what'd happen if you and that wife of yours caused any more trouble, so now you've got forty-eight hours to get your shit out – or my lads will be moving it for you.'

Jeff felt his body go hot and cold with fury, and when he

spotted Val taking her time to get into her car he almost lost it. 'You still here, you nosy bitch? Aren't you supposed to be fixing the damage you've done and finding my daughter?'

Val climbed behind the wheel without replying. Jeff glared at her when she started the engine and drove away.

'More trouble?' Ford sneered, shaking his head. 'Just can't help yourself, can you, Benson?'

'Go fuck yourself!' Jeff spat. 'And you can fuck that, an' all,' he added, snatching the paper out of Ford's hand and tearing it in half. He flung both pieces back at the man, and then slammed the door in his face.

'Forty-eight hours,' Ford called through the letter box. 'I still want the two months' rent you owe me, *and* I'll be billing you for the cost of whatever damage you've done while you've been here!'

Behind the door, Jeff slid down to the floor and pressed his hands over his ears.

7

It was gone six p.m. before Skye received the text she'd been waiting for. After leaving the house that morning, she had gone to the local park and found herself a hiding place in a thick clump of bushes, far away from the play area where mothers and their children had been coming and going all day. The sky was a stormy shade of grey by now, and the temperature had plummeted, so she was almost crying as she pulled the phone from her pocket with frozen hands.

Where are you? the message read.

In the park, she replied.

Can you meet me at side of Brookes Bar station in half hour?

Yeah. But how will I know you?

Don't worry, I'll find you xxx

A little miffed that she'd been left waiting for so long, but also relieved that her ordeal was almost over, Skye slipped the phone back into her pocket and fought her way out of the bushes. The station was a fair distance away, but she'd have walked to London and back if it meant having somewhere warm and safe to sleep – even if it *was* only on the floor beneath her new friend's bed.

The station entrance was situated midway down a dead-end sloping path off a busy main road. A solitary street lamp at the road's end provided the only light, and the further Skye walked down the path when she got there fifteen minutes later the darker it became. Glad of the cover, she quickly found a hiding place behind a skip from where she had a clear view of the entrance but couldn't be seen by the station staff or passengers.

An hour later she was still there. Sure that she hadn't missed Jade, because everybody who'd come out of the station so far had been much older than them, she began to wonder if her friend had changed her mind – or had ever intended to come in the first place.

Unwilling to accept that Jade would do something like that, Skye tucked her chin down inside the collar of her jacket and watched as the latest batch of commuters streamed out from the entrance and hurried up the path. She envied them because they were all heading for the warmth and comfort of home, and she wished that she could do the same. But she no longer *had* a home, thanks to her stupid mum.

As she scanned the now-deserted area she jumped when a guard suddenly pulled a metal shutter down over the entrance, plunging her into almost total darkness. Stiff and sore, she stood up and tugged the phone out of her pocket, intending to text Jade and ask where she was. But her hands were so cold that she lost her grip, and she cried out in despair when it slipped from her fingers and smashed onto a rock at her feet before bouncing out onto the path. Rushing out from her hiding place, she snatched it up off the floor and was devastated to see that the screen had shattered.

'*No!*' she cried, frantically pressing the buttons to no avail. 'Why are you doing this to me?'

A bright light suddenly sliced through the darkness from the road's end, and Skye breathed in sharply when she glanced up and saw a car coming slowly towards her. Scared that it might be the police, she darted back behind the skip and watched as it drove past. It turned around at the end of the path and came back, and she thought that it would continue back on up to the road. But when it stopped just a few feet away, and she saw the driver staring at her through his open window, the hairs rose on the back of her neck.

'Are you Skye?' the man called out to her. 'I'm Jade's brother Tom. She got held up and asked me to come and get you.'

When Skye didn't move after a few seconds, he held a mobile phone out through the window, saying: 'You can ring her if you don't believe me.'

Skye bit her lip. She wasn't stupid – she knew better than to get into a car with a stranger. But he *had* known her name, *and* that she was supposed to be meeting Jade. And she doubted he'd be offering to let her use his phone if he wasn't telling the truth.

'Sorry if I scared you,' Tom said when she walked over to the car and climbed in beside him. 'Jade didn't give me a description, so I wasn't sure who I was supposed to be looking for. Have you been waiting long?'

'Not really,' Skye mumbled, finding it difficult to speak because her lips were so numb. 'About an hour.'

'Sorry about that,' Tom apologised, setting off when she'd buckled her seat belt. 'Jade said she sent you a text to let you know I'd be coming instead of her, but you didn't answer.'

'I dropped my phone,' Skye told him, her cheeks smarting as the warm air from the heater vents thawed them.

'Ah, right.' Tom nodded and fixed his gaze on the busy road, looking for a gap in the traffic.

Skye cast a hooded glance at him from the corner of her eye when he drove on. QTPye – *Jade* – had never

mentioned him, but they'd usually been too busy talking
about their parents to have got around to the subject of
brothers and sisters. Tom looked like he was in his twen-
ties, which was a bit of a gap considering that Jade was
the same age as Skye; and he wasn't particularly good-
looking, from what she could see in this light. His nose
was a bit big, his Adam's apple was sticking out quite far
over the collar of his shirt, and he had curly hair, which
she'd never really liked on boys. It surprised her that his
hair looked quite fair, because she'd imagined Jade as
being dark-haired for some reason – although she wasn't
sure why, considering that she had never seen a picture
of her.

'Oh, by the way, there's been a change of plan,' Tom
suddenly said. 'I don't know how much Jade's told you, but
our folks are going through a bit of a rough patch and they've
been arguing all day, so she thought it'd be best if you waited
at my place until she can come for you.'

Skye was embarrassed to have nearly been caught staring
at him, but she also felt guilty for putting him and his sister
out when they had troubles of their own to deal with, so she
said, 'You don't have to do that. You can drop me off here;
I'll walk back.'

'No chance.' Tom smiled. 'Jade's dying to meet you, and
she'd kill me if I let you slip away. Anyway, it's nice to have
a bit of company when I'm driving, so relax; we'll soon be
there.'

Skye settled back in her seat and gazed out of the window
as they crawled along in the heavy traffic. The combination
of the heat and the soft classical music that was drifting out
from the speakers made her feel sleepy and she began to
drift off. But she jolted awake when Tom picked up speed

again, and she gazed out of the window to see that they were heading into a more rural area.

The further they went, the more spaced out the houses and street lamps became. By the time Tom left the road they had been travelling along and turned in through a set of broken gates, she hadn't seen a single sign of life in a full ten minutes.

The silhouetted shapes of trees and bushes lined the long, bumpy driveway, and Skye squinted through the windscreen when a house came into view up ahead.

'Is that yours?'

'It's my cousin's place,' Tom told her. 'He's in the army, so I look after it when he's stationed overseas. It's falling to bits, but it's quiet, so it suits me.'

Skye gazed at the house as they drew near and saw that he hadn't been lying about the state of it. Even in the darkness, she could see that the roof was badly bowed, and the porch over the front door was listing to one side, while the wonky window frames looked like they were in danger of falling apart at any second.

Tom came around to Skye's side when he'd parked at the back of the house, and offered his hand to help her out. She was about to take it, but shrank back at the sound of muffled barking.

'Is that a dog?'

'Yeah, but it's okay,' Tom assured her. 'Come on, let's get inside. It's freezing out here.'

Skye climbed nervously out of the car and grimaced when her foot sank into something squelchy. She could hardly see anything, but there was an unpleasant smell in the air and she hoped she hadn't trodden in dog muck. Nose wrinkled in disgust, she tugged her foot free and quickly followed Tom over to the house.

Terrified that the dog might be waiting to pounce, Skye took a cautious step inside when Tom unlocked the door and waved for her to go in ahead of him. But she stumbled back at the sound of yet more barking, and clutched at his arm.

'It can't get me, can it?'

'Don't worry, I'll protect you,' Tom assured her as he reached over her shoulder and flicked a switch.

A light flickered on, and Skye saw that they were in a kitchen; every surface of which was littered with empty bottles, cans, and microwave-food cartons, while the sink was crammed with dirty pots and pans. There was a bad smell in the air, and she guessed it was coming from the overflowing bin that was standing beside the grease-splattered cooker.

A skittering sound made her jump, and she was terrified when she turned her head and saw a long-haired Alsatian with a matted coat coming towards her. Tom ordered it to get to bed before it reached her, and she was relieved when the dog immediately turned and slunk over to a filthy blanket in the far corner of the room.

Tom slipped his jacket off, tossed it over the back of a chair, and then opened a cupboard and took out a tin of dog food.

'Hungry?' he asked, glancing back over his shoulder at Skye as he peeled back the lid.

Skye caught a whiff of the meat and shook her head.

'I didn't mean *this*.' He grinned. 'I picked us up a takeaway when Jade asked me to come and get you. Hope you like sweet-and-sour?'

Embarrassed when her stomach rumbled, Skye folded her arms over it and nodded shyly. Sweet-and-sour was her absolute favourite, but they rarely had the money for takeaways in their house so she couldn't remember the last time she'd had it.

After feeding the dog and tossing the empty can onto the ledge, Tom wiped his hands on his trousers before taking a couple of takeaway cartons out of the fridge. He peeled the lids off and placed them in the microwave, then frowned when he glanced over at Skye and saw her still standing by the door.

'I hope you're not going to stand there all night? You're making me nervous.'

'Sorry.' Skye pulled a chair out from under the table and sat down to watch as Tom moved over to the sink and pulled out two plates from the crockery heaped in it. After giving them a quick rinse under the tap, he wiped them dry with a grubby tea-towel. He took the cartons back out of the microwave when it pinged, and shared out the food.

'Sorry about the mess,' he apologised, using his elbow to shove a pile of old newspapers off the table so that he could put Skye's plate down. 'I meant to clean up before you got here, but I didn't have time.'

'It's okay,' Skye murmured. She was sure he'd told her that he'd come straight from work when he picked her up, but she guessed that he must have come back here first.

Tom handed a fork to her, and then sat down and got stuck into his food. After a while, he glanced over at Skye and gave her a questioning look when he noticed the way she was picking at hers.

'What's up?' he asked, his mouth full, his cheeks bulging. 'Don't you like it?'

'I'm not very hungry,' she lied, reluctant to admit that the mouldy-looking thing that was stuck between the prongs of her fork was putting her off.

'Don't worry; he'll have anything you can't manage.'

Tom gave a backwards nod in the dog's direction, and Skye shivered when she saw that it had finished its own food and was now lying with its head on its paws, its dark gaze riveted to her plate.

When dinner was over, Tom reached for her plate and dumped it and his own in the sink.

'Do you want me to wash up?' she offered.

'Nah, it'll keep,' he said. 'Come through here. I'll get a fire going.'

Skye edged around the table and followed Tom into a small, shabbily furnished living room. It smelled strongly of the dog in there, and the threadbare sofa was coated in its fur. 'Do you think Jade will be long?' she asked, perching on the edge of a cushion.

'I'll ring her in a minute,' Tom said, switching on a standard-lamp before kneeling in front of the soot-blackened fireplace. After piling some lumps of coal into the grate and shoving a little pile of kindling under them he lit it, and watched to see that the flame had caught before pushing himself back up to his feet and heading back into the kitchen.

Skye looked around when he'd gone. Apart from the sofa she was sitting on, there was one battered armchair in the room, the ancient-looking lamp with its old-lady-style shade, a heavily scarred coffee table, and a bookcase – one shelf of which contained a row of dusty old books, while the rest seemed to be crammed with letters, yellowed newspapers, tobacco tins, and empty beer bottles. There was no TV or hi-fi, and if there was a house phone she couldn't see it. In fact, the only thing in the room that looked as if it actually belonged in this century was a laptop that was sitting on a small table beside the armchair – and even that looked battered.

Torn from her observations by the sound of Tom's voice

floating through from the kitchen, Skye cocked her head to listen as he hissed, 'You're joking! What am I supposed to tell her? She thinks you're on your way.'

He went quiet for several moments after this. Then, sounding irritated, he said, 'All right, but you'd best get here first thing. And let me know if it gets any worse.'

Skye looked up when he walked back into the room, and gave him an innocent smile. But it quickly slipped when he said, 'I'm really sorry about this, but Jade's not coming. My mum's kicked the old man out, and now she's insisting our Jade stays with her in case he comes back and tries any funny business.'

'Oh, right,' she said, sitting forward. 'I'd best go, then.'

'You don't have to,' Tom assured her. 'It's not your fault, is it? Anyhow, Jade asked if you could stay the night, and I've already said yes.'

'I don't mind,' Skye insisted, feeling awkward for putting him out. 'You probably want to go to your mum.'

'Like hell!' Tom snorted. 'I had enough of them when I was living there. Anyhow, it's freezing, and I haven't got enough petrol to get back to Manchester. It's up to you if you fancy walking, but I'm not going out again tonight.'

Skye was torn. She desperately didn't want to outstay her welcome, but she didn't have a clue where they were, and the thought of trying to find her way home in the pitch dark terrified her.

'I've got a spare room, if that's what you're worried about,' Tom went on persuasively. 'Jade sleeps there when she stays over, so it's no problem you using it.'

Relieved that she wouldn't have to go back out into the cold, Skye gave him a grateful smile. 'Okay, then. Thanks.' Then, shyly, she said, 'Can I use the toilet, please?'

'Course,' Tom said. 'Come on, I'll show you where it is. It's a bit of a mess, though,' he warned as he opened another door and went out into a dark, narrow passageway.

'It's okay,' Skye said as she followed him. 'I'm used to it.'

After leading her up a steep flight of stairs, Tom pushed open a door and pulled a light cord, revealing a manky old bathroom.

'Feel free if you want to take a bath,' he said, stepping aside to let Skye enter. 'It might take a while for the water to get hot, though, 'cos the boiler's a bit knackered. That's your room,' he said then, pointing out a door at the other end of the landing. 'And I think our Jade might have left some nightclothes last time she was here.'

'Thanks,' Skye murmured, going into the bathroom and closing the door.

She'd been desperate for a wee for ages, but when she saw the state of the toilet she wasn't sure she wanted to sit down on it. Tom had warned her that the room was a mess, but that was an understatement. The floor was littered with soggy newspapers, socks and towels; the old bath and sink unit had deep, ingrained tidemarks, and both sets of taps looked crusted and green; the window-ledge was cram-packed with old bottles of shampoo, razors, and various other junk. As for the toilet, the upturned seat was spattered with urine stains, and there were loads of tiny hairs stuck to the rim and the basin, while the water in the filthy bowl looked dark and murky.

Unable to hold it in any longer, Skye reluctantly unzipped her jeans and hovered over the seat, but almost jumped out of her skin when Tom tapped on the door.

'I've left a towel out here for you,' he called through the wood. 'Come down when you're finished; I'll make us a drink.'

'Okay,' she called back, looking around for a toilet roll. Seeing none, she was forced to use a sheet of newspaper instead.

When she'd heard Tom going back down the stairs, she opened the door and reached for the small towel he'd left on the floor outside. She ran water into the sink and washed herself quickly, using the sliver of soap she'd found stuck down beside the bath taps. Then, ashamed of how greasy her hair was when she glanced into the pitted mirror, she dipped her head into the water and scrubbed it with the soap.

The house was freezing, and she shivered as she made her way to the room that Tom had pointed out to her. He had turned on the bedside lamp, and a nightdress and a dressing gown were laid out neatly on the bed. Skye gazed around in amazement. The wallpaper in here was every bit as faded and old-woman-like as in the other rooms, and the furniture was just as ancient. But in contrast to those rooms, this one was tidy, and the nightclothes and girly bedding looked so clean that they could have been brand new.

Skye guessed that Jade must obviously be tidier than her brother, and she smiled when she spotted the boy-band posters pinned to the wall facing the bed, most of which were of Blue – the band over which she and QTPye had first bonded on WhisperBox, and from where Skye had taken her screen-name BlueBabe. Hayley preferred One Direction, but Skye and Jade had better taste, which was probably why they had got on so well from the start – and why Hayley had always been jealous of their friendship.

At the thought of Hayley, Skye sighed and touched her angel. They had been best friends for as long as she could remember, and she missed her; but she just couldn't shake off the niggling little thought that Hayley could have helped her if she'd really wanted to. Jade didn't even really know her, but she hadn't hesitated to offer Skye a place to stay when she'd heard how bad things were – and that made her a *real* friend, in Skye's eyes.

Determinedly pushing Hayley from her mind, Skye towel-dried her hair and combed it with her fingers before changing into Jade's nightclothes and heading back down the stairs.

Tom was sitting in the armchair with the laptop on his knee when she walked into the living room. He looked up and smiled when he saw her. 'Feeling better?'

'Yeah, loads.' Skye smiled shyly back and took a seat on the couch.

'Hope you don't mind wine?' Tom nodded towards a cup sitting on the coffee table in front of her. 'I was going to make tea, but the milk's off.'

'It's fine,' Skye lied, reaching for it. She'd only tasted wine once before, and had absolutely hated it. But she wasn't about to say no, because it was a thrill to be treated like a grown-up after being pushed around and treated like a kid by all the other adults she'd come into contact with recently.

'I'm just catching up on some work,' Tom told her. 'Won't be long.'

Skye nodded and sipped her wine. It tasted every bit as disgusting as she'd thought it would, but she forced herself not to grimace and took another sip.

The open fire made this room far warmer than the rest of the house, and Skye felt the tension slide off her shoulders as she gazed into the crackling flames. After a few minutes, she cast a surreptitious glance at Tom and decided that he wasn't quite as ugly as she'd initially thought. He was nowhere near as handsome as her dad, who was the best-looking man in the whole world, in her opinion; but his eyes were quite nice, and she liked the way he talked to her: as if she was *his* friend as well as Jade's. An only child herself, Skye couldn't help but envy her new friend for having a big brother like him to look out for her.

She dipped her gaze when Tom suddenly looked up and smiled at her. She took another sip of her drink. It still tasted nasty, but she liked the heat as it slid down her throat; and the floaty sensation that was starting to settle over her was quite nice, too.

8

'Help! Someone help me!'

Skye's harsh breath seared her raw throat, and she cried out in pain when her bare foot snagged on the exposed roots of a tree. She crashed to her knees but, terrified when she heard heavy footsteps pounding the ground close behind, scrambled back up quickly and forced her legs to carry her on.

A buzzing noise was coming from the darkness up ahead, and she raced towards it, praying that somebody was there who could help her. But just as she opened her mouth to scream again, she was blinded by a piercing white light.

'Morning.'

Skye's eyes popped open at the sound of the voice, and she breathed in sharply when she saw the hazy figure of a man standing in the doorway.

'Nightmare?' Tom smiled as he switched off the electric razor he was holding.

Skye nodded, and drew the quilt that was covering her up to her throat. Now that her vision was clearing and she was able to see his face, she remembered who he was. But she had absolutely no memory of having come upstairs and climbed into bed.

'You must have been wiped last night 'cos you were flat out when I finished working, so I had to carry you up.' Tom answered her unspoken question. 'I thought about leaving you on the couch, but I figured you'd be more comfortable up here. Hope you slept okay?'

Skye nodded and slid her chin lower beneath the quilt to cover her burning cheeks.

'I've taken the day off work,' Tom went on. 'Thought I'd get something special for tea, since I've got a guest. What do you fancy?'

Skye cleared her throat, and said, 'I should probably go home. My mum and dad will get worried if I stay out again.'

'No, they won't.' Tom smiled and walked over to the bed. He squatted down beside her and peered into her eyes, saying softly, 'Don't get upset, but Jade's told me what's going on, so I know all about your folks, and you getting put into a home and running away.'

'Oh,' Skye murmured, blushing some more. 'Is – is she here?'

'No, she rang while you were asleep and we had a long chat.' Tom reached out and stroked a stray hair off her face. 'Stop worrying – we're going to look after you. Okay?'

Skye nodded, but she was too embarrassed to look him in the eye.

'Right, I'd best get moving.' Tom straightened up and backed towards the door. 'Help yourself if you want anything. But don't try and open the door while I'm gone, 'cos the dog might go for you.'

'I won't,' Skye croaked, shuddering when a vision of the mangy dog leapt into her mind.

After Tom had left, she waited until she heard the sound of his car starting up before she slipped from the bed and peeked out through the grimy net curtain. The back garden looked more like a scrapyard, cluttered as it was with broken cars, rusted old washing machines, fridges and bicycle frames.

An expanse of wildly overgrown grass lay behind this, and yet more grass and trees beyond that.

Wherever they were, it was far away from home, and that both comforted and scared Skye. On the one hand, there was no chance of anybody she knew spotting her and telling the police that she was here; but on the other, if Jade didn't turn up again and Tom asked her to leave, she had absolutely no clue how to get home. And, as much as he was insisting that he didn't mind her being here, he was bound to get fed up if she stayed too long.

Tom had turned his car around by now, and when he leaned forward in his seat and peered straight up at her Skye stepped quickly back from the window. But he'd obviously seen her, so when he smiled and waved she forced herself to wave back.

Too scared to venture downstairs in case the dog went for her, she climbed back into the bed and gazed around the room. It was comforting to think that Jade had lain here before her, and she wished that the girl would hurry up and get here.

Skye had dozed off by the time Tom came back, but she woke with a start when she heard him running up the stairs.

'What's wrong?' she asked, sitting bolt upright when he burst through the bedroom door as if he had the Devil at his heels.

'I just saw you on the news,' he panted, clutching at his chest as if he'd been running for miles. 'I was walking past a TV shop and you popped up on the screen, so I went in to see what it was about, and . . .' He sat down heavily on the bed and reached for her hand. 'I'm really sorry, but they're saying you stabbed your dad.'

'*What . . .?*' Skye gripped the edge of the mattress with her free hand as the room went into a spin.

'I know you didn't do it,' Tom went on, sounding every bit as shocked as she felt. 'But the police think you did, and they've put a warrant out for your arrest. They're in town right now, handing out posters with your picture on.'

'But it wasn't me,' Skye cried. 'It was my mum.'

'I know.' Tom gave her a regretful look before adding, 'I didn't want to have to tell you this, 'cos I knew it would upset you, but they were on the news as well.'

'Who?'

'Your mum and dad. She was crying, and he had his arm round her. They both said it was you who stabbed him. They said you've always been difficult, and they knew you'd do something terrible one day; they just never thought you'd turn on them.'

'*No.*' Skye shook her head in disbelief. 'They wouldn't do that. I haven't done anything wrong.'

'I'm so sorry,' Tom said quietly. 'I wouldn't have told you, but I thought you needed to know.'

'I don't understand,' Skye murmured numbly. 'My mum was holding the knife when the police came in – that was why they arrested her. They *know* she did it.'

'She reckons she took it off you after you did it, because she was trying to protect you,' said Tom. 'And that's not all,' he added grimly.

'What do you mean?' Skye gazed up at him, wondering what else there could possibly be.

'Remember that home you got sent to? Well, the people who run it have said that you threatened *them* with a knife as well, and then stole a load of money before you took off.'

'That's not true!' Skye squawked, her eyes flooding with tears. 'They're lying!'

'I know.' Tom squeezed her hand between his. 'But the police believe them, and they're going all out to hunt you down.'

'What am I going to do?' Skye's face crumpled as the tears spilled down her ashen cheeks.

'You're going to stay here with me,' said Tom, pulling her into his arms and holding her close. 'I promised Jade I'd look after you, and that's exactly what I'm going to do.'

At the mention of his sister, Skye peered fearfully up at him through her tears. 'What if she sees the news and tells the police I'm here?'

'She'd never do that.' Tom was adamant. 'Trust me, I know my sister, and she won't tell a soul. I'd best ring her, though,' he went on thoughtfully. 'Tell her to stay away while all this is going on. It was all right when you were just talking to each other online, but I don't want her getting dragged into this.'

'No, she can't be,' Skye agreed guiltily. 'I shouldn't have asked her for help. It wasn't fair on her.'

'You didn't ask, she offered,' Tom reminded her. 'And she'll be fine – as long as you deleted those messages like she told you to?'

Skye nodded and wiped her nose on the back of her hand.

'Where did you leave your computer?'

'I hid it in the attic, under the floor stuff.'

'Good girl.' Tom rocked her gently. 'Now, stop crying, everything's going to be okay. You'll be safe here with me while we find a way to prove your innocence.'

'Thank you,' Skye croaked, clinging to him as if her life depended on it.

Tom held her for a while longer before gently easing her away, saying, 'Lie down and try to relax while I ring Jade. I'll bring you a drink when I'm done; it'll make you feel better.'

After everything she'd just heard, Skye doubted that anything would ever make her feel better again. She just couldn't believe that her mum and dad had said all that awful stuff about her – although she didn't know why she was so surprised, considering how many times she'd seen them lie to the police in order to protect each other in the past. They would have a fight and her mum would scream blue murder, only to retract her statement as soon as she calmed down and say she'd made it all up – or even deny that she'd said it in the first place. It was like some kind of game to see how far they could push each other; how far they could push the police. But it was serious this time. A knife had been involved, and her dad could have died. And they must have known that the police wouldn't let it drop, so they'd concocted this plan to pin the blame on Skye, knowing that she wasn't there to defend herself. And, for some reason that Skye just couldn't get her head around, the staff at the children's home had said that she'd pulled a knife on *them* as well. So now nobody would believe a word she said, and she would go to prison for the rest of her life, even though she hadn't done a single thing wrong.

'Hey, I thought I told you to stop that,' Tom chided when he came back a few minutes later carrying a cup and a bunch of roses and found her sobbing into her pillow. He laid the flowers on the floor and sat beside her on the bed. 'Here, drink this.'

Chest still heaving, Skye swiped at her tears and sat up.

'It's brandy,' Tom said, guiding the cup towards her lips.

'I was going to make tea, but I figured you needed something stronger.'

Skye sipped it and grimaced. It tasted even worse than the wine, but Tom had said it would help and he was the only person in the world that she could trust right now, so she drank some more.

'Attagirl.' Tom smiled when she'd finished and took the cup from her hand. 'Now relax. You'll feel better in a minute.'

Skye lay back against the pillows and shivered as a warm, tingling sensation began to creep up from her toes.

'I got you these while I was out.' Tom reached for the flowers. 'Thought they might cheer you up.'

Skye's heart fluttered in her chest as she gazed at the red roses. 'Are they for me? No one's ever bought me flowers before.'

'Well, they should have,' said Tom, laying them on the bedside table and stroking her cheek. 'You're a lovely girl, and you deserve to be treated like a princess.'

'Thank you.' Skye felt the words float up from her throat and out through her lips. She was starting to feel really, really strange; as if she had slipped out of her skin and was floating, weightless, towards some kind of beautiful dreamscape.

'You're welcome,' Tom whispered, lowering his face and pressing his lips gently onto hers.

Back in Manchester just then, unaware of what was happening to his daughter, Jeff was thoroughly pissed off. He'd rung his solicitor this morning, only to be told that he stood no chance of having the eviction order overturned, so now he had just over twenty-four hours to pack up and get out. Then he had the problem of finding somewhere else to live – which wasn't going to be easy, considering he was flat broke.

Furious with life, he was cramming the contents of his bedroom drawers into the few boxes he'd just managed to scrounge from the local supermarket. But he immediately abandoned his task when he heard his phone ringing downstairs and, hoping that it was Skye, ran down to the kitchen to get it.

Jeff had been confused yesterday when he'd turned his phone back on after coming home from the hospital and had seen a couple of texts from Andrea. When he'd read them and realised they were actually from Skye, he knew that she had been back to the house and must have found Andrea's phone. It had been switched off when he'd tried to call it back, but he hoped that Skye had seen his missed call and was trying to reach him again.

'Hello . . . Skye? Is that you?' he gabbled when he snatched his phone up off the ledge. 'Where are you, sweetheart?'

'Sorry, it's just me,' the caller said apologetically. 'You said you were going to call me back.'

'Oh, yeah, sorry.' Disappointed to hear Shirley Dawson's voice instead of Skye's, Jeff pulled a chair out from under the table and sat down. 'Things have been a bit crazy since you called, and I haven't had a chance.'

'It doesn't matter.' Shirley excused him. 'Are you still in hospital? Can I come and see you?'

'No, I'm at home,' Jeff told her, shaking a cigarette out of his pack and looking around for his lighter. 'But it's not really a good time right now, to be honest. I've been evicted, and Skye's gone missing.'

'Oh, God, that's awful,' Shirley said concernedly. 'Where do you think she's gone?'

'No idea.' Jeff lit up and inhaled deeply. 'The police are looking for her, so there's not a lot I can do except wait.

She'll be okay, though,' he added, sounding more convinced than he felt. 'She's probably just staying with a mate.'

'Yes, probably,' Shirley agreed. Then, sensing that he wanted to change the subject, she asked, 'Why have you been evicted?'

''Cos my landlord's an arsehole,' Jeff replied bitterly. 'But he's done it by the book, so I haven't got a leg to stand on.'

'How long have you got?'

'A day, so I should really get back to the packing.'

'Do you need any help?'

'No, I'll be okay, but thanks for offering,' Jeff said gratefully.

'Do you have somewhere to go?' Shirley asked. 'Only, you know you're more than welcome to stay at mine if you're stuck.'

Jeff thanked her again. Then, standing up when he heard a knock at the front door, he said, 'Best go – someone's here.'

'Just a minute,' Shirley said quickly. 'I need to talk to you about something.'

'It'll have to keep,' Jeff said, already walking out into the hall. 'I've got an appointment with the doctor tomorrow afternoon, so I'll see you when I bring my sick note in.'

'That's what I'm trying to tell you,' said Shirley. But Jeff didn't hear the rest, because he had already cut the call.

When he opened the door, the woman who was standing outside smiled up at him and said, 'I hope I'm not disturbing you, but are you Skye's dad?'

'Who wants to know?' Jeff grunted, all set to send her away with a flea in her ear if she turned out to be another nosy social worker.

'I'm Kathy Simms,' she told him. 'Hayley's mum.'

'Oh, right.' Jeff felt guilty for having been so snappy. 'Sorry, my head's all over the place at the moment.'

'I can imagine,' Kathy said sympathetically. 'It's a terrible business; you must be so worried.'

'Just a bit.' Jeff sighed. 'So, what can I do for you, Kathy?'

'I promised Hayley I'd come round. She's not very well at the moment, and she's been fretting about Skye, so I thought it might cheer her up if there was news. But I'm guessing there hasn't been any?'

'Not yet, no.'

'I'm so sorry.' Kathy gazed up at him with genuine concern in her eyes. 'I can't begin to imagine how hard this must be for you.'

Jeff gave a tight smile and cast a surreptitious glance at his watch. It was kind of her to call round but he wished she'd hurry up, because time was running out fast and he still had tons to do.

'Hayley was so upset when she got ill again just before Skye's birthday,' Kathy was saying now. 'She'd already bought her present, but she thought she wouldn't be able to give it to her, so she was made up when Skye called round last Friday.' She smiled fondly now, and said, 'It was only a cheap little necklace, but Skye seemed to like it.'

Jeff gave her a blank look. He didn't know anything about a necklace, but he was more bothered to think that he might have missed Skye's birthday. He couldn't for the life of him remember its date but he wasn't about to admit that to this woman and have her thinking he didn't care about his daughter.

Embarrassed when she remembered that Skye had received the gift immediately before finding him that day, Kathy said, 'Oh, I'm sorry, you probably didn't see it. It was just a little angel, nothing special. Hayley told her to wish on it whenever she feels low and it will lift her back up. Daft, I know, but that's girls for you.' She stopped talking at last and gave Jeff an apologetic smile. 'Sorry. You've got enough on your plate without me going on.'

'It's fine,' Jeff assured her. 'But I am kind of in the middle of something, so I should really get back to it.'

'Oh, of course, sorry,' Kathy apologised again. She turned to leave, but then hesitated and turned back. 'Before I go, can I just say that I know Skye, and she's a sensible girl, so I'm sure she'll turn up safe and sound.'

'I hope so,' Jeff murmured. 'Thanks again for coming round, love. And I hope Hayley gets better soon.'

'Me too,' said Kathy, smiling wanly. 'Bye, then.'

Jeff nodded goodbye and watched as she walked away. He'd written Hayley off as a posh kid when he had met her that time, but her mum hadn't struck him as being at all stuck-up. She just seemed like a genuinely nice, caring woman, and he was glad that Skye was mates with her daughter because God knew she needed at least *one* good female role model in her life.

When Kathy had turned the corner, Jeff closed the door and made his way back up the stairs. In his bedroom he cast a thoughtful gaze at Andrea's clothes still hanging in the wardrobe. He had been so pissed off with her for landing him in this mess that he had contemplated leaving her stuff behind for the landlord to dispose of. But as he looked at her dresses and blouses now, he knew he couldn't do it. She was a nightmare, but they had worked their way through some pretty tough times in the past and he was sure they could get through this, too.

He would just make damn sure that Andrea couldn't get

her hands on any more knives when she came home. And it would be a long time before he trusted her enough to turn his back on her again.

Reaching a decision, he lifted Andrea's clothes out of the wardrobe and laid them inside a box. If he got cracking, he reckoned he could have most of it done by morning. He would then have to throw himself on Alan Ford's mercy and ask if he could leave the boxes here until he'd found a new place, because there was no way he could lug everything around the streets by hand. And if Jeff had to swallow his pride and beg the smug bastard on his knees, so be it. He just hoped he found somewhere fast, because he needed to get everything sorted before Andrea and Skye came home.

9

'No, don't!' Skye gasped, struggling to push the man off. His breath was hot on her neck, and the stench of sweat was suffocating. 'I can't breathe! Stop it! Please!'

She woke with a start, and a little whimper of fear escaped her lips as the pitch darkness weighed down on her. She was alone, but as her vision began to sharpen and silhouetted shapes came into focus she knew that something wasn't quite right. Everything was in a different place. No, not just that. It was different furniture. In a different room.

Terrified when the door creaked open slowly, she pushed herself up the bed with her heels until her back struck the metal bedstead. As dim light from the landing began to creep in, she saw Tom in the doorway and cried out with relief.

'Hey,' he crooned, rushing to the bed when she burst into tears and taking her in his arms. 'What's all this?'

'I didn't know where I was,' Skye sobbed, clinging to him. 'I thought – I thought a m-man . . .'

'Ssshhh.' Tom stroked her hair as she gulped back her tears. 'It was just a nightmare, but you're safe now. I'm here.'

Glad of his presence, Skye stayed in his arms until the fear had subsided. Then, easing herself free, she wiped her eyes and asked, 'Is this your room?'

'Yeah. It seemed a bit daft, you sleeping in there after we . . .' Tom trailed off and smiled as he looped a lock of her hair behind her ear. 'I wasn't sure you liked me at first, but you do, don't you?'

Skye thought it was a strange thing to ask, but she did like him, so she nodded.

'Good, because I liked you as soon as I saw you,' he went on. 'But I didn't think I stood a chance, because you're so pretty. Then, when you kissed me last night, I just knew it was meant to be.'

Skye felt as if someone had just dripped ice water down her spine. She didn't remember kissing him. Oh, God, what had she done? And why did she keep falling asleep and forgetting everything? Was she going crazy – like her mum?

'Don't worry, my beautiful princess,' Tom was saying now. 'Your mum and dad might not love you, but *I* do, and if anyone ever tries to hurt you again, I'll kill them. You're mine now, and we love each other.'

Skye had started to tremble. He was talking as if they were boyfriend and girlfriend, and something had obviously happened if he was saying that she had kissed him. But she couldn't remember a thing after him giving her that brandy yesterday. Maybe she was an alcoholic? There had to be *some*thing wrong with her.

As he gazed down at her, a flicker of a frown crossed Tom's brow. 'You're not regretting it, are you?'

Skye was more confused than she had ever been in her life before, and she felt guilty when she saw the uncertainty in his eyes. Her mum had always said that the truth came out in drink, so she guessed that she must like him even more than she'd thought she did. It was the only explanation, because she would never have thrown herself at him otherwise.

'Have you changed your mind?' Tom was peering deeply into her eyes.

Skye bit her lip and shook her head. This all felt very, very weird, but she had to admit that it *was* kind of nice to know that Tom liked her so much.

She stiffened when he raised her chin and lowered his face to hers, but she tried her hardest to relax when he whispered, 'Don't fight it – this is what being in love feels like.'

She didn't really enjoy the kiss. Tom's lips were wet and sloppy, and she hated the feel and taste of his tongue poking around inside her mouth. But she closed her eyes and let him carry on, telling herself that it was different from the kisses she'd shared with boys in the past because they obviously hadn't known how to do it properly.

Excited more by the thought that Tom saw her as a woman than by what he was doing to her, she didn't resist when he fondled her breasts. But when he slipped his hand down between her legs, she winced and pulled back.

'It's okay,' he whispered, pushing her down gently onto her back and climbing on top of her.

'It's sore,' she cried, struggling to push him off as he unzipped his fly and pushed his knee between hers to part them. 'Don't, Tom! I don't want to!'

'That's not what you said the first time.' Tom's voice was breathy in her ear. 'Stop fighting, you'll just make it harder. It'll be easier this time, I promise.'

Skye was crying by now, and she struggled with all her might to stop him from peeling her knickers down. But he was too strong, and she felt as if she was being ripped apart when he entered her roughly.

'God, that feels good,' he said hoarsely, pushing deeper.

Skye squeezed her eyes shut and bit down hard on her

lip as the tears rolled down her face and soaked the pillow. It hurt, a lot, but she couldn't stop him so she had no option but to lie still and pray that he would hurry up and finish.

Ten agonising minutes later, Tom's body stiffened and he clamped his lips down hard on hers, almost choking her when he thrust his tongue deep into her mouth. Then, at last, he sighed and rolled onto his back.

'Are you okay?' he asked, reaching out after a while and pulling her towards him.

Still sniffling, Skye nodded and laid her head on his chest. Like the man in her nightmare, Tom smelled of stale sweat and cigarette smoke, but she was just glad that it was over and he was being nice to her again.

'You're so special,' Tom murmured sleepily as he stroked her hair. 'I just know we're going to be together for ever.'

Skye closed her eyes and listened as his heartbeat gradually began to slow to normal. She hadn't liked the sex one little bit, but she didn't dare risk upsetting Tom by telling him that. Now that the police were looking for her, and her mum and dad had turned against her, she had absolutely nowhere else to go if he kicked her out.

Skye fell asleep in Tom's arms, but she was alone when she woke up the next morning, and she was mortified to see dried blood on her thighs and the sheet. Desperate to wash away the shameful evidence of what she had done, she pushed the quilt off her legs and lowered her feet to the floor. But she hesitated when she saw the roses that Tom had bought her sitting in an old vase on the bedside table. A folded note was propped against it and, guessing that it was for her, she reached for it.

Morning, Princess, it read. *You look so beautiful sleeping I wish I didn't have to leave you, but I've had to go to work. I'll be home as soon as I can get away. Try not to miss me as much as I'm going to miss you. All my love, your Tom.*

He'd put ten kisses at the end, and had drawn a love-heart with an arrow through it. It was the most romantic thing Skye had ever seen, and it made her feel guilty for having tried to resist him last night. She'd thought that her mum and dad loved her, because that was how parents were supposed to feel about their children; but she had never felt as loved by them as she did by Tom.

She just wished that the sex didn't have to hurt so much.

Still clutching the note, Skye got up and wandered over to the window when she heard the sound of birdsong outside. It made a pleasant change from the noise of cars racing up and down, neighbours arguing, and drunks singing or shouting abuse as they made their way home from the pub – which was all she ever heard through her window at home.

It was a bright day, and she felt the heat of the sun on her face as she gazed out at the countryside. It was so peaceful out there, and she felt safe knowing that nobody had a clue where she was. It still hurt to know that her mum and dad had betrayed her, but she had Tom now so she didn't need them any more.

Even as she thought it, Skye knew that she was lying to herself. She still loved her parents, and probably always would. Not that they deserved it after what they had done, but she couldn't control what her heart felt.

Determined not to think about them, because she knew it would ruin her fragile mood, Skye went to the bathroom and ran water into the sink. As she waited for it to fill, she gazed around at the mess and decided to do some cleaning before

Tom came home. It was the least she could do to repay him for his kindness. And, anyway, if he'd meant what he said about them being together for ever, then this was her home now, too; and it was her duty to do the housework while he was out earning money to feed her.

After washing, Skye went back to the bedroom and got dressed before tackling the bed. But just as she was pulling the soiled sheet off, she heard a snuffling sound behind her and almost wet herself with fear when she turned and saw the dog standing between her and the door. She hadn't been downstairs since that first night, and it looked even bigger and more dangerous up close.

'Sit!' she squeaked, praying that her voice wouldn't spur him on to attack her. When the dog cocked its head but remained standing, she tried to imitate the firm way she'd heard Tom speak to it, and repeated her command more sternly: 'I said *sit*!' Amazed when the dog obeyed this time, she edged around the bed, murmuring, 'Good boy. Now stay there. *Stay*!'

Her plan was to get out of the room and lock it in, but she stopped in her tracks when the dog suddenly stood up again, and whimpered, 'Please don't bite me' when it came towards her.

Shocked when it sniffed her feet and then licked her leg before sitting down, she reached out tentatively and patted its head. Feeling braver when it gazed up at her with mournful eyes, she squatted down and held out her hand. Delighted when it plonked its paw onto her palm, she laughed. 'Wow! You're just a big softie, aren't you?'

An old leather collar was buried beneath its fur, and Skye squinted at the disc that was hanging from it when she noticed faded lettering etched onto it.

'Bernie,' she said when she was able to make it out.

At the sound of its name, the dog licked her face, and Skye grimaced as she wiped the slime off with the back of her hand. 'God, you stink!' she complained, wrinkling her nose in disgust. 'I think you need a bath when I've sorted this place out.'

She stood up now, and smiled when Bernie followed her out onto the landing and down the stairs. When they reached the kitchen he went straight to the back door, and she guessed that he wanted to go outside to do his business.

'Sorry, boy,' she told him when she saw that there was no key in the lock. 'You'll have to wait till Tom gets home.'

Bernie ran around her when she tried to walk away, and then sat down and barked up at a shelf that was screwed to the side of the cabinet. Skye followed his gaze and saw a rusted old biscuit tin. Intrigued, she reached for it, and was amazed to see a load of old keys nestled among the buttons, reels of cotton and various other bits and bobs that it contained.

'Oh, you clever boy,' she exclaimed, laughing when Bernie ran back to the door. 'Come on, then; let's see if we can find one that fits.'

Bernie waited patiently as she tried the keys one by one. But as soon as she found the right one and started to open the door, he shoved his nose through the gap and squeezed his way out. Nervous of following in case someone should happen to be passing, Skye watched from behind the door as he emptied his bladder against an old bicycle. Alarmed when he then trotted into the long grass and she lost sight of him, she hissed, 'Bernie, come back! *Bernie!*'

Annoyed with herself, because Tom had told her not to open the door, and now she had lost his dog, Skye stuck her head outside and peered around to make sure that nobody was around. Then, calling '*Bernie?*' in a loud whisper, she made her way across the cluttered yard. He was nowhere in sight, but she heard a scratching sound and followed it through the long grass and around the side of an old shed.

Bernie was pawing at the door, but he sat down when he saw her, as if waiting for her to let him in. She glanced at the cobwebs and shuddered. 'I don't think so, mate. Come on.' She patted her thigh and turned to go back to the house, but hesitated when he didn't follow. 'What's up, boy?'

When Bernie barked and then lay down with his head on his paws, Skye groaned. 'Come on, you don't want to go in there. Let's go back to the house and I'll find you something nice to eat. Would you like that? Some nice din-dins?'

She sighed when Bernie still didn't budge. She really didn't fancy getting attacked by an army of spiders. But he seemed desperate to go in there, for some reason, and if letting him have a quick look around would get him to come back to the house she supposed it wouldn't hurt.

The door was locked when she tried the handle, so she said, 'Okay, wait there while I go and get those keys. But if you're not here when I get back, you're in big trouble.'

Amused with herself for talking to Bernie as if he could understand a word she was saying, Skye made her way back to the house. She heard a car approaching just as she reached it and, terrified that it might be the police, she ran inside and peeped out through the dirty net curtain. Her legs shook with relief when she saw that it was Tom, and she quickly opened the door again.

'You scared me half to death,' she said, smiling as Tom stepped out of the car. 'I thought you were at work.'

Anger blazing in his eyes, he strode towards her, demanding, 'How did you unlock that door?'

Her smile slipping, Skye said, 'I found some keys. Bernie wanted to go out.'

'Where is he?' Tom peered around.

Skye pointed in the general direction of the shed but decided not to mention that she had ventured round there, too. She wasn't sure why Tom was so annoyed with her, but she didn't want to make him even more so.

'*BERNIE*!' Tom yelled. 'Get back here!'

'He only wanted a wee,' Skye murmured, hugging herself when she heard the harshness of his tone. 'It's my fault, not his.'

'I told you not to open the door,' Tom snapped. 'If anyone had seen you, you'd be going straight to prison – and so would I for letting you stay here. Is that what you want?'

'No.' Skye shook her head and dipped her gaze guiltily. It was no wonder he was angry. He was trying to protect her, and she had risked being caught and getting them both into trouble. 'Sorry, I didn't think.'

'Well, you need to listen to me in future,' Tom said, pushing her back inside when the dog came slinking back. 'All it'll take is for one person to see you, and that's it – game over.'

'I know,' Skye said contritely. Then, wincing when he kicked out at Bernie, she cried, 'Don't do that! I just told you it was my fault.'

'He knows he's not allowed out unless I'm here.' Tom eyed the dog as it scampered inside with its tail between its legs. 'Last time he got loose he tried to attack someone, and the police said they'll shoot him if it ever happens again.'

'God, that's horrible,' Skye gasped.

Tom gave her a dark look and then went back to the car

and took several bulging carrier bags out of the boot before following her inside.

'I got out of work early so I could do some shopping,' he told her, dumping the bags on the ledge. 'Thought I'd best stock up, seeing as we don't know how long this is going to go on for.'

Desperate to get back into his good books, Skye said, 'I'll put it away, if you want?'

Tom relocked the door and slipped his jacket off. Then, breathing in deeply to shake off his bad mood, he held out his arms and said, 'You can do it in a minute. I want my kiss first.'

Skye closed her eyes when he pulled her close and forced his tongue between her teeth. She didn't like it any more than she had the first time, but she told herself that she would get used to it – eventually.

When it was over and Tom let her go, she waited until he turned to get something out of his pocket before quickly wiping her mouth on the back of her hand. She gave him an innocent smile when he turned back to her, and said, 'I was going to do some cleaning. Have you got any bleach, and cloths, and that?'

'Look under the sink,' Tom told her, squinting as he lit a cigarette.

Bernie was lying on his blanket. He was visibly trembling, and Skye felt guilty when he flicked a nervous glance at her as she knelt down to search the cupboard. He would never have been kicked if she hadn't let him out, but she sensed that Tom wouldn't approve if she made a fuss of him. So she ignored him and rooted through the ancient bottles and cans until she found some bleach and a crusty old dishcloth.

Tom was staring at her when she stood up and turned

back to him. 'They've been talking about you on the news again,' he said. 'It was on the radio when I was driving back just now. They reckon you're dangerous, and they're warning people not to approach you if they see you.'

'Why?' Skye was stunned.

'Your mum and dad told them that you threatened to kill them in their sleep, so now the police think you're some kind of psychopath.'

Skye's face drained of colour and her legs went weak. 'That's not true.'

'*We* know that, but they've only got your parents' word to go on so they're taking no chances.' Tom took a deep drag on his cigarette and shook his head. 'I just wish they knew you like I do, then they'd know it was all lies.'

Grateful that he still believed in her, Skye sat down heavily on the chair facing his and tried to make sense of this latest news.

'Look at you, all upset.' Tom reached across the table and took her hand in his. 'Your parents should be ashamed of themselves. They've got a lovely daughter, but it's like they just want to get rid of you any way they can. It's cruel, and they don't deserve you. And when they said that about you being promiscuous . . .' He trailed off and clenched his jaw.

'What does that mean?' Skye croaked.

'That you sleep around,' said Tom. 'Makes me so mad hearing stuff like that when I know I was your first. I was tempted to stop the car and ring that radio station when I heard what they were saying, but I couldn't risk it, because then everyone would know that you're here. I might *have* to, though, if they keep on saying it.'

'No, you can't!' Skye begged, terrified that she would get caught.

'It's really hard to hold it in when I know they're lying,' Tom said, gazing into her eyes. 'But I won't say anything if you don't want me to. They'll find out the truth eventually, but you're all I care about right now.'

'Thank you.' Skye gazed down at their hands as he entwined his fingers through hers. 'I just don't understand why they're doing this. What have I done to make them hate me so much?'

'They're idiots, and you're better off without them,' Tom said supportively, flicking his ash into the saucer he'd been using as an ashtray. 'I saw Jade earlier, by the way.'

'Oh?' Skye looked up. 'Did she ask about me?'

'Yeah, but I don't think you're going to like what she told me.'

'Why, what did she say?'

'Something about a girl called Hayley. Do you know who she meant?'

Skye nodded and waited for him to go on.

'She reckons she talked to her in that chat room you two used to go on.'

'WhisperBox,' said Skye, praying that Jade hadn't told Hayley that she was here, because Hayley might tell her parents, who would probably tell the police.

'Yeah, I think that's what she called it. Anyway, she said the girl was slagging you off; saying how she's never really liked you, and only pretended to be your friend because she felt sorry for you.'

Skye's brow creased in disbelief. 'She wouldn't say that. She's my best friend.'

Tom shrugged. 'Only telling you what Jade told me. And she's got no reason to lie, has she?'

'No, but . . .' Skye trailed off and subconsciously touched

her angel. She would never have dreamed that Hayley would turn on her like that. But as Tom had just said, why would Jade lie about it? It was Hayley who was jealous of Jade, not the other way round; and Jade had never tried to turn Skye against her before, so why would she start now?

'I'm sorry, babes.' Tom raised her hand to his lips and kissed it. 'I hate seeing you upset, and I really wish I didn't have to keep telling you all this stuff.'

'It's not your fault,' Skye murmured. 'You and Jade are the only ones I can trust.'

'I'm glad you know that,' Tom said quietly. 'Because we'd have nothing if you didn't trust me.' He gazed at her for a few more seconds, then said decisively, 'Right, enough of this. They can say what they want, but we're not going to let them get to us any more. From now on, it's just you and me against the world.'

Skye smiled, but dropped it quickly when Tom pulled her to her feet and started leading her towards the door. 'What about the shopping?' she asked, guessing that he was heading for the bedroom. 'I was supposed to be putting it away.'

'It can wait,' Tom said, gripping her hand firmly as he walked up the stairs.

In the bedroom, Skye averted her gaze shyly when Tom stripped down to his underpants and climbed beneath the quilt. This would be the first time they had done it when she was stone-cold sober, and she was dreading it because she knew that it would hurt. But then, she supposed the pain was a small price to pay for the security and love that Tom was offering her. So, taking a deep breath, she undressed quickly and climbed in beside him.

'Wait!' she said, sitting back up quickly when Tom reached for her.

'Why are you taking it off?' he asked, watching as she unclipped the necklace.

'Hayley gave it to me,' she told him, pulling a face as she dropped it onto the bedside table. 'But now I know what she really thinks of me, she can get stuffed. They *all* can.'

Tom gave her a slow smile and pulled her into his arms.

10

'Mr Benson?'

Jeff had been staring at the floor, but he jerked his head up when he heard his name being called, and rose quickly to his feet when he saw Barbara, the housing officer who had been dealing with his application, gesturing for him to join her in the tiny interview room.

He'd been seen fairly quickly when he arrived at lunchtime, but after getting him to fill out a raft of forms Barbara had told him to sit in the waiting room. It was now four p.m. and his back was aching from sitting around for so long. He just hoped she wasn't going to tell him to sling his hook, because that really would piss him off.

'Sorry for keeping you waiting,' Barbara apologised. 'We're a bit short-staffed at the moment.' She took her seat and linked her hands together on the desktop as she waited for Jeff to sit down across from her. 'Right, we've looked into your application,' she said then, 'and I'm pleased to tell you that you've been accepted onto our list.'

'Great. So what do I do now?'

'Start bidding on properties. I'll talk you through the process, and give you your ID number for logging onto the system. However, I do have to warn you that you may be waiting a while before you're offered anything because you don't have many points.'

'But I'm homeless,' Jeff reminded her.

'I appreciate that,' she conceded. 'But we have a high demand for rehousing in this area, and a lot of our applicants are in greater need.'

'How much more in need can you be than having nowhere to live?'

'I can give you the numbers of some hostels,' Barbara suggested. 'But please let me know when you get a place so I can contact you if anything comes up.'

Jeff stared at her in disbelief. 'I'm not being funny, love, but I've been sat here all day. Surely you can do better than this?'

'In all honesty, you're lucky you've been accepted at all,' Barbara informed him. 'When people make themselves homeless, as *you* did by ignoring your landlord's warnings about antisocial behaviour, we're under no legal obligation to rehouse them.'

'Hang on,' Jeff cut in indignantly. 'For a start, I did not *make* myself homeless, and there was no antisocial behaviour; the landlord was just looking for an excuse to kick us out.'

'Which you provided.'

'What, by getting myself stabbed?'

'You've already told me you received two warnings prior to the eviction order being issued,' Barbara reminded him. 'And in my experience, the court wouldn't have granted it unless your landlord had been able to provide sufficient proof to back up his claims.'

'I don't even know what he said to the court, 'cos he did it when I was in hospital,' Jeff told her. 'He could have said anything.'

'That's something you'd have to take up with him and the magistrate,' said Barbara. 'As I said, you're lucky we've agreed to accept you. But as an adult with a regular wage and no dependants, you are not considered a priority.'

'But I'm *homeless*!' Jeff was starting to raise his voice. 'And I *have* got dependants – my wife and daughter.'

'One of whom, according to you, is currently in hospital, and the other in the care of Social Services.'

'My wife could be out any day, and when my daughter's found she'll be coming back to me.'

'*If* that happens, we'll reassess your housing needs,' Barbara assured him. 'But there's nothing to stop you from renting privately in the meantime.'

Frustrated that she didn't seem to have listened to a word he'd said when she had initially interviewed him, Jeff balled his hands into fists beneath the desk.

'I've already told you I've been trying to do that, but there's nothing going,' he said through gritted teeth. 'If there was, do you think I'd have bothered coming here?'

'Mr Benson, you're in full-time employment so you should have no problem getting a landlord to take you on,' Barbara replied coolly. 'The majority of our applicants are unemployed and don't have that option.'

'You mean scroungers?' spat Jeff. 'So I work my backside off and I've got to suffer, but they can sit on their arses all day popping out kid after kid and they get everything handed to them on a plate?'

'I think we're done here.' Barbara stood up. 'If you'd like to take a seat outside, I'll get you those numbers.'

Jeff wanted to tell her where to stick her numbers, but he held his tongue and made his way back out to the waiting room. It was a massive knock-back to be told that he wasn't considered a priority despite being homeless, and he loathed the idea of having to move into a hostel. But it looked as if he didn't have much choice. He'd rung every local letting agent and scoured the newspapers in search of a private place, and there was absolutely nothing going – at least, nothing that didn't require a massive deposit that he had zero chance of getting his hands on any time soon. The council was his only hope, but now it looked as if he was going to be waiting a long, long time for them to come up with a place for him.

Already thoroughly pissed off, Jeff was gutted when he walked out of the office a short time later and discovered that he was down to his last cigarette. No money, no smokes, no home – and if he didn't get a move on, he'd miss his appointment with the GP and have no sick note to take into work.

Sure that his day couldn't possibly get any worse, he set off for the surgery.

An hour later, tired, hungry, and desperate for another cigarette, Jeff walked through the gates of Ripley Autos and, nodding hello to the shirt-and-tie guys who worked in the showroom and were currently shadowing the lone customer who was strolling around the lot, made his way to the service station at the back.

An Audi estate was up on the ramps, and Jeff saw that all three of his fellow grease-monkeys were working on it: Chris and Phil at the back tinkering with the exhaust, Des at the front with his head under the bonnet.

Des glanced up when he heard Jeff's footsteps, and flicked a hooded glance at the others before quietly asking, 'What are you doing here?'

Jeff sensed an atmosphere and frowned. 'Yeah, I'm all right, thanks, mate. Nice to see you, too.'

'You'd best go,' Des urged in a whisper. But it was too late; the others had already seen Jeff and were walking towards him.

'Didn't think you'd have the nerve to show your face round here again,' Phil said coldly, wiping his hands on a dirty rag.

'What you on about?' Jeff gave him a questioning look.

'Don't come the innocent,' Chris chipped in angrily. 'We know all about it.'

'All about what?' Jeff gazed from one to the other of them in confusion.

'You know what gets to me?' spat Phil. 'All them times you've had us all feeling sorry for you, making out like your missus kicked you out for nowt when all along you've been beating the shit out of her. It's no wonder she stabbed you.'

'My missus would slit my fucking throat if I ever tried that crap on her,' Chris joined in. 'But I'd never do that, 'cos I'm not a lowlife piece of shit like you.'

'Are you serious?' Jeff stared at the pair in disbelief. 'How long have you known me?'

'Too fucking long, now we know what you're *really* like.' Phil stepped forward now and pressed his forehead against Jeff's. 'You'd best do one before we give you a taste of your own medicine,' he snarled. 'You might scare the shit out of your missus, but it ain't gonna wash with us. Or do you only try it on with defenceless women?'

'Back off!' Furious that they had made up their minds about him without giving him a chance to explain, Jeff shoved Phil away roughly. 'If you're trying to wind me up, it's worked,' he snapped. 'But you can fuck off if you think I'm letting you goad me into a scrap, 'cos you've got this dead wrong.'

'You're bound to say that,' Chris said scathingly. 'Hardly going to admit it, are you? Cunts like you never do.'

'I'm saying it 'cos it's *true*,' Jeff retorted angrily. 'You can believe what you want, but I'm no wife-beater – never have been, never will be.'

'Not what we heard,' said Phil. 'My wife's mate lives on your road, and she reckons the police are at yours every other night 'cos of you knocking Andrea around.'

Jeff turned to Des – the only one who hadn't actually accused him of anything yet – and asked, 'Do *you* believe this bullshit?'

Des shrugged. 'I don't know what to think, mate. I wouldn't have thought you was like that, but why would the lass say it if it wasn't true?'

'It's your Skye I feel sorry for.' Phil jumped back in. 'The shit that poor kid must have had to live with, watching her dad beat up her mum. I swear to God, if there wasn't a camera in here, I'd . . .' He bared his teeth and, growling, smashed his fist into his palm.

The door that led to the offices and showroom opened behind them just then and the owner's son, Tony, strode in. A real gym-bunny, he looked like a typical nightclub bouncer – and had the temper to match the bruiser image.

'I thought I heard your voice,' he said, marching over to Jeff with a scowl on his face. 'What do you want?'

Jeff clenched his teeth when he heard the coldness of the man's tone. Obviously the lads weren't the only ones who had heard rumours and condemned him in his absence.

'I brought my sick note,' he said, pulling the slip out of his pocket. 'Hey!' he protested when Tony snatched it from him and ripped it in half. 'You can't do that.'

'I just did,' said Tony, giving him a fierce look. 'You're sacked. Now fuck off while you can still walk.'

Out of the corner of his eye, Jeff could see Chris and Phil

smirking and it infuriated him. 'I'm not having this,' he said angrily. 'I've done fuck-all wrong, and you're out of order for treating me like this.'

'Are you fuckin' *deaf*?' Tony bellowed. 'I said do one!'

'You can't sack me.' Jeff stood his ground. 'I've got rights.'

Tony gave a sinister smile and stepped closer. Nose to nose now, he stared menacingly into Jeff's eyes, and said, 'So take me to a tribunal, you fuckin' muppet. But I guarantee you won't make it to court in one piece – *if* you make it there at all.'

Jeff was no coward but he was also no fool, and this was a battle that he instinctively knew he would lose. So, stepping back, he cast a look of betrayal at his so-called mates and walked out with his head held high. He had worked alongside those men for almost two years, and had probably spent more time with them than he had with Andrea and Skye. He knew their wives and kids, had celebrated their birthdays, and even supported them when they had suffered losses in their families. And they had done the same for him, so he didn't get how they could change their opinion of him so suddenly and so completely.

Shirley Dawson was at her desk, finishing off some paperwork before she packed up for the day. She glanced up when a shadow passed her office window and leapt to her feet when she saw Jeff walking past with a thunderous look on his face.

'Wait!' she called, running to the window and waving to catch his attention. 'Jeff! *JEFF*!'

He didn't see her and carried on walking, so she dashed from the office and, ignoring the receptionists who asked what was wrong as she ran past, raced outside.

'Jeff!' she called again, running after him as he strode toward the gates. 'Wait!'

At last Jeff stopped and turned around. Out of breath when she reached him, Shirley gasped, 'You should have called me back. I was trying to warn you.'

'Go back inside,' Jeff said, flashing an angry look back at the showroom when he spotted Tony watching through the window. 'No point you getting into trouble as well.'

'Sod him,' said Shirley, after glancing back to see what Jeff was looking at. 'I'm more concerned about you. Are you okay?'

'Not really,' Jeff replied tightly. 'But there's nothing I can do about it, 'cos he's made it quite clear what'll happen if I try to make a case of it.'

'I'm so sorry,' Shirley said sympathetically. 'You know if there was anything I could do . . .'

'I know.' Jeff sighed and ran a weary hand through his hair. Then, giving a defeated smile, he said, 'Oh, well, back to the drawing board.'

'What are you going to do?'

'No idea. But don't worry about it, I'll sort something.'

'My offer's still there if you need somewhere to stay,' Shirley reminded him.

Jeff nodded. 'Thanks, love.'

'No, really,' Shirley insisted, sensing that his pride would prevent him from accepting. 'And nobody need know if you'd rather they didn't. I've got a spare room – you can stay as long as you need to.'

Touched, Jeff reached out and squeezed her arm in a gesture of gratitude. Then, desperate to get out of there, he turned and walked away.

Resigned, by the time he got home, to the fact that he was now out of a job as well as a home, Jeff rolled up his sleeves and carried all the boxes he'd packed into the living room. There were nine in total, and they were all heavy, because he'd crammed as much as possible into each one. His back was killing him by the time he'd finished, and he wasn't looking forward to shifting them again when – *if* – he found a place to take them to. He was just glad that the furniture belonged to the landlord so he didn't have to worry about tackling that as well.

He spent the next few hours cleaning, but it was a futile task. Things had been pretty good when they had first moved in here; Andrea had been reasonably stable, and he'd just landed the job at the garage after months of struggling in part-time warehouse positions. But it hadn't taken long for the cracks to appear, and as he went from room to room looking at the evidence of Andrea's furious outbursts he knew he had a cat in hell's chance of getting his deposit back. There were holes in almost every door, the wallpaper was ripped and stained, several pieces of furniture were broken, and both the fridge and the washing machine were dented from the kicks and punches that had been rained on them at one time or another. And then there was the bloodstained living-room carpet to replace on top of all that, so it was going to take for ever to pay it all off.

Thoroughly depressed by the time he'd done everything that could be done to make the place look half presentable, Jeff sat on the couch with his head in his hands. He jumped when his phone beeped a short time later, and sighed when he saw a message from Shirley on the screen.

I've got a bottle of wine, it read. *And there's a huge stuffed-crust pepperoni pizza in the oven that I can't possibly eat all by myself. So what time should I expect you?*

She had written her address at the end, and finished off

with a smiley face. Jeff couldn't help but smile himself as he gazed at it. Shirley was a good woman, but more than that she was a good friend – and God knew he could use one of them right now.

Having decided, Jeff slipped his jacket on and picked up the small bag he'd packed. Then, sure that the neighbours would probably watch him leave from behind their nets and cheer with joy to be rid of him, he switched off the lights and set off for Shirley's place, calling in at a shop on the way to buy some much-needed cigarettes with the change he'd found down the back of the couch.

Shirley's ground-floor flat was a good twenty-minute walk from Jeff's house and he was exhausted by the time he got there.

'At last!' she said, opening the door before he had a chance to ring the bell and giving him a huge smile. 'I was starting to think you weren't coming.'

'Sorry,' Jeff apologised, stepping inside and putting his bag down. 'I was sorting the house out. Or should I say *trying* to,' he added, rolling his eyes as he slipped his jacket off.

'That bad?' Shirley asked, taking the jacket from him and hanging it up.

'Nothing a bulldozer wouldn't fix,' he quipped.

He looked at her now, and frowned when he saw that she had changed out of her work blouse and skirt. She looked fresh and feminine in jeans and a baby-pink T-shirt, with her usually pinned-up auburn hair loose around her shoulders. 'I haven't stopped you from going out, have I?'

'Oh, yeah, 'cos I'd look *really* hot bopping at the Ritz in these babies, wouldn't I?' Shirley teased, lifting her foot to show him her pink fluffy slippers. 'Anyway, I invited you,' she reminded him. 'So, come on, let's get you sat down; you look wiped.'

Two table lamps were casting a warm glow around the small living room, and the TV was on in the corner with the volume turned down low. Shirley rushed over to the couch and positioned some cushions in the corner, then ordered him to take off his shoes and lie down.

Jeff couldn't help but smile as he slipped his feet out of his trainers. He'd had his reservations about coming here, mainly because of the conclusions that people would inevitably jump to if they found out. But any misgivings were already melting away, and he sank down onto the couch with a sigh of relief.

'Thanks for this,' he said gratefully. 'I really appreciate it.

'You're more than welcome,' Shirley said softly. 'And, like I said, you can stay as long as you like.'

'I'm hoping it'll only be for a few days,' Jeff assured her. 'Just until I can get into a hostel.'

'A hostel?'

Jeff shrugged. 'Wouldn't be my first choice, but I can't afford a deposit on somewhere private so I haven't got much option. Don't worry, I'll pay my own way while I'm here,' he added quickly, in case she thought he was expecting her to feed him as well as give him a temporary roof over his head.

'Jeff, it's fine,' Shirley insisted. 'And I don't want your money. You're still recuperating, so I just want you to relax and stop worrying. And tomorrow I'll drive you over to pick up the rest of your stuff.'

'No, it's all right, the landlord says I can leave it there for a week,' Tom told her. 'I'm hoping I should have somewhere by then. No point shifting it twice, is there?'

'Well, the offer's there if you change your mind.' Shirley smiled. Then, gesturing with a nod towards the kitchen, she said, 'Best go and check on that pizza.'

Jeff rested his head back against the cushions when she'd gone and closed his eyes. He already felt more relaxed than he had in days, and he was so tired that he could easily have skipped dinner and gone straight to bed. Life was a living nightmare at the moment, and he dreaded to think what was going to get thrown at him next. But he'd be able to cope better if he could have one good undisturbed night's sleep.

His eyes were still closed when Shirley carried their plates through a short time later, and she smiled fondly as she gazed down at him. He was a good man, and he didn't deserve what people were saying about him. The guys at work were supposed to be his friends, but they obviously didn't really know him if they thought he was capable of what he'd been accused of. But then, he wasn't the kind of man to reveal his private business to all and sundry, so they didn't know the half of what his wife had put him through. Shirley knew some of it, because Jeff had trusted her enough to confide in her when things had been really bad and he'd needed someone to talk to. She had no doubt that it was even worse than he had intimated, but she refused to believe that he was the aggressor he'd been made out to be. He just wasn't like that.

When Jeff suddenly opened his eyes and looked up at her, Shirley blushed and quickly put the plates down on the table. 'I thought you were asleep. I was just wondering if I should wake you and let you know dinner's ready, or cover you with a quilt and leave you there for the night.'

'I was only dozing.' Jeff pushed himself upright to give

her room to sit down, and grimaced as a sharp pain ripped through his back.

'Are you okay?' Shirley asked. 'Do you need a painkiller?'

'Yeah, I think I'd better,' Jeff said, dropping his feet to the floor. 'I forgot to take them earlier. And I missed my antibiotics, as well.'

'Stay there, I'll get them. Where are they?'

'In my bag, front pocket. Thanks, love.'

'Will you stop thanking me?' Shirley chided. 'I'm your friend, not Mother bloody Teresa.'

She left the room and came back a few moments later carrying the pharmacy bag containing Jeff's medication, along with a glass of water. Jeff took them from her and popped two capsules and two tablets out of the foil strips. When he'd washed them down, Shirley took the glass and placed it on the table before passing his plate to him.

'You don't have to wait on me,' he said amusedly. 'I'm not a complete invalid.'

'No, but you need to rest,' she insisted. 'Anyway, I like looking after people. I always secretly wished I'd trained to be a nurse instead of getting into accounts. At least I'd have been doing something useful.'

'You'd have been a great nurse,' Jeff agreed, lifting a slice of pizza to his mouth. 'You've got a great bedside manner.'

He winced as soon as the words had left his mouth, and bit down on the pizza. This was another reason why he'd been hesitant about staying here: because he and Shirley had a tiny bit of history. It was only a drunken kiss at the works' Christmas do, and he had immediately regretted it so they had agreed never to mention it again. But it was still there, hanging between them like an invisible veil, and the mention of bed – as innocently as it had been meant – brought the guilt rushing back.

Beside him, Shirley's heart was pounding. Determined to act as if everything was perfectly normal and she hadn't noticed his discomfort, she turned up the TV volume and settled back in her seat to eat her dinner. She had liked Jeff from the moment they'd met, and had always thought him extremely attractive with his black hair, deep blue eyes, and quiet aura of strength. And she wasn't the only one, because the receptionists at work had gone into flirt over-drive when they'd first laid eyes on him. He had made it clear from the off that he wasn't interested in any of them, and Shirley respected him for that. But even though they had never spoken about the kiss since it had happened, he had to have guessed that she still fancied him if his reac-tion to the mention of bed just now was anything to go by. She knew it was selfish, but it had been a long time since she'd enjoyed the company of a decent man in her home. She had been looking forward to seeing Jeff tonight, so the last thing she wanted to do was scare him off and send him running for the hills.

When they had finished eating, Shirley opened a bottle of wine and was relieved when the tension gradually evaporated. She and Jeff made small talk for a while, and watched a bit of TV. But when she caught him stifling the third yawn in as many minutes, she smiled, and said, 'I think I'm ready to hit the sack. I've made up the spare bed for you, but feel free to stay up if you're not ready to go to sleep yet.'

'No, I'm shattered,' Jeff admitted. 'I need to make an early start on looking for a place tomorrow. And I want to call in at the police station to see if there's any news on Skye.'

Flooded with guilt at the mention of his missing daughter, Shirley gave him an apologetic look. 'Oh, God, I totally forgot to ask about that. Have you heard anything yet?'

Jeff shook his head and sighed. 'I'm actually starting to wonder if they're deliberately keeping me out of the loop because social services are involved.'

'Social services?' Shirley gave him a questioning look.

'The police called them in,' Jeff explained, remembering that they hadn't really spoken about what had actually happened that night. 'A social worker came to see me in hospital and took my key so she could pick up some of Skye's stuff from the house. She got me to sign some forms while she was there, agreeing to let them look after Skye,' he went on bitterly. 'It was supposed to be a voluntary arrangement, but the bitch shifted the goal posts while I was laid up and applied for a protection order, so now I'm going to have to fight to get Skye back – *if* they find her.'

Once he'd started, he couldn't seem to stop and Shirley listened in silence as he poured out the whole story. Sad by the time he'd finished, she said, 'I'm so sorry. I had no idea things were so bad.'

'Worst thing is, it's my fault,' Jeff murmured, thoroughly drained by now. 'I knew Andrea was in a bad way, but I let her get to me and that was stupid. I should have just kept my mouth shut and made her start taking her tabs again, then none of this would have happened.'

'Maybe not this time,' Shirley said softly. 'But I've got to admit I kind of agree with what that copper said. I know you don't really like talking about Andrea, so I only know a fraction of what goes on day to day; but even *I* can tell that she's got a serious problem. And if she could do that to you, what's to say it wouldn't be Skye next time?'

'No.' Jeff shook his head adamantly. 'She'd never hurt Skye.'

'She already did, when she hit her in the face with that ashtray,' Shirley reminded him.

Annoyed with himself for having told her about that, because it made Andrea sound like an out-of-control monster, Jeff said, 'That was an accident. We thought Skye was asleep and didn't hear her coming downstairs. Nothing like that has ever happened since.'

Shirley could see that he was struggling and gave him an understanding smile. 'I'm not bad-mouthing Andrea, I'm just saying it's something you need to think about. She might get better now, but there's always a chance that she'll get ill again, and you have to be prepared for that – for Skye's sake, if not your own. The good thing is, the police and social services must have dealt with thousands of cases like this, so they'll know it's not your fault and they won't take Skye away from you permanently.'

'You reckon?' Jeff gave a derisive snort. 'You haven't heard the way they've been talking to me, or seen the way they keep looking at me, like I'm some kind of lowlife.'

'I'm sure they don't think that,' Shirley said kindly. 'They're just trying to look out for Skye.'

'Maybe,' Jeff conceded bitterly. 'But who's looking out for her now they've lost her?'

Shirley instinctively reached for his hand when she saw the pain in his eyes, and said, 'I know this must be tearing you apart, but I honestly think she'll be fine, wherever she is. If she's anything like her dad, she'll be a strong, sensible girl who knows how to take care of herself. And, as bad as it sounds, if something awful had happened, I'm sure you'd have heard by now. It's not like America, where kids go missing and never turn up again. This is a tiny country, and there are CCTV cameras everywhere these days. She'll be spotted soon and brought home, you'll see.'

'I hope so,' Jeff murmured. Then, squeezing her hand, he

said, 'Thanks, love. I needed to hear that.'

'Any time,' Shirley said sincerely.

Aware that there was really nothing more to be said on the subject for now, they said goodnight and went to their separate beds. But as tired as Jeff had been before their chat, it took him an age to get to sleep. He *had* been worried that something bad must have happened to Skye, so Shirley's words had given him a little comfort, because the police would definitely have told him by now if Skye had turned up at a hospital, or – God forbid – if a body had been found. So no news was definitely good news, he supposed. But he still wanted to know where she was, and wouldn't be able to rest until she was found.

'Big girls don't cry . . . bi-ig gi-irls, they don't—'

Skye abruptly stopped singing when the music died, and groaned when she realised that she had drained the Walkman's batteries.

Behind her on his blanket, Bernie sighed as if to say *Thank God for that*, and she smiled as she peeled off her rubber gloves. She hadn't known any of the songs when Tom had given her Jade's old Walkman and Four Seasons CD after finding them in the bedroom cupboard. But after being bored out of her skull without a TV to watch, she'd been playing the album non-stop as she cleaned the house and now knew every song by heart. She thought she sounded great singing along, but Bernie obviously didn't agree.

Skye brushed her damp hair out of her eyes with the back of her hand now, and gazed around the kitchen. Determined to earn her keep in case Tom thought she was sponging off him and chucked her out, she had set herself the task of cleaning the house from top to bottom. This was the last room on her list, and it was proving to be the hardest by far. It had taken all morning just to clear the mess off the ledges, and she'd been on her hands and knees ever since, trying to scrub through the thick layer of ingrained dirt and grease that seemed to be coating everything. There was still a way to go before it would be as clean as she wanted it to be, but it would have to wait until tomorrow because Tom would be home from work in a couple of hours. She needed to decide what they were having for dinner and then take a quick bath to rid herself of the smell of bleach.

After putting the cleaning equipment away, Skye took Bernie's lead off the hook behind the door. She had never made the mistake of letting him out on his own again after that first time, but she saw no harm in *taking* him out. Tom didn't know about it, and she had no intention of telling him since he'd as good as forbidden her to pay the dog any attention. Bernie was a guard dog, he'd said, and if she softened him up by making a fuss of him he wouldn't protect her if the police came or someone broke in. That thought terrified her, but she still couldn't bring herself to ignore the poor animal.

Used to their new routine, Bernie trotted over to her and sat patiently at her feet as she clipped the lead to his collar before reaching for the key that she kept hidden inside an old clock. Tom had confiscated the first one she'd found, but he didn't know about the other one she'd found in a drawer a few days later. It had taken her a good week to pluck up the courage to use it, because she'd been scared that he might come home early again and catch her. But she knew the sound of his car by now and was sure that she could get back inside before he got anywhere near the house.

Confident that nobody would spot her, because she'd been here for several weeks now and hadn't seen a single soul apart from Tom, Skye stepped outside and led Bernie around to the back of the house. The sun was high, and she raised her face to soak up its warmth as Bernie snuffled around. The nastier smells of the countryside no longer bothered her, and she smiled as she picked up the sweet scent of the wild flowers that had started to spring up in the long grass. Her parents had only ever lived in high-rise flats, or terraced houses with tiny backyards, so she'd never had the luxury of sunbathing in an actual garden before. She wished she could spend a whole day out here but she knew that would be a risk too far, so these few stolen minutes would have to do.

When Tom arrived home that evening, Skye had re-hidden the key and wiped up the muddy paw-prints before taking her bath and getting changed. Unaware that she had been outside, he smiled when he saw that she was wearing his favourite pink dress and had tied her hair up in bunches – just how he liked it.

'Smells good,' he said, dropping the bags he was carrying onto the table and coming up behind her as she waited for their microwave dinners to finish heating. 'What we having?'

'Chicken Korma,' she told him, grimacing when he planted a wet kiss on her neck.

She could feel the hardness of his penis pressing against her buttocks and prayed that he wasn't about to demand sex. It wasn't so bad at night after a couple of cups of wine because the alcohol went straight to her head and stopped her from feeling anything, and the darkness meant that she didn't have to see his face while he was doing it – or he hers. She still found it strange that she could never remember anything the following morning, but if the confusion blocked her from remembering the gory details she could live with it.

'I lit the fire,' she told him now, wriggling free of his grasp when the microwave pinged. 'Why don't you go and sit down while I plate up. I'll fetch it in for you.'

'In a minute,' Tom said. 'I've got something for you.'

'Oh?' Hoping that it wasn't another dress, Skye lifted the hot cartons out of the microwave and laid them on the ledge before turning to face him. His taste in clothes was awful, and she hated the new wardrobe he'd bought her after throwing her jeans away. She'd never been one for wearing dresses and skirts, but the ones he'd chosen were particularly flouncy and – it had to be said – childish-looking. She'd have died of shame if any of her old friends were to see her in them.

'Close your eyes,' Tom ordered, smiling mysteriously.

Skye did as she'd been told and listened as he rustled around in one of the plastic bags he'd brought in. Confused when he told her to open her eyes and she saw that he was kneeling in front of her, her eyes widened when she saw the small box in his hand containing a ring with a blue stone surrounded by tiny diamonds.

'Skye Benson,' he said, gazing up into her eyes. 'Will you do me the honour of being my wife?'

This was the very last thing Skye had ever expected, and she didn't know quite how to respond. 'But I'm not old enough,' she reminded him when she found her voice.

'Don't worry, I'll wait for you,' Tom said, grinning as he stood up and pulled her into his arms. 'I told you we'd be together for ever, and I meant it. I just had to know that you'd say yes if I asked. You *are* saying yes, aren't you?'

Skye swallowed deeply when he peered down into her eyes. She did like him, but she'd been a little wary of him since he'd caught her outside and gone mad that day, so the thought of being married to him for ever and ever unnerved her.

'What's wrong?' Tom demanded, a note of irritation creeping into his voice. 'You don't look very excited for someone who's just been proposed to.'

'I am,' Skye lied, scared that he might think she was being ungrateful. 'I just don't know how we'd manage it. I'd have to leave the house, and someone might recognise me and tell the police.'

'No one's going to see you,' Tom assured her, plucking the ring out of the box and sliding it onto her finger as if it were a done deal. 'No one from Manchester, anyway. We're going to Gretna Green.'

'Where's that?'

'Somewhere where people can get married without anyone sticking their noses in. We just have to apply for a copy of your birth certificate and wait till you turn sixteen, then fill the car with petrol and go. And once you've got my name, you'll never have to worry about going to prison because no one will know who you used to be.'

Skye bit her lip and gazed down at her ring. It was lovely, and she was flattered that Tom had spent so much money on her because no one had ever bought her anything so precious before. But a little voice in her head was telling her that it was all happening too fast.

'I've got another surprise for you,' Tom said suddenly. 'Jade's coming with us; she's going to be your bridesmaid.'

'Really?' Skye jerked her head up at this. 'Wow, that's great. I've been dying to meet her.'

'She's dying to meet you, too,' said Tom. 'You're her best friend, and she misses talking to you.'

'I miss that too,' Skye murmured.

In truth, she missed quite a lot of things about her old life. As badly as they had treated her, she still got a bit tearful whenever she thought about her mum and dad. And she even missed Hayley, despite having learned that the girl had never really liked her. Several times over the last few weeks, when

Tom had been at work and the boredom of being stuck in the house on her own had threatened to overwhelm her, she had fantasised about going home. Not to stay, because she knew that couldn't happen; just to see everyone from a distance. She had actually made it as far as the gate on a couple of occasions, but the fear of being arrested and spending the rest of her life in jail had always sent her scurrying back to the house.

'This wasn't quite the reaction I was expecting,' Tom complained, frowning again as he watched the troubled thoughts flit through Skye's eyes. 'Me and Jade have been planning this for weeks, so the least you could do is look happy about it.'

'Sorry,' Skye apologised. 'I'm just a bit shocked.'

'Are you sure that's all it is?' Tom demanded. 'Only, if you don't want to marry me, there's no point making me and Jade go to all this trouble to make it perfect for you, is there?'

Skye knew she had upset him, and tried quickly to make amends. 'Course I want to marry you,' she lied, forcing a smile. 'I can't wait.'

'I hope you mean that,' Tom muttered sulkily. ''Cos I've put my neck on the line for you, and so has Jade.'

'I know,' Skye murmured.

'Yeah, well, forget about it.' Tom abruptly let go of her and pulled his cigarettes out of his pocket.

Unsure what he'd meant, Skye felt a thrill of apprehension course through her. Forget about what? The misunderstanding, or the wedding?

'Reheat that while I get changed,' Tom ordered after lighting his smoke, nodding towards the food that was still sitting on the ledge. 'And hurry up, 'cos I'm starving. It's all right for you, lounging around all day doing nothing, but I've had a tough day.'

Sure now that she had hurt him, Skye said, 'I'm sorry, Tom; please don't be angry with me. I really love my ring, and I can't wait to be your wife – honest.'

'You've got a funny way of showing it,' he snapped. 'Me and Jade spent hours choosing that ring, and you've ruined it in two seconds flat with your sour face. Don't know why I bothered. And I *was* going to give you these,' he added, snatching a bag off the table and throwing it at her, 'but you'll probably just chuck them back in my face as well.'

Skye felt guilty when several magazines spilled out of the bag and she saw that they were wedding brochures. She hugged herself when Tom marched out of the room and stomped heavily up the stairs. Apart from the time when he had caught her outside, he treated her pretty well and had only snapped at her a few times since she'd been here. It made her feel isolated and vulnerable when he got like this, but she knew from experience that there was only one sure-fire way to lift his mood. So, as sickened as she was by the thought of what she was about to do, she put the food back into the microwave and followed him up the stairs.

12

A month after moving in with Shirley, Jeff was still no closer to finding a place of his own, despite having scoured the internet and local estate agents for rental properties and placing bids on the council website. There was nothing available, and when even the hostels had told him that he would be waiting months for a room, he'd conceded defeat and allowed Shirley to drive him over to the old house to pick up his boxes.

He had been walking back there every day since, to check for post and see if there were any signs that Skye had been there. His main concern was that she wouldn't know how to find him if she turned up and saw that he'd moved out – or, worse, that she would think he'd abandoned her. He had tried to call Andrea's phone several times and had left numerous messages telling Skye where he was and begging her to get in touch. But the phone was always off, and she hadn't replied to any of his messages, so he had resigned himself to the thought that the phone was either dead or lost.

As he turned the corner onto his old road today, Jeff was dismayed to see a skip outside the house. He'd seen Alan Ford a few days earlier and the man had warned him that he was about to start working on the place. But Jeff hadn't expected it to be this soon, and the thought that new tenants would soon be installed depressed him. It was one thing to pop in when builders were around, but he very much doubted that the new family would appreciate him calling round every day.

The front door was open when Jeff reached the house and he could hear the muted sound of a radio coming from the kitchen. Aware that he no longer had the right to be here, he walked down the hall and tapped on the door before pushing it open. Three builders were in there, ripping out the units, and loud bangs coming through the ceiling told him that more were at work upstairs, while yet more were out in the yard shovelling up the debris.

Ford had yet to tell Jeff what he owed for repairs over and above his deposit, but if he ran true to form Jeff guessed that Ford would probably claim that a complete overhaul had been needed because of the damage they had caused while living here. He wished he'd thought to take photos before he left, to prove that it hadn't been that bad. But it was too late now.

'Can I help you?' one of the builders asked.

Jeff turned to him, and smiled. 'I, er, used to live here, and I thought I'd check if there's been any post while I was passing.'

'I haven't seen any,' the builder told him. 'You'll have to ask the landlord. He'll be here in a bit.'

'Didn't you get it redirected?' one of the others asked, glancing down at Jeff from the ledge he was standing on. 'That's what me and my missus always do when we move.'

'I haven't had time,' Jeff replied, too embarrassed to admit that he couldn't have afforded the fee even if he had remembered. 'I'll get onto it when I get home.'

'Hope you told the leccy board you moved,' the man went on as he leaned down to plug his drill into a wall socket. 'We might be on this for a while, and you don't wanna get whacked for the juice we'll be using.'

'Yeah, that's sorted,' Jeff lied, making a mental note to do it as soon as he was out of earshot.

'That it?' the first builder asked. 'Only we'll be pulling the ceiling down in a minute, so I'll need you out of here.'

Jeff nodded and said, 'Yeah, sure.' Then, spotting a scrap of paper on the floor, he leaned down and picked it up, saying, 'Don't suppose anyone's got a pen?'

The man on the ledge took a pencil from behind his ear and tossed it over. Jeff caught it and quickly jotted down Shirley's address. Then, holding the paper out to the first builder, who he'd guessed was the gaffer, he said, 'If a young girl should happen to come looking for me, could you give her this? Only my daughter's missing, and I want her to be able to find me if she turns up.'

'Put it on there.' The builder nodded towards the window ledge. 'If I see her, I'll make sure she gets it.'

Jeff thanked him and put the paper down. Then, taking one last wistful look at his old kitchen, he went back out into the hall – just in time to see a man walk out with Skye's quilt and laptop in his arms.

'Wait!' he called, rushing down the hall.

The quilt was already in the skip by the time he reached the pavement, and the man was carrying the laptop to a van parked across the road. Jeff ran after him and snatched it out of his hands.

'Oi, what's your game?' the builder protested, trying to snatch it back.

'It's mine,' Jeff told him, holding onto it and wondering why he hadn't seen it when he was packing, because he was sure he hadn't missed anything. 'Where did you find it?'

'In the attic.'

Jeff's heart lurched when he remembered that the social worker had wanted to check the attic. He asked, 'Was there anything else up there, like a mobile phone? It's really important,' he added, hoping that the man would pick up on his urgency and hand over the phone if he'd pocketed it. 'You see, my daughter's missing, and I haven't been able to get hold of her, so it'd really help if I could find her phone so I'd know who she's been contacting.'

'Nah, mate, I only found that and the quilt,' the man told him.

Jeff sensed that he was telling the truth, and nodded. 'Thanks. And sorry if it sounded like I was accusing you of nicking it – I'm just really worried about her. I've left my address with your mate in case she turns up, but can you keep an eye out for her as well? Her name's Skye; she's blonde, about five-two, and she's fourteen.'

Or is she fifteen now? he wondered, remembering that Hayley's mum had mentioned something about a birthday present. Ashamed to admit that he didn't know his own daughter's age, he didn't correct himself.

'Yeah, course,' the man agreed, giving him a sympathetic look. 'My little 'un's twelve, and I'd go off my head if I didn't know where she was, so I know how you must be feeling. Look, tell you what,' he said then. 'Why don't you give us your number, and I'll bell you if I see her.'

Jeff gave the man his mobile number, and then set off back to Shirley's with the laptop clutched to his chest. He vaguely recalled that it had been loaned to Skye by her school, so he knew he ought to return it to them. But, right now, it was his only link to her and just holding it in his arms was a comfort to him.

* * *

Shirley was tired when she got home from work that evening, and her head was banging from the stress of having spent yet another day pretending not to notice the dirty looks and snide comments being aimed her way by the lads in the garage and the snotty bitches on reception.

She couldn't believe they had turned on Jeff so viciously on the strength of a few rumours. They had known him for as long as she had, so they ought to have known better than to listen to malicious gossip. But they had not only condemned him without giving him a chance to give his side of the story, they had also sentenced him to a lifetime of having to look over his shoulder in order to avoid getting his head kicked in should they chance upon him in some quiet place.

Shirley hadn't done herself any favours by speaking up for him in the pub the day after he'd been sacked. In hindsight, she should have kept her mouth shut and waited for them to get bored of talking about him. But it had pissed her off to hear them trashing him, and she'd got up on her soapbox and given them a good old tongue-lashing: berating the guys for so quickly forgetting all the times Jeff had supported them and helped them out, and reminding the bimbos that it hadn't been so long since they were all batting their fake eyelashes at him and trying to worm their way into his bed.

She could care less that none of them had spoken to her since, but it wasn't so easy to ignore the rumours that were beginning to circulate about her and Jeff. Somehow – and Shirley had no idea where it had come from, considering that she had never socialised with any of her colleagues outside of work and hadn't thought that any of them knew her address – they had found out that Jeff was staying with her and now seemed determined to make her life at work even more uncomfortable.

It was hard to keep going in such a toxic environment, but if they were hoping to make her quit they were in for a very long wait because she was made of stronger stuff than that. And the boss, who had made his own fair share of snide asides since it had all kicked off, knew better than to try and sack her because he knew she would haul him up before a tribunal without pausing for breath. Apart from which, she did the accounts, and he *definitely* wouldn't want the taxman to find out about the numerous ways in which he avoided paying his due. Still, it was unpleasant, all the same, and Shirley wished there was a way to prove Jeff's innocence so that life could get back to normal.

She hadn't mentioned any of this to Jeff, though, because he was depressed enough already without her adding to his woes. He would only end up blaming himself for dragging her into it if he knew, and then he'd probably leave, which wouldn't benefit anyone – least of all him.

With that in mind, Shirley adopted her usual bright smile as she let herself into the flat tonight, and chirped, 'Honey, I'm home!'

Surprised not to pick up the scent of furniture polish or hear the whirr of the vacuum cleaner, because Jeff had become quite the dab hand at cleaning while he'd been staying with her, she dropped the bag of takeaway food she was carrying onto the kitchen table and walked through to the living room.

Jeff was slumped on the couch with a dejected look on his face. Worried that he might have received bad news, Shirley draped her jacket over the back of the chair and sat down beside him.

'Are you okay? Has something happened?'

'I'm just a bit down,' Jeff told her. 'The landlord's got the builders in at my old place, and it was sad to see them ripping everything apart. Kind of felt like the end of an era.' He sighed now, and shook his head, before adding, 'I'll be forty in a couple of years, and what have I got to show for it? No wife, no kid, no house, no job – nothing. I'm a failure; a complete and utter failure.'

'No, you're not,' Shirley argued, relieved to hear that this wasn't about Skye, as she had feared. 'You're a good man, and none of this is your fault.'

'Course it's my fault,' Jeff countered miserably. 'It was my job to look after them, and I let them down.'

'How?' Shirley demanded. 'You didn't stab anyone, and you weren't to know that Skye would run away. You're a good husband and father, and that's a damn sight more than I can say for most of the men I've met – believe me.'

Jeff knew that she was trying to raise his spirits, but it wasn't going to work, because the truth was the truth and he couldn't shrug it off.

'If I was such a good husband I'd have had Andrea sorted out a long time ago,' he admitted. 'All I had to do was make sure she took her tabs, but I couldn't even do that. As for Skye, I don't even know how old she is. How disgusting is that? I'm her father, and I don't even know when her birthday is.'

Shirley's heart went out to him when she saw the anguish in his eyes, and she reached for his hand. 'It's not your fault,' she reiterated gently. 'You worked long hours, and you had Andrea's illness to contend with. You couldn't be expected to keep track of every little detail.'

'Her birthday's not a little detail, it's important,' Jeff countered guiltily. 'She's my only child, and I was there when she was born, so how could I just forget it like it meant nothing?'

'I forget birthdays all the time,' Shirley told him. 'Even managed to forget my own last year.'

'It's not the same,' Jeff said quietly. 'I've been sat here all day thinking about her, and I've realised that I don't know the first thing about her. What she likes to eat, what music she listens to, what year she's in at school – nothing. I couldn't even tell you the last time I sat down and actually talked to her one on one. It's like she was just some kid who lived upstairs.'

'You're being too hard on yourself,' Shirley insisted. 'This has been a really stressful time for you, but you must know there was nothing you could have done. It was out of your hands.'

Jeff disagreed. 'I'm not the man you seem to think I am, love. There's a lot that I could have done different, and I'm ashamed that I let it get to this. But I'll make up for it when they come home,' he added with conviction. 'As soon as we're all back together, I'll do whatever it takes to keep them safe and happy.'

'I know you will,' Shirley murmured, battling envy as she heard the passion in his voice. Andrea didn't deserve him, in her opinion. The woman's illness was manageable but she'd chosen *not* to manage it, seemingly preferring to torture Jeff with her unnecessary outbursts. And God only knew what their daughter had endured at her mother's hands while Jeff had been breaking his back to keep food on the table and a roof over their heads.

'I'll get out of your way,' Jeff said, pushing himself forward on his seat. 'You're supposed to relax when you get home from work, not have to sit here listening to my problems.'

'That's what friends are for.' Shirley gazed up at him when he rose to his feet. 'And I like listening to you.'

'Thanks, but I'm really not the best company right now.' Jeff gave her a wan smile. 'Don't worry; I'll be okay once I shake myself out of this.'

'It's not healthy to bottle things up,' Shirley reminded him. Then, smiling slyly, she added, 'Anyway, you can't go, 'cos I got a takeaway, and there's way too much for just me.'

'You didn't have to do that,' Jeff murmured, feeling guilty all over again.

Shirley rolled her eyes in mock exasperation. She knew he was broke and felt bad about being unable to contribute, but she didn't have a problem with it and wished that he would stop fretting.

'You don't honestly think I'd let you stay here if I wasn't getting something out of it, do you?' she asked, trying to lighten the mood. 'In case you hadn't noticed, I'm a lazy cow who'd rather chew off my own arm than lift a duster, so it's been great having my own live-in housekeeper. And don't even get me started on how much it would have cost me to get someone in to do all the other jobs you've done since you got here,' she went on, warming to her theme. 'I've had quotes from plumbers and electricians, and they all wanted thousands – which is why I never got anything fixed. I sometimes wonder why I bothered buying the damn place. Should have stayed with the council and let them deal with it.'

'Okay, I get it.' Jeff held up his hands when she paused for breath. 'I'll eat the bloody takeaway.'

'Good!' Shirley gave a nod of satisfaction. 'Now go and run yourself a bath and relax,' she ordered, standing up and bossily pushing him towards the door. 'I'll put the food in the oven to keep it warm.'

'I don't need a bath,' Jeff protested, amused by her

uncharacteristic assertiveness because she was one of the most laid-back women he'd ever met.

Shirley raised an eyebrow, and said playfully, 'Er, I think you'll find that you do, mister. And I don't know how long you've been wearing those jeans, but I'd be surprised if they don't start walking around of their own accord before too long.'

'Ouch!' Jeff winced. Then, smiling sheepishly, he admitted, 'I guess they are a bit ripe, aren't they? Keep meaning to put them in the wash, but then I'd have to find something else to wear while I'm waiting for them to dry, and it'd be a ball-ache having to go through all the boxes to find the one with my stuff in it.'

'I *was* joking,' Shirley told him, adding diplomatically, 'but I do think you'd feel better if you got changed. And I can help you go through the boxes if it's too much for you.'

'No, you're all right,' Jeff said quickly. 'I need to open them, anyway. They found Skye's laptop in the attic back at the house, and I need to check if I packed her charger before I take it back to the school.'

'Why was it in the attic?' Shirley asked. 'You don't think she's been up there this whole time, do you?'

'I did wonder, especially when I saw the builder carrying her quilt out with it,' Jeff replied. 'But he reckoned he didn't find anything else, so even if she had been up there she's definitely not there now.'

'Have you told the police?'

'No. Why? Do you think I should?'

'I would,' said Shirley. 'You never know, it might give them a lead.'

'How?' Jeff frowned.

'Well, if Skye's anything like my niece she's probably got

a whole other life on the net that you and Andrea knew nothing about,' Shirley explained. 'In my day, we used to pour out our hearts into our diaries and hide them under the mattress. But girls these days spill out all their troubles and secrets on Facebook and Twitter, don't they?'

'Skye couldn't have done that,' Jeff told her. 'We didn't have internet.'

Shirley drew back her head and gave him a disbelieving look. 'You do know this is the twenty-first century, don't you? *Every*one's got internet.'

'Not us,' Jeff murmured, cringing at the memory of Andrea having had their Sky account cut off before smashing up their computer, after taking it into her head that the Devil was using it to access their souls – or some weird kind of shit like that. The laptop had only escaped because Skye had managed to convince her mum that it had been blessed by a priest at school – which, surprisingly, considering they weren't Catholic, Andrea had fallen for.

'Have you looked on it yet?' Shirley asked thoughtfully. 'Skye might not have been able to go online, but she still could have been keeping some kind of journal on there, and it might give you an idea of where her head's been at lately. She might even have mentioned her friends, which would give us a chance to figure out where she's gone.'

'I haven't been able to look on it,' Jeff told her. 'I tried turning it on when I got back, but I think the battery's flat. At least, I *hope* that's why it didn't come on,' he added grimly. 'God knows how much the school'll whack me for if she's broke it.'

'Only one way to find out,' said Shirley, already planning to help him out by paying the school off from her savings if that turned out to be the case.

'I'll go and look for the charger,' Jeff said decisively.

'It can wait till you've had your bath,' Shirley said firmly, figuring that he'd have a better chance of picking up on potential clues if he was refreshed and relaxed. 'But please try not to fall asleep in there again,' she added, the twinkle of amusement in her eyes belying the pained expression on her face. 'Old Mo from upstairs said she heard you snoring last time and thought she was back in the Blitz.'

'I don't snore,' Jeff protested.

'You so do!' Shirley laughed. 'Why do you think I bought so much cotton wool last time I went to Superdrug?' Grinning when Jeff gave her a horrified look, she said, 'Only joking. I bought proper earplugs the day after you moved in.'

Amused when she turned and sauntered into the kitchen, Jeff shook his head and went into his room. The bed, wardrobe, and chest of drawers that had already been in there when he arrived took up the majority of the floor space, but his boxes had taken up every other spare inch and he groaned as he squeezed past them now. He'd been so sure that the landlord would rifle through them that he had used far too much tape to secure them and it was going to take an age to get into them. He'd also forgotten to mark them to say whose stuff was in which, so he was going to have to go through them one by one to find which were Skye's.

It would have been a lot easier with Shirley's help, but he'd refused out of loyalty to Andrea. She was obsessive about many things but privacy was way up at the top of the list, and she would absolutely hit the roof if she ever found out that he'd allowed another woman to rummage through her personal belongings. But that would be the least of his problems if he still hadn't managed to find a place by the time she was released from hospital, because she was always accusing him of having affairs so there was no way she would ever believe that this was an innocent arrangement. And even though nothing had happened between him and Shirley, Jeff had to admit that *he* would be suspicious if the shoe were on the other foot.

Shirley was an attractive woman, and she was great company, so Jeff couldn't deny that he liked her – probably a little more than he ought to, if he were really honest. They had always got on well, and she was the only one he'd felt comfortable confiding in when things had been bad at home and he'd had nowhere else to turn. He could never have told his male friends the truth because they would have marked him down as a complete wuss; and there was no way he would ever have trusted the shallow dolly-birds on reception with such personal stuff. But Shirley had not only listened without judging, she had also offered him the use of her spare room when he hit rock bottom, and had effectively been keeping him ever since – which made her a true friend in Jeff's eyes.

Unlike Andrea, who was constantly on edge as if waiting for the world to fall on her head, Shirley was easygoing and pleasant, and Jeff would miss her when this was over and he had to say goodbye. But that was exactly what he would have to do if he and Andrea were to stand any chance, because there was no way she would allow him to maintain a friendship with the woman he'd been living with in her absence.

In some ways he wished he could wipe his hands of his dysfunctional marriage and start afresh on his own. But his conscience wouldn't allow him to abandon Andrea. Despite everything she'd put him through she was his wife, and he'd vowed to stick by her in sickness *and* in health. And there was Skye to consider, too. If he turned his back on her mother, what would become of her? When she turned up – and he had to keep telling himself that she would, or he'd go crazy – he and Andrea needed to present a united front in order to make Social Services back off and let them get their family back on track.

And that was why Jeff had decided that, as soon as they were reunited, they were moving to someplace where nobody knew them and they wouldn't be dogged by rumours and speculation.

But he'd still be sad to say goodbye to Shirley.

13

Shirley had been about to dish out the takeaway food when the doorbell rang a short time later. She was peeping through the spyhole at the two police officers who were standing outside when the bathroom door opened behind her, and she blushed when she turned her head and saw Jeff walk out with a towel wrapped around his waist. She'd only ever seen him fully clothed before, and the sight of his toned stomach and muscular tattooed arms reminded her of a dark-haired version of David Beckham in an aftershave ad that she'd once seen.

'What's up?' Jeff gave her a questioning look when he noticed the way she was staring at him.

'The police are here,' she whispered, quickly pulling herself together and fixing her gaze on his face.

Jeff raked his wet hair back with his fingers and walked over to take a look. Unaware of Shirley almost swooning beside him as she inhaled the musky scent of his shower gel, he tutted softly when he saw his old adversary PC Andy Jones standing alongside PC Dean on the step.

'They're here for me,' he said flatly. 'Let them in; I'll go and get dressed.'

Shirley waited until he'd gone into his room before she opened the door. Unnerved by the way one of the cops immediately looked her up and down, she asked, 'Can I help you?'

'Is Jeff Benson staying here?' the other one asked.

Shirley nodded and stepped aside to let them in. 'He'll be out in a minute,' she said, showing them into the living room. 'Can I get you a drink while you're waiting?'

'No, we're okay, thanks,' Jones said coolly as they sat down on the couch.

Unsure what to do with herself, Shirley perched on an armchair and crossed her legs. It was clear from their expressions that they weren't here to deliver good news, but if something really bad had happened she'd have expected them to have their sympathetic faces on. So maybe it was just a routine call. She hoped so, because Jeff was just starting to get back on his feet and she didn't want to see him get knocked back down again.

When Jeff came in a few minutes later, he sat on the armchair beside Shirley's and rested his elbows on his knees. Then, clasping his hands together, as if to steel himself for the worst, he said, 'Have you found her, then?'

'Not yet,' Dean replied, casting a wary glance towards Shirley. 'But this might be better done in private.'

Glad of an excuse to escape, because the atmosphere was making her feel jittery, Shirley was on her feet in a flash. 'I need to put the washing in the dryer before something runs,' she said when Jeff told her that she didn't have to leave. 'I'll be in the kitchen if you need anything.'

Jeff sensed that she would rather not be here and nodded. He didn't blame her for wanting to get away; Jones was a cocky bastard at the best of times, but he had a particularly sly look in his eye tonight, and Jeff could only assume that the idiot had jumped to the conclusion that he and Shirley were at it.

He was right. As soon as she had left the room, Jones

gave a slow, knowing smile, and said, 'Proper landed on your feet here, haven't you, Benson? Nice little gaff; pretty little bird to keep your bed warm while the missus is out of the way. You must think all your Christmases have come at once.'

'She's a friend,' Jeff informed him curtly. 'And I'm staying in the spare room – not that it's any of your business.'

'Yeah, course you are,' Jones drawled sarcastically.

Dean, hoping to avoid a repeat of the sniping that had occurred between the men during the hospital visit, sat forward in his seat. 'We need to talk to you about some allegations that have been made.'

Jeff tore his gaze from Jones and frowned. 'What kind of allegations?'

'We've received a report to the effect that you assaulted your daughter on a number of occasions,' Dean explained.

'*What?*' Jeff felt as if he'd been punched square in the face. 'I've never laid a finger on Skye in my life! Who the hell told you that?'

'We can't disclose the source,' said Dean. 'We just need to hear your side of the story.'

'There is no story, 'cos it's not fucking true,' Jeff asserted furiously.

'Is that the same kind of *not true* as all those times you beat the shit out of Andrea and then made her retract her statement?' asked Jones, making quote marks in the air with his fingers.

'Fuck off!' Jeff glared at him.

A nasty glint sparked to life in Jones's eyes and he said, 'Swear at me like that again and I'll have you in a cell so fast your head'll spin right off your shoulders.'

'I take it you're denying it?' Dean chipped in.

'Of course I am,' Jeff replied sharply. 'And when I find out where it came from . . .'

He left the rest unsaid, but his meaning was clear, and Jones said, 'Don't even *think* about using this as an excuse to give her another kicking, 'cos I'm gonna be watching you like a hawk, and if you so much as *look* at her in a funny way I'll have you.'

Jeff's stomach churned. They weren't supposed to reveal the source of their information, but Jones had just as good as admitted that it had come from Andrea. Stunned, he turned to Dean. 'This is a joke, right?'

Annoyed with his loose-tongued colleague, Dean shook his head.

'And you're taking her seriously?' Jeff was incredulous. 'Even though you *know* she's not right in the head.'

'We have to take any allegation concerning the abuse of a minor seriously,' Dean replied evenly.

'So when was this so-called abuse supposed to have happened?' Jeff demanded. 'And what exactly am I meant to have done?'

Unconvinced by Jeff's show of indignation, Jones said, 'Let's just cut to the chase, eh? Where is she?'

'Where's who?' asked Jeff, his teeth tightly clenched.

'Don't play games.' Jones steadily held his gaze. 'You know exactly who I'm talking about.'

'And you know I've got no idea, 'cos I was in hospital when she went missing,' Jeff reminded him.

'You could have set it up from in there,' Jones argued. 'All it would have taken is one phone call telling her where to meet you when you discharged yourself.'

'She hasn't got a phone.'

'She could have called you from a box.'

'Well, she didn't.'

'You won't mind us checking your phone, then, will you?'

Jeff dipped his gaze at this, and inhaled deeply through his nose. 'All right, she did try to contact me,' he admitted, aware of how bad it must sound after he'd just denied it. 'She sent me a couple of texts, but I was still sedated after the op so I didn't see them.'

'And you didn't think to mention this when we saw you at the hospital?' Dean asked.

'I didn't find them till I got home,' Jeff told him truthfully. 'I'd switched my phone off so it didn't disturb the other patients.'

'Thought you said Skye didn't have a phone?' Jones threw his words back at him.

'She must have got hold of Andrea's, 'cos that's where the texts came from,' Jeff explained. 'And, yes, I did try to call her back, before you ask, but her phone was dead by then – and it hasn't come back on since.'

'How convenient.'

'Here, look for yourself if you don't believe me.'

Jeff passed his phone over and watched as Jones read Skye's messages before checking the call log.

'So,' Jones said when he'd finished. 'We've established that she *did* go home after she ran away, *and* that she let you know she was waiting for you there. And then you discharged yourself and went straight to her.' He paused there and peered at Jeff with open suspicion in his eyes before asking, 'Is that when you did it?'

'I didn't *do* anything,' Jeff replied tersely, his knuckles turning white as he clenched his fists. 'She wasn't there, and I haven't seen or heard from her since.'

'And you didn't think we'd want to know about it?' Jones

shook his head in disgust. 'You wanna know what I think happened? I think Andrea stabbed you 'cos she caught you at it with Skye, and you knew she was going to blow you up as soon as she was able to talk to us without you breathing down her neck, so you panicked and got rid of Skye before we could question her. Isn't that the truth of it?'

'This is crazy,' Jeff spluttered. 'I've never touched Skye, and I don't know why Andrea's saying that I did. Take me to her,' he demanded. 'She won't be able to lie while I'm standing in front of her – then you'll know I'm telling the truth.'

'I'm afraid that's not possible,' said Dean.

'Why not? She's my wife, and I've got a right to see her.'

Jones gave a snort of disdain. 'Come off it, mate. It's been weeks since she was sectioned, and you haven't asked to see her once, so you can drop the concerned-husband act.'

'I was a bit busy having surgery and getting evicted,' Jeff retorted angrily. 'But I want to see her now. Which hospital is she at?'

'None,' Jones said smugly. 'She was released two weeks ago, and we got her into a refuge – where you can't get at her and *persuade* her to retract her statement.'

'What?' Jeff was stunned. 'How come I wasn't told she'd been released?'

'Firstly, because nobody knew where you were until we called round to your old place on the off-chance this afternoon and got this address off a builder,' Jones told him. 'And secondly, because she didn't *want* you to know. And who could blame her after all the crap you've put her through? I knew you were a vicious bastard, but some of the stuff she's told us . . .' He trailed off and gave Jeff a look of pure disgust, before saying, 'Men like you make me sick to my stomach.'

'This is bullshit, and you know it,' Jeff protested. 'You're just trying to get back at me 'cos you couldn't make me say it was her who stabbed me. What did you do – cut her some kind of deal to get her off with it and land me in it instead?'

'She's not trying to get off with anything,' Jones informed him smoothly. 'She's standing by her admission, and it's looking like she'll get a verdict of self-defence now she's decided to tell the truth. And the psych docs have said she's fit to stand trial, so if you were hoping to get away with it on the grounds of her mental instability, forget it.'

'Get away with what?' Jeff yelled. 'I haven't fucking done anything.'

'So where's Skye?'

'I don't *know*!'

The door opened and Shirley marched in, her face drained of colour, her eyes blazing.

'I'm sorry,' she apologised to Jeff. 'I wasn't eavesdropping, but I could hear everything, and I can't listen to any more of this rubbish.'

She turned to the officers now and said, 'Whatever Andrea's told you, it's all lies. I've known Jeff for two years, and he is one of the nicest, gentlest men I've ever met. And he would *never* hurt his child – it's just not in his nature.'

Jones smirked at her before turning his attention back to Jeff. 'Hasn't taken you long to pull the wool over this one's eyes, has it? Mind you, you've only been here a few weeks so she probably hasn't had time to piss you off enough to get a kicking yet, has she?'

'Are you serious?' Shirley gasped. 'You can't talk to him like that. You're supposed to be a professional.'

Jones peered up at her and said, 'You seem like an intelligent woman, love, but you obviously don't know him half as well as you think you do. If I was you I'd get him out of here before you find out why his wife's in the state she's in.'

'You cheeky bastard!' Jeff roared, leaping to his feet.

'Calm down, Mr Benson,' Dean cautioned, also rising. 'This isn't helping.'

'Am I under arrest?' Jeff demanded through clenched teeth. ''Cos if I'm not, you'd best get him out of here right now, or I swear to God I'll—'

'You'll what?' challenged Jones, getting up and facing him. 'Lay one on me? Go on, then, fella – right here.' He jutted out his chin. 'Come on, what's keeping you? Why don't you try it on with a man for a change, and see what you get!'

'Right, that's enough!' Dean barked, physically pushing his colleague towards the door. 'Go and wait in the car – I'll finish up here.'

Aware that he'd gone too far, Jones flashed Jeff a last look of disgust before stalking out. When he'd gone, Dean offered his apologies to Shirley before turning to Jeff.

'The investigation is ongoing, and we will need to speak with you again, so make sure you let us know if you leave this address in the meantime.'

'Why bother waiting?' spat Jeff. 'If you think you've got something on me, you can arrest me right now. Here . . .' He held out his hands. 'I'll even let you cuff me.'

'That won't be necessary,' said Dean. Then, nodding goodbye, he left.

'I can't believe this,' Shirley croaked, in a complete state of shock. 'Why would Andrea *say* those terrible things? And why have they let her go if she's still pleading guilty to stabbing you?'

Equally shocked, and desperately trying to get his head around this latest turn of events, Jeff was pacing the floor. 'I don't know what the hell's going on in that crazy head of hers,' he muttered. 'But there's no way I'm having her say I've been hurting Skye. That's an absolute, bare-faced lie.'

'Of course it is,' Shirley agreed, reaching out and touching his arm in a gesture of support. 'Don't worry – the truth is bound to come out and they'll realise you're not capable of any of this.'

Jeff stopped pacing and breathed out shakily. 'I can't leave it to chance. This is too serious. I need to talk to Andrea and find out what she's been saying.'

'She doesn't want you to know where she is,' Shirley reminded him. 'The good thing is, they obviously haven't got any evidence or they would have arrested you. But I think you should seek legal advice nevertheless.'

'I know,' Jeff agreed, feeling as if the world was falling down around his ears. 'That bastard's had it in for me for years, and it'd make his miserable career if he could get me sent down for this.'

'Well, we'll just have to make sure that he can't, then, won't we?' said Shirley.

'How?' Jeff gave her a hopeless look. 'The only one who can tell them the truth is Skye, and we don't have a clue where she is.'

'I don't know,' Shirley admitted. 'But I think we should start by taking a look at her laptop. It's a long shot, but I've been thinking about it and I don't believe she'd have bothered taking it up into the attic to do homework. Teenagers aren't that conscientious at the best of times, and I'm sure that school would have been the very *last* thing on her mind in a situation like this.'

'You're right,' Jeff agreed, narrowing his eyes thoughtfully.

'Right, I'll put the food back in the oven while you look

for the charger,' Shirley said decisively. 'We can eat while we're looking for clues.'

Eager to find out if their hunch was right, Jeff reached for her hand as she stepped around him and gave her a grateful smile. 'Thanks, love. I honestly don't know how I'd be coping with all this if you weren't here.'

'Don't be daft.' Shirley blushed and, slipping her hand free, pushed him towards the door. 'That's what friends are for. Now hurry up so we can get started.'

It took Jeff almost an hour to find the charger, and the floor and the bed were both covered in clothes and personal items by the time he'd finished. He wasn't looking forward to having to repack it all again but it would have to wait. Right now, he just wanted to plug the laptop in and find out what was on there that Skye had thought important enough to make her take it up into the attic.

As Shirley had said, it was unlikely to be schoolwork because no one in their right mind would think about something like that while they were on the run. And it couldn't be an online thing, either, because they hadn't been connected to the internet. So that just left the journal that Shirley had suggested Skye might have been keeping – and Jeff truly hoped that would turn out to be the case, and that Skye might have written something in it which would prove that her mother was lying. He knew he hadn't spent anywhere near as much time with her as he ought to have over the last few years, but he had never hurt her. So even if she'd been disappointed by his seeming lack of interest, he couldn't imagine that she would have said anything damning about him.

The laptop came on as soon as he plugged it in, and

Shirley, who was sitting beside him on the couch, uttered a jubilant, 'Yes!' when the screen lit up a few seconds later.

'What's this?' Jeff frowned when a wall of text appeared.

'It looks like she was in the middle of something when the battery died,' said Shirley, leaning forward to read it. 'Hate to say I told you so, but this looks like a chat-room conversation.'

'How could it be?' Jeff was confused. 'I already told you we didn't have internet.'

Shirley smiled, and said, 'You really are clueless, aren't you? All it takes is for somebody nearby to have an unprotected Wi-Fi signal, and anyone who knows about these things can access it. Skye obviously did, and I'd bet she'd been secretly logging on the whole time you and Andrea thought she was up in her room doing her homework.'

'Wow, I had no idea.' Jeff shook his head in amazement and stared at the screen again. 'Her name's not on there,' he said after a moment. 'You don't think someone else was using her laptop, do you?'

'These are just screen-names,' Shirley explained. 'People use them to protect their real identities when they're chatting with strangers on these things. My guess would be that Skye is the one calling herself BlueBabe,' she went on thoughtfully. 'And the laptop battery probably died just after she sent the last message, which is why it was still on the screen when we turned it back on. Is that Andrea's number?'

Jeff snatched up his phone and checked Andrea's mobile number against the one on the screen. 'Yeah.'

'Okay, well, it looks like this QTPye might have been offering her somewhere to stay,' said Shirley. 'Just let me see if I can get the rest of the conversation up, in case there's an address.'

As soon as she touched the mouse-pad, the text on the

screen was replaced by a notice informing them that the session had timed out.

'Damn!' she muttered. 'We'll have to log in to get it back. Don't suppose you know her password, do you?' Immediately answering her own question, she said, 'No, of course you don't. You didn't even know she'd been going online.'

'Is there no other way of getting into it?' Jeff asked.

'Probably,' said Shirley. 'But I'm afraid my computer skills don't stretch that far. You could try making an educated guess,' she suggested. 'Most people tend to go for the obvious: date of birth, name of a pet – that kind of thing.'

'We didn't have any pets, and I can't remember her birthday,' Jeff reminded her shamefacedly.

'Okay, well, the mother's maiden name is another common one. What was Andrea's surname before you got married?'

Jeff pursed his lips and tried to remember, but his mind was a complete blank. 'Christ, that's bad,' he said guiltily. 'I should know these things.'

'Stop beating yourself up,' Shirley said softly. 'It's not easy to remember details when you're under pressure.'

Shoulders slumping, Jeff fixed his gaze on the laptop screen. Shirley was too nice to admit it but even *she* couldn't deny that he was a complete waste of space as a father and husband.

'We could let the police look at it,' Shirley said after a while. 'They have special departments for this kind of thing, so I'm sure they'd have no problem hacking into her account.'

'No way.' Jeff shook his head. 'They already think I'm guilty, and if she's written anything bad on there I'm done for.'

'Why would she have?' Shirley frowned. 'You haven't hurt her.'

'I know, but she might have thought I'd been hurting her

mum,' Jeff murmured resignedly. 'She was always in bed when it kicked off, but she must have heard Andrea screaming blue murder. The neighbours used to hear her, and they all thought it was me knocking her about, so what's to say Skye didn't think the same?'

'I'm sure she knows you weren't the aggressor,' Shirley said supportively. 'And I very much doubt that she'd have gone home and tried to contact you if she was scared of you.'

'I still can't risk letting the police see it until I know for sure,' said Jeff. 'What if we're wrong and she's said something bad about me on there? That's bound to make them take Andrea's allegations even more seriously, isn't it?'

Shirley gave him a sympathetic look but didn't say anything. She understood his concerns but she just didn't know what else to suggest.

'Hayley!' Jeff said when the name suddenly popped into his head. 'She's Skye's best mate – she might know her password.'

'She might even be QTPye,' Shirley mused. 'Do you know where she lives?'

'Her mum did tell me when she called round after I got out of hospital,' Jeff said. 'I can't remember the number but I know the road, so I can ask around when I get there. It's only a few streets from my old place.'

'I'll drive you over there when we've eaten,' Shirley offered, pushing his as yet untouched plate towards him. 'The sooner we get this sorted, the sooner we'll clear your name.'

Kathy Simms was on her way home from the shops when Shirley drove onto her road a short time later. Jeff cried, 'Stop!' when he spotted her.

'That's Hayley's mum,' he said, peering out through the side window when Shirley pulled over. 'At least, I think it is,' he added, a little less certain now that he could see her more clearly. He'd only met her once, but he was sure she hadn't been as skinny or gaunt-looking as this woman.

'Go and ask,' Shirley urged. 'If it's not her, she might still know where they live.'

Jeff nodded and unbuckled his seat belt.

Kathy had put her bags down and was about to slot her key into her front door when she heard her name being called. She turned her head and squinted at the man who was walking quickly across the road. Then, a wary look leaping into her eyes when she recognised him, she asked, 'What do you want?'

Jeff could see now that he had got the right woman, but she looked even worse up close; her cheeks were sunken and the bags under her eyes were dark and deep, as if she hadn't slept in weeks.

'Sorry if this is a bad time,' he said, a little thrown by her frostiness considering how nice she'd been when she had called round to his place that time. 'I just wondered if I could have a quick word with Hayley.'

'Absolutely not.' Kathy opened the door and reached for her bags.

'It won't take a minute,' Jeff promised.

'I said *no*,' spat Kathy, tossing the bags into the hall and then turning back to glare at him. 'You've got a damn nerve coming round here.'

'You told me to call round if I ever needed anything,' Jeff reminded her, guessing that she must have heard the rumours about him and Andrea since their last meeting. 'I just need to ask Hayley if she's been talking to Skye on some chat room, and if she knows her password. Please, love, it's really important.'

'Are you deaf?' Kathy snapped. 'Just go away, and don't come near me or my family again.'

'Look, I don't know what you've heard,' Jeff said when she stepped inside the house. 'But it's not true.'

'Oh, really?' Kathy crossed her arms. 'So the police were lying when they said they're investigating you for abusing Skye, were they?'

Furious to hear this, and guessing that it was Jones's doing, Jeff's nostrils flared. 'He had no right to say any of that stuff to you.'

'So you're *not* under investigation?' Kathy raised an eyebrow and waited for him to answer. When he didn't, she gave a snort of disgust. 'And to think I actually felt sorry for you.'

'Wait!' Jeff reached out and pushed the door back when she tried to close it.

'Remove your hand right now or I'll call the police,' Kathy squawked, genuine fear in her voice now.

'Just hear me out first,' Jeff implored, gazing up at her. 'I know you've probably already decided that I'm guilty, but I swear on my life I've never laid a finger on Skye. She's my daughter, and I'm worried sick about her, so please just let me ask Hayley if she knows where she is. Or *you* ask her if you don't want me to see her. Please, I'm begging you: just do this one thing for me, and I swear I'll never bother you again.'

A flicker of uncertainty flashed through Kathy's eyes. Jeff saw it and hoped that he'd got through to her. But she shook her head after a moment, and said, 'I'm sorry, but Hayley was really upset when the police questioned her and I can't put her through that again.'

'The police questioned her?' Jeff repeated, a sickly feeling of dread stirring in his stomach. 'About what?'

Kathy didn't answer this. Instead, her eyes now glittering with tears, she said, 'Look, I don't know if you're lying, but if you are innocent I'm sure you'll be able to prove it without involving us and ruining what little time we've got left.'

When Jeff gazed blankly back at her, her chin started to quiver and her shoulders seemed to fold in on her.

'I'm only telling you this so that you'll understand the damage you'll be doing if you insist on coming back,' Kathy said quietly. 'Hayley's got leukaemia. We only found out a couple of weeks ago, and the consultant doesn't think she's strong enough for treatment, so we're not sure how long we've got left with her.'

'Oh, jeezus.' Jeff instinctively reached out to touch her arm. 'I'm so sorry, love. I had no idea.'

'Don't!' Kathy sobbed as the tears spilled over and ran down her cheeks. 'I'm sorry I can't help you, and I really hope that Skye turns up soon. But I can't let our last days with Hayley be tainted by this, so please just respect my wishes and stay away from us.'

Shocked and saddened by what he'd heard, Jeff shoved his hands into his pockets when she slammed the door shut. He made his way back to the car.

'What's wrong?' Shirley asked, instantly concerned when she saw his gloomy expression. 'What did she say?'

Jeff didn't answer. He couldn't. He just sat in stunned silence for several long moments. Then, his voice hoarse, he said, 'Can we go home, please?'

Shirley didn't hesitate; she put the car into gear and drove back the way they had come.

Already concerned, because he had clearly been disturbed by whatever that woman had said to him, she was even more so when he went straight into the bathroom when they got back to the flat and she thought she heard him crying. She didn't want to pry but this was the first time she had ever seen him this upset, and it broke her heart to see him so defeated.

'Are you okay?' she asked, still waiting in the hall when he came out some time later.

'Not really,' Jeff muttered, embarrassed that she'd witnessed him breaking down like that. 'I think I just need to be on my own for a bit. Sorry.'

'Don't apologise,' Shirley said softly. 'Take as long as you need. I'll still be here when you're ready to talk.'

Dark eyes filled with pain, Jeff gazed at her and said, 'You're a good woman, Shirley, and you'll never know how much I appreciate everything you've done for me. I just wish . . .'

Shirley held her breath and waited for him to go on. But when he gave her a sad smile and then walked into his room, she sighed and went into her own room. There, deep in thought, she lay on the bed and stared up at the ceiling. She wished she could find a way to help him out of this mess, but she just didn't know where to start. The officers who had called round earlier had made it blatantly clear that they thought he was guilty, and she already knew that the idiots at work thought the same. And if that woman's reaction to seeing him just now was anything to go by, the rumour mill was obviously running at full throttle.

It was so unfair, and Jeff didn't deserve any of it, but there was nothing she could say or do to show them what a huge mistake they were all making.

In the next room, Jeff was also lying on his bed, his mind reeling as he tried to make sense of everything. He couldn't understand why Andrea was doing this to him after he'd supported her through numerous breakdowns and suffered years of misery, never knowing what mood she would be in when he got home from work or what accusation she would throw at him next. Her own family had long ago washed their hands of her, as had any friend she'd ever managed to make, but he had stood by her the whole way, and this was how she repaid him – by accusing him of abusing their daughter. And the police might not have specified the nature of this so-called abuse, but he was no fool; he knew they meant sexual – and the very thought sickened him to his stomach.

'Skye, where are you?' he moaned as a tear trickled slowly down his cheek. 'Please come home, baby; you're my only hope.'

14

'I'm sorry.' Skye trailed miserably behind Tom as he strode into the kitchen. 'I didn't know it was special.'

'Stop whining!' he snapped, grabbing his jacket off the back of the chair. 'I hate it when you do that.'

'Sorry,' she murmured, modifying her tone so he wouldn't shout at her again as she perched on a chair and slotted her hands between her knees to keep them from doing any more damage. 'If you get some glue while you're out, I'll try and fix it.'

'Forget it.' Tom picked his keys up from the ledge and unlocked the door. Flashing an unimpressed look back at her, he said, 'Do something about your hair while I'm out.'

'Like what?'

'I don't know? Cut it, or something.'

'Short?' Skye was horrified.

'I don't care, as long as it looks better than *that* when I get back,' Tom sniped. 'You're going to make me go off you if you don't start making an effort. Is that what you want?'

Skye shook her head and sniffed back the tears that were stinging her eyes. Her shoulders sagged when he walked out, relocking the door behind him. It was three weeks since he had proposed, and he still hadn't forgiven her for what he called her ungrateful response. Hurt that she'd thrown his love back in his face after he had opened his home and his heart to her, he'd taken back the engagement ring, telling her that she couldn't have it back until she had proved she was worthy to wear it. And she had been trying really, really hard ever since, but nothing seemed good enough – not even when she let him do bottom sex without crying all the way through. But now she'd broken the vase that he said he'd inherited off his dead grandmother, he would probably never forgive her.

When Bernie came and sat beside her, she gave him a sad smile and stroked his head, murmuring, 'At least you still love me. But I can't take you out, if that's what you're after. He might come back, and then I really *will* be in trouble.'

Skye got up when Bernie slinked back to his blanket, and took the scissors out of the drawer. There was no way she was cutting her hair short, because she didn't want to end up looking like a boy, but she supposed a trim wouldn't hurt. It would help if she had some shampoo, because she'd been washing her hair with soap and washing-up liquid since the last bottle ran out, and it made her already fine hair look even more limp and straggly. But Tom was refusing to buy her anything at the moment, because he said she'd taken his generosity for granted and needed to be taught a lesson.

She didn't blame him, because he had been really good to her when she first moved in and she had held herself back from really opening up to him. His coldness towards her these last few weeks had given her a serious reality check, and she'd have given anything to have the nice Tom back. Even the prospect of getting married no longer scared her, because it was infinitely preferable to the thought of spending the rest of her life in prison – which, Tom had been reminding her every day, was where she was going to end up if she didn't buck up.

Determined not to let it come to that, Skye went upstairs to try and make herself look more presentable for when he got home. And then she would make him a special dinner, she decided: to show him what a good wife she would be if he could only find it in his heart to forgive her.

Tom was smiling as he drove into Manchester after leaving the house. Skye didn't know if she was coming or going since he'd started punishing her for her bad attitude, and it was good to see her struggle because girls like her, with their pretty faces and innate sense of entitlement, had taken the piss out of him during his entire life. She had been jumping through hoops to win back his affection these last few weeks, and he had thoroughly enjoyed watching her go through the wringer. But with every victory came a loss, and his was that he no longer felt quite the same level of excitement he'd felt when he was first trying to woo her. Now she was his, body and soul, he needed a new source of entertainment; a new challenge.

The MOT stations and garages that were situated in the old railway arches beneath the Mancunian Way flyover were all closed on Sundays, and that made it the perfect spot for prostitutes and drug dealers to ply their trades. Tom would never have dared to walk through there on foot, and if his car had been even semi-decent he'd have thought twice about driving through there, too. But his clapped-out old Vectra hadn't attracted any unwanted attention on his previous visits so he wasn't too worried about parking up there now.

A group of hooded youths were gathered at the far end of the street. They hadn't spotted him because it was already starting to get dark by then and his car was concealed behind a row of industrial skips. If they did see him and made a move, he would reverse out the way he'd come and make a quick getaway. But, until then, he was happy just to sit and wait.

And he didn't have to wait too long. Less than half an hour after he'd parked up, a girl came shuffling round the corner and Tom sank lower in his seat to watch as, arms folded over her skinny stomach, a ten-pound note clutched in her filthy hand, she headed towards the youths – exactly as she had done the last time he'd seen her, a week earlier.

She had caught his attention that time because of her similarity to Skye. Both blonde, slim and of average height, they could have been sisters; although this girl looked a little younger, maybe thirteen or fourteen. And, unlike Skye who had an air of innocence about her, this girl looked what Tom could only describe as feral: as if she'd been born on the streets, and had never seen, never mind used, a bathtub or a washing machine.

As he'd seen her do the previous time, the girl approached the youths and handed her money over in exchange for something that Tom couldn't see from this distance. But then, he didn't need to see it to know that it was drugs. And, given the low price, and her unkempt appearance, he'd hazard a guess that it was either heroin or crack.

After doing her deal, the girl walked quickly back up the road towards him. But this time, instead of going off around the corner as she had done the last time, she ducked into a set-back doorway and settled herself in the corner.

Close enough to see that her hands were shaking, and her skinny legs trembling beneath her baggy camouflage trousers, Tom watched as she carefully opened the wrap she'd just bought. For such a young girl, she was in a bad way and even if he hadn't witnessed the score he'd have known that she was a junkie.

She took a small blackened piece of silver foil out of her jacket pocket now, and Tom watched as she tipped the contents of the wrap onto it with an expression of intense concentration on her pinched little face. Then, slotting a rolled-up piece of paper between her lips, she flicked a lighter to life beneath the foil and sucked on the smoke that rose from it.

She repeated the process several times, turning the foil around and around in order to get every last bit. Tom watched in fascination as her whole body seemed to sag – her legs sliding out in front of her, her chin falling forward onto her chest. She looked like a little rag doll, and if anyone had found her and decided to attack her she would have been absolutely helpless to defend herself.

He flicked a glance back along the road after a while and felt a little thrill of excitement in his gut when he saw that the youths had gone. As, too, had the older prostitute who had been leaning against the wall a little further down from them when he had first arrived. Apart from him and the girl, the area was now deserted. It was time to make his move.

Chloe Lester wasn't so far gone that she couldn't hear foot-steps, and she gazed groggily up when a shadow fell across her face.

'Whaddaya want?' she slurred at the grinning man who was standing over her.

'Depends what you're offering,' Tom said, squatting down beside her.

'Shop's shut,' she said, her voice whispery, her eyes rolling as she struggled to keep them open. 'Come back in half an hour.'

'That's too long,' said Tom. 'I need it now. How much?'

When he pulled his wallet out of his back pocket and took out two twenty-pound notes, Chloe forced herself to sit up a little straighter.

'What you after?' she asked, her gaze riveted to the money.

'Whatever I can get,' he replied. 'But not here.' He leaned back and glanced both ways along the road to make sure they were still alone. 'You'll have to come in the car.'

Chloe didn't usually get into cars. But then, she didn't usually come across men who had this much cash to splash.

'Okay,' she agreed. 'But I want dropping back here after we're finished.'

'Of course.'

Tom stood up and offered his hand to help her to her feet, but she shunned it and got up on her own.

'Where's the car, then?'

'Just over here.' Tom jerked his head at her to follow, and quickly made his way across the road.

Skye felt very proud of herself as she put the spaghetti Bolognese into the oven to keep warm. She'd never made anything more complicated than beans on toast before moving in here, so it was a real achievement to have made this meal from scratch and she couldn't wait to see what Tom thought of it when he got home. If that didn't show him how much of an effort she was making, nothing would.

She had just finished washing the pots when she heard his car pull up outside. Quickly drying her hands, she smoothed her freshly washed and trimmed hair and turned to face the door with a smile on her lips. But it slid straight off when Tom walked in and she saw that he wasn't alone.

'This is Chloe,' he said, ushering the girl into the kitchen. 'She's in a bit of trouble, so I said she could stay with us for a while.'

Skye gaped at him in disbelief, wondering why he had brought someone here when he knew what would happen if she got recognised. Didn't he care that she could end up in prison for life?

'She needs a bath and something to eat,' Tom was saying now, seemingly unaware of Skye's distress. 'And you'll have to give her something of yours to wear while you wash her clothes.'

Skye flicked a glance at the girl as he spoke. Her grubby clothes looked far too big for her, and her trainers were practically falling apart on her feet.

'Have you been cooking?' Tom asked, sniffing the air as he slipped his jacket off and looped it over the back of a chair. 'What is it?'

'Spaghetti Bolognese,' Skye told him, still warily eying the girl.

'Really?' Tom raised an eyebrow. 'I'm impressed. Is there enough for three?'

'I'm not sure,' Skye murmured, aware that her hands were shaking as she reached for a tea-towel to take the plates back out of the oven. She would ordinarily have been thrilled by his approval, but any pride she had been feeling before he came in had now been replaced by fear.

'Just share some onto another plate,' Tom said, strolling over to wash his hands.

Skye nodded. Then, casting a hooded glance back at the girl, she whispered, 'Can I talk to you for a minute?'

When she put the plates down on the ledge and walked into the living room, Tom told Chloe to make herself comfortable before following Skye out.

'What's up?' he asked, leaving the door ajar.

Skye pushed it shut and hissed, 'Why did you bring her here? What if she recognises me?'

'Don't panic.' Tom gave an unconcerned grin. 'She hasn't got a clue who you are.'

'How do you know?' Skye peered up at him with dread in her eyes. 'She might have seen me on the news, or on those posters the police were handing out.'

'I doubt anyone would recognise you from them,' he scoffed. 'They're not that good.'

'But she *might*,' Skye whined.

'Calm down,' Tom crooned, pulling her into his arms. 'I'll ask her if she's seen you before, and if she has we'll deal with it.'

'How?' Skye sniffed and rested her head on his chest, grateful that he was no longer angry with her. It had been a lonely few weeks.

'We'll think of something,' he promised, stroking her hair. 'But I guarantee she doesn't know anything. Anyway, she's in trouble herself so she's not likely to want to talk to the police, is she?'

'Why, what's she done?'

'Nothing. She's a victim, like you. And that's why I said she could stay.' Tom drew his head back and grinned down at her. 'You're not jealous, are you?'

'No.' Skye blushed. 'I'm just scared she'll grass me up and I'll get sent to prison.'

'You're going nowhere.' Tom raised her chin with his finger and peered into her eyes. 'You're mine, and I'll kill anyone who ever tries to come between us. Okay?'

Skye nodded, and Tom kissed her on the forehead before easing her away. 'Right, let's go and eat,' he said. 'And be nice to Chloe,' he added as he reached out to open the door. 'She's young and scared, and we need to make her feel welcome.'

Skye took a deep breath and, forcing a smile onto her lips, followed him back into the kitchen where Chloe was now slumped in a chair with her hands shoved deep into her jacket pockets and a look of boredom on her face. Unnerved by the unfriendly look the girl gave her, Skye took an extra plate out of the cupboard and set about sharing a portion from each of her and Tom's meals onto it.

Annoyed when she glanced back over her shoulder and saw that Tom hadn't taken his usual chair but was sitting next to Chloe, she gritted her teeth. He had been teasing when he'd asked if she was jealous just now, but maybe she was, a little. She'd felt like an outsider at home, always stuck in her room while her mum and dad got on with their own lives down below. And it had been no better at school, where most of the other kids had looked down on her because of her scruffy clothes. Hayley had been her only real friend – or, at least, Skye had *thought* she was. But even Hayley hadn't made her feel as special as Tom did, and she resented that he was now paying so much attention to this girl.

Determined to let this cuckoo know that she wasn't welcome in *her* nest, Skye carried their plates over to the table and slammed Chloe's down in front of her.

'Hey, watch it,' Tom scolded when sauce splashed onto Chloe's jacket. 'Look what you've done.'

'My hand slipped,' Skye lied, sitting across from them.

'Not good enough,' Tom snapped. 'She's a guest, and you need to apologise.'

'Sorry,' Skye murmured, afraid of putting him back into

a bad mood so soon after winning back his affection. 'I didn't mean to spill it – the plate was hot.'

Tom accepted this and nodded his approval. Then, reaching for his fork, he twirled spaghetti around it and shifted sideways in his seat to look at Chloe.

'So, you were telling me about your dad. I take it you didn't get on too well?'

'He's a pig,' Chloe said, mimicking his action and twisting spaghetti around her own fork. 'I don't blame my mum for walking out on him; I just wish she'd taken me with her so he wouldn't have started doing all that stuff.'

'What stuff?'

'You know.' Chloe shrugged, and pushed her laden fork into her mouth. 'Sex, an' that.'

Irritated to see that Tom didn't look bothered about Chloe talking with her mouth full, when just two days earlier he'd criticised her for accidentally doing the same, Skye jabbed her fork viciously into her own food.

'He used to beat me and my mum up all the time,' Chloe went on. 'He got worse after she left, but I was used to it by then, so I wasn't really fussed. I just didn't like it when he started making me sleep in his bed.'

'Did you tell anyone?' Tom asked, his gaze riveted to her face.

'Nah.' Chloe shook her head. 'What's the point? No one ever believes me.'

Skye listened in silence as the girl continued to pour out her tale of woe. If it was true, then it was terrible because fathers weren't meant to do those disgusting things to their own daughters. But there was something not quite right about this girl, and Skye wasn't sure she believed her.

After dinner, Tom showed Chloe up to the bathroom,

leaving Skye to clear up on her own. She washed the plates quickly, and was about to go up to see what they were doing when Tom strolled back in. When he saw the sulky expression on her face, he drew his head back and gave her a questioning look.

'What's up with you?'

'I don't like being ignored,' she complained. 'I'm supposed to be your fiancée, but you've just sat there talking to her like I wasn't even here.'

'Don't be so stupid,' Tom said dismissively. Then, looking around, he asked, 'Where's that wine I left on the ledge?'

'In the fridge.'

'Why have you put it in there?' He stalked over and yanked the door open. 'Red wine's supposed to be drunk at room temperature.'

'*Sorry*,' Skye muttered under her breath. 'How was *I* supposed to know?'

'Stop being so childish,' Tom scolded, taking three cups out of the cupboard. 'You're not off probation yet so you'd better drop the attitude, 'cos you're getting on my nerves.'

Chloe appeared in the doorway just then, wearing Skye's dressing gown. Tom smiled when he saw her and nodded his head towards the living-room door, saying, 'Go and make yourself comfortable in there; I won't be a minute.'

When she'd gone, he turned to Skye and said, 'Go and keep her company while I do this. And be nice: she's a guest.'

A little mollified that he had again described the girl as a guest, Skye went into the living room. But her hackles rose all over again when she found Chloe sprawled on the couch puffing on the cigarette she'd just lit.

'Is that one of Tom's?' she demanded, perching on his

armchair when it became clear that the girl wasn't about to move over for her.

'What if it is?' Chloe retorted cockily. 'He told me to help myself, so I did. Got a problem with that?'

'No,' Skye lied. 'I was only asking.'

Chloe smiled to herself and blew a smoke ring. 'I think I'm going to like it here,' she said, poking her finger through it.

'You're only staying, not moving in,' Skye reminded her.

'We'll see,' Chloe said cryptically.

Skye frowned when the girl shot her a challenging look. Tom had said she was scared, but she didn't seem scared to Skye. There was an air of hardness about her that was reminiscent of the bullies who had made Skye's life a misery at school and in the home.

Tom joined them a couple of minutes later and handed a cup of wine to Skye, and then a second one to Chloe before sitting down with his own at the other end of the couch. Skye took a sip and almost choked on it when she noticed Chloe slide one of her feet towards him and press the tips of her toes against his thigh. It was clearly deliberate, but Tom didn't seem to have noticed.

'I was just saying that I think I'm going to like it here,' Chloe said, gazing innocently over at him. 'Did you mean it when you said I could stay as long as I want?'

'Course I did,' he affirmed.

'Thought so.' She cast a sly glance at Skye.

'She's not moving in, though, is she?' Skye blurted out, determined to put the cocky cow in her place.

'Don't be so selfish,' Tom scolded.

'It's all right.' Chloe adopted a wounded expression and placed her cup on the table before dropping her feet to the floor. 'She obviously doesn't want me here, and I don't want to cause any bother, so I'll go.'

'No, you won't,' Tom insisted. 'This is my house, and I decide who stays or goes.'

Already upset that he was taking the girl's side over hers, Skye was furious when Chloe smirked at her. But she knew it would be pointless to say anything, so she took another deep swallow of wine.

All innocence again when Tom turned back to her, Chloe smiled and said, 'Thanks for letting me stay. It's been ages since I slept in a real bed.'

'You're more than welcome,' Tom said, picking her cup up and handing it back to her. 'I promised I'd look after you, and I will. Now just relax and drink your wine, then I'll run you a bath.'

Skye drank the rest of her wine in one go and stood up.

'Where are you going?' Tom asked when she started walking towards the door.

'To get another drink,' she told him clippily.

'I'll get it.' He jumped up and snatched the empty cup from her hand. 'How about you, Chloe? Ready for another one?'

Chloe finished her drink and handed her cup to him. Then, lounging back when he'd left the room, she looped her hands together behind her head, and said, 'Yep, I'm definitely going to like it here.'

Thoroughly agitated, Skye sat back down and rapped her fingernails on the arm of the chair. This was going to be a long night, and she couldn't wait for it to be over.

15

Bright sunlight was streaming through a gap in the curtains when Skye woke up the next morning, and her head throbbed painfully when it hit her eyes. Desperate to escape its line of fire, she rolled onto her side and pulled her pillow down over her face. She hadn't felt this bad since her first night here, when she hadn't been used to alcohol and had got really, really drunk. And, just like that time, she couldn't remember having come up to bed last night. Guessing that Tom must have carried her upstairs again, and hoping that he wasn't annoyed with her, she slid her hand over to his side of the bed.

'Tom . . .? Are you awake?'

He wasn't there and the sheet felt cool to her touch, as if it had been some time since he left the bed – if he'd even slept there at all.

Sick at the thought that he might not have done, Skye squinted at the alarm clock he kept on his bedside table. Her head felt woolly, but she was pretty sure it was Monday. He always left for work at seven a.m. and it was only 6:45, so she might still catch him.

Tom wasn't in the kitchen when she got downstairs, but she could see his car through the window so she knew he hadn't left yet. She looked into the living room, wondering if he might have slept on the couch, but he wasn't in there either. About to withdraw her head, she hesitated when she spotted a filthy pair of trainers lying upturned on the floor. Confused, because they weren't hers, and they were far too small to be Tom's, she breathed in sharply when a vision of a young girl suddenly flashed into her mind.

Chloe.

The name came on the heels of the vision, and Skye rushed back out into the hall as a sickening wave of suspicion washed over her.

'Tom?' she yelled, racing up the stairs. '*TOOOOM!*'

'Sshhh!' Tom hissed, walking out of the bathroom just as she reached the landing. He was bare-chested, and was rubbing his wet hair with a towel. 'What are you shouting for?'

'I – I didn't know where you were,' she croaked, feeling a little foolish for having thought that he was with Chloe. 'I wanted to see you before you went to work.'

'I'm not in work today,' he told her, strolling into the bedroom. 'It's a bank holiday.'

'Oh, right,' Skye murmured, following him and sitting on the end of the bed. 'Are you going out?' she asked when he pulled a T-shirt over his head and shoved his feet into his trainers.

'Yeah, I need to get Chloe some new clothes.'

'Why?'

Tom had just started combing his hair but he twisted his head around when Skye asked him this, and said, 'I hope you're not questioning me?'

Skye shivered when she heard the anger in his voice, and mumbled, 'No. I just don't see why you've got to buy clothes for her, that's all.'

'Because she needs them,' he replied irritably. 'Her stuff was too dirty, so I threw it out. Anyway, like I said last night, this is *my* house and I won't have you tell me what I can and can't do. I don't see why you've got such a problem with her, anyway. She hasn't done anything to you.'

'Yeah, she has,' Skye countered sulkily. 'She was horrible to me last night.'

'No, she wasn't.'

'She *was*. You didn't see the way she kept looking at me when you weren't watching.'

'Right, pack it in!' Tom barked, slamming the comb down on the dresser. 'I've tried to be nice, but you obviously haven't learned your lesson yet. She's staying, and that's the end of it. Have you got that?'

When Skye nodded, he took two small paper wraps out of his pocket and tossed them onto the bed, saying, 'Give one of those to Chloe when she gets up. And make sure she has something to eat.'

With that he left, leaving Skye to fume in silence.

Chloe felt terrible when she woke up a couple of hours later, and she was confused to find herself in bed because she didn't remember having come upstairs. In fact, she didn't remember much of *any*thing after Tom had brought out the wine last night, so she guessed that she must have had too much and this was the hangover.

When an all too familiar itching sensation began to crawl over her skin, she sat up and scratched her face as she looked around for her jacket. Tom had talked her into coming here yesterday with the promise of food and a bed, and she had only agreed on condition that he let her stop off on the way to score a couple of wraps. She'd guessed that he was some kind of do-gooder who thought he was going to 'save' her from her life on the streets, and she had no doubt that he would probably try to get her off the smack while she was here. But there was no way she was going cold turkey. She'd been there and done that, and had no intention of putting herself through it again.

Her clothes were nowhere to be seen, so she got up and made her way downstairs to the kitchen.

'Where's my clothes?' she asked when she saw Skye on her hands and knees scrubbing the life out of the lino. 'My head's killing me, and I need my stuff.'

Skye shot a frosty look back over her shoulder and, sloshing the scrubbing brush into the bucket of soapy water, sniped back, 'It's your own fault for drinking so much. You're obviously too young to handle it.'

'I'm not that much younger than you,' Chloe retorted churlishly.

'I'm nearly sixteen,' Skye lied. 'What are you, *twelve*?'

'Fifteen, *actually*.' Chloe gave her a smug smile.

'Maybe so, but I'm more grown-up,' snapped Skye.

'Whatever,' Chloe said dismissively, looking around. 'So where's my stuff?'

'In the bin,' Skye told her. 'Tom said he didn't want it in the house 'cos it stinks.'

'You'd better be kidding me!' Chloe gasped, rushing over to the bin. 'My gear's in the pocket.'

'Not that one,' Skye said when the girl yanked the bin lid up. 'It's in the outside one. And that's locked,' she added when Chloe ran to the back door. 'So don't bother trying it.'

When Chloe turned and rushed out into the hall, Skye guessed that she was going to try the front door, and called, 'That one's locked, as well. And the windows are nailed down, before you start on them.'

'This isn't funny,' Chloe said, visibly shaking when she

came back after running around the house looking for exits. 'Why's everything barricaded? It's locked up tighter than fucking Strangeways.'

'Tom likes to know I'm safe when he's out,' Skye told her. 'But don't worry,' she added resentfully. 'He took your stupid drugs out of your pocket before he binned your stuff.'

'Where is it?' Chloe asked, looking around the spotless ledges before pulling a drawer open.

'Don't root,' Skye scolded. 'Nothing in there belongs to you.'

'It don't belong to you, neither,' Chloe said irritably as she rifled through the drawer's contents. 'It's Tom's house, not yours.'

'Me and Tom are engaged,' Skye informed her tartly. 'So everything is mine as well as his.'

'I don't see no ring on your finger,' Chloe sneered, resuming her search.

'It was too big, so he's getting it changed,' Skye lied, her cheeks flaming. 'We're getting married next year, so there!'

'If you say so.'

Infuriated, Skye threw the brush into the bucket and stood up. 'What's that supposed to mean?'

Unfazed by her aggressive stance, Chloe said, 'It means you're dreaming if you think he's gonna marry you. If I wanted him, I could take him off you like that.' She clicked her fingers.

Skye's chest was heaving, and her eyes were glinting with anger. 'I *knew* you were after him,' she hissed. 'But you're never going to get him, so you'd better just give up and get lost.'

Chloe shook her head. 'You're proper thick, you, aren't you?'

'And you're a slag,' Skye shot back. 'Don't think I didn't see you touching him with your feet last night.'

'Didn't stop me, though, did he?' Chloe slammed the drawer shut and opened the cupboard above it instead.

'Get out of there!' Skye squawked, rushing over when the girl started pushing her neatly stacked tins around. 'I spent ages sorting that out.'

'Don't try and boss me around, you stupid bitch,' Chloe yelled. 'I just want my gear.'

Skye instinctively lashed out when Chloe shoved her, but she missed her mark and yelped with pain when Chloe grabbed her by the hair. 'Get off me!'

'Make me!' Chloe hissed, dragging Skye's head down and trying to kick her. 'You've been looking down your nose at me ever since I got here, but you've picked the wrong one to mess with, bitch!'

Skye had never liked fighting, mainly because she wasn't very good at it, but she knew she had to do something or she was going to lose half her hair. So, twisting her neck, she reached up and raked Chloe's cheek with her nails.

Bernie had started barking as soon as the fight began but he jumped up when Chloe screamed, and ran towards them. Chloe saw him coming and darted behind the table, crying, 'It's gonna bite me! Call it off!'

For a split second, Skye felt like letting Bernie go for the other girl. But she quickly snapped out of it and shouted, 'It's okay, boy! Go back to bed.'

At the sound of her voice, Bernie turned and went back to his blanket. But he continued to eye Chloe as he lay back down, and growled deep in his throat when she stepped out from behind the table.

'Sorry,' Skye murmured, feeling guilty when she saw the

blood-dotted welts on the other girl's cheek. 'I shouldn't have done that.'

'Fuck off.' Chloe glared at her as she placed a hand over the stinging flesh. 'You're just lucky you've got that mutt to protect you, or I'd have done for you.'

'I'm trying to apologise,' Skye argued. 'And I don't have to, 'cos you started it.'

'*I'm trying to apologise*,' Chloe mimicked nastily. 'You make me sick, you snotty cow. My old school was full of bitches like you, always looking down their noses at me. But I showed them, and I'll show you. You just wait till *that*'s not around.' She nodded in Bernie's direction. 'You'll be sorry you ever messed with me.'

'You're not the only one who's had it hard,' Skye snapped, losing patience with the girl's self-pitying attitude. 'I got put in a home before I came here, and had to run away.'

'Big *wow*,' Chloe retorted sarcastically. 'I've been kipping in a doss house with a load of crackheads and winos.'

'Yeah, well, my mum stabbed my dad,' Skye shot back, a *beat that* look on her face.

'Why?' Chloe asked. 'Catch him touching you, did she?'

Skye's cheeks reddened with indignation at the very suggestion that her dad would ever do something like that to her. 'No, she did not!'

'Yeah, she did.' Chloe gave a knowing smile. 'I can always tell when someone's lying, and it's written all over your face.'

Furious that the girl was bad-mouthing her father, Skye hissed, 'Shut your dirty mouth, you! My dad's not like yours. He's lovely, and he'd *never* do anything like that.'

'So lovely that your mam stabbed him,' Chloe reminded her nastily. 'Normal people don't go around stabbing people for nothing.'

'She's ill, if you must know,' Skye admitted, her eyes glittering with tears of anger. 'And don't you ever talk about my dad again, or I'll—'

'You'll what?' Chloe challenged, fronting up to her and giving her a shove. 'If you're gonna do it, do it – don't just stand there saying it.'

'You'd best back off.'

'Or what?'

Neither girl had heard Tom's car pulling up outside, and they both jumped when the door suddenly opened and he marched in.

'What the hell's going on in here?' he demanded, dropping the carrier bags he was holding and placing his hands on his hips. 'I could hear you from outside.'

Offended that he was directing his angry glare at her, Skye spluttered, 'It's not *my* fault. She's the one who started it!'

'No, I didn't,' Chloe protested. 'All I did was ask for my gear, and she went for me.'

'You liar!' Skye squawked. '*You* went for *me*!'

'Look what she did.' Chloe rushed over to Tom and raised her cheek to show him the fingernail marks. '*And* she tried to set the dog on me.'

Skye's mouth fell open in disbelief. 'I did not! He was only trying to protect me 'cos you were ripping my hair out.'

'I was scared,' Chloe whimpered, clutching at Tom's arm. 'I thought they were going to kill me.'

Tom placed a protective arm around her shoulder and said, 'I'm here now. Don't worry; I won't let them hurt you.'

Skye felt as if a knife had been plunged into her heart when Chloe flashed a triumphant grin at her, and she burst into tears and ran for the door.

'Where do you think you're going?' Tom demanded,

pushing Chloe out of the way and stepping in front of Skye to block her path.

'Away from *her*,' she sobbed, struggling to get past him.

Tom gripped her firmly by the arms and peered down into her tearful eyes. 'Are you forgetting that you're wanted for attempted murder, you stupid girl? You'll go to prison for life if the police get their hands on you.'

'I don't care!' Skye tried to wrench herself free. 'I'd rather go to prison than put up with her.'

'Pack it in!' Tom shook her roughly. 'If you think I'm just going to let you walk out of here and land me in it, you can forget it. You're going nowhere!'

'You're hurting me,' Skye cried, wincing when he dug his fingers into her arms.

'I'll do more than hurt you if you ever try to leave me again,' he warned her. 'You're mine, and I'll never let you go. *Never.*'

The breath caught in Skye's throat when she saw the fury in his eyes, and she immediately stopped struggling, scared that he might hit her.

'Go upstairs and wait for me,' Tom ordered, loosening his grip at last. 'I'll be up to see you when I've dealt with *him*.'

More afraid now for Bernie than for herself when Tom glared at the dog, Skye asked, 'What are you going to do?'

'What I should have done a long time ago,' he hissed, marching over and kicking Bernie viciously in the ribs.

'Stop it!' Skye cried. 'It's not his fault! He hasn't done anything!'

'Shut up,' Tom snarled, seizing the squealing dog by the scruff of its neck and hauling it off its blanket. 'He needs to learn who's boss round here.'

'Leave him alone!' Skye ran after him when he dragged

the dog to the back door, and pummelled his back with her fists, screeching, 'Don't you dare hurt him, or I swear I'll go and I'll never come back!'

Tom pushed her away roughly, sending her flying back against the table. Then, dragging Bernie outside, he slammed the door and locked it from the outside, preventing her from following. Helpless, Skye stumbled over to the window and let out an anguished sob when she saw him pick up a stick and start beating the dog with it.

Chloe hadn't spoken during the confrontation, but she wandered over to stand beside Skye now and shook her head as she watched what was happening outside. 'Wow, I wouldn't like to be that mutt right now.'

'This is *your* fault!' Skye reminded her accusingly. 'He's only doing it 'cos you lied about me trying to set Bernie on you.'

'I know,' Chloe admitted guiltily. 'Soz. I didn't think he'd flip out like that. Are you okay?'

Unable to stand it, Skye shook her head and moved away from the window. Watching as she paced the floor, Chloe asked, 'Was it right what he said about you being wanted for attempted murder?' A look of admiration came onto her face when Skye nodded, and she said, 'Cool. No wonder he didn't want to let you leave. He'd probably get life for hiding you.'

'I know,' Skye croaked, wiping her nose on the back of her hand. 'But he knows I'd never tell on him.'

'Who did you try to kill?' Chloe quizzed. 'Your dad?'

Offended that the girl clearly thought she was guilty, Skye said, 'I didn't try to kill *any*one, you stupid cow. I'm not like *you* – I don't go round attacking people for no reason.'

'You must have done something,' Chloe argued. 'The police wouldn't be after you if you was innocent.'

'Oh, think what you like,' Skye snapped. 'Just hurry up and leave, 'cos me and Tom were fine before you came and ruined everything. And here,' she said then, pulling one of the wraps that Tom had given her out of her pocket. 'Have your dirty drugs if you're that desperate.'

Chloe snatched the wrap and ran over to the drawer where she'd seen a roll of tin foil when she'd been rooting around a little earlier. Blind to the look of disgust that Skye flashed her before marching upstairs, she grabbed the lighter that was sitting on the ledge beside the cooker and settled at the table to prepare her fix. She could easily have done the whole lot in one go, but she decided to have just enough to take the edge off her craving.

She had pegged Tom as a weirdo when he'd claimed not to want sex after getting her into his car yesterday, and had only flirted with him when they got back to the house in order to wind Skye up for treating her like something that had crawled from under a stone. But as much as she had enjoyed watching the jealous cow go off like a rocket, this set-up was a bit too freaky even for her and she didn't plan on sticking around for too long. As soon as she found something worth nicking, she'd be off.

Skye was sitting on the bed when Tom walked into the bedroom a short time later, her knees drawn up to her chest, her tear-swollen eyes downcast. He sat down beside her and held out his arms, but Skye shook her head and refused to come to him.

'Stop being so stubborn,' he said, pulling her towards him and holding her tight against his chest. 'I'm sorry for shouting at you, but this fighting has got to stop. You've got no reason to be jealous of Chloe. She's not special like you, is she?'

'So why do you keep taking her side?' Skye asked, torn between relief that he was being nice to her again and resentment that he had automatically blamed her for the fight that Chloe had started.

'I don't,' Tom insisted. 'I'm just trying to make her feel welcome, because she's had a really tough time and she's got no one else to turn to. You know how that feels, so you should understand why I'm doing this.'

'I don't like her,' Skye said sulkily. 'She's trying to take you off me.'

'Well, it's not going to work, is it?' said Tom. 'You're my number one, and you always will be.'

'Promise?'

Tom sighed and gazed down at her. 'You should already know without me having to keep telling you. But if you don't trust me, what's the point? I can't just keep on giving if all you ever do is take. I need to know you love me as much as I love you.'

'I do,' Skye told him sincerely. 'It's just *her*. She keeps laughing at me behind your back.'

'Right, I'm getting sick of this.' Irritated again, Tom pushed her away. 'I promised Jade that I'd look after you, and I have; but how do you think she'd feel if she knew you were behaving like this towards that young girl down there after she went out of her way to help you? She wouldn't be very happy to hear that, would she?'

'No,' Skye admitted. 'But—'

'But nothing.' Tom cut her off sharply. 'This stops now, so go and say you're sorry and we'll say no more about it.'

'But I haven't done anything wrong,' Skye protested. 'It was her who started it.'

Tom raised an eyebrow. 'Have I been wasting my time?'

Skye bit down on her resentment and shook her head.

'Good girl.' Tom kissed her on the forehead and then stood up, pulling her up with him.

Chloe was rifling through the books on the shelf unit when the pair came back downstairs, and she narrowed her eyes when she spotted that they were holding hands. The dirty bastard had to be at least thirty, and she'd bet the police would be very interested to know about him shacking up with a wanted fifteen-year-old.

'Skye's got something to say.' Tom pushed Skye forward.

'Oh?' Chloe turned her head and gazed innocently over at them.

'I'm sorry.' Skye forced a tight smile. 'I shouldn't have scratched you, and it won't happen again.'

''S'all right.' Chloe shrugged. 'It was my fault as much as yours. And soz for messing your drawer up. I'll help you tidy it, if you want.'

'No, it's okay.' Skye folded her arms. 'I'll do it.'

'There we go.' Tom gave them an approving smile. 'Now isn't that better?'

'Yeah, loads,' Chloe agreed.

'Mmmm,' murmured Skye.

'Right, well, since you've decided to behave I'll show you what I bought while I was out,' Tom said, heading back into the kitchen.

The girls gave each other a wary look before following, neither of them convinced that the other's apology had been sincere.

Tom passed one of the carrier bags to Chloe and the other to Skye, and then sat down to watch as they opened them.

'Oh, wow,' Chloe gushed when she pulled out a frilly

flower-print dress. 'Thanks, Tom, it's gorgeous. No one's ever bought me anything like this before.'

'Well, they should have,' he said magnanimously. 'You're a pretty girl, and pretty girls deserve to have nice things.'

He glanced at Skye now, and raised an eyebrow when he saw that she hadn't opened her bag yet. 'Aren't you going to look at yours?'

Skye had been staring at the dog's empty blanket, but she turned to him when he spoke, and asked, 'Where's Bernie?'

'Chained up outside,' Tom told her. 'And that's where he'll be staying,' he added firmly, letting her know that he wouldn't tolerate any argument on the matter. 'I warned you not to spoil him, so you've only got yourself to blame.'

Upset to think that she was the cause of Bernie's suffering, Skye vowed to herself that she would sneak out to see him as soon as she got the chance.

'Oh, wow, this is ace,' Chloe exclaimed just then, lifting a polka-dot blouse from the bag and holding it against herself.

Sure that she had to be joking, because the blouse was Tom's usual flouncy, childish style, Skye flashed a disbelieving glance at her. Shocked to see that Chloe seemed to genuinely like it, she decided that the girl was either a really good actress or was even younger and more stupid than she looked.

Annoyed, when she opened her own bag, to see that Tom had bought her a dress identical to the one he'd chosen for Chloe, Skye gritted her teeth. But, determined not to make the mistake of under-reacting and have Tom accuse her of being ungrateful again, she forced a smile, and said, 'Thanks, Tom, I love it.'

'I knew you would.' He grinned and lit a cigarette. Then, his eyes gleaming darkly, he said, 'Why don't you go and get changed, then you can do a little fashion show for me.'

'Ooh, yeah,' Chloe cooed, as if she was really excited by the idea. 'Come on, Skye.'

Suspicious of this sudden friendliness, Skye followed as Chloe galloped up the stairs. When they reached the landing and the girl headed towards her and Tom's room, she said, 'Don't go in there – that's ours. You can get changed in the spare room.'

A spark of anger flared in Chloe's eyes, but she quickly blinked it away and gave Skye an innocent smile. 'Okay, you're the boss. But have you got a brush so I can do my hair? Only I don't want to look a mess when I've got my new dress on.'

'Wouldn't you have been better off having that bath you were supposed to have last night?' Skye suggested, flicking a look of disgust at the other girl's greasy locks. 'There's no shampoo but you can use soap, like I do.'

'Yeah, it could probably do with a wash,' Chloe agreed. 'But only if *you* don't mind. I mean, it *is* your house, and I wouldn't want you thinking I'm taking liberties.'

Sure that she was being sarcastic, Skye narrowed her eyes. 'Are you trying to be funny?'

'No, course not,' said Chloe. Then, sighing, she said, 'Look, I know we got off on the wrong foot, and I probably shouldn't have got so lippy – but I can't help it. People always think they can treat me like shit, and it makes me dead defensive. Girls are the worst,' she went on bitterly. 'They act like they're your best mate and get you to tell them all your secrets, then run round telling everyone. I hate them.'

Skye knew exactly how that felt, because it had torn her heart in two to learn that Hayley had been slagging her off on WhisperBox – and she imagined that the bitch had probably gone back to school and told everyone what she'd been saying about them behind their backs, as well.

'We've both said nasty things,' she conceded, giving Chloe the first genuine smile since they'd met. 'Let's forget it and start again, eh? Friends?' She held out her hand.

'Friends.' Chloe grinned and shook it. 'And don't worry, I'm not after your Tom,' she added quietly. 'I only said that to wind you up 'cos I thought you didn't like me. But I wouldn't bother trying it on with him, 'cos he's mad about you.'

'Do you think so?'

'God, yeah, it's dead obvious. Wish *I* could find someone nice like him, but all I ever get is horrible old pervs like me dad.'

Unaware that Chloe's last comment had been a dig at her and Tom's relationship, Skye said, 'Don't worry about your dad: he can't get to you here – me and Tom will make sure of that.'

'You're ace, you,' Chloe gushed, lurching forward and giving her a hug. 'We're gonna be best mates, I can tell.'

Skye wasn't sure she'd go *that* far, but it was a start, she supposed. Disentangling herself when she caught a whiff of Chloe's smelly head, she said, 'Right, go and wash your hair. Then you can come to my room and I'll give you the brush.'

'Will you do it for me?' Chloe asked, gazing up at her with a mixture of gratitude and adoration. 'I want it like yours, 'cos you look dead pretty like that.'

'If you like,' Skye agreed, blushing at the unexpected compliment.

Alone in the bathroom a few seconds later, Chloe's gushing smile was replaced by a smirk as she gazed at her reflection in the pitted mirror. Skye was thick if she thought they were going to be friends, because Chloe didn't do friends – not female ones, anyway. Every bitch she'd ever made the mistake of trusting had stabbed her in the back, so men were her only pals these days. Men with wallets, who didn't mind shelling out for a bit of the magic her young body could bring into their sad, perverted lives.

And she fully intended to get her sticky little fingers on Tom's wallet before she was done here. But after the way she'd just seen him flip out on Skye and the dog, she knew she would have to tread carefully. She had made the mistake of underestimating freaks like him before, and she didn't fancy getting a kicking before being booted out empty-handed if she tried to strike too soon.

Tom was getting impatient. It was only mid-afternoon but he was in the mood for a party, so he'd poured the wine, closed the living-room curtains, switched on the lamp, and pushed the couch and table back to create a little runway.

When, after waiting almost an hour, the girls still hadn't come back down, he went out into the hall and called, 'What's taking so long?'

In the bedroom, Skye was kneeling on the mattress behind Chloe, a look of concentration on her face as she teased the girl's fine hair into shape. 'Just coming,' she called back.

'Bet that's what *he*'ll be doing after he's copped a look at you,' Chloe teased, grinning round at her.

'Don't be cheeky,' Skye chided, tugging gently on Chloe's hair to make her turn her head back around.

A little tap came at the door just then, and Tom said, 'I've poured you some drinks, but I'll leave them out here so I don't ruin the surprise. Hurry up – I'm dying to see you.'

Chloe jumped down off the bed and rushed over to the door. After pressing her ear against it to make sure that Tom had gone back downstairs, she reached out for the cups of wine he'd left on the floor outside and handed one to Skye before sitting back down with her own.

'Do you like wine?' Skye asked, watching as she swallowed a large mouthful.

'Nah, it's minging,' Chloe admitted, wiping her mouth on the back of her hand. 'But it's better than nothing, and you don't notice the taste so much if you drink it fast. Why? Don't *you* like it?'

'Not really.' Skye pulled a face and returned to her back-combing.

'So why do you drink it, then?'

''Cos Tom likes it.' Skye shrugged.

'Doesn't mean *you* have to have it,' said Chloe, gazing at her in the mirror. 'Just tell him you want something different. If he loves you, he'll get you anything you want.'

'No, it's okay; I don't really mind it,' Skye murmured, reluctant to admit that she wouldn't dare ask Tom for anything right now in case he went into another mood with her.

'You proper love him, don't you?' Chloe asked. When Skye nodded and reached for her drink, she took another swig of her own, and then asked, 'So what's it like, shagging him?'

Almost choking, Skye gasped, 'You can't ask *that*! It's private.'

'I just want to know if it's any good,' Chloe persisted. 'Has he got a big one?'

Skye didn't answer this. The truth was that she didn't know, because she had nothing to compare it with. Anyway, it was ugly, so she avoided looking at it unless she absolutely had to. But it did hurt if they did it when she was sober, so she supposed it must be quite big.

'Bet it feels good doing it with someone you love,' Chloe went on wistfully. 'I went out with a lad once, and it was kind of nice with him. His mam worked at a newsagent's, and he used to smuggle sweets and cigs out for me. But then my dad found out and warned him off, so he spread it round school that I had Aids.'

'That's horrible,' Skye said sympathetically.

'I didn't care.' Chloe shrugged. 'He was a dickhead, and I only went with him for the cigs.'

'Yeah, but telling people you had Aids?'

'It stopped them bullying me, 'cos they were scared of catching it if they touched me,' Chloe said philosophically. 'Anyhow, I moved out of that school a few weeks after and then I ran off, so it made no odds to me what they were saying. I might go back one day and blow the place up,' she said then, as casually as if she were talking about paying an old friend a visit. 'Or get a gun and shoot all the teachers, like them American nutters you see on the news.'

Skye didn't know if Chloe was joking, but she was starting to understand why the girl had been so aggressive when they had first met. It sounded like she'd had an even worse time at school than Skye, and then she'd had her dad to contend with when she got home. It was horrific, and Skye felt really sorry for her.

'You know when you get married?' Chloe said, abruptly changing the subject. 'Can I be your bridesmaid?'

'Tom's already said his sister's going to be my bridesmaid,' Skye told her. 'But I can ask him if it's okay to have two.'

Even as she said that last bit, Skye was half-hoping he'd say no. As nice as it was to have another girl to talk to after weeks of seeing nobody but Tom and Bernie, she wasn't sure how she felt about Chloe staying from now until the wedding next year. The girl had displayed two extremely different sides to her personality, and Skye would have to see which one was the real Chloe before she let down her guard completely.

'Is this yours?' Chloe leaned over the bed and picked up the angel necklace that was still sitting where Skye had left it on the bedside table.

'Mmmm.' Skye nodded and averted her gaze quickly. It had been three full weeks since she'd taken it off, and she had vowed never to wear it again. But still, she couldn't bring herself to throw it away. Just as she couldn't deny that, at times, she still missed her old friend.

'Can I try it on?' Chloe asked, already looping it around her neck.

Skye sighed, and said, 'I suppose so. But you can't keep it, 'cos my friend gave it to me for my birthday. She reckons it's a guardian angel, and when you need something you ask it to help you get it.'

'Cool.' Chloe smiled and rubbed the little angel between her fingers. 'I'm going to ask it for fags.'

'Good luck with that.' Skye snorted softly. 'The stupid thing's never answered any of my prayers, so I can't see it answering yours.'

'We look like sisters, don't we?' Chloe remarked, changing the subject yet again.

Skye glanced at their reflections and had to admit that they did look alike; especially so since they had decided to model the matching dresses and style their hair the same way.

'Yeah, a bit.'

'Wonder what Tom'll say when he sees us,' Chloe mused, twisting her head this way and that to check her hair. 'Do you think he'll like us in our dresses?'

'Probably, seeing as he chose them,' Skye said, climbing down off the bed and reaching for her cup.

'Race you,' Chloe challenged.

'Okay, go on, then.' Skye took a deep breath and finished her drink in one.

Chloe did the same, and grinned when she finished a fraction of a second faster. 'Winner!' she crowed, placing the empty cup upside down on her head.

'Get it off, you nutter,' Skye ordered, laughing. 'You'll ruin your hair.'

Chloe did as she'd been told and said, 'Told you it's not as bad if you drink it fast.'

'Suppose not,' Skye agreed, giggling when she felt it go to her head. 'I think I'm getting tipsy.'

'Me, too,' Chloe said, linking arms with her. 'Come on. Let's go get another one before it wears off.'

Tom was drumming out an agitated beat with his fingertips on the arm of his chair. He stopped abruptly when the girls stumbled into the room, and his eyes lit up when he saw that they were wearing the matching dresses. He'd noticed a similarity between them from the start but dressed like this they could almost have been twins, and the thought thrilled him.

'Oh, wow,' he murmured as the stiffness in his trousers strained against the zip. 'Look how beautiful my girls are.'

'Can we have some more?' Chloe asked, thrusting her empty cup towards him. 'We want to get pissed – don't we, Skye?'

Tom pulled his jumper down over his crotch and leapt to his feet. 'Good job I got a few bottles,' he called back over his shoulder as he rushed into the kitchen. 'We can have a party.'

'What for?' Skye asked, wondering if it was even possible

to have a party with just three people. She'd only ever been to Hayley's birthday parties in the past and while there weren't usually too many guests there because her friend – *ex*-friend – more often than not would be suffering one of her imaginary illnesses there were always more than three people there.

'A welcome Chloe into the family party,' Tom said, coming back with their refilled cups.

'Yay!' Chloe grinned. 'No one's ever had a party for me before.'

Skye smiled when she saw the joy in Chloe's eyes, and she felt stupid for having been so jealous of her. She looked like an excited little twelve-year-old, so of course Tom wouldn't fancy her.

'We need music if we're going to have a proper party,' Chloe was saying now as she bounced on the spot. 'Can you play something on your laptop, Tom?'

'I can't get music on there,' he told her. 'But we don't need it; we'll make our own fun.'

'Oh, aye?' She gave him a knowing smile. 'And what kind of fun did you have in mind, exactly?'

'I thought we were supposed to be doing a fashion show,' Skye reminded them. 'What do you think, Tom?' She put a hand on her hip and twirled around. 'Does it suit me?'

'And me?' Chloe joined in, adopting the same stance as Skye and strutting the length of the room with her lips pushed out in a parody of a sexy pout.

'Not like that,' Skye asserted, pushing her out of the way. '*This* is how you do it.'

Laughing when Skye pranced past her, lifting her knees high with each step, Chloe spluttered, 'What's that supposed to be? A *horse*?'

'This is how they do it on *America's Next Top Model*,' Skye

informed her, stopping at the window and making a flam-
boyant turn. 'They all walk funny on there; and the weirdest
one always wins.'

'Have another drink and then do it again,' Tom ordered,
his eyes gleaming as he sat back in his seat. 'I'll be the judge.'

'What does the winner get?' Chloe asked, reaching for her
cup.

'It'll be a surprise.' He grinned.

Excited by the thought of winning a prize, Skye and Chloe
downed their wine and then took it in turns to walk up and
down the room, each trying to outdo the other with their
exaggerated pouts and turns.

Tom made them do it several times before declaring Skye
the winner.

'Aw, that's not fair,' Chloe protested, flopping down sulkily
onto the couch. 'You only picked her 'cos she's your
girlfriend.'

'You're both my girls,' said Tom. 'But I had to give Skye
an extra point because she's the eldest.'

Chuffed that he had chosen her, Skye sat down beside
Chloe and gave her a playful dig in the ribs with her elbow.
'Shut up moaning, you,' she slurred. 'This is your party, so
crack a smile before your face gets stuck like that.'

'Who's ready for another drink?' Tom asked, standing up
again.

'Me!' Skye and Chloe said simultaneously.

When they burst out laughing and fell into each other's
arms, Tom snatched up their empty cups and carried them
quickly into the kitchen.

16

Chloe woke with a start, and let out a whimper of confusion when the pitch darkness pressed down on her like a lead weight. She had been dreaming that she'd been kidnapped and tossed into the boot of a car. At least, she'd *thought* it was a dream but now she wasn't so sure, because her body was still jumping around.

It took several moments before she realised that she was lying on her back in bed, and that her body was jumping because Tom was bouncing on top of her.

'What are you doing?' she demanded, trying weakly to push him away. 'Gerroff.'

'Sshhhh,' he gasped, his breath coming in short bursts as he picked up speed. 'Just stay like that . . . stay like – *aaggghhh*!'

He stiffened and arched his back, and Chloe felt nauseous when she saw the gargoyle-like grimace on his heavily shadowed face. But when he then flopped down on her she released an involuntary whoosh of breath, and croaked, 'I can't breathe!'

'God, that was good,' Tom panted as he pushed himself up onto his elbows and gazed down at her. 'And you enjoyed it, too – didn't you?'

Chloe didn't answer: she was too busy wondering what was going on. She noticed a tiny red light winking at her from the dresser at the side of the bed and twisted her head to squint at it. 'What's that?'

'Just my alarm clock.' Tom jumped up and rushed over to switch it off. 'I thought I'd best bring it in case I fell asleep.'

He reached for his dressing gown, which was draped over a chair, and took a pack of cigarettes out of the pocket after slipping it on. Lighting two, he passed one to Chloe and then sat down on the bed again, with his back against the metal bedstead and his legs stretched out.

'That was great, but I think it's probably best if we don't tell Skye. She'll only get jealous, so we'll keep it our little secret for now – okay?'

Chloe frowned and took a deep pull on her cigarette. This was her second night at the house, and the second time she'd woken up in bed with no memory of having walked up the stairs. The last thing she remembered was that they had been having a party, and she and Skye had done a fashion parade for him. After that it was a complete blank, and she guessed that the wine must have knocked her out again. It definitely wasn't the smack, because she'd deliberately not had very much, so that was all it could be.

Tom was staring at her in the darkness. 'I hope you're not regretting it,' he said, the glow from her cigarette making his eyes gleam eerily. 'I only did it because you said you wanted to.'

'Eh?' Chloe squinted up at him. 'When did I say that?'

'Last night, after Skye went to bed. Don't you remember?'

'*No.*'

'Well, you did,' Tom insisted, a hurt expression coming onto his face. 'And then you kissed me, so what was I supposed to do?'

'Did I?' Chloe screwed up her face. She didn't even like

kissing, because it reminded her of her dad, so that *definitely* had to have been the wine's doing.

'I should have known you didn't mean it,' Tom said, lowering his feet to the floor. 'Why would a beautiful girl like you be interested in someone like me? I'm such an idiot.'

'I thought you were supposed to be madly in love with Skye?' Chloe reminded him.

'I am.' Tom turned and peered down at her. 'But that doesn't mean I can't love you as well.'

'You've only known me a couple of days,' Chloe pointed out, thinking that he must be even weirder than she'd originally thought if he believed that he was in love with her already.

'You've told me all I need to know,' Tom said quietly. 'That's good enough for me.'

'I haven't told you everything,' said Chloe, rubbing at her arm when it started itching.

Tom gave her a piercing look. 'I hope you're not keeping secrets from me? That wouldn't be very nice after everything I've done for you.'

'No, but there's stuff girls tell each other that we wouldn't tell blokes,' said Chloe, adding, 'Like about periods, and that,' in the hope that it would put him off asking any more questions.

'I know about periods,' Tom informed her. 'We're not all Neanderthals like your father.' He stubbed out his cigarette on a plate that was sitting on the dresser and said, 'Anyway, I won't have secrets in my house.'

'*You*'re keeping one,' Chloe reminded him indignantly. 'You don't want me to tell Skye about this.'

'Only because it would upset her,' Tom said, as if it were a perfectly reasonable explanation. 'You know what she's like.

She'd only fly off the handle and make me kick you out, and then what would you do?'

'Go back to the doss house.' Chloe shrugged and sucked on her cigarette. 'Or go home.'

'*No!*' Tom slammed his hand down on the mattress. 'I will not let you go back to that filthy life. You're staying here with me where I can keep you safe, and that's final.'

Unlike Skye, who jumped to Tom's every command because she was terrified that he might kick her out and she'd end up in prison, Chloe was unfazed by his outburst. She wouldn't get into trouble if she decided to leave – at least, not with the police. If she went home her dad would probably give her a beating to teach her a lesson for running away again. The bruises only lasted a few days, so everything would soon be back to normal. But if Tom was that desperate for her to stay, she saw no harm in playing him along for a bit.

'Will you get me a telly if I stay?' she asked. 'Only it's dead boring without one, and I'm missing '*Ollyoaks*.'

'Olly what?' Tom frowned.

''*Olly*oaks,' Chloe repeated. Then, rolling her eyes, she said, 'God, don't tell me you've never seen it? *Every*one watches it. So can we get one, or what?'

Tom shook his head. 'There's no signal out here. That's why I haven't already got one – or a house phone.'

Chloe's shoulders slumped with disappointment. Then, perking up again, she said, 'We can still get one to watch DVDs on. My dad's mate's got one with a built-in player; it's massive.'

'We haven't got the room,' Tom told her. 'Anyway, it's not good for you to watch too much TV; it strains your eyes.'

'So do laptops,' Chloe sniped. Then, frowning when

something occurred to her, she said, 'Here, how come you can get a signal for that but not for a telly?'

'It's not connected to the internet,' Tom told her. 'It's for work, not for messing around on.'

'Oh, right,' Chloe murmured, accepting this. 'I still don't see why we can't get a telly for DVDs, though. We don't even need a big one; one of them little flat-screen ones will do.' She gave an exaggerated sigh now, and added, 'I don't really want to go home, 'cos I like it here with you and Skye. But I'll go out of my head if I've got nothing to do.'

'Okay, I'll think about it,' Tom conceded. 'But only if you promise not to tell Skye about us.'

'Course I won't,' Chloe said without hesitation.

Tom stood up now and, guessing that he was going to bed when he reached for his alarm clock, Chloe said, 'Can you leave us a couple of cigs? Oh, and can you get some beer tomorrow, 'cos that wine's horrible.'

'No beer,' Tom said, taking three cigarettes from his pack and laying them on the bedside table. 'Skye likes wine, and I don't want her to think I'm favouring you by changing it.'

'Okay,' Chloe agreed, deciding not to bother telling him that Skye hated the wine even more than she did. 'As long as I get my telly.'

Tom reiterated that he would see what he could do, and then quietly eased the door open and crept back to his and Skye's room.

Alone, Chloe stubbed out her dog-end and groped around in the dark for her wrap and tinfoil. After chasing a quick line, she lay back against the pillow and gazed up at the shadowed ceiling as she waited for the hit to kick in. The house was a dump and, so far, she hadn't seen anything of any real value. But Tom obviously had money, and if she played her cards right she would probably be able to wheedle a tidy sum out of him in exchange for her silence. And when she was ready for the off, she'd have no problem carrying a nice little TV with a built-in DVD player out under her arm.

17

Jeff ought to have been getting back up to full physical strength now that his wound had healed and he'd finished his course of antibiotics. But the weight seemed to be dropping off him, and Shirley was becoming increasingly concerned as, day after day, she came home from work to find him slumped on the couch. The accusations that Andrea had levelled against him had knocked the stuffing right out of him, and he seemed to have resigned himself to the thought that Skye was dead.

Shirley had tried everything to cheer him up, but even she couldn't deny that things were looking grim as each day passed with no news of the girl. So when the same two police officers who had called round a week earlier knocked on her door one evening she thought her fears had been realised and they had come to tell Jeff that Skye's body had been found.

She didn't notice the rest of the coppers who were behind Jones and Dean until she opened the door. Her legs turned to jelly when one of them informed her that they had a warrant to search the flat while the rest of them piled in.

She stumbled into the living room and watched in horror as Jones dragged Jeff roughly up off the couch and handcuffed him before reading him his rights and informing him that he was being arrested on suspicion of murdering his daughter and unlawfully disposing of her remains.

'He's innocent,' she protested, following when Jones and Dean then hauled Jeff outside to a waiting van. 'You know his wife's lying, so why are you doing this? And how can you arrest him for murder if there isn't even a body?'

'Back off,' Jones grunted, pushing her aside as Dean hustled Jeff into the cage at the back of the van and slammed the door shut.

'My God,' Shirley gasped when she saw the jubilant expression on his face. 'Jeff was right about you; this *is* personal.'

Residents from the surrounding flats and maisonettes had started to gather on the pavement by then, and Jones cast a hooded glance in their direction, before saying quietly, 'Listen, love, I don't know if you're just an idiot who's fallen for Benson's bullshit, or whether you're in on this and have been helping him to cover his tracks. But I'll find out, and if you *are* involved I'll have you. Now back off and let us do our jobs, eh?'

'How dare you threaten me,' Shirley spluttered indignantly. 'Your attitude is appalling. I'm going to report you.'

'Knock yourself out,' Jones drawled unconcernedly. 'But it won't get your boyfriend out any faster – I'll make sure of that.'

Outraged, Shirley turned on her heel and started marching back to her flat. But when she heard the mutterings passing through the crowd, she stopped in her tracks and glared at them.

'Haven't you lot got anything better to do than revel in an innocent man's misery? You should be ashamed of yourselves.'

'We ain't the ones who should be ashamed,' a man who lived in a flat on the floor above shot back nastily. 'You're the one who's been screwing the beast who killed his own kid. Help him hide the body, did you?'

'Probably her idea to have his missus put away, an' all,' a woman asserted loudly, letting Shirley know that the gossip had well and truly reached them. 'Brass-necked tart, that one; flouncing round like Lady bleedin' Muck, just 'cos she can afford to buy her gaff while the rest of us are renting. Not so high and mighty now, though, is she?'

When several of the others voiced their agreement, Shirley shot the smug-looking woman a hateful glare and, raising her chin proudly, stalked up to her front door – only to be stopped from entering by the policewoman who was standing guard.

'This is my flat,' Shirley said, thinking that the woman hadn't realised who she was. 'I need to get my phone.'

Forced to step back when another copper walked out just then, carrying both her and Skye's laptops in clear plastic bags, she said, 'You can't take that one, it's mine.'

'We're seizing all computer equipment,' he told her. 'But everything's being listed, so you should be able to claim back anything that's yours when the case is over with.'

'Jeff only used it a few times to look for jobs and a place to rent, so there won't be anything on there that's useful to you,' Shirley argued. 'And I need it for work.'

'Sorry.' The copper stepped around her and continued on his way.

Almost in tears by now, Shirley stamped her foot in frustration when she glanced down the hall and saw a gloved policeman pawing through the drawers in her bedroom.

'That's my room, not Jeff's,' she told the policewoman. 'And those are my personal belongings.'

'This is a murder investigation,' the woman reminded her coolly. 'Personal doesn't come into it.'

'But I've not been charged with anything,' Shirley shot

back self-righteously. 'So I don't understand what you think you'll gain by searching my things.'

'Won't know till we've looked, will we?' The policewoman shrugged and stood her ground.

'I'm going to get my phone,' Shirley said furiously, lunging towards the door.

'Step back, madam.' The policewoman put a hand on her chest and shoved her. 'You're not going in, and if you try again I'll arrest you.'

Infuriated, Shirley balled her hands into fists, and yelled, 'Will you people *please* stop pushing me around! This has got to be illegal.'

'If you want to make a complaint, I'll be happy to give you the details of who you need to contact before we leave,' the woman told her smoothly.

'Right, fine. I'll wait.' Shirley folded her arms. Then, raising an eyebrow when the copper stared at her, she said, 'What? I'm outside, aren't I? Or are you going to tell me *that*'s against the law now, as well?'

'Can I have a word?'

Shirley jerked her head around at the sound of Jones's voice and glared at him. 'I bet you're loving this, aren't you?'

'Oh, boy, he's done a proper job on you, hasn't he?' Jones said. Then, sighing, his expression weary, he jerked his chin up at her. 'Come to the car for a minute.'

'Why? Am *I* under arrest now?'

'Not yet. But I still want a word.'

Shirley stubbornly stayed put and watched as he walked over to a squad car and climbed behind the wheel. But curiosity got the better of her after a few seconds, and she followed reluctantly.

'Go on, then,' she snapped when she had climbed in beside him. 'Say whatever you've got to say.'

'Look, I know you think I'm a hard-nosed bastard and this is some kind of set-up,' Jones started. 'But I promise you it isn't like that. And I'm only telling you this to save you a load of grief, because I've dealt with Benson loads of times in the past and I know how he operates.'

When Shirley rolled her eyes and tutted, he went on: 'Believe it or not, I actually get why you fell for his Mr Nice Guy act, 'cos he even fooled *me* to start with. But I've seen the other side of him since then, and he's not the mild-mannered bloke he makes himself out to be. He's a thug who gets a kick out of beating his wife up and then scaring the shit out of her to make her retract her statement.'

'No.' Shirley shook her head. 'You're wrong about him.'

Jones gave her a pitying look. 'You know what, you were right about this being personal. It is. But do you want to know why?'

'Not really,' Shirley muttered clippily. 'But I suppose you're going to tell me, anyway.'

'I'm pissed off, that's why,' said Jones, anger glowing in his eyes as he spat the words out. 'Pissed off that I spent so much time concentrating on Andrea, trying to make her see sense and let the assault charges stand, that I completely missed what was happening to that kid of theirs right under my nose. *That*'s why I want him to get what's coming to him now. Not because of some stupid vendetta he's invented in his head, but because I let that girl down – and I refuse to do it again.'

Shirley heard the sincerity in his voice and knew that he believed what he'd said. But she couldn't accept it, because she knew the truth.

'You do know it wasn't Jeff who was beating Andrea up, don't you?' she told him. 'It was the other way round. I've seen the bruises, and he confides in me.'

'Come on, love.' Jones gave a cynical little smile. 'You don't seriously believe a tiny woman like Andrea could beat up a big bloke like him, do you? Or that he'd have *let* her. Anyway, if that was true, how come he never mentioned it all those times she had him collared?'

'Would you have believed him?' Shirley asked. 'No, I didn't think so,' she said when she saw the answer in his eyes. 'Anyway, I can't imagine many men would want to admit to something like that and have people think them weak, can you?'

She raised an eyebrow and waited for Jones to deny what she'd said. But when he just gazed evenly back at her, she sighed and said, 'Look, Jeff might be guilty of being too proud for his own good, but that doesn't mean he's guilty of this. He's one of the sweetest, gentlest men I've ever met, and he's been out of his mind with worry about Skye these last few weeks. As for *Andrea*,' she spat out the name, 'she's clearly still ill if she can say such terrible things, and I don't understand why you're giving her the time of day, if I'm honest.'

'She's got her issues, I'll grant you that,' Jones conceded. 'And if she'd done her usual U-turn we wouldn't be having this conversation. But she's got nothing to lose by telling the truth this time, has she? When she found out about you and him, she knew it was over, and that's when she decided to put an end to the lies.'

'What do you mean?' Shirley drew her head back and frowned at this. 'There is no me and him. We're just friends. I *swear*,' she insisted when Jones gave her a disbelieving look.

Then, blushing, she added, 'Okay, I'll admit that I do find Jeff attractive. But he's never shown the slightest interest in me, so if that's why Andrea's doing this she needs to be told that it's not true before this goes any further.'

Jones admired her loyalty, but it was wasted on a weasel like Jeff Benson and he said, 'I actually feel sorry for you. I can see you've totally fallen for whatever line he's been spinning you. But, believe me, when Skye's body turns up and you see him for what he really is you'll thank God we got him out of here before he started on you. And I guarantee he *would* have done, 'cos blokes like him can't help themselves.'

'No.' Shirley shook her head. 'He's a good man.'

Jones sighed, then shrugged in a gesture of defeat. He had tried, but if she was determined to blindly support the man there was nothing more to be said.

After the police had gone and she was able to get back into the flat, Shirley sat on her armchair and gazed around numbly. They had turned the place upside down and waltzed off not only with Jeff's mobile phone and Skye's laptop, but hers too. And God only knew what else they had taken – or what possible use they thought any of it was going to be to the case. But she wasn't so much bothered about the loss of physical possessions as about the invasion of her privacy. She felt completely and utterly violated to know that those uniformed strangers had pawed through every single thing she owned, and she doubted that she would ever feel secure again in her once cosy home.

As her gaze came to rest on the couch, where Jeff had been sitting when the police arrived, she was saddened all over again at the memory of the defeated look on his face as he was hauled out. He was already depressed, and she hoped that he had been allocated a duty solicitor who would make sure he was seen by a doctor because she was scared that he might do something stupid if he became overwhelmed by it all.

An almighty crash suddenly shattered the silence. Shirley screamed when a brick flew in through the window and bounced across the floor, missing her feet by mere inches.

'Get out while you still can!' A rough voice followed the brick. 'We don't want your sort round here!'

Shaking violently, Shirley snatched up the house phone and dialled 999.

18

'You're a fool,' Shirley's cousin Mel chided as she handed a glass of neat brandy to her a short time later. 'You should have stayed out of it.'

Shirley swallowed a large mouthful and grimaced when it scorched her throat. The police had advised her not to stay at the flat tonight, so after giving her statement and waiting for the glazier to board up the smashed window she'd phoned Mel and asked if she could stay here. But she was already starting to regret her decision, because it was obvious that Mel, just like the rest of them, had already mentally tried and convicted Jeff.

'He didn't do it,' Shirley murmured, sick and tired of hitting brick walls at every turn in her battle to prove his innocence. 'His wife is just punishing him because she thinks he's having an affair with me.'

'And is she right?' Mel raised an eyebrow and gave Shirley a questioning look as she sat down beside her.

'*No.*' Shirley sighed wearily. 'We're just friends. But if my own family don't even believe me, what chance have I got with everyone else?'

'I do believe you,' Mel said, the cynical expression on her face belying her words. 'But you've got to admit it looks bad, hon. You said it yourself, he's been arrested loads of times.'

'And never been charged,' Shirley reminded her defensively.

'Mmmm,' Mel murmured. She didn't know the man personally but she doubted whether the police would have arrested him for murder if they didn't have firm evidence.

Shirley took another sip of her drink and flopped her head back against the cushions. 'You should have seen him when they took him away, Mel. He was like a lamb to the slaughter – no fight left in him whatsoever. I felt so helpless.'

'I know you don't want to hear this,' Mel said gently. 'But have you considered that he might have decided there was no point resisting, because he knew he'd been caught?'

'No.' Shirley shook her head adamantly. 'I've been with him a lot these last few weeks, and I've seen what this is doing to him. He hasn't done anything. I'd know if he had.'

Aware that she was getting nowhere, Mel shrugged, and said, 'Well, you know your own mind, so I'm not going to beat on about it. But there's nothing you can do for him now, so you need to forget him and start thinking about yourself.'

'You mean turn my back on him?' Shirley gave her an anguished look. 'I can't do that. He needs me.'

'And *you* need to be safe,' Mel stated firmly. 'No one can get at him now he's locked up, but you don't have that same protection. I mean, look what happened tonight: you're not even safe in your own home. And I guarantee that won't be the end of it.' She gave Shirley an imploring look when she saw the resistance in her eyes, and said, 'Please, Shirl – I'm worried about you. You're burying your head in the sand, but this isn't going to go away. Everyone thinks he's guilty, and if they see you standing by him that'll make *you* guilty in their eyes, too. You have to take that seriously, because it might not just be a brick through your window next time.'

Shirley squeezed her eyes shut. She couldn't dispute what

Mel had said, because her cousin was dead right. This was a dangerous situation and her neighbours had made it clear that they thought she was involved in Skye's disappearance. And if the people who had known her for years thought her capable of shielding a supposed child-murderer, God only knew what everyone would think when they got wind of this latest development. Her workmates, for example: they had already stopped talking to her, but they would make her work life a living hell over this.

Mel watched as the grim thoughts flashed through Shirley's eyes. She hadn't wanted to upset her and would support her in any way that she could, but it had needed to be said. Shirley obviously cared deeply about Jeff Benson, and truly believed that he was innocent. But her obstinate loyalty would be the rope that hanged her if he were found guilty, and she would have to deal with the fallout for the rest of her life.

Even more depressed now than when she had first arrived, Shirley finished her drink and put the glass down on the coffee table.

'Thanks for letting me stay, but I think I need to be on my own for a bit,' she said quietly as she pushed herself forward on her seat. 'You don't mind if I go to bed, do you?'

'Course not,' Mel assured her. Then, guessing that her cousin might have a problem getting to sleep with all this playing on her mind, she said, 'There's a pack of Nytol in the bathroom cabinet if you need it.'

Shirley nodded and leaned over to kiss her on the cheek before making her way up to bed.

In a holding cell at the police station just then, Jeff felt as if his head was about to explode as he struggled to come to terms with what the duty solicitor Malcolm Fitch had told him.

It seemed that the police were not only planning on charging him with murdering Skye and disposing of her remains, despite having no body to substantiate the claim; they were also looking into adding an extra charge of attempted murder, since Andrea had apparently decided to tell them that *he* had been trying to stab *her* that night, and that she'd been forced to wrestle the knife from him and stab him in self-defence.

'Don't worry too much about that one,' Fitch had said. 'Her statement is pretty damning on the face of it, but I'm planning to discredit it on the grounds of mental incapacity, *and* the fact that she has completely changed her version of events since making the initial statement.'

If that had been intended to give Jeff hope, the man had squashed it flat when he'd gone on to say: 'If that was all they had on you, I'm confident we'd get an acquittal; but I'm afraid your wife's testimony is only a small part of the main case. Now that they think you've been systematically abusing your daughter, they're going to hammer you any which way they can. Which means dredging up not only your record of arrests for domestic violence, but also anything that has ever been logged regarding Skye's well-being. Teachers who have expressed concerns about her; friends she confided in; hospital staff who have ever treated her; social workers; the foster-parents; the staff from the children's home she was placed in – they'll all be called to the stand.'

'But I haven't done anything,' Jeff had insisted for what felt like the millionth time. 'Andrea's lying through her teeth; and they haven't even got a body, so how can they charge me with Skye's murder? It's crazy.'

'The CPS obviously believe that the circumstantial evidence is strong enough to secure a conviction,' Fitch had told him, going on to warn: 'And they'll undoubtedly cite your affair with Shirley Dawson as a motive for you wanting Andrea dead, so you should prepare yourself for the probability that she'll be called to appear as a witness for the prosecution.'

Jeff had tried to tell the man that he had not been having an affair with Shirley. But Fitch clearly hadn't believed him – about that, *or* about Andrea's outrageous claims that he'd been abusing Skye. And that was worrying, because if his own brief thought he was lying what chance did he stand with a judge and jury?

The guilt he'd already been feeling about having involved Shirley in this mess had intensified a thousandfold since that conversation, and he was cursing himself for ignoring his instincts and taking her up on her offer of a place to stay when he got evicted. If he'd only gone and found himself a bridge to sleep under none of this would be happening, because Andrea wouldn't have jumped to the conclusion that he'd been seeing Shirley behind her back and started this malicious campaign.

It almost made him wish that he *had* gone for it with Shirley, because at least then he'd have had one good memory to hold onto as he rotted his life away in prison. She was the only one who believed in him, and he would never be able to thank her enough for being there in his darkest hour. But she had to start thinking about herself now, and if she was called as a witness he prayed that she would have the sense to distance herself from him and say whatever she had to say in order to deflect the fingers of suspicion that were already being pointed in her direction – even if she incriminated him further in the process.

Drawn from his thoughts by the sound of the grille in the door being scraped back, Jeff pushed Shirley out of his mind and glanced up at the eyes that were peering in at him. They had placed him on suicide watch and had been checking on him every fifteen minutes, so even if he had been able to sleep they would have made damn sure that he didn't.

'Don't worry, I haven't tried to top myself,' he assured the officer quietly. Then, 'Any chance of a drink yet?'

'Does this look like a fucking cocktail bar?' the man behind the eyes retorted sarcastically.

'I only meant tea or water,' Jeff said evenly, refusing to be drawn because he suspected that they were dying for him to kick off so they'd have an excuse to beat the shit out of him. 'I haven't had anything in hours, and my throat's sore.'

'That how your daughter felt before you did for her, was it?' the copper hissed. 'Make her suffer before you cut her up and scattered her all over the countryside, did you? And you've got a nerve to whinge about a sore throat? You wanna think yourself lucky there's a fuckin' camera in there, you lowlife piece of shit, or you'd find out how much of a fuck we give about your throat!'

Jeff didn't bother replying to this. What was the point? So much for innocent until proved guilty: it was a done deal as far as this lot were concerned. But if the cops were being harsh, it was nothing compared with the treatment he could expect in prison. Classified as a nonce and a child-murderer, he'd be made to suffer in ways that he didn't even want to think about. And not just by the screws but by his fellow cons, too.

He lowered his head and rested his forehead on his knees as the weight of the world threatened to crush his shoulders. The solicitor had told him not to give up hope, that there was still a possibility of Skye turning up in time to blow her mother's claims to pieces. But it wasn't going to happen.

She'd been missing for too long and, even if she had been hiding out at a mate's place the whole time, Jeff knew that she must have seen the news reports appealing for information and would have found a way to let him know that she was okay.

Already more or less resigned to the fact that he was never going to see Skye again, Jeff vowed that, even if a miracle occurred and he was found not guilty, this was the end of the line for him and Andrea. He would never forgive her for this. *Never.*

19

Skye crept down the stairs and tiptoed across the kitchen to retrieve the chicken pieces from last night's dinner that she'd stashed beneath the rubbish in the bin.

It was a fortnight since Chloe had arrived and Bernie had been banished to live outside, and she had been sneaking out to see him whenever she got the chance. It was bad enough that the poor thing was chained to the concrete washing-line post in the middle of the scrapyard section of the garden, without him starving to death as well. But that was what would happen if Skye didn't give him the scraps she saved, because Tom seemed to have forgotten about him now that he was no longer in the house, and often didn't feed him.

She had just taken the key out of the back of the clock and was about to slide it into the lock when she felt a tap on her shoulder. Terrified that Tom had discovered her secret and had only pretended to leave for work this morning so that he could lie in wait and catch her red-handed, she turned around, her face scarlet with guilt.

'You idiot!' she gasped when she saw that it was Chloe and not Tom. 'What are you sneaking up on me like that for? You nearly gave me a heart attack.'

'All right, keep your hair on.' Chloe chuckled. 'I heard you creeping round and wanted to know what you were up to.'

'Nothing,' Skye lied, palming the key and sliding it up her sleeve. 'Just making sure Tom locked the door properly.'

'Yeah, right, like he'd go out without triple checking it,' Chloe scoffed. 'He's so paranoid that someone's gonna break in and take you away from him, it's like a prison in here.'

'I know, but there's no harm checking.' Skye gave her a tight smile and walked over to the kettle. 'I'm making a coffee. Do you want one?'

'Mmmm,' Chloe murmured, taking a seat at the table and watching her through narrowed eyes. 'How come you're so jumpy?'

'I've got a headache,' Skye told her. 'It's making me feel tense.'

'You've always got a headache, you,' Chloe mused. 'You wanna watch that. My nan was always getting them and they said it was migraines, but it turned out to be a massive brain tumour.'

'Don't say that,' Skye spluttered, taking a pack of paracetamol out of the drawer.

'It's true,' Chloe insisted. 'She lost three stone overnight when they told her; went from fat to thin, just like that.'

Skye jumped when the girl clicked her fingers loudly, and shuddered as she popped two tablets out of the strip. 'No one loses weight that fast,' she muttered, pouring herself a cup of water. 'You're making it up.'

'Don't call me a liar,' Chloe said sharply. 'I was there, I saw it.'

'Okay, whatever.' Back turned, Skye rolled her eyes and shoved the tablets into her mouth. 'How come you're up?' she asked then. 'You don't usually come down so early.'

'Couldn't sleep,' Chloe told her. 'I had a bad dream and it woke me up.'

'I used to have them all the time when I first moved in,'
Skye said sympathetically as she spooned coffee into two
cups. 'But they go away after a while. What was yours
about?'

'My dad,' Chloe said quietly. 'He found out I was here
and came to get me, but I said I didn't want to go with him
so he started booting the door in. He was proper angry. I
thought he was gonna kill me.'

'I wouldn't worry about it,' Skye said reassuringly as she
carried the coffees over to the table and sat down. 'There's
no way he could find out you're here – unless you told
someone you were coming?'

'How could I have done that when *I* didn't even know till
I got here?' Chloe asked. She rested her elbows on the table
now and cupped the hot mug between her hands. 'What were
you really doing at the door just now?'

'I've already told you, I was checking it.' Skye lowered her
gaze and sipped her coffee.

'What you lying for?' Chloe asked. 'And don't say you're
not, 'cos I can tell. You've got one of them faces that can't
hide nothing.'

'I'm not lying,' Skye insisted, forcing herself to look the
other girl in the eye.

Chloe gave a sly smile. 'Bet you were trying to pick the
lock, weren't you? I wouldn't blame you 'cos I was thinking
about doing it myself, I'm that bored stuck in here all the
time. Doesn't it do your head in?'

'Not really.' Skye shrugged. 'I keep myself busy.'

'What, cleaning and cooking, and running round after
Tom?' Chloe said sarcastically.

'It's better than being in prison,' Skye reminded her.
'Anyway, that's what wives are supposed to do,' she added

piously. 'The man goes to work, and the woman looks after the house.'

'Yeah, but for the *rest of your life?*' Chloe placed heavy emphasis on these words, as if it was a death sentence – which, to her, was exactly how it seemed. 'I think I'd rather go to prison. At least they let you out every day, *and* you get to watch telly.'

'I used to feel like that,' Skye told her. 'But it's not so bad once you get used to it, and I kind of like the quiet now.'

'Well, I don't,' Chloe countered. 'And Tom best hurry up and get me that telly he promised or I'm out of here.'

'We can't get a signal out here,' said Skye, wondering why Tom would have promised to get a TV when he knew full well that it wouldn't work.

'That's why I told him to get one with a built-in DVD player, so we can watch films,' Chloe explained. 'He keeps saying he's looking, but if he doesn't get one soon I'm going home. At least I can do what I want there.'

'You can't go back there,' Skye blurted out, horrified that Chloe was even thinking about it. 'Your dad *rapes* you,' she added, as if she thought that the girl had forgotten. 'At least you're safe here.'

'You reckon?'

Skye frowned when Chloe gave her a loaded look, and said, 'What's that supposed to mean?'

'Nothing.' Chloe shook her head and stared down into her cup. 'It's just that dream. It freaked me out, and I can't help wondering what'd happen if my dad *did* find out I was here.'

'He's not going to, so stop worrying,' Skye said reassuringly. 'Me and Tom will look after you. Anyway, I'd miss you if you left. I don't like it that you're still doing drugs, and I wish you'd stop, but you're like my little sister and I love looking after you.'

Chloe took another sip of coffee without answering. She had nothing against Skye, and actually thought she was quite nice now that she'd got to know her a bit better. But it did her head in that Skye acted like a big woman and treated her like a kid when, in truth, there were only a few months between them. And for someone who considered herself so mature, Skye was so naive where Tom was concerned that it was laughable. Chloe had only resisted telling her the truth about him because Tom had been keeping her sweet with smack and cigarettes. But this was the second time he'd gone to work without leaving any cigs for her, and she only had enough gear left for a couple of little hits. If he didn't sort it out soon, he was going to be sorry.

Skye was peering at her thoughtfully across the table. 'If I tell you something, will you promise not to tell Tom?'

'Yeah, course.'

'Would you feel better about staying here if you could go outside?'

'Dunno.' Chloe shrugged. 'Maybe. Why?'

Skye bit her lip. The front door had already been barricaded when she first got here, but then Tom had nailed all of the windows shut as well, and it could be unbearable in here when it got really hot outside. She understood why Chloe was going stir-crazy because she probably would, too, if she weren't able to go out for those few minutes each day. Tom would go ballistic if he found out about the key, but if it changed Chloe's mind about leaving it was a risk that Skye was willing to take.

Making her mind up, she shook her sleeve to make the

key drop into her hand and then placed it on the table between them.

Chloe gazed down at it for a second, and then back up at Skye. 'What's that?'

'The back-door key. But you absolutely can't tell Tom, 'cos he'll go mad if he finds out.'

'How long have you had it?'

'Not long,' Skye lied. 'I found it in the drawer the other day. I was going to tell you, but I was scared you might tell Tom.'

'We're supposed to be best mates,' Chloe reminded her. 'You should know I'd never do that to you.'

'I know,' Skye murmured guiltily. 'I just . . .' She trailed off and shrugged, unable to come up with a reasonable excuse for not having told her.

Offended, Chloe crossed her arms. 'I've told you every-thing, and I really thought I could trust you. But I should have known you were just like all them other bitches. You all say one thing to my face, then take the piss out of me behind my back.'

'I'm not like that,' Skye insisted. 'And I *was* going to tell you.'

'So you've been going out this whole time, while I've been locked in here, *dying*.'

'Only a couple of times. But I promise I haven't been having fun behind your back. All I do is feed Bernie, then come straight back in.'

'I knew you cared more about a dog than you do about me,' Chloe said petulantly.

'Of course I don't,' Skye lied. 'But you've got food and a bed, so you're okay. He'd have nothing if I didn't go out and see to him.' She paused now, and sighed before asking, 'Have you fallen out with me now?'

'I'll have to think about it,' Chloe muttered, snatching the key off the table and standing up.

'You're not going to tell Tom, are you?' Skye asked worriedly, also rising.

'I said I wouldn't, so I won't,' Chloe told her as she slotted the key into the lock. 'But I don't see what the big deal is. He don't own you, so he can't stop you going out.'

'You know why I can't go out,' Skye said lamely as she followed Chloe over the step. 'And he wouldn't stop me if it wasn't so dangerous – he's just protecting me.'

'From what?' Chloe spread her arms and turned in a circle. 'I can't see no one out here, can you?'

'We can't take any chances,' Skye replied quietly. 'And we can't stay out too long,' she added, glancing nervously around the corner. 'If Tom comes home early we'll be in trouble.'

'You mean *you* will be,' Chloe retorted unconcernedly. 'He can't say nothing to me 'cos I'll just leave if he tries.'

'Please don't,' Skye implored. 'I only told you about the key so you'd stay.'

Chloe was no longer listening; she was too busy soaking up the rays of the sun on her face. 'God, that's ace,' she murmured, as if it were the first time she had ever been outside – which was exactly how it felt after two weeks of being locked inside the stuffy house.

Bernie had sat up when he saw Skye come out of the house, and his tail was batting the soiled ground now as he waited for his treat. Leaving Chloe to luxuriate in the warmth, Skye took the scraps out of her pocket and tiptoed carefully around the mangled bikes and rusted washing machines.

'Hey, don't let it off the chain,' Chloe called nervously when she saw where Skye was heading.

'I couldn't even if I wanted to,' Skye called back. 'But I

wouldn't come too close, if I was you,' she added when Bernie gave a low growl at the sound of Chloe's voice. 'I don't think he's forgiven you yet.'

'Don't worry, I ain't going nowhere near it.' Chloe cast a hateful look in the dog's direction. 'Ugly, smelly bastard wants its teeth kicking out, if you ask me.'

'Don't be horrible,' Skye said protectively, squatting down when she reached Bernie and giving him a cuddle.

'It wants a cork up its arse, an' all,' Chloe went on, staring in disgust at the heaps of dog muck that were scattered around. 'Why can't it shit in the grass, like normal dogs? It proper stinks out here.'

'It's not his fault he can't move far,' Skye reminded her. Then, smiling when Bernie licked her face, she put the scraps on the floor in front of him, and stroked his head as he gobbled them up. 'That nice, is it, boy? You like that?'

'Anyone would think it was a baby, the way you talk to it,' Chloe sneered, edging past them and making her way into the long grass.

'Where are you going?' Skye asked, glancing up as she passed. 'There's nothing down there, and I told you we can't stay out too long.'

'I'm having a mooch,' Chloe called back over her shoulder. 'What's in that shed over there?'

'Spiders,' Skye told her, wiping her hands on her thighs and standing up. 'Come on, Chloe, don't go too far. Tom might come back any minute.'

'So?' Chloe had disappeared from view by now, and her voice had grown fainter.

'Seriously, Chloe, we need to go back,' Skye implored, beginning to regret having told the other girl about the key. When no answer came, she tutted and set off after her.

Chloe was standing on her tiptoes when Skye turned the corner of the old shed, her hands cupped over her eyes to shade them as she peered through the filthy window.

'There's a load of stuff in here,' she said when Skye joined her. 'Boxes, and all sorts. Wonder what's in them?'

'I don't know and I don't care,' said Skye, crossing her arms and shivering when she noticed the tiny insects that were caught in the web next to Chloe's cheek. 'It's Tom's, not ours.'

'I'm going in,' Chloe declared, dropping onto her heels and reaching for the door handle. After rattling it a few times to no avail, she said, 'Where did you say you found that key?'

'In the drawer,' Skye told her. 'But there's no more in there, if that's what you're thinking.'

Disappointed, Chloe gazed at the door again. 'D'you reckon I could kick it in?'

'No, I do not!' Skye spluttered, horrified that Chloe was even contemplating it, because then Tom would definitely know they had been out of the house. 'Look, whatever's in there, it's none of our business, so come on, we're going back. *Now*, Chloe.'

Reluctantly, Chloe followed Skye back to the house, but there was no way she was leaving it at that. People only went to the trouble of locking stuff away like that when it was worth something, and if there was something in that shed that she could make money out of she was having it.

Skye's headache got worse after they went back inside, and Chloe was glad when she announced that she was going to take a nap to try and clear it. Free to search for more keys, Chloe went through all the drawers and was about to start on the cupboards when somebody knocked loudly on the front door. Scared that it might be her dad, or the police looking for Skye, she crept out into the hall and, crouching low even though there was no chance of anybody seeing her through the mishmash of bars that Tom had nailed across the back of the front door, tiptoed up the stairs.

'Skye!' she hissed, dashing into the bedroom and shaking her friend's shoulder roughly. 'Skye! Wake up! *SKYE*!'

Roused by the violent shaking, Skye peeled her eyes open and gazed confusedly up at her. 'Wha's up?'

'Someone's at the door,' Chloe whispered urgently.

'*What*?' Shocked out of her fug, Skye sat bolt upright. 'Who is it?'

'I don't know!' Chloe twisted her hands together nervously as another round of knocking echoed through the hallway below.

Skye kicked the quilt off her legs and stumbled over to the window.

'Don't!' Chloe squawked when she started to ease the curtain back. 'They might see you!'

'I need to know if it's the police,' Skye told her. 'If it is and they know I'm here, they'll kick the door in.'

'Will they be able to get through them bars?' Chloe gazed at her as if she held all the answers.

'I don't know,' Skye admitted, her voice quivering with fear.

More knocking made them both jump, and Chloe clutched at Skye's arm as Skye pressed her ear up against the curtain to listen out for voices or the crackle of a radio. Skye held her breath when she heard two male voices, but they were two low for her to hear what they were saying.

'I think they're going,' she whispered when, a few seconds later, she heard the crunch of footsteps on the rough gravel.

'Be careful,' Chloe cautioned when Skye eased the curtain back with the tip of her finger. 'Can you see anything?'

'There's a van by the gates,' Skye told her. 'But I can't see anyone. They must have gone round the back.'

The muted sound of barking coming from the back garden just then confirmed her suspicions and, dragging Chloe along behind her, Skye rushed down the landing to Jade's room at the back, where Chloe had been sleeping since she moved in.

It was an absolute tip in there; clothes strewn around the floor, the bed unmade, and a heap of dirty cups and plates on the dust-covered dressing table. Skye wrinkled her nose in disgust when the strong odour of sweat and unwashed sheets hit her in the face, and rushed over to the window.

'Who is it?' Chloe asked when Skye twitched the curtain aside.

'Don't know,' Skye murmured, staring down at the two men who were standing below. 'I don't think it's the police, though,' she said, taking in the overalls and clumpy boots they were both wearing.

Bernie was still barking madly, and Skye was afraid that he would do himself an injury as he threw himself around, straining against the chain that was binding him to the post. When one of the men suddenly turned and stared up at the house, she let out a little cry and dropped to her haunches, pulling Chloe down with her.

'Do you think he saw us?' Chloe asked fearfully.

'I don't know!' Skye whispered. 'Sshhh, I need to listen.'

'What do they want?' Chloe persisted. 'You don't think they'll try and break in, do you?'

Irritated that the girl was still talking, Skye shuffled closer to the wall. One of the men had a little coughing fit, and she pulled a face when she heard him hawk up in his throat and spit out the phlegm. This was followed by the sound of trickling water, and she guessed that one of them was taking a piss.

'Dirty pigs,' Chloe muttered.

Skye nodded her agreement and placed a finger on her lips to quieten the girl. The men stood and talked beneath the window for a couple of minutes. Skye strained to hear what they were saying, but again couldn't make out a single word. When, at last, they began to move away, she jumped back up to her feet and ran back to her own room, with Chloe hot on her heels.

The girls watched as the men ambled back down the path and climbed into the van. But just as it started to reverse out onto the road, Tom's car turned in and forced it to stop.

'What's he doing?' Chloe asked when Tom climbed out from behind the wheel.

'I don't know,' Skye murmured, chewing on her thumbnail as the men got out of the van and walked towards him.

'Hope he's not gonna try and start a fight. They'd kill him – size of them to him.'

Skye didn't reply to this, but she was thinking much the same thing. From here, Tom looked a lot smaller and skinnier than the burly workmen, and she was terrified that they might beat him up and then take his keys off him and let themselves into the house to rob them.

Tom spoke with the men for several minutes, and then climbed back into his car and reversed out to give them space to get their van back on the road. When they had gone, he drove onto the path and jumped back out to close and secure the rusted gates before continuing on up to the house.

Skye and Chloe had run down to the kitchen by the time

he pulled up, and they were standing side by side facing the door when he let himself in.

'What did they say?' Skye asked.

Tom lunged for her without answering and grabbed her by the throat.

'Oi! Get off her!' Chloe protested when Skye squealed with fear. 'She hasn't done nothing!'

'Shut up or you'll be next!' Tom warned, flinging Skye down onto a chair.

'You wouldn't bleedin' dare!' Chloe retorted, darting round to the other side of the table. 'My dad'll beat the shit out of you if you ever touch me!'

Nostrils flaring, chest heaving, Tom ignored the threat and lowered his face to Skye's, snarling, 'Why were you showing yourself at the window like that?'

'I wasn't,' Skye squawked. 'They couldn't see me.'

'Well, *I* fucking did,' he yelled, his eyes bulging with rage. 'Were you deliberately trying to get their attention?'

'*No!*' she spluttered, tears running down her cheeks. '*Ow!*' she cried when he grabbed her hair and yanked her head back. 'You're hurting me!'

'I think that's exactly what you were doing,' he spat. 'I think you were hoping they'd come and rescue you – *weren't you?*'

Tom shouted this last bit, and Skye grimaced when his spittle sprayed her face.

'How far would you have gone if I hadn't got here when I did?' he demanded. 'Would you have flashed your breasts at them, like the dirty little slut you are? I bet you'd have *loved* it if they'd got their ladders out of the van and climbed up to you, wouldn't you?'

'You're off your fuckin' head,' Chloe piped up. 'She didn't

do nothing. I'd tell you if she did, but she didn't. And you're bang out of order having a go at her over it, 'cos she was terrified.'

Tom's eyes were still blazing, and his breath was fiery on Skye's face as he carried on staring at her for several moments. But, gradually, his breathing began to slow, and after a while he released her.

'You want locking up,' Chloe muttered, going over to stand behind Skye. 'Look at the state of her neck, and she didn't even do nothing.'

'I'm sorry,' Tom muttered, casting a shamefaced glance at the marks on Skye's throat. 'I shouldn't have done that, but I was scared they might have seen you. You know we'll all go to prison if we get caught.'

'*I* won't,' Chloe reminded him tartly, placing her hand on Skye's shoulder in a show of support. 'But I'll make sure *you* do if you ever do anything like that again.'

Teeth tightly clenched, cheek muscles twisting, Tom eyed her for several long moments. Then, breathing in deeply, he said, 'It won't happen again. We're a family, and we've got to stick together no matter what.'

'It was my fault,' Skye murmured guiltily. 'I shouldn't have gone to the window.'

Chloe gazed at her in disbelief, then shook her head and sat down. Some people were just too stupid for their own good.

'Forget it,' Tom said quietly. 'Just make sure it doesn't happen again.' He held out his arms now and summoned Skye to him with a jerk of his chin.

Still sniffling, she got up and fell against his chest.

'I'm sorry,' he crooned, stroking her hair. 'I'm just so scared of losing you.'

'I know,' Skye murmured. 'But I'd never do anything to put us in danger on purpose, you know I wouldn't.'

Chloe struggled to conceal her contempt as she watched the pair cuddle up to each other. Tom was what her dad called a 'snapper': calm one minute, a raving maniac the next, then back to calm again in a heartbeat. As for Skye . . . well, if Tom ever dared to treat Chloe the way he'd just treated *her*, she'd stab him right in the balls.

Tom glanced up just then, and tilted his head when he saw Chloe staring at them. 'Come here,' he said, still holding Skye with one arm while extending the other to Chloe.

'Nah, I'm all right.' She stayed put.

'Don't be like that,' Skye said, holding out her own hand to urge the girl to join them for a comforting hug. 'You were just as scared as I was, so you don't have to put on a brave face. And Tom's here now, so we're safe.'

Chloe couldn't think of anything worse than a group hug. But she didn't want either of them to guess what she was thinking right now, so she reluctantly went over and allowed them to include her in their embrace.

She pulled away again quickly when she felt Tom's erection pressing against her thigh. It was one thing shagging him behind Skye's back, but if he thought they were on for a threesome he had another think coming. She'd never done it with another girl, and she wasn't about to start now.

'I need a fag,' she said when she'd extracted herself. 'You forgot to leave me some when you went out this morning, and I've been gasping all day.'

'Maybe it's time you thought about quitting.' Tom flashed a look of disapproval at her as he took his arms from around Skye and fished his cigarettes out of his pocket. 'My dad used to say: if you can't afford to buy them, you can't afford to smoke them.'

Chloe held out her hand, daring him to refuse, and a tiny light of victory flared in her eyes when he handed one over without another word.

'Right,' Tom said, shelving his annoyance at having been blackmailed. 'Have you made dinner yet, Skye?'

'No, not yet,' she admitted. 'I had a really bad headache and went for a lie-down, and then those men turned up, so I—'

'It's okay,' Tom cut her off. 'I was going to say I'll get a takeaway. I think we all need a treat after that shock, don't we?'

Skye smiled and nodded, relieved that she wasn't in trouble again. She tried to be sensible and mature, but she just kept on doing stupid things and she hated herself for it, because one wrong move on her part would be all it took to blow their world apart.

Chloe sucked on her cigarette to keep herself from gagging when she saw the grateful look on Skye's face. Tom had throttled her and practically accused her of being a whore, and yet she was looking at him now like he was some kind of superhero. What was *wrong* with this girl?

'Did those men say what they wanted?' Skye asked.

'They reckon they're looking for places to buy round here, but I told them this house isn't for sale,' said Tom. 'How long were they here before I got back?' he asked then. 'Did they try any of the doors or windows?'

'No, they just knocked, then went round the back,' Skye told him. 'They were only here about ten minutes. I think Bernie scared them off, 'cos he was going mad.' She paused now, and looped her fingers together before saying tentatively,

'I was thinking, it might be safer to let him back in now – to protect us while you're out. Only, now they've seen him, I bet they wouldn't dare try to break in if they came back and heard him barking inside.'

Tom nodded thoughtfully, and said, 'I'll think about it.'

Delighted to think that she might have bought Bernie a passage back into the house, Skye smiled. But when she saw the look of horror on Chloe's face, she said, 'Don't worry, I won't let him go anywhere near you.'

'He'd better not, or I'll stab him,' Chloe warned.

A couple of hours later, after they had eaten and Skye had washed the plates, the three settled in their usual places in the living room: the girls on the couch, flicking through the wedding magazines for the millionth time; Tom on his armchair with his laptop on his knee.

After a while, he closed the lid and placed the laptop on the table beside his chair before heading into the kitchen. Chloe waited a couple of minutes and then stood up casually, telling Skye that she needed a drink of water. It was the first chance she'd had to talk to Tom on her own since he got home, and she was intending to ask for her gear and ramp up the pressure about the TV he'd promised but still hadn't got. But she forgot all about that when she walked into the kitchen and saw him shaking something from a little bag into one of the cups that were standing on the ledge.

'What are you doing?' she asked, instantly suspicious.

Tom's shoulders stiffened, and he looked like a child who'd been caught with his hand in the cookie jar when he turned to face her. But he quickly composed himself and hissed, 'Close the door.'

Chloe did as he'd asked and gave him a questioning look.

'You can't tell Skye about this,' Tom whispered, his eyes darting every which way as he tried to think up a feasible-sounding explanation. 'It's for those headaches she keeps getting. I called in to see my doctor on my way home this evening, and he reckons it might be high blood pressure.'

'You told your doctor Skye was here?' Chloe frowned. 'What if he tells the police?'

'No, of course I didn't tell him,' Tom said irritably. 'I just described the symptoms and said it was me who was having them, and that's what he said it was. And he said it can kill you,' he went on gravely. 'It's caused by stress, and if it gets too bad it makes your blood vessels explode. That's why Skye can't know about this – because she'll get scared, and that'll be really dangerous for her.'

'So what's that?' Chloe glanced down at the little bag he was holding.

'Medicine to bring the pressure down,' he told her. 'Don't worry, it won't hurt her. She'll just feel a lot more relaxed after she's had it.'

'Why don't you just tell her?'

'Because it'll work better if she's not sitting there waiting for something to happen,' Tom replied with authority. 'It's a psychological thing. If you expect something and it doesn't happen, you end up feeling worse.'

Chloe still looked doubtful, and Tom smiled. 'There's absolutely nothing to worry about; you know I'd never do anything to hurt her. I just want to make her feel better.'

'She'd have felt a lot better if you hadn't tried to strangle her,' Chloe reminded him accusingly.

'I know,' he said quietly. 'But I've apologised, so what more can I do?' He sighed now, and said, 'Anyway, you'd best go back in there and let me get on with this before she starts wondering what we're up to.'

Skye glanced round when Chloe came back into the room, and held up the magazine she was reading. 'Here, look at this – isn't it gorgeous? I thought I'd decided on that other one, but I think I prefer this one now. What do you think?'

Chloe sat down and glanced at the frothy dress that Skye was gushing over. 'Yeah, lovely,' she said distractedly, her mind still on Tom and the powder she'd just seen him tipping into the cup. If it had come from the doctor, why was it in a bag and not a prescription box or bottle? And how had he managed to see his doctor *and* stop off at a pharmacy, but still get home at the usual time?

'How about these for you and Jade?' Skye was asking now, showing Chloe some bridesmaids' dresses. 'But not in orange, obviously, 'cos that's just nasty. I'd want them to be pink.'

Chloe murmured, 'Mmmm' and nodded without even looking at them.

When Tom came back a few seconds later and handed a cup of wine to each of them, Chloe peered down at the dark liquid and felt a thrill of realisation course through her when she saw several tiny white flecks floating on the surface. The light was always dim in here so she'd never noticed it before, and Skye was so naive she would probably have thought that wine was supposed to have flecks in it if *she* had noticed. But Chloe had been doing smack for a year and had tried numerous other drugs before that, so she should have recognised the signs. That weird sense of confusion every morning; Tom claiming that she'd given him the come-on when she didn't even fancy him; Skye's headaches . . . It all made sense now. He'd been spiking their drinks.

When Tom sat back down and resumed whatever he'd

been doing on his laptop, Chloe glanced at Skye out of the corner of her eye to make sure that she was still engrossed in her wedding dresses and accessories. Then she carefully tipped her cup and spilled some of her wine down the side of the cushion. She knew Tom would guess what she'd done when he discovered that the cushion was wet but she planned to be long gone by then.

Skye had already started to look a little sleepy by the time she finished her first drink, and Chloe mimicked her as she handed her empty cup to Tom when he offered them a refill. Then, when Skye's eyes started to roll just a few sips into her second drink, and the magazine fell from her hand, Chloe let her own head loll back against the cushion and mimicked her friend's heavy breathing.

The hairs on the back of her neck stood on end when she peeped out through her lashes and saw the way Tom was staring at them over the top of his screen. And when he laid the laptop down and walked over to her, she had to force herself not to resist when he grasped her chin in his hand and rocked her head from side to side. Seemingly satisfied that she was asleep, he slid his hands beneath her and picked her up.

She lay floppy in his arms as he carried her up the stairs, but as soon as he laid her on her bed and went back downstairs to get Skye she sat bolt upright. She had to get out of here, but how? She wasn't stupid enough to think that Tom was going to let her walk away without a fight, but she just wasn't up to fending him off right now. She'd finished her last little bit of smack after dinner but it was already wearing off, and she knew that she would soon start shaking and feeling sick. Tom had promised to score for her on his way home from work, but she could hardly ask him for it now because then he'd know that she'd been faking being unconscious. And she didn't even have the wine to take the edge off the withdrawal.

The house was locked up tight, and she had no idea where that spare back-door key was because that paranoid cow Skye had hidden it after they came back inside this afternoon. But, even if she had known where it was, she wouldn't dare try and sneak out while Tom was home. He'd already proved he was a nutter by drugging the pair of them, so he'd be bound to come after her to stop her from telling anyone. And, out here in the middle of nowhere, there would be nobody to help her if she screamed.

At the sound of a floorboard creaking outside her door, Chloe quickly lay back down and listened as Tom came quietly into the room and walked around the bed. She struggled not to shudder when he leaned over her and his hot stale-smoke breath scorched her cheek. When at last he moved away, she watched through slitted eyes as he placed something on the dresser at the side of the bed.

Almost giving herself away with a sharp intake of breath when she saw a blinking red light and realised that it was a camcorder and not the alarm clock that Tom had previously claimed it to be, she squeezed her eyes shut when he turned back to her. The sick bastard! Not content with drugging her, he been filming himself having sex with her as well!

Tom had undressed after placing Skye in their bed, and he slipped his dressing gown off now and draped it over the back of a chair before climbing naked onto the foot of the bed.

'You've been a very bad girl, and I'm not very happy with you,' he said, his voice husky as he pushed Chloe's knees apart and shuffled up between her legs. 'You might look like my princess, but that's as far as it goes. She's innocent, but your father has ruined you, so now I'm going to have to teach you how to behave like a lady.'

Chloe didn't resist when Tom reached for one of her hands and raised it above her head, but when she felt him start to wrap something around her wrist, she guessed what he was about to do and snapped her eyes open.

'Oh, so you *are* awake?' He grinned down at her in the darkness. 'I thought so. What did you do with the wine?'

'I spilled it,' she informed him, a note of victory in her voice. 'Now get off me, or I swear I'll tell Skye everything!'

'No, you won't,' Tom replied unconcernedly, pressing his elbow down hard on her chest and grasping her wrist firmly.

'Wanna bet?' she spat, trying with all her might to bring her knee up between his legs. 'Get off me, you ugly big-nosed bastard! I hate you! You make me sick, and I'm going to tell everyone about you!'

'And that's exactly why you're going nowhere,' said Tom. 'Because you can't be trusted.'

Frustrated, because he had her pinned down too tight for her to do him any damage, Chloe released a strangled scream and thrashed her head from side to side. Shocked when Tom slapped her hard across the face, she stopped briefly. But she quickly recovered, and hissed, 'You just wait till my dad finds out about this, you freak. You're *dead*!'

'Don't make me laugh.' Tom snorted. 'He doesn't care about you. *I'm* the only one who cares. But I've tried to help you, and you just keep on throwing it back in my face.'

'So let me go, then,' Chloe demanded.

'Just like that?' Tom tilted his head and gazed down at her as if he were seriously considering it. Then, shaking his head slowly, he said, 'I don't think so.'

Scared when he fed the end of the curtain tie-back he'd just wrapped around her wrist through the metal struts of the bedstead behind her head, Chloe said, 'All right, I'm sorry, and I swear I won't say nothing. I only said that 'cos I was mad at you, but I'd never grass you up. I just want to go home.'

'And you really think I'd take your word after the way you tried to blackmail me?' Tom wrenched her other arm up over her head. 'See, that's the problem with girls like you: you just don't know a good thing when you see it. You have to go and ruin everything by being greedy and demanding. Anyway, I'm saving you from yourself, because you'd only end up back on the streets if I let you go; selling yourself to any man who gives you the time of day. Your mother obviously taught you well.'

'My mum's no prostitute,' Chloe protested, anger momentarily overriding her fear. 'And you've got no right to talk about her like that when you don't even know her!'

'I know enough.' Tom smiled nastily as he looped a second tie-back around her other wrist. 'And I seem to remember that you weren't so reticent about bad-mouthing her the other night, were you? You had *plenty* to say about her then. What was it you said now . . .? She's "a big fat slag who shouldn't have been allowed to have kids if she wasn't going to bother taking proper care of them".'

'I said that to Skye, not you. It was none of your business.'

'*Every*thing is my business. And the last bitch who questioned my authority had to learn her lesson the hard way – just like you're going to.'

Chloe's blood ran cold, and her tears spilled over when Tom wriggled back down to the end of the bed and picked up another cord before grabbing her ankle.

'Please don't hurt me,' she begged, trying desperately to sound innocent and guileless, like Skye. 'I'll do anything you want, and I promise I won't tell. I love you.'

'If only I could believe that,' Tom said regretfully. 'But you're a liar, Chloe, and I know exactly what you'd do if I let you go. You'd go straight back to your scummy friends and tell them about me and Skye.'

'No, I wouldn't,' Chloe insisted. 'I swear on my nan's life I won't say a word.'

'Would that be your *dead* nan?' Tom asked sarcastically.

'You know what I mean,' Chloe sobbed. 'I promise I won't tell anyone.'

'Sorry, I can't take the risk,' said Tom.

Aware that nothing she said was going to make any difference, Chloe kicked out at him and strained with all her might to pull her hands free of their restraints. Then, throwing her head back, she screamed at the top of her lungs.

'Pack it in!' Tom hissed, scrabbling back up the bed and clamping his hand over her mouth. 'You asked for this,' he told her, peering down into her panic-stricken eyes. 'Ever since you got here, you've done nothing but flaunt yourself and push the boundaries of my generosity and patience. But I've had enough. Do you hear me? *Enough!*'

Unable to breathe, Chloe's face turned crimson, and her eyes began to bulge.

'I'll take my hand away,' Tom told her. 'But if you scream again, I *will* hurt you. Do you understand?'

Chloe nodded again, and then drew in a deep gasping breath when he withdrew his hand.

'It's a pity it had to come to this, because I was starting to like you,' he said. 'But sometimes you just have to admit when something isn't working and let it go, don't you?'

'I'm sorry,' Chloe whimpered, truly scared for her life now. 'I swear I won't tell. Skye's my best friend, and I'd never do anything to hurt her. Please, Tom, just let me go and I'll never say nothing – cross my heart.'

Tom stroked her hair back off her face and gazed down into her tear-filled eyes. 'If you do exactly as you're told and prove you can be trusted, I'll think about it. Okay?'

He smiled when she nodded her agreement, and said, 'Good girl. Now relax, and let's have some fun.'

20

Skye's stomach was churning when she woke up, and she clamped a hand over her mouth and ran to the bathroom just in time.

After throwing up violently several times, she rested her sweaty cheek on the cold toilet seat. She knew this couldn't be just a hangover because, as bad as the wine often made her feel when she'd had too much, it had never made her *this* sick. She guessed that she must have got food poisoning from last night's takeaway.

Either that or she had a brain tumour, like Chloe's grandmother.

'Chloe!' she croaked, scared that she might actually be seriously ill. 'Please get up! *CHLOE*!'

When no answer came, she groaned and pulled herself to her feet. Chloe's bed was empty when she looked into her room and, thinking that the girl must have had another nightmare and got up early again, she made her way downstairs in need of some TLC.

Shocked to see Bernie lying on his blanket when she walked into the kitchen, Skye temporarily forgot about her sickness and ran over to give him a cuddle.

'What are you doing in here?' she asked, laughing when he excitedly licked her face. 'Did Tom let you in? Oh, it's so good to see you, boy. I've missed you.'

Chloe wasn't in here and, guessing that she must have got scared when she saw Bernie, Skye gave the dog one last cuddle and then popped her head around the living-room door to let her know she was safe to come out. That room was empty, so she walked out into the hall, calling, 'Chloe, where are you? I'm up now, so you can come out.'

She frowned when no answer came and walked down the hall. Using her shoulder to force open the door of the tiny front room that they couldn't use because it was so crammed with rubbish, she looked inside, and then turned and checked the cupboard under the stairs before going up to check the bedrooms again.

Scared now that Bernie might have attacked Chloe and she was going to find the girl lying injured somewhere, she looked under the beds and in every cupboard and drawer, and even crouched down to check the space beneath the bath. But Chloe was nowhere to be found.

Baffled as to how the girl could have vanished into thin air, Skye suddenly remembered that Chloe now knew about the back-door key. If she'd seen where Skye had hidden it, she might have taken it into her head to sneak out to break into the shed – which would land them in a whole heap of trouble, because Tom was bound to notice if she messed up anything in there.

Cursing Chloe under her breath, Skye ran back down to the kitchen and grabbed the clock off the shelf – only to be baffled all over again when she saw that the key was still in it. And the back door was locked when she tried it, so she knew that Chloe couldn't have unlocked it and then put the key back to fool her.

'Oh, God,' she moaned, sitting down heavily on a chair as the realisation settled over her that Chloe must have found another way out and was probably halfway back to Manchester by now. Tom was going to go absolutely mad when he found out.

Right on cue, Tom's car pulled up at the side of the house, and Skye bit nervously on her lip as she waited for him to come in.

Surprised to see her downstairs, Tom paused when he stepped inside, and drew his head back. 'How come you're awake? You were fast asleep when I went out.'

'I felt sick,' she told him. Then, wringing her hands together, she said, 'Don't get mad, but I can't find Chloe. She wasn't in her room when I got up, and I thought she might have come down here and got scared when she saw Bernie. But I've looked everywhere, and she's just not here.'

'I know,' Tom said, slipping his jacket off. 'She went home last night. Well, this morning, to be more accurate. I took her.'

'To her dad's?' Skye gasped. 'But I thought we agreed she shouldn't go back there.'

'She wanted to go,' Tom said, shrugging as he lit a cigarette and sat down at the table. 'And to be honest, I thought it was probably for the best.' He patted the seat beside his and waited for Skye to sit down before continuing. 'Don't get upset, but you were right about her: she *was* trying to take me away from you.'

'What do you mean?' Skye was confused. 'She said she only flirted with you to get back at me, and she promised she wouldn't do it again.'

'She lied,' Tom said flatly. 'But that's what girls like her are like: they'll say anything to get their own way.'

'What did she do?' Skye asked, folding her arms over her stomach when it started to churn again.

'She tried to seduce me when you fell asleep last night,' Tom told her. 'And when I said no, she threatened to tell you that *I'd* tried it on with *her*. That's when I decided she had to go.'

'Bitch,' Skye muttered, unable to believe that the girl had been lying to her face after she'd gone out of her way to help her settle in. She'd treated her like a little sister, and had even let her wear the angel necklace.

'My necklace!' she gasped, raising her hand to her bare throat. 'I lent her my necklace. Did she give it to you when you dropped her off?'

Tom shook his head and gave her a regretful look. 'I didn't know she had it, or I'd have taken it off her. Sorry.'

'It's not your fault,' Skye said, sniffing back the tears that had begun to glisten in her eyes. She might not have wanted to wear the stupid thing, but she hadn't wanted to lose it for ever. If she ever saw Chloe again, she would kill her for stealing it.

'I should have listened when you told me what she was like,' Tom said, reaching out to wipe an escaped tear from her cheek. 'But I promise it'll never happen again.'

'What if she tells someone I'm here?'

'She won't. I made her swear on the Bible before she got out of the car. Just trust me on this. I guarantee she won't tell a soul.'

Skye nodded, but the thought of what would happen if Chloe *did* tell was terrifying.

'Are you all right?' Tom asked.

Skye shook her head and swallowed loudly. 'I feel really sick. I think I've got food poisoning off that takeaway.'

'Doubt it, or I'd have it, too,' said Tom. 'You probably just had too much to drink. Anyway, this should make you feel better.' He took a last drag on his cigarette and stubbed it out. Then he reached into his pocket. 'Now we've got rid of the troublemaker, I thought it was time you had this back.'

Skye's face lit up at the sight of her ring, and she smiled when Tom slipped it onto her finger.

'Carry on behaving yourself like you have been lately, and I won't have to take it off you again,' he said. 'Happy?'

Skye nodded vigorously and beamed as she gazed down at the tiny twinkling diamonds surrounding the dark sapphire. She had forgotten how beautiful it was, and she was determined never to lose it again.

'Oh, and I've got another surprise,' Tom said casually. 'I'm taking you to meet some old friends of mine in a couple of weeks. Don't worry,' he added quickly when a look of panic leapt into Skye's eyes. 'I've told them my sister is staying with me, so they'll think you're her.'

'But what if they recognise me?' Skye asked.

'They won't,' Tom assured her. 'And it'll give you a chance to show me what a good little wife you're going to be.'

'How?'

'Just by being you,' Tom said, taking her hand in his and giving it a reassuring squeeze. 'Stop worrying, you'll be great. Just dress yourself up in one of your pretty dresses, and tie your hair up how I like it, and they'll fall in love with you, just like I did. Okay?'

Skye nodded, but she was already dreading it. He'd said that everything would be all right when he brought Chloe into their lives, and look how that had turned out. The girl had already betrayed her by trying to get off with Tom behind her back. And if she could lie about that, what was to say she hadn't lied when she'd promised Tom that she wouldn't tell anyone about them?

'I'm going to be sick,' she spluttered, yanking her hand free and jumping to her feet.

Tom sat back in his chair and watched thoughtfully as Skye rushed from the room and clattered up the stairs. She was his third attempt, and the only one, so far, that he'd been properly able to control. It had been a mistake to think that he could subdue a streetwise girl like Chloe, but he still wished it hadn't had to end so badly.

He heard Skye throwing up in the bathroom on the floor above, and lit another cigarette before wandering into the doorway to listen. He hoped it wasn't what he thought it was, because that would throw a serious spanner in the works. The men he'd lined up for the first face-to-face meet were expecting an innocent little girl, not a used, pregnant teenager. But it was too late to find a fresh one now, so Skye was his only option. She looked the part right now, so he'd have to put her to good use while he could because it would only be a matter of months before she was completely useless.

If he allowed it to get that far.

21

As he strolled into the station. PC Andy Jones was laughing at a joke that one of his colleagues had just told. It was his first day back on duty after a fortnight's break, and he looked tanned and healthy after lounging around at his mum and dad's caravan park in Devon. When he retired from the force, he planned to up sticks and move down there permanently; maybe set up a little detective agency so that he could keep his hand in while he waited for the old man to bow out of the business. But, until then, he was happy to be back in Manchester – and eager to get stuck into whatever delights or horrors lay in store.

'Hey, Andy. Over here.'

Jones looked round when he heard Dean's voice, and grinned when he spotted his partner standing by the coffee machine.

'Okay, Bud?' He walked over and clapped a hand on Dean's shoulder. 'Missed me?'

'Like a hole in the head,' Dean quipped. 'It's never been so peaceful out there.'

'So you've got nothing to tell me?' Jones feigned disappointment. 'No big arrests? Nothing juicy?'

'You want juicy, take a look at this,' DS Janice Holden said, walking out of her office just then with a photograph in her hand.

'What's this?' Jones tilted his head and peered at it.

'CEOP just faxed it over,' she told him, holding it up so they could both see it. 'They think it's that girl whose dad you arrested for murdering her. Apparently, they were image-matching stills from some vids on a paedo website they've been investigating, and her name flagged up.'

'You're kidding me!'

Jones snatched the picture from her hand and stared at it. The girl who was featured in it was fair-haired, and looked to be around the same age as Skye Benson, but the image was too grainy to see any clear facial detail. Naked, and seemingly asleep – or, more likely, he guessed, unconscious – she was spread-eagled on a bed, with her wrists and ankles manacled to the foot- and headboards. A bright circle of light had been directed onto her exposed vagina, and Jones felt sick when he saw that a wine bottle had been inserted into her.

'Do they know where this shit's coming from?' he asked, his jaw tight with fury.

'They're working on it,' Janice told him. 'It seems this particular site first popped up a year ago, but it went dormant for a while so they lost track of it. It reappeared a couple of months ago, and they've been trying to get a hook into it ever since. But they reckon that whoever's behind it is juggling fake IP addresses, so they haven't been able to pin it down to a specific location.'

'Is it a pay-per-view site?' Dean asked. 'If it is, they should be able to trace where the money's going.'

'They didn't mention it,' Janice told him. 'But I'm assuming they're having problems with that, too, or I'm sure they'd have had him by now.'

'When was this filmed?' Jones asked, unable to make out

the digits on the time-and-date stamp in the bottom right corner.

'A week ago,' said Janice.

Jones and Dean looked at each other as the implication of her words sank in.

'So she's not dead, then?' Dean said quietly. 'And Benson can't be behind it, because he's been in lock-up for weeks.'

'Doesn't mean he didn't organise it,' Jones muttered, wondering how he could have got this so badly wrong. 'He could have sold her on, for all we know.'

'We won't know for sure until they track down whoever's running that site,' Janice told them. 'I just thought you should know.'

Jones thanked her and handed the picture back.

'What do you reckon?' Dean asked when Janice had gone back into her office.

'I don't know, mate.' Jones shook his head. 'I just don't know.'

'Well, whether or not Benson's involved in her disappearance, he obviously hasn't murdered her,' Dean pointed out. 'So that charge'll have to be dropped.'

'*If* it's her.'

'I doubt the CEOP guys would have sent it over if they weren't absolutely sure.'

Jones groaned and looped his fingers together behind his head.

'I think we need to speak to the chief,' Dean said quietly.

'You mean jump before we're pushed?' Jones sighed, and his shoulders sagged as he lowered his arms. 'Come on, then. Might as well get it over with.'

22

Two days later, Jeff was lying on his bunk re-reading Shirley's letter for the tenth time when his cell door was suddenly unlocked.

'What's up?' he asked, sitting up when Officer Smethwick walked in. 'It's not my turn to go out in the yard yet, is it?'

'Get your stuff together,' Smethwick ordered. 'And hurry up; the Governor's waiting.'

'What does he want?' Jeff asked, trailing down the landing behind Smethwick after hastily shoving his scant possessions into the prison-issue plastic bag.

'Don't ask me,' Smethwick grunted. 'I'm just the lackey who got sent to fetch you – like I've got nothing better to do than escort nonces round like it's some sort of fucking holiday camp.'

Jeff didn't bother saying anything else. Most of the screws had been at least civil if not actually friendly since he got sent here to wait for his court date, but he'd been doing his best to keep his head down nevertheless, in order to avoid the beatings and baitings he'd been expecting. Smethwick was a colder fish than most, and Jeff knew that any further questioning would earn him a backlash of some sort later on.

The Governor, Mr Owen, was seated at his desk with the telephone clamped to his ear when they reached his office.

His door was open and he glanced up when he saw them. He waved for them to come in.

Jeff perched on the chair facing the desk, and held his bundle to his stomach. Conscious of Smethwick standing behind him, he scratched his neck and waited for the Governor to finish his call.

'Sorry about that,' Owen said when he'd hung up at last. 'The wife's having problems with the builders. But anyhoo . . .'

He smiled now, and Jeff frowned. It was the first time *any*one had smiled at him since he got here, and it unnerved him. 'What's going on, Mr Owen?' he asked politely. 'Am I in trouble?'

'On the contrary,' said Owen. 'You're leaving us.'

'Eh?' Jeff's frown deepened, causing a deep crevice to split his forehead down the middle. He'd lost even more weight since being sent here, and he had aged twenty years.

'There appears to have been a significant development in your case,' Owen told him. 'I'll leave the police to explain the details, but the upshot is: the murder charge has been dropped.'

'*What*?' Jeff's head reeled, and he gripped the edge of the Governor's desk to steady himself.

'Straighten up!' Smethwick barked, jabbing him in the shoulder.

'It's all right.' Owen held up his hand to tell the man to back off. 'No harm done.'

'Does this mean they've found Skye?' Jeff asked when he felt able to speak again.

'I don't know the specifics,' Owen admitted. 'All I know is that the charge has been dropped and I've been told to release you.'

'What about the other stuff?' Jeff asked, struggling to take in the news. 'The attempted-murder thing?'

'You'll have to speak to the police about that,' said Owen. Then, glancing at his watch, he stood up and extended his hand across the desk. 'I have an appointment, so I'll have to go. Good luck, Benson; I sincerely hope our paths never cross again.'

'Me, too,' said Jeff, numbly rising from his seat and shaking the man's hand.

Head still reeling, Jeff found himself on the pavement outside the prison an hour later, his bag of belongings in one hand, a travel pass in the other – although he had absolutely no idea where he was supposed to travel *to*, seeing as he had no home of his own and no friends or family to turn to.

He hadn't yet moved when a police car pulled up alongside him a few minutes later, and his heart sank when PC Jones climbed out from behind the wheel.

'What's this?' he asked resignedly as the man walked towards him. 'Come to arrest me for something else I haven't done?'

'No, but I have come to take you to the station,' Jones said, feeling awkward because this was the first time they had met since their last unpleasant encounter. 'We need to talk to you.'

'About what?' Jeff stayed put.

Before Jones could explain, another car pulled up behind the squad car and Jeff's solicitor, Malcolm Fitch, stepped out.

'Sorry I'm late,' he called, extending his hand as he rushed over to them. 'I was just about to go into court when I got the call, and I'm afraid I couldn't get out of it. How are you, Jeff?'

'Okay,' Jeff muttered as he shook Fitch's hand. 'But they want me to go to the station with them. They reckon they need to speak to me about something.'

'I was under the impression that all charges had been dropped?' Fitch raised a bushy eyebrow at Jones. 'Didn't Mrs Benson retract her statement after being updated re the latest developments?'

Jones nodded. 'She did, sir. But this isn't about that.'

'What's going on?' Jeff looked in confusion from one to the other of the men. 'What latest developments? Has Skye been found, or not?'

Fitch's expression suddenly became grave, and he asked, 'Haven't you been told anything yet?'

'No, nothing,' said Jeff, an unpleasant feeling of apprehension stirring in his gut. 'They have found her, though, haven't they? She's . . . she's not dead?'

'Not as far as I'm aware,' Fitch reassured him. 'But I'm not sure we're in the best place to discuss this, so maybe we should accompany the officers back to the station where they can explain in more detail.'

Jeff nodded his agreement and walked over to the squad car without another word, desperate to find out what had happened to make them all act so cagey.

Shirley was on her way home from work that evening when her mobile phone started ringing. She never answered calls when she was driving, but she'd sent a text before she set off and the phone was still on the passenger seat, so she flicked a quick glance at it – and was shocked to see Jeff's name on the screen. Quickly pulling over, because he was the very last person she had expected a call from, she snatched the phone up.

'Hello, Jeff? Is that you?'

'Yeah, it's me, love,' he answered wearily. 'I've been let out.'

'Really?' Shirley gasped. 'Why? What's happened?'

'I don't really want to explain on the phone. Can we meet up for a coffee?'

'Where are you? I'll come and get you.'

Jeff went very quiet for several moments, and Shirley drew the phone away from her ear to check if the call had been disconnected. When she saw that it hadn't, she said, 'Jeff? Is everything all right? Talk to me. You're worrying me now.'

'I'm okay,' he replied at last. 'Just feel like my head's about to explode.'

'Where are you?' Shirley asked again. 'I'm coming for you.'

After cutting the call, Jeff walked over to the bus stop on the opposite side of the road so that Shirley wouldn't have to turn her car around when she saw him. He sat down on the thin bench beneath the shelter and pulled his tobacco out of his pocket to make himself a smoke while he was waiting.

His hands were shaking as he rolled his cigarette, and he felt self-conscious when he noticed a woman who was standing outside the shelter casting hooded glances at him. He guessed that she'd either recognised him and was wondering what a man who had supposedly murdered his own child was doing out on the streets, or she'd taken one look at his gaunt face and trembling hands and had pegged him as a junkie.

Either way, she was wrong. But Jeff supposed he'd have to get used to this kind of reaction because this was how everyone would probably look at him from now on. The 'no smoke without fire' mentality was alive and kicking around these parts, and the fact that the charges had been dropped would do nothing to turn that tide of opinion. If anything, it would probably make people feel even more anger towards him. Rather than accept that he might actually be innocent – which meant that everything they had been saying about him since his arrest was wrong and their theories completely out of whack – they would be more inclined to take the line that he had somehow got away with it.

Jeff was on his third roll-up by the time Shirley's car came into view some fifteen minutes later. The suspicious-eyed woman had long since gone about her business, but she'd left him with a bad taste in his mouth, so when Shirley pulled up he didn't immediately climb into the car when she leaned over and pushed open the passenger-side door.

'Aren't you getting in?' Shirley asked, gazing expectantly out at him.

'I'm not sure I should,' he said, glancing around to see if anyone was watching. 'I don't want to drag you back into my mess. That's why I suggested going somewhere for a coffee – so we can talk without you worrying about your neighbours seeing us together.'

Shirley's gaze hardened at the mention of her neighbours, few of whom were speaking to her still; although, thankfully, no further threats had been made.

'Do you really think I give a damn what those small-minded idiots think?' she said scathingly. 'They can all rot in hell as far as I'm concerned.'

'Has something happened?' Jeff asked, unaware of the incident with the brick shortly after his arrest.

'Nothing I can't handle,' Shirley assured him. 'Anyway, get in. There's a bus coming, so I need to move.'

Jeff climbed in reluctantly and buckled his seat belt as she pulled away from the stop. 'Sorry about this,' he murmured.

'I probably shouldn't have called you, but my head's in a mess, and I just needed to talk to someone who's not connected with the law.'

Shirley flashed him a sideways glance and said, 'Let's just get home and put the kettle on, then we can put our feet up and you can tell me everything. Okay?'

Jeff nodded and settled back in his seat. Her plan sounded good, but he had no idea where he would go from there. Malcolm Fitch had given him the numbers for some hostels, but he had no credit on his phone to call them and no money to buy any. Right back where he'd started after getting evicted, it looked like he was going to spend the night looking for a bridge to sleep under.

Shocked by his gaunt appearance, Shirley chattered about the traffic, the weather, and any other trivial thing she could think of on the journey home. Once there, she held her head high and walked alongside him to the front door, even though she could see nets twitching at several windows in the block.

'Tea or coffee?' she asked, going straight into the kitchen after dropping her handbag, kicking off her shoes and hanging her jacket behind the door.

'Coffee, please.' His own jacket still zipped up to the throat, his hands shoved deep into the pockets, Jeff stood awkwardly in the doorway as she filled the kettle.

'Why don't you go and put the telly and the lamps on,' Shirley ordered, sensing that he was still shell-shocked about having been released. 'Oh, and, take this.' She pulled a take-away menu out of the drawer and pushed it into his hand. 'I was going to cook, but I can't be bothered now so we'll order something in.'

'Don't,' Jeff said, giving her a pained look as he tried to

hand the menu back. 'You did enough when I was staying here, I can't let you start subbing me again.'

'Suit yourself.' Shirley shrugged. 'But don't blame me if your mouth starts watering when I'm stuffing myself with pepperoni pizza and garlic bread.'

Jeff smiled and wandered into the living room. His already heavy heart slumped a little lower as he switched the lamps on and gazed around. It was a small flat, but Shirley's personality was stamped all over it and everything about it was feminine and homely. He had enjoyed the time he'd spent here before his arrest, but that was over now and he couldn't afford to let himself get too comfortable again.

'So,' Shirley said, sitting beside him on the couch when she'd brought their coffees in a few minutes later. 'Tell me what's happened.'

Jeff sighed heavily and ran a hand through his hair. 'I don't even know where to start.'

'Well, I'm assuming something must have changed with the case, or they wouldn't have let you out,' Shirley prompted. 'Why don't you start there?'

'They dropped the charges.'

'Really?' Shirley smiled widely. 'That's great. Is that because they've found Skye?'

'Kind of.'

Concerned when Jeff lowered his head and started chewing on his lip, as if struggling to control his emotions, Shirley said, softly, 'What do you mean, Jeff? Don't tell me she's . . .?'

'No. God, no.' Jeff shook his head. 'At least, they don't think so,' he added grimly. 'But they won't know for sure until they trace whoever's uploading the videos.'

'Videos?'

'They're on some paedophile website the police have been investigating,' Jeff told her, feeling sick to his stomach just saying the words. 'Apparently there's some kind of special department that deals with these sites, and they've been trialling some program that compares images from the videos against pictures they've got stored on a central database and they got a positive hit on Skye's picture. They realised it couldn't have been me doing it, because they were filmed and uploaded while I was inside. And she was alive in them, so they had to drop the murder charge.'

Shirley didn't know what to say. It was wonderful that he'd been exonerated, but absolutely dreadful that it had taken something like this to prove his innocence.

'I'm so sorry,' she murmured, reaching for his hand. 'I can't even begin to imagine how you must be feeling. But they'll have her back in no time now that they've got a lead – you'll see.'

'It's not that easy,' Jeff told her. 'They reckon this bloke – or blokes, 'cos they're not sure if it's just one, or a whole gang of them – must be some kind of tech-head, 'cos he's blocking them from getting any solid information.'

'They'll get him,' Shirley said with certainty.

'I hope so,' Jeff said plaintively. 'I just want her back, Shirl.'

'I know, love,' Shirley murmured. 'But you need to stay strong because Skye's going to need you more than ever when she's found, and you'll be no use to her if you make yourself ill.' She paused at this, and peered deep into his eyes before suggesting, 'Why don't you stay here?'

'No, I can't.' Jeff shook his head. 'I shouldn't have stayed last time; look at all the trouble it caused.'

'I don't care what anyone thinks,' Shirley said firmly. 'Your stuff's still here, and no one else needs the bed so there's absolutely no reason why you shouldn't use it. Anyway, what kind of friend would I be if I left you to face something like this on your own?'

Jeff felt the sting of tears at the back of his eyes. After everything he'd put her through already, she *still* wanted to support him.

'You are one truly special lady,' he said quietly. 'And God only knows why you're still single. All I can think is that your last boyfriend must have been some kind of idiot not to have put a ring on your finger when he had the chance.'

'He tried, but I said no,' Shirley told him, smiling shyly.

'Lucky me.' Jeff's eyes were dark and piercing as he stared into hers.

Suddenly acutely aware of their entwined fingers and her heart pounding fiercely in her chest, Shirley gasped when Jeff leaned over and kissed her.

'I'm so sorry,' he said, pulling away quickly after a moment. 'I shouldn't have done that; it was totally out of order. I'd best go.'

'Wait!' Shirley jumped to her feet when he stood up and, blushing, admitted, 'I've wanted to do that again ever since the first time, but I never dreamed you'd ever feel the same way about me as I do about you. I know you're probably feeling guilty about Andrea, but please don't, because it was more my fault tha—'

Jeff pulled her into his arms and kissed her again before she could finish the sentence – and this time he didn't stop.

23

The dog's head was buried in the grass a couple of hundred yards away, his tail sticking up in the air. He was foraging, and Bob hoped he wasn't worrying a rabbit or some other small creature. He knew it was nature, but he hated seeing animals in distress, and he really didn't have the time to rescue it *or* put it out of its misery.

'Leave it,' he ordered as he approached. 'Let's go.'

The dog wagged his tail at the sound of his master's voice but carried on digging and whining. Bob pushed the long grass aside and saw an ancient sewage-outlet pipe, the mouth of which was stacked with debris that had gathered there over the years. Guessing that Oscar had probably chased a rat into the pipe and was trying to go after it, Bob gripped the dog's collar and tried to tug him away. But, just as he was about to clip the lead on, something caught his eye that caused him to freeze for a second.

Sure that he had imagined what he'd glimpsed, Bob reached into his inside pocket for his key-ring torch. He leaned forward and directed the faint beam at the heap of tin cans and bottles that were snagged behind a mangled bicycle wheel. As his vision sharpened, a sickly taste flooded his mouth. He tried to tell himself that it was an animal that had crawled into the pipe and died, but no animal he'd ever seen had long blonde hair like that.

'Oh dear lord!' Legs almost giving way with shock, Bob staggered back onto the path. 'Oscar!' he barked when the dog seized the opportunity to go back to his digging. '*Stop that!*'

The dog obeyed and Bob quickly clipped its lead on. Then, hands shaking wildly, he fumbled his mobile phone out of his pocket.

'Police!' he blurted out when his call was answered. 'I've found a body. I th-think it's a young girl.'

'What's your name, sir?'

'Bob. Bob Wilks.'

'And where are you, sir?'

Bob gave his location, and then asked, 'Will somebody be here soon? Only I should really be getting home to my wife. She has Alzheimer's, and she'll be confused if I'm not there when she wakes up.'

'A unit is on its way,' the operator assured him. 'Could you go back up to the road so they can see you, please?'

'Yes, of course,' Bob agreed, tugging on Oscar's lead. 'I do hope I haven't called you out on a wild-goose chase,' he said then, doubt beginning to creep in as he scrambled back up the bank. 'It *looked* like a body, but I didn't get too close, so I could have made a mistake.'

'You were right to call us,' said the operator. 'And don't worry, nobody will mind if it turns out to be a false alarm.'

The road that separated the canal from the woodland was usually rammed with traffic by 8.30 a.m. as commuters from the outlying villages headed to their jobs in the city. But there was an eerie silence along the road this morning, because the area had been cordoned off. Squad cars blocked the road to prevent vehicles other than emergency ones from entering the search zone, while police tape had been strung across both ends of the towpath to prevent unwitting ramblers from tainting potential evidence.

After the markers had been set in place, and numerous crime-scene photographs taken, the corpse had been extracted from the outlet pipe where the dog had discovered it and was now laid out on the towpath so that the attending pathologist could do a quick examination.

Thanks to the high summertime temperatures, and the shallow layer of stagnant water in the base of the pipe, the body was in an accelerated state of decomposition; its bloated, green-tinged flesh was already beginning to split. The pathologist had handled many such cases, but rarely were the victims quite as young as this one. He wouldn't know her exact age until he was able to conduct a thorough examination, but he assessed her to be within the 14–16 age range. And she was naked, which implied that the motive for the attack had been most probably sexual.

What disturbed him most was the damage that had been inflicted on the body post-mortem. And he sincerely hoped that it *had* been done after she had died, because he dreaded to think what the poor child would have suffered had she been alive when her attacker had battered her face almost to a pulp, smashed out her teeth, and crudely cut off her fingertips. It was an obvious attempt to prevent the police from making an identification, but the perpetrator had overlooked one crucial piece of evidence.

24

The list of missing children in the Greater Manchester area was depressingly long, but only seven of them matched the general description of 'Canal Girl' – as the victim had been dubbed by the police – in terms of gender, hair colour, approximate age, and height. No clothing had been found at or near the scene, and no potential murder weapon had yet been located, so the necklace that had been recovered from around her throat was all they had to go on, and each team of officers who had been tasked with visiting the missing girls' families the following morning were given a photograph of it for identification purposes.

PCs Jones and Dean had been assigned the two families who lived local to their patch: those of Chloe Lester and Skye Benson. And as the Lesters' place was closest, they went there first.

Dennis Lester wasn't pleased to be woken by the police at such an early hour, and he made his displeasure clear by yelling, 'Fuck off, I ain't done nothing!' through the door when they knocked.

Only when Dean had explained via the letter box that they were here about his daughter did he relent and open up for them. But after looking out and seeing no sign of Chloe on the landing behind them, he said, 'Where is she, then? You usually fetch her back after she's done a runner.'

'Can we come in?' Dean asked.

'Nah, I'm not in the mood for visitors,' Lester drawled, scratching his belly through a hole in his stained vest. Then, narrowing his eyes when something occurred to him, he said, 'Here, I hope she hasn't been telling tales, 'cos she's a born liar, that one, and you don't wanna be taking no notice of anything she says.'

'We've found a body,' Dean told him, opting for the blunt approach, because it was clear that nothing else was going to work. 'So, if we could just come in for a minute . . .?'

Lester released a heavy sigh, as if he really couldn't be doing with this, and said, 'All right. But give us a minute to put the dogs in the kitchen. They don't like you lot, and I ain't gonna be held responsible if they savage you.'

He left the door slightly ajar, and Jones and Dean exchanged a bemused glance when they saw him go into the living room and come back out carrying two ancient, scabby-looking Jack Russell dogs by the scruffs of their scrawny necks.

After tossing them into the kitchen and slamming the door shut, Lester called over his shoulder for the officers to come in as he made his way back to the living room.

Both men wrinkled their noses when the stench of sweaty feet, stale cigarette smoke, and dogs hit them in the face, and neither of them particularly fancied sitting on the filthy couch when Lester waved for them to take a seat after himself flopping into a tatty armchair. But, mindful of why they were here, they pushed their concerns about their uniforms and the probability that they were going to be flea-bitten by the time they left to the backs of their minds, and sat down.

As Dean explained what little they knew and showed Lester the photograph to see if he recognised the necklace, Jones gazed around in disgust. The man clearly spent the majority of his waking life in that chair, because it was surrounded by heaps of crushed beer cans, dirty plates, and mouldy kebab and pizza remnants; and Jones guessed that the dogs, who were both barking now and scratching at the kitchen door, didn't get out much, either, judging by the little heaps of shit he could see among the rubbish covering the floor. His eye was drawn to a stack of porn magazines partially hidden beneath Lester's chair, and he frowned when he made out the title of the top one: *Teen Sluts*.

'She ain't got no jewellery, so it deffo ain't hers,' Lester said as he handed the photo back to Dean after glancing at it. 'And even if it had been, it wouldn't be no more, 'cos she never keeps nothing for two minutes, her. If it's worth more than a quid, she'd have flogged it first chance she got.'

'Would you be willing to come and do a formal ID of the body?' Dean asked, adding, 'But I have to warn you that it won't be pleasant, and you wouldn't be allowed to go into the room with her.'

'What, go and look at a stiff?' Lester pulled a disgusted face. 'I don't think so, mate.'

'If you're not up to it, you could always provide a sample of DNA for comparison,' Dean suggested.

'Yeah, right,' Lester snorted, fishing a can of beer out from down the side of his cushion and tearing the tab off. 'I know what you lot are like. Soon as you've got it, you'll be trying to pin every robbery and mugging from the last fifty years on me. Fuck that for a game of soldiers.'

He paused to take a swig of beer. Then, rifling through the dimps in the ashtray that was sitting on the arm of his chair, he said, 'It wouldn't help, anyhow, 'cos her mam was a slag, so Chloe's probably not even mine. I've always thought she was more like the cunt her mam was knocking off round the time she got caught. Ken Brown, I think his name was. And he had a few bob, if I remember right, so you'd be better off tracking him down if you're after someone to pay for the funeral.'

Outraged by his callous attitude, Jones said, 'A child has been murdered, and she could be your daughter. Don't you care?'

'Why should I?' Lester shot back unrepentantly. 'Bitch never gave a toss about me. She's as bad as her mam, that one: coming and going like I'm running some kind of hostel for fuckin' whores. If that body is hers, I'm just surprised it's taken this long for someone to do her in, 'cos she's always been more trouble than she's worth.'

Dean saw the warning glint of anger spark in Jones's eyes and stood up quickly, saying, 'We'll leave you to think about it. Just call if you change your mind.'

'I won't,' Lester said adamantly, staying put as Jones too rose to his feet.

Jones gave him a scathing look and then stared pointedly down at the magazines. 'That's some hobby you've got there, fella. Always go for the young 'uns, do you?'

'Fuck off,' Lester growled. 'Them's all legal, them.'

'I bet,' drawled Jones, looking around the room now. 'No computer?' he asked after a moment. 'I wouldn't mind taking a look to see what kind of stuff you've got on there.'

'Do I look like I'd know how to use a computer?' Lester sneered. 'Even if I could afford one, I wouldn't want it,' he went on. 'Leaves you wide open for people to find you, that internet shit; and I'm fucked if I'm having all the birds I've ever shagged coming after me for child maintenance.' He shook his head now, and smirked as he took another swig of his beer. Then, belching loudly, he raised an eyebrow. 'You still here?'

Jones gave a snort of disgust and stalked out, and Dean gave Lester a curt nod before following quickly.

'Lowlife bastard,' spat Jones, still furious as they made their way down the communal stairs. 'I'm going to look him up on the system when we get back to the station; see if I can get anything on him.'

'Just leave well enough alone,' Dean cautioned as they exited the block and walked back to the car. 'You're already facing a complaint of harassment if Jeff Benson decides to go ahead with that, so I wouldn't be adding another one to the list if I were you.'

'Yeah, well, let's just hope this poor girl doesn't turn out to be Chloe Lester,' Jones muttered. ''Cos I'd hate to see what kind of send-off she'd get if it was left to that heartless cunt to arrange it.'

Dean nodded his agreement and climbed into the passenger side as Jones got behind the wheel. 'Did you manage to find out where Jeff Benson's staying?' he asked as they buckled their seat belts.

'No.' Jones shook his head and started the engine. 'His brief reckons he was going to try and get into a homeless hostel, but I didn't have time to ring around before we set out. I thought we could call in at that garage where he used to work after we've spoken to Andrea; see if he's been in touch with that friend of his – Shirley.'

'Good idea,' said Dean, reaching through the middle of the seats to put the photograph in the back. 'If he's contacted anyone, it'd be her, I'm sure. Nice woman,' he remarked then, gazing out of the window as they set off.

'Yeah, she is,' Jones agreed. 'Shame she had to go through all that shit with her neighbours after we arrested him, 'cos she didn't deserve that.'

'Neither did he,' Dean said quietly.

Jones drove on without replying. But he couldn't deny what Dean had said, and he'd felt guilty about the way he had treated Jeff Benson since it had come to light that he could not have murdered his daughter. Not only that, but Andrea had also confessed to having made up the abuse allegations to get back at him for his supposed cheating. And then she had retracted her statement about him trying to stab her, so Jones no longer believed a word she'd said and was actually beginning to wonder if Shirley had been right about Andrea being the real perpetrator all those times he'd been called out to domestics at their place.

Whatever the truth, Jones just hoped that the twisted bitch didn't fall apart when they saw her now and told her about these latest developments, because he really didn't think he'd be able to dredge up an ounce of sympathy for her.

25

Shirley had taken the rest of the week off work. Unlike her colleagues, who all regularly went down with mysterious illnesses the morning after a major football match or a hen or stag party, she had never taken one single sick day in the entire time she had worked for Ripley Autos. But she was damned if she was going to leave Jeff on his own at a time like this so she'd got up early and left a message on her boss's answerphone, telling him that she had flu.

After making the call, she had gone back to bed and gazed at Jeff as he lay sleeping. She had always liked and respected him, but her feelings had deepened considerably after he had moved in that first time and she'd had a chance to really get to know him. She had never imagined that he might ever feel the same way about her, so she'd been stunned when he had kissed her last night; and the lovemaking that had followed had been incredible.

She just hoped he didn't wake up with regrets and think that she had taken advantage of him when he'd been at his most vulnerable.

Determined not to ruin the beautiful memory of their night together by allowing herself to become paranoid about it, Shirley got up after a while and took a quick shower before going into the kitchen to make Jeff a cup of coffee and some toast. Prison had taken a huge toll on him physically but he was as proud as ever, so she knew she'd have a fight on her hands getting him to accept her hospitality. But he needed building up, and she was determined to get him properly back on his feet again.

She had just slotted the bread into the toaster and was reaching into the cupboard for cups when someone knocked loudly and insistently on the front door.

A slim blonde woman was standing on the step, and she looked Shirley up and down when she answered the door. Then, a sneer on her lips, she said, 'So you're the bitch who destroyed my life, are you?'

'Sorry?' Shirley folded her arms defensively, conscious that she must look a mess with the towel around her hair and her satin dressing-gown damp in patches from where she hadn't properly dried herself. 'Do I know you?'

'I'm Jeff's wife,' Andrea informed her icily. 'Where is he? And don't say he's not here, because I *know* he is.'

Thrown, because this was the first time she had ever seen the woman, Shirley wondered what to do for the best. She didn't want to invite Andrea in, but she also didn't want to leave her out here if she was going to cause a scene. Her nosy neighbours would be bound to notice, and the last thing Jeff needed right now was for it to turn ugly again.

'Wait there a minute,' she said, deciding that it would be best to let Jeff deal with it. 'He's in the spare room. I'll go and get him.'

Cheeks flaming, Shirley closed the door and rushed back along the hall. She didn't know why she'd thrown that in about him being in the spare room, and it was obvious that the woman hadn't believed her. But she'd panicked, and the words had come out before she could stop herself.

'Jeff, wake up.' She shook his shoulder gently. '*Jeff!*'

He woke with a start and peered groggily up at her. 'What's up?'

'Andrea's here,' she told him. 'She wants to see you.'

'*What?*' Jeff sat up and rubbed his eyes. 'Are you joking?'

'No.' Shirley shook her head and re-tightened her dressing-gown belt. 'She's on the step. I didn't know whether I should let her in or not.'

'No, you shouldn't,' Jeff said, an uncharacteristic hardness creeping into his voice as he pushed the quilt off his legs and looked around for his clothes. 'She had no right to come here.'

'I told her you were in the spare room,' Shirley murmured as he pulled his jeans on. 'I thought . . .' She trailed off, shrugged, and then said, 'Well, I didn't think you'd want her to know about – you know.'

'It's none of her business,' Jeff said, standing up to zip his fly before pulling his T-shirt over his head. 'But I don't really care who knows, 'cos me and her are done.'

'I know you might feel like that now,' Shirley said understandingly. 'But you might change your mind when you talk to her, so please don't say anything you might regret. She's very beautiful,' she added quietly, letting him know that she wouldn't hold it against him if he took one look at Andrea and realised he'd made a huge mistake last night.

Jeff reached out and gently tilted her chin up. 'She's nowhere near as beautiful as you,' he said softly. 'She might look good on the outside, but your beauty is inside *and* out; and even if you change your mind about us and tell me to leave, I'll never go back to her now I know how good it can be with someone decent.'

Shirley shook her head when she saw the sincerity in his eyes, and murmured, 'I'd never tell you to leave.'

Jeff smiled and kissed her. Then, taking a deep breath when Andrea started hammering on the door and shouting his name through the letter box, he said, 'Suppose I'd best go see what she wants.'

Andrea's eyes were wild when Jeff opened the door. His heart sank, because it was clear from her stance that she was gunning for a fight.

'How could you?' she spat.

'How could I what?' he replied evenly, determined not to let her goad him into a slanging match.

'You *know* what!' she screeched. 'Screwing that bitch behind my back! How long has it been going on?' she demanded now, her words flying like machine-gun fire. 'I bet you were at it the whole time you were working there, weren't you? Is she the reason you were always late home? Is that where all the money went? Were you spending it on *her*, while me and Skye were scraping for crumbs?'

Conscious that some of Shirley's neighbours had come outside and were gathering across the road, Jeff lowered his voice and said, 'We're not together any more, Andrea, so even if I *was* with Shirley it'd have nothing to do with you. But, *no*, I have not been screwing her behind your back. I *never* cheated on you – though God knows I wish I had, considering how many times you accused me of it. You made my life hell, but it's over now and I want a divorce, so leave me alone.'

'You can't get a divorce,' Andrea cried, tears spurting from her eyes as her anger dissolved in the face of his coldness. 'I won't let you! I'm your wife, and you promised to be faithful to me for life.'

'You tried to kill me, and then told the police I'd been

abusing my own daughter,' Jeff reminded her incredulously. 'You can't seriously think I'd take you back after that?'

'I was *ill*,' Andrea sobbed, her usually pretty face a crumpled mess as she clutched at the front of his T-shirt. 'You know I don't know what I'm doing when I get like that. And I was desperate 'cos I thought I'd lost you. But I didn't mean it, and I've told them it's not true. Please don't hate me. I can't live without you.'

'You've been living without me all right for the past few months while I've been laid up in hospital and prison,' Jeff reminded her, trying to prise her fingers off his T-shirt without hurting her, because he had no doubt that she would probably have him arrested for battery again as soon as she realised that she wasn't going to get her own way this time. 'You went too far; there's no going back from this.'

Shirley had decided to nip out to give them some privacy. Dressed now, her hair roughly dried, she came out into the hall to get her coat. But when she glanced out through the door and saw the growing crowd across the road, she touched Jeff's arm, and said, 'Why don't you bring her in and make her a coffee to calm her down? Then you can talk to her without that lot listening in.'

Jeff didn't want to talk to Andrea while she was in a state, because he knew from experience that it wouldn't end well. But he didn't want Shirley to suffer any more gossip because of him, so he nodded and jerked his chin up at Andrea to tell her to come in.

Still sobbing, Andrea stumbled over the step and clutched at Shirley's arm. 'Please don't take him off me. He's my husband, and I need him.'

Embarrassed, Shirley mumbled, 'It's got nothing to do with me. You need to talk to each other.'

She pulled her arm free and rushed out. But, just as she closed the door, a police car pulled up at the kerb ahead. When Jones and Dean got out and walked over to her, she said, 'If you've come to see Jeff it'll have to wait. Andrea's here, and she's a bit upset.'

Jones was surprised to hear this. The refuge staff had said that she had gone out when he and Dean had called round there, but it had never occurred to him that she might have come here. They had only come themselves because Shirley's boss had told them that she'd taken the rest of the week off and they had guessed that Jeff must be here.

'So they're both here?' Dean asked.

'Yes.' Shirley nodded and shifted her handbag onto her other shoulder. 'But, as I said, she's a bit upset, so you should probably give them a few minutes.'

'I'm afraid this can't wait.'

Shirley's instincts prickled when she heard the gravity of his tone, and she murmured, 'Oh, no. It's not Skye, is it?'

'Do you think we can do this inside?' Dean asked without answering her question.

'Of course.' Hands shaking, her legs like jelly, Shirley pulled her keys from her handbag and unlocked the door, then rushed inside, calling, 'Jeff, where are you?'

'In here,' he called back from the kitchen. 'What's up?'

'Where's Andrea?' she asked.

'In the spare room,' Jeff told her. Then, frowning when he noticed the tears glistening in Shirley's eyes, he asked, 'What's wrong, love?'

Shirley bit her lip as her chin began to quiver. But one of the officers tapped on the front door before she could tell him, and she reached back to open it, murmuring, 'Sorry, come in.' Then, turning back to Jeff, she said, 'Go and get Andrea while I take them through.'

Andrea's face was tear-stained when Jeff led her into the living room, and she clung to his arm like a frightened child when she saw Jones and Dean sitting on the couch.

'What do they want? Don't let them take me away.'

'It's okay, they just want to talk,' Jeff reassured her, pushing her gently towards the armchair beside the one where Shirley was already sitting.

When Andrea grasped his hand and pulled him down beside her, he flashed Shirley an apologetic look as he sank onto the arm of the chair. Then he turned to the officers, asking, 'So, what's happened? Have you found Skye?'

'We're not sure,' Dean told him truthfully. 'The body of a young girl who matches her general description was found yesterday morning, but—'

'What do you mean, *general description*?' Jeff interrupted. 'You've got her picture – you must know if it's her or not.'

'I'm afraid there was damage to the face which made it difficult to establish the identity by picture alone,' Dean told him, trying to make it sound less horrific than it actually was.

Jeff clenched his teeth when he heard this, and raised his chin. 'So how do you know it's her?'

'We don't,' said Dean. 'You're just one of the seven families who are being visited today. This was recovered at the scene,' he said then, holding out the photograph. 'Do you recognise it?'

Jeff gazed at the picture for a second and shook his head. 'No, I've never seen it before.'

'Mrs Benson?'

Wide-eyed with fear, Andrea flicked a quick glance at the picture and also shook her head.

'Hang on,' Jeff said when a memory flitted through his mind. 'I think someone mentioned something about a necklace to me recently. Hayley's mum,' he said when it suddenly came to him. 'She said Hayley gave Skye a necklace on the day I . . .' He paused and licked his dry lips, before finishing: 'On the day I got stabbed.'

Dean exchanged a hooded glance with Jones, and then asked, 'Would you be willing to view the body?'

Jeff breathed in deeply. The last thing he had ever expected to happen in his life was that he would be asked to identify a dead child. But somebody had to do it, and Andrea certainly wasn't up to it. So he nodded.

'Yes, I'll do it. When?'

Dean saw the pain in his eyes, and said, 'Look, I can see this is difficult, so why don't we pay Hayley a quick visit to make sure it's the same necklace before we put you through that? And that will also give us a chance to check if any of the other units have had a positive response in the meantime.'

'*Skyyyeee* . . .' Andrea suddenly moaned, as if the news had only just filtered through. 'Where's Skye . . .? I want Skye.'

Jeff put his arm around her shoulder when she started wailing, and gently held her to him, whispering, 'It's okay, love; they don't even know if it's her yet, so let's not jump to conclusions, eh?'

'I can have someone from the family-liaison team come over, if you like?' Jones offered. 'They're trained to deal with these situations.'

Jeff didn't answer so Shirley did it for him, saying, 'Thank you, that's probably a good idea. Andrea can stay here while we're waiting. I'll look after her.'

Jones and Dean both stood up, but as Dean made his way out to the car Jones called Jeff out into the hall.

'I'm not being funny,' he said when Jeff joined him, 'but I think Andrea should see a doctor. I know it's tough on both of you, but she's taking it really hard, and with her history I wouldn't want to take any chances.'

'I know,' Jeff murmured, glancing back into the living room, where Shirley was now holding Andrea in her arms. 'She was already acting a bit weird before you got here, to be honest. Do you know if she's been taking her meds while she's been in that refuge?'

'I couldn't tell you,' Jones admitted. Then, lowering his voice another notch, he said, 'I know we've had our rucks in the past, and you probably think I'm a cunt. But if it's awkward having Andrea here after everything that's happened, I'd be happy to take her back to the refuge for you.'

Jeff's heart was heavy as he gazed back at Andrea and Shirley again. As much as he resented his wife for what she'd put him through during these last few weeks, it was obvious from the way she'd been behaving since she got here that she was still ill. And if the staff at the refuge weren't able – or willing – to make sure she took her meds, he dreaded to think what she might do if it did turn out to be Skye's body they had found.

'I can't let her go back there on her own,' he said resignedly. 'She needs me.'

'Okay,' Jones said, respecting him all the more for standing by his wife after everything she'd put him through. 'We'll come back as soon as we've seen Hayley, and let you know what she says.'

He reached out and opened the door now. But before he stepped out, he extended his hand, and said, 'I'm really sorry it's come to this, mate. I wouldn't wish it on anyone.'

It was an olive branch, but Jeff was hesitant about accepting it because he couldn't forget how massive a part

Jones had played in ruining his life. But then, he supposed that he had himself played an even bigger role. He'd had numerous opportunities to set the record straight, but pride and misguided loyalty had prevented him from telling the truth about his and Andrea's volatile relationship, so who could blame Jones for having marked him down as a wife beater?

'Thanks,' he said, shaking Jones's hand. 'I appreciate that.'

After showing the man out and closing the door, Jeff leaned back against it, wondering how he was going to tell Shirley about the decision he'd just made.

He was still standing there, staring up at the ceiling, when Shirley came out into the hall a few minutes later.

'Are you okay?' she asked.

He was far from feeling that but he didn't want to burden her any more than he already had, so he pulled himself together and said, 'Yeah, I was just thinking things over. What's Andrea doing?'

'Lying down,' Shirley told him. 'She dropped her bag and her tablets fell out. I noticed some Valium and persuaded her to take a couple. I hope that was okay?'

'That's fine; it'll help a lot,' Jeff said. Then, a look of regret in his eyes, he said, 'We need to talk.'

Shirley shook her head. 'No, we don't,' she said softly. 'She needs you, and I understand that you've got to be there for her. And please don't worry about me, because I'll be fine. Friends?' She gave him a tiny smile.

'Always,' Jeff whispered, taking her in his arms to give her one last hug.

'Fuck!' Jones muttered, a deep frown creasing his brow when he turned onto Hayley's road fifteen minutes later and saw a long line of cars parked right the way down, in the middle of which were a hearse and two black limousines. 'Trust us to turn up with news like this when they've had a death on the street.'

'I'll do it,' Dean said, already opening his door as the car crawled to a stop in the middle of the road outside the Simms's house. 'Go and find somewhere to park – I'll be in and out in a minute.'

'All right, but don't get waylaid,' said Jones, making the sign of the cross on his chest. 'Funerals give me the heebie-jeebies.'

Dean nodded and jumped out of the car. Then, head down as a mark of respect, he walked quickly over to the Simms's house.

The door opened just as he was about to knock, and he stepped back quickly when a black-suited funeral director came out. Thrown, he looked around to see where Jones had gone but just as he spotted him and was about to make a hasty retreat, another man came out and asked, 'Can I help you?'

Dean took in the man's red nose and swollen eyes and guessed that he must be closely connected to the deceased. 'It's okay,' he said. 'I can come back tomorrow.'

'You're here now, so you might as well tell me what you want,' the man said, taking a cigarette out of his pocket and lighting up with visibly shaking hands.

'Terry, do you know where I put that—' Kathy Simms came into the doorway and abruptly stopped speaking when she saw Dean. She swallowed loudly, and folded her arms before asking, 'You're the one who came to see Hayley about Skye, aren't you?'

'Yes,' Dean affirmed. Then, feeling awkward, because she

looked every bit as upset as the man, he said, 'I'm sorry for disturbing you; if I'd known, I would have left it for another day. Please accept my condolences.'

'Wait,' Kathy said when he turned to leave. 'What did you want?'

Dean hesitated. This felt so disrespectful under the circumstances, but they were both curious to know why he was here and he didn't want to leave them worrying on a day like this. So, turning back, he said, 'Skye's dad mentioned that Hayley gave her a necklace.'

'That's right.' Kathy nodded. 'For her birthday. What about it?'

'I wondered if I might ask her to take a look at a photograph,' said Dean. 'It should only take a second, and it would be really helpful to our investigation.'

Kathy bit down hard on her lip as tears immediately flooded her already swollen eyes, and Dean's heart sank when he suddenly realised whose funeral this was. He had no idea why, considering some of the untimely deaths he'd seen in his line of work, but he automatically thought of old people whenever he saw a funeral procession and he had assumed that the deceased must be one of the couple's parents. But, now that he thought about it, he supposed he really ought to have guessed, because Hayley had been unwell when he and Jones had visited that time to ask if Skye had ever mentioned anything about her father abusing her, and her mother had asked them to leave because she was concerned that the child might get worse if they upset her too much.

'I'm so sorry,' he said quietly. 'I had no idea.'

Kathy sensed his distress and shook her head. 'You weren't to know,' she said kindly. 'It was leukaemia, but we didn't find out until it was too late so we've just been hanging on day by day, minute by minute. Anyway, she's out of pain now, and that's all that matters,' she finished, raising her chin in an effort to show that she was coping, although she clearly wasn't. 'So, what was this photograph you wanted to show her?'

Dean could really have done with the ground opening up and swallowing him right about now. But he held the photograph out, saying, 'Would you know if this is the necklace?'

'Yes, it is,' Kathy affirmed, smiling sadly as she gazed at it.

'Are you sure?' Dean asked.

'Absolutely,' she said. 'I was with her when she bought it. Such a pretty little thing. The lady who sold it to us said it was the only one she had left, so Hayley just had to have it. You know, I actually think she knew she was dying even then, and wanted Skye to have something nice to remember her by,' she went on wistfully. 'She never actually said it, but it's just a feeling I've got.'

Kathy's husband had been peering intently at the photograph as they spoke. 'Is that blood?' he asked.

Dean had forgotten about that, and he quickly withdrew the picture and rolled it up.

'Blood?' Kathy repeated, genuine concern leaping into her eyes as she peered at Dean. 'Oh, no,' she moaned when he didn't confirm or deny it. 'Please don't tell me that was her they were talking about on the news last night? The body they found by the canal in Worsley?'

'We don't have a positive identification as yet,' Dean told her truthfully. 'But this necklace was found at the scene.'

'Poor baby,' Kathy sobbed, pulling a tissue out of her pocket as her husband put his arm around her. 'Hayley would have been heartbroken; she loved Skye so much. They were more like sisters than friends, and she never stopped checking her Facebook page for messages. And Skye's poor dad must be in agony,' she went on guiltily. 'I was so horrible to him last time I saw him. Please tell him I'm sorry, and if there's anything I can ever do he's more than welcome to come round.'

Dean nodded, and said, 'I'll tell him.' Then, stepping aside when the funeral director came back and told the couple that it was time to start thinking about setting off, he said goodbye and rushed up the road.

'What's up?' Jones asked when he climbed quickly into the car.

'Just drive,' Dean muttered, afraid that he might fall apart if he had to watch the coffin being brought out of the house. 'For God's sake just get me out of here. I'll explain on the way.'

Dean explained the procedure as Jones drove them over to the mortuary a short time later, but nothing could have prepared Jeff for the overwhelming pain he felt when the technician drew back the curtain and he saw the girl's body on the other side of the window.

At first it didn't seem real, and he almost felt as if he were watching a scene out of some TV show. But then he saw the wispy blonde hair that Skye had inherited from her mother, and tears clouded his eyes as he forced his gaze down to her face. Her poor battered, bloodied, just about recognisable face.

'It's her,' he sobbed. 'That's my Skye.'

Jones put a comforting hand on Jeff's shoulder as the façade of strength that he'd been trying so desperately to maintain crumbled.

'Are you sure?'

Unable to answer in words, Jeff nodded, and then turned from the window and sank to his knees with his face in his hands.

26

Skye's funeral was held three weeks later. The sky was dark and overcast, as if a storm was brewing. It felt apt to Jeff because it wouldn't have seemed right to say goodbye to his daughter in bright sunlight, with the sound of children's laughter floating into the cemetery from the park across the road and the peal of ice-cream vans creating a farcical backdrop to the vicar's sombre words.

Jeff had barely slept a wink the night before, and was dressed and waiting several hours before he saw the hearse and funeral car pull up outside the B and B where he and Andrea had been staying while they waited for the council to find them somewhere permanent. It was a low-end place that felt more like a war zone than a safe refuge. Fights were constantly kicking off in the surrounding rooms, drunks argued loudly throughout the night, and the stench of neglect hung over the entire place like a damp blanket.

Andrea hated it there, but Jeff couldn't have cared less where he was living right now. Time seemed to have stood still as a multitude of emotions dominated his every waking moment. Grief, guilt, anger, rage, guilt again, and always grief . . . It was never-ending, and he couldn't see the faintest glimmer of light at the end of the tunnel. He'd had it all, and now he had nothing.

Andrea was back on her meds, and they had stabilised her

to the point where she was no longer flipping from high to low every few minutes. Now she was just sad, and Jeff was drained from having constantly to comfort her without getting any comfort himself. It wasn't easy after everything she'd done and, as hard as he tried, he just couldn't shake off the niggling suspicion that she was a little more sad about the fact that she knew he no longer felt the same way about her than she was about losing Skye.

But he was determined not to allow those thoughts to cloud his mind today. For Skye's sake, he just wanted to get through this with as much dignity as he could muster.

The chapel service was mercifully short, and Jeff was glad of the chance to have a few moments of privacy on the short drive to the cemetery afterwards. The hearse had arrived a few minutes before them, and Jeff could see as they made their way along the path that Skye's coffin had already been placed on the supports over the grave. In a bitter-sweet twist, her plot was on the same row as Hayley's and he gazed with sadness at the flowers still adorning Skye's friend's grave as they traipsed slowly past. Two young lives, gone in the blink of an eye. It was so very wrong. But at least they were as close to each other in death as they had been in life, so that was some small comfort.

The few members of Jeff's family who had turned up had been keeping a respectful distance throughout the day, afraid of upsetting Andrea who had made it clear as soon as she saw them that they weren't welcome. None of her side had even been informed about Skye's passing, much less invited to the funeral, so the rest of the mourners were mainly made up of a scattering of old neighbours and some of Skye's old school friends – who were all crying as if she had been the most popular girl in school.

Jeff found the girls' emotional wailings a little hard to swallow since Hayley's mum had told him about the bullying that both of their daughters had suffered, but he kept his thoughts to himself. He was determined not to do anything to make this already bad day worse.

The social worker, Val Dunn, had turned up at the end of the service, and Jeff had struggled to contain his anger when she'd come over to offer her condolences as he and Andrea left the chapel. He had wanted to scream at her that this was her fault; that Skye would never have run away and ended up getting murdered if Val hadn't gone back on her promise and dumped her in that children's home instead of placing her with a nice family. But, again, he had kept his mouth shut.

Jones and Dean had both come along to pay their last respects, and Jeff was touched that they had taken the time out to support him and Andrea when they had both done so much already. In the weeks since that awful viewing of Skye's body, not a day had gone by when Jones hadn't rung, if not actually called round to the B and B to ask if there was anything they needed, anything he could do. But what Jeff was most grateful for was the money that the two officers had raised from their colleagues at the station to put towards the funeral. They had called round yesterday to give him the cheque, and he had been totally blown away by their kindness.

When at last they reached the graveside, Andrea broke down at the sight of the coffin and fell to her knees in a sobbing heap. Battling his own breaking heart, Jeff pulled her firmly back up to her feet and held her close, whispering, 'It's all right, she's at peace now. Let's just get through this last bit, then it'll all be over.'

As the vicar blessed Skye's soul and prayed over the coffin as it was lowered into the ground, a verger made his way through the mourners with a box of earth for them to throw into the grave. But just as Andrea had thrown her handful in, she spotted Shirley standing to the back of the crowd and screamed, 'What's *she* doing here? She's got no right! Tell her to go, Jeff! Tell her to go! I don't want her here!'

Jeff hadn't noticed that Shirley was there, so he didn't immediately know who Andrea was talking about. But when he glanced round and saw Jones approaching her, his stomach did a little flip. Shirley and Jeff hadn't spoken since he and Andrea had left her place that day and gone to the B and B, but Andrea had been quizzing him about her ever since. Desperate to keep his wife on an even keel so that they could bury Skye without drama, Jeff had adamantly denied that anything had happened, but he knew that Andrea didn't believe him. And he supposed it hadn't helped that he'd been making excuses whenever Andrea tried to get him to have sex with her, but he just couldn't bring himself to do it. Too much had happened, and the scars of what he'd been through were still too raw.

When Shirley nodded her agreement to whatever Jones had said and walked away, Jeff sighed and turned back to the grave to throw his handful of dirt in. Jones had obviously asked her to leave and, respectful woman that she was, Shirley had gone without questioning why she wasn't welcome after everything she had done for Jeff and Andrea. But that was her all over: always putting others before herself – whether or not they deserved her consideration.

When it was all over, Andrea declared that she wanted to go straight back to the B and B. Jeff would have preferred to go to the pub to get slaughtered, but no amount of alcohol was going to shift the cloud of gloom that had been hovering over his head for the past few months. And now that he didn't even have the hope that Skye would be found and brought home to hold onto, the future held no joy for him.

As the mourners said their farewells and began to drift away, and the gravediggers began to shovel the dirt back into the grave, Jeff stared down at the coffin one last time and whispered, 'Goodnight, God bless, sweetheart,' before leading Andrea back to the car.

27

'You're dead.'

'What?' Confused by Tom's words, Skye stared up at him from her seat at the kitchen table.

'I said you're dead,' Tom repeated, grinning as he slapped a photograph down on the table in front of her. He'd cut it from the front page of the *Manchester Evening News* after seeing the headline on a newspaper stand on his way home from work, and he'd been dying to show it to her.

Skye stared down blankly at the picture, unsure at first what she was looking at. But her stomach gave a sickening lurch when she gazed at the headline: *Murdered Local Girl Laid To Rest*. And when she then saw the face of the man and woman who were standing beside the grave, her heart started to pound so hard in her chest that she feared it might explode.

'That's my mum and dad,' she gasped, gazing back up at Tom with shock in her eyes. 'I don't understand.'

'It's quite simple,' he said, squatting down beside her with a strange little smile on his lips. 'They've given up on you.'

'But there's a coffin,' Skye croaked. 'How can they have a coffin if I'm not there?'

'It's what they call a mock funeral,' Tom explained. 'People do that when someone's gone missing and they're fed up of waiting for them to come back. They want to get their own lives back on track, so they bury an empty box to tie up the loose ends. They probably took out life insurance on you after you first went missing,' he went on. 'But they wouldn't have been able to claim on it until they buried you.'

'But they can't bury me if I'm not there,' Skye protested, horrified to think that her parents had written her off like this.

'It's perfectly legal,' Tom told her. 'After so long, the law lets you declare someone as dead so you can get on with your own life. But this is good,' he went on, taking her hand in his. 'Now we don't have to worry about anyone recognising you, because they all think you're dead.'

'But I'm not,' Skye said plaintively as tears began to slide down her cheeks. 'And why did they have to say I'd been murdered? That's just horrible.'

'They always say that when they haven't got a body,' said Tom. 'It makes it look better in the news. *And* gets them more sympathy,' he added scathingly.

'But I don't want them to think I'm dead,' Skye moaned. 'That makes it feel like I'm never going to see them again.'

The smile slid from Tom's lips, and the expression in his eyes hardened as he peered into hers. 'Why are you still thinking about seeing them again after everything they've done? Have you forgotten that they tried to frame you for attempted murder?'

'No,' Skye sobbed. 'But—'

'But nothing,' snapped Tom. 'They never loved you. They said you were the child from hell and they wished you'd never been born. Why do you think they didn't bother looking for you after you ran away? They only tried to find you after the police got involved, so they could have you locked up instead of your mum and get you out of their lives once and for all. Does that sound like love to you?'

Skye shook her head and looked down at the floor.

'*I'm* the only one who's ever loved you,' Tom went on bitterly, 'but nothing I do is ever good enough for you, is it? I gave you that ring and bought you all those lovely clothes; I even got rid of Chloe for you. But you haven't changed. You're still an ungrateful little bitch.'

'I'm not ungrateful,' Skye croaked, shocked by how fast his mood had turned. 'I'm just sad.'

'Well, you've got no reason to be.' Tom dropped her hand and pushed himself back up to his feet. 'This could have been the start of a whole new life for us, but if all you're going to do is cry about the past, what's the point? If you'd rather be with them, you might as well just go. See how sad you feel when they chuck you in prison and leave you to rot.'

'Don't say that,' Skye cried, her chest heaving.

'Why not? It's true,' said Tom. 'But then, you're too stupid to accept the truth, aren't you?' he went on nastily. 'You just want to lie around like a beached whale, taking, taking, taking. You make me sick – do you know that? I mean, look at you.' He drew his head back and sneered at her. 'Fat, ugly, *and* stupid. Who would ever put up with you, apart from me? Your mum and dad already hate you, so how do you think they'd react if you turned up looking like that?'

'Stop it,' Skye sobbed, rocking to and fro on her chair as he ranted. 'You're scaring me.'

'You deserve it,' spat Tom. 'After everything I've done for you, I can't believe you can betray me like this.'

'I haven't done anything,' Skye protested.

'You didn't need to,' Tom hissed. 'Your reaction to that

picture said it all. I thought you'd be happy, but now I know you don't really care about me, I can't even bear to look at you.'

'Where are you going?' Skye asked when he snatched his keys off the ledge and stalked towards the door.

'Don't question me,' he barked over his shoulder. Then, hesitating before opening the door, he turned and glared at her, saying, 'You've had it too easy for too long, that's your trouble. I've gone easy on you lately, but it's time I started putting my foot down, seeing that's the only time I ever get any respect round here. Things are going to change from now on, so you'd better get ready.'

'What do you mean?' Skye asked, unnerved by the intensity in his eyes as he spoke.

Tom walked out without answering, and she jumped when he slammed the door so hard that it rattled the shelves and caused the clock in which she kept her secret key to fall over. Tears still rolling down her cheeks, she couldn't even muster up the energy to stroke Bernie when he came over and rested his head on her thigh after Tom's car had screeched away from the house. Everything just felt too painful right now.

Sobbing again when the all too familiar taste of bile flooded her mouth, she got up and ran to the bathroom. She'd been sick for weeks, and anything and everything set her off. The smell of Tom's cigarettes, food, drink – everything. Tom said she must have picked up a stomach bug, and had been buying all sorts of foul-tasting medicines for her to take. None of them worked, and some even made her feel worse, because they gave her stomach cramps as well as the relentless nausea.

Secretly terrified that she might be seriously ill, she longed to be a child being looked after by her mum and dad again. She knew they didn't love her or they would never have betrayed her like they had; but she had created a romanticised scenario in her mind of them welcoming her home with open arms and telling the police that they had got it wrong and she shouldn't go to prison.

It was just a dream, though. A stupid, ridiculous dream that was never going to come true – especially not now they had decided to declare her dead.

Skye didn't understand how any parent could do something like that to their own child, but she supposed Tom had been dead right when he'd said that they hated her and wanted that chapter of their life to be over with so they could move on without her.

When she stopped vomiting at last, she traipsed wearily back down to the kitchen and slumped down onto the chair before reaching for the photograph. She wished Tom hadn't cut it out, because she would have liked to have been able to read the story that went with it. But it would probably be a pack of lies from her mum and dad; pretending to be sad, when really they were glad.

Skye stared long and hard at the faces of the people who were standing by the grave alongside her parents, but the photo was very grainy and she couldn't really see them clearly enough to gauge if she recognised them or not. The one she was really looking for definitely wasn't there, though. She'd have known Hayley even if her back had been turned, and it saddened her all over again to think that her one-time best friend hadn't even bothered to put on an act and go to her mock funeral.

As another wave of self-pity washed over her, Skye angrily scrunched the picture up in her hand. She might as well have died for real, for all they cared. But they could all go to hell. If ever she had doubted Tom when he had said that they had never loved her, this was all the confirmation she needed that they were glad to be shot of her. And they hadn't even done it nicely; they'd had to go and claim that she'd been murdered so that people would take pity on them and overlook what bad parents they had been. They disgusted her, and she was never going to think about them again.

And this time she meant it.

After his row with Skye, Tom drove further out into the countryside. He'd done a drive-around a few days earlier and had spotted several derelict barns that looked interesting. It was dark enough this evening so that he could take a closer look without fear of being spotted by any suspicious farmers or passers-by.

The barn he'd been particularly keen to check out was set much further back from the road than the others, and the pathway which led to it had more or less merged into the untended field it occupied. It was pretty much obscured from view by the high, unkempt hedgerow which separated it from the road, which made it perfect for people who didn't want to be seen coming and going in the middle of the night. But, best of all, the farmhouse to which it belonged was no longer occupied.

He drove slowly up to the farmhouse now and got out to take a look through the windows. It was much larger than his house, and he might actually have considered moving into it if it hadn't been in such a bad state of disrepair. Huge chunks of the roof seemed to be missing, which meant there would probably be a serious damp problem to contend with; and the windows and doors were so badly bowed it would be impossible to keep the place warm when winter hit. So, no, the house was out of the question. But the barn was definitely usable.

Skye was fast asleep on the couch when Tom arrived back home later that night. He gazed down at her for a while, taking in the powdery white streaks of dried tears on her flushed cheeks, and the protective way she was cradling her belly in sleep even though she didn't even seem to have realised yet that she was pregnant.

That thing that was growing inside her was a major drawback to Tom's plans, and he resented the sight of her slowly swelling stomach. He needed it to be gone before he started his next venture, but he was quickly running out of time and nothing seemed to be shifting the damn thing.

He had taken down his website after having had second thoughts about the last video he'd uploaded of Chloe. His customers enjoyed watching the girls being abused while they were unconscious, because children were at their most helpless when they were tied up and knocked out. But he supposed that some might feel funny about watching a child being abused after death. The lead-up to it was okay, because it was undoubtedly a turn-on to see a child begging for its life. But showing the actual act had been a step too far, so he had taken it down before anyone could think about reporting him.

Since then, he had gone back to trying to connect with girls on WhisperBox, but he still hadn't found a suitable replacement for Skye. And that was disappointing, because there was a great market out there just waiting to be tapped. All he'd needed was a venue where the men could meet the girls in private, without it being connected to Tom in any traceable way. And now he'd found the perfect barn, he was eager to get started. But Skye's growing stomach would be a major turn-off for his clients, and it pissed Tom off to think of all the money he could potentially lose because of her.

As he stared down at her now, the anger churned his stomach. And before he could stop himself, he fisted his hand and rammed it into her belly.

Skye screamed as the pain woke her immediately. She pulled her knees up to cover her stomach as tears spurted from her eyes.

'It's okay,' Tom said, squatting beside her and stroking her terrified face. 'You were having a bad dream, but I'm here now – you're safe.'

Skye gaped confusedly up at him through her tears. She didn't know what was going on. It didn't feel like she'd been dreaming, but if Tom said she had then she must have been. But if it had been a dream, why did it hurt so much?

'Are you okay?' Tom asked as he watched the doubts flit through her eyes.

'My stomach hurts,' she sobbed.

'That's because you were hitting yourself when I came in,' Tom told her. 'I was just about to stop you when you woke up screaming. You must have been having a nightmare. I'll go and get you a drink to calm you down.'

Confused, Skye cradled her aching stomach when Tom went into the kitchen. When he came back a couple of minutes later and handed a cup to her before sitting next to her, she raised it to her lips. But then she gagged when she caught the scent of the wine.

'I don't think I can drink it,' she moaned, her mouth flooding with saliva. 'The smell's making me feel sick.'

'I've put something in it to settle your stomach and help you relax,' Tom told her, guiding the cup back up to her lips. 'You've let yourself go lately,' he went on as she drank some.

'But I'm going to help you get back on your feet, 'cos we can't have you going to your wedding looking like this, can we? No one likes fat brides.'

'Do you really think I'm fat?' Skye asked, mortified. 'I knew I'd put a bit of weight on, 'cos some of my clothes are getting tight. But I didn't think I was that bad.'

'Well, you are,' Tom said bluntly. 'And I'll probably go off you if you get any bigger, so you need to stop being so greedy. Drink up.'

Skye forced herself to take another sip. Then, frowning, she said, 'You don't think I could be pregnant, do you? Only I think I might have missed a period. Or maybe even two,' she added uncertainly. 'And with all the sickness . . .'

'Don't be daft,' Tom scoffed, jabbing his finger hard into her belly. 'That's fat, not a baby. Anyway, I can't have them, so if you are it can't be mine.'

'I haven't slept with anyone else,' Skye blurted out.

'You'd better not have,' said Tom, gazing down at her with suspicion in his eyes. 'Because I'd kill you if you ever betrayed me like that.'

'I haven't!' Skye insisted. 'I haven't even seen anyone.'

'Then you're just fat, like I said in the first place,' said Tom. 'And you need to stop being so greedy.'

'But I hardly eat anything,' Skye murmured. 'Everything makes me sick.'

'You must be doing it in your sleep,' Tom told her, a look of concern in his eyes now. 'If you're doing that, *and* punching yourself as well, I'll have to keep an eye on you.'

'What do you mean?' Skye asked, unnerved by his serious tone.

'It could be a symptom of mental illness,' Tom explained grimly. 'Like your mum.'

His words sent a chill through Skye, and she gripped the cup a little tighter.

'If you do it again we'll have to think about taking you to a doctor, because it's definitely not normal,' Tom went on. 'But don't worry about it for now. Just finish your drink and let's go to bed. It's been a long day, and I think we could both do with a rest.'

28

The next few weeks were harrowing for Skye as, morning after morning, she woke with fresh marks on her stomach. Tom was being supportive, but she just couldn't understand why she was trying to hurt herself in her sleep and the thought that she might have the same illness as her mum terrified her. And on top of the worry of that, she was still being sick and she felt bloated all the time.

Sure that Tom was going off her, because she kept catching him giving her funny looks, she took all the different medicines he bought for her and prayed that one of them would eventually work and she could go back to normal.

Unable to clear the gloomy thoughts from her head when she was alone in the house, Skye started working her way through the books from the living-room shelf unit. They all seemed to be historical romances, which she thought was an odd choice for Tom's soldier cousin to have made, given that he must be – she assumed – fairly young. But the tales of downtrodden scullery maids being hauled through the fires of servitude by their evil masters before finding true love quickly caught her imagination. She found herself yearning to run carefree through a cornfield before falling into the arms of a real-life Prince Charming who would whisk her away from her troubles and devote his life to making her happy.

But it was just a dream and, no matter how much Skye lost herself in the fantasy while she was reading, reality was always lurking in the background, waiting to slam her back down to Earth as soon as she put down the book.

The pains started five weeks after Tom had told her about her parents 'burying' her. Terrified that the punches she'd been raining on herself during the night had seriously damaged her stomach, Skye took four paracetamol and then ran a bath, hoping that a relaxing soak in the warm water would soothe the awful pain.

Not five minutes after she had climbed in and started reading her latest book, she heard Bernie barking in the kitchen below. Immediately nervous, because he never barked as loudly or as insistently as that, she climbed quickly back out and pulled on her dressing gown. She hadn't heard anybody knocking at the door but she crept into her bedroom and peeped out of the window all the same. Nobody seemed to be out there, so she tiptoed down the landing to check out back. Again, she saw nothing, so she went downstairs to see if Bernie had hurt himself.

The dog was standing at the back door, still barking, the fur on the back of his neck standing on end.

'What's the matter, boy?' Skye asked, cradling her aching stomach with her hand as she walked over to him. 'Has something spooked you?'

He stopped barking when she stroked him, and wagged his tail. But he was still edgy, and she noticed that he kept cocking an ear as if listening to something she couldn't hear. Guessing that an animal must have come too close to the house for his liking, she made herself a hot drink after giving him a cuddle, and carried it back up to the bath.

★   ★   ★

Outside, as Skye re-immersed herself in her latest romance, the man who had crept into the garden via the untended field beyond ran up the path with a pair of bolt cutters in his hand. After cutting through the thick chain that was securing the gates, he pulled them quickly open and waved to the man behind the wheel of the van that was parked a little way down the road.

'All clear?' the driver, Eric, asked when he'd reversed the van through the gates and onto the drive.

'Yeah, the car's not here, and the dog's inside,' his son John told him as he hopped into the passenger seat. 'Best hurry, though,' he cautioned, glancing nervously around for approaching vehicles. 'There's a shed round the back with a load of boxes in it. You start loading up while I check it out.'

Eric nodded and reversed on up the path towards the house. They had meant to come back a lot sooner than this, but a short prison stint after being caught with a van full of stolen cable had forced them to put their plans on hold. Eager now to get his hands on the potential gold mine of scrap metal he'd seen the last time they were here, Eric parked up and jumped out, then opened the van's back doors to start chucking stuff in while his son ran over to the shed.

John gave the shed door a couple of kicks after finding that it was locked, but quickly realised that wasn't going to do the trick when he saw that it opened outwards instead of inwards. Running back to the van, he grabbed the crowbar from under his dad's seat and then ran back to jemmy his way in.

A foul stench smacked him in the face when at last the door opened, and he grimaced as he batted his way through the cobwebs that were laced at eye level across the frame. As his vision adjusted to the dimness inside the shed, he noticed the black carcasses of a load of flies littering the floor and guessed that something must have died in here. Most probably a stray cat, he thought; or a rabbit, or a badger, or something like that. Whatever it was, it smelled disgusting, and he couldn't wait to check out the boxes and get the hell out of there.

A load of rusted old lawnmowers and other gardening equipment was standing in the far right corner of the shed. John gave these the once-over and made a mental note to have his dad take a look at them when they were done, because they might fetch a couple of quid – if they had any room left in the van.

The first of the boxes that were stacked in the left-hand corner yielded nothing but old, musty-smelling clothes, so he pushed them aside and started on the boxes that were sitting behind them. It quickly became apparent that these were all empty, and he was pissed-off to think that he'd wasted all that time breaking in here for nothing. About to go and help his dad, he hesitated when he realised that the buzzing sound he'd been hearing since he came into the shed was coming from the old chest freezer that most of the empty boxes had been stacked on top of. Curious to know if the house owner was keeping roadkill in there, and that was where the smell was coming from, he raised the lid gingerly to take a peek.

Eric was struggling to heave an old motorbike chassis into the back of the van when he heard John cry out. He dropped the bike, hopped out of the van, and rushed through the grass – colliding with John who was running hell for leather the other way.

'What the hell's up with you?' he asked when he saw the look of horror on his son's face.

'There's a fuckin' body in there,' John spluttered, pointing back at the shed. 'Let's get out of here!'

'Don't talk daft,' Eric scoffed, sure that John must have imagined whatever he thought he'd seen. 'It's that film you had on last night. I told you not to watch it on your own.'

'It's not the fucking film,' John squeaked. 'It's a body – I saw it. Go and have a look if you don't believe me!'

A bemused smirk on his lips, Eric pushed his son aside and walked round to the shed. 'I can't see no bodies,' he called, after standing in the doorway for a moment and squinting at the assorted junk.

'It's in the freezer at the back,' John told him, keeping his distance.

Muttering 'Chicken-livered idiot' under his breath, Eric made his way over to the freezer and raised the lid.

At first, he didn't realise what he was looking at. But when he leaned over to take a closer look and saw a pair of eyes staring back up at him through the thick layer of ice, a sharp pain tore through his chest.

'Holy fucking shit!' he gasped, taking a stumbling step back. 'John! *JOHN*!'

'I'm not coming back in there,' John called from the doorway. 'Let's just sack it off. Come on, Dad, this is heavy shit.'

'I think I'm having a heart attack,' Eric moaned, clutching at his chest as he staggered back outside. 'You'll have to drive.'

John put an arm around his dad's waist and helped him back to the van. Then, mindless of the still-open back doors, and the things his dad had thrown inside falling back out as he drove, he gunned the van back onto the road, the wheel in one hand, his mobile phone in the other.

'Police!' he yelped when his call was answered. 'I've just found a dead body.'

'What the fuck are you doing?' the old man hissed, trying to snatch the phone away from him.

Swerving wildly onto the other side of the road as he switched the phone to his other hand, John told the operator what he'd seen and where to find it. Then, disconnecting the call, he opened his window and tossed the phone into the field they were passing.

'What did you do that for?' Eric gasped, his face pale and sweaty as the pain in his chest increased.

'Don't worry, it was a pay-as-you-go so they won't be able to trace the call back to me,' John assured him. 'But I told you that fella looked like a weirdo when we spoke to him that time, and if you die 'cos of whatever he's done I'm gonna make sure the fucker goes down for it.'

'I'm not fucking dying,' Eric protested.

John cast a sideways glance at his father and thought otherwise. But he kept the thought to himself, and drove on in search of a hospital.

29

'Please stop it, Bernie,' Skye moaned, clutching at her aching head when the dog jumped up from his blanket and started barking again. 'It's probably just a fox or something. But it can't get in, and you're not allowed out, so just give it up – *please*.'

It was an hour since she'd got out of the bath and she felt no better than when she'd gone in. If anything, she felt worse and, as much as she often these days dreaded the sound of his car pulling up outside, she wished desperately that Tom would come home early today, because she was getting seriously scared about these pains.

Slumped over the table with her hands covering her ears to shut out the sound of Bernie's barking, she didn't hear the shuffle of feet outside. But when a loud bang came at the door a few seconds later, she almost fell off her chair with shock.

Her mouth bone-dry with terror when another bang shook the floor, she pulled herself up to her feet and gasped with fear when she saw the flashing lights of a police vehicle outside. Immediately sure that Chloe must have grassed her up, she ran towards the larder to try and hide in the cellar. But the back door flew open before she'd taken two steps and she fell to her knees as the kitchen became a blur of uniforms and shouting policemen. Then, curling into a ball when another pain ripped through her belly, she gritted her teeth.

'What's your name, love?' a policeman asked, kneeling beside her.

'Skye,' she sobbed. 'But please don't arrest me, I didn't do it, I swear I didn't.'

'Okay, calm down,' the officer said as one of his colleagues dragged Bernie past with a wire loop around his neck and the rest of the cops spread out to search the house. 'Is anybody else here with you?'

Skye shook her head as the tears streamed down her cheeks. She cried, 'He's at work. But it's not his fault – he didn't know.'

'Didn't know what, love?'

'That my mum stabbed my dad then blamed me,' sobbed Skye. 'I didn't do it, though,' she insisted again, giving the officer an imploring look. 'Honest, I didn't.'

'All right, take it easy,' he said, concerned when he saw a pool of blood spreading out on the floor around her thighs. 'Let's just get you looked at, then you can tell us all about it. Okay?'

Skye nodded. Then she screamed when another wave of pain swept over her.

30

Jeff was packing his things into a holdall when a knock came at the door later that evening. He'd tried, he really had, but he just couldn't take it any more. The B and B was so depressing that it was starting to make him feel ill, and Andrea was doing his head in, pretending that she was still ill when he knew for a fact that she was completely stable because he'd been making sure that she took her tablets.

He knew exactly why she was doing it. She knew his feelings had changed, and she couldn't bear it that she was losing him. It was sad, and he wished with all his heart that he could feel differently. But there was no use denying it. He just didn't love her any more, and the longer they stayed together, the longer it would take for Andrea to accept it and let him go.

That was why he had decided to leave. He had no idea where he was going to go from here, but a park bench would be preferable to spending one more night in a bed with a woman he no longer loved. And once he was gone, she would get all the help and support she needed from her case workers to get back on her feet.

It still hurt, though, and his expression must have reflected his pain when he opened the door to find PCs Jones and Dean in the corridor, because they both gave him a concerned look.

'Is this a bad time?' Jones asked, flicking a glance over Jeff's shoulder at the closed bathroom door, from behind which they could hear the sound of Andrea crying.

'You could say that,' Jeff said quietly. 'I've just told her I'm leaving, and she's not taking it too well.'

'Sorry to hear that, mate,' Jones murmured, giving him a sympathetic look.

Jeff gave a resigned shrug. 'It's not easy, but she'll be better off without me in the long run. Anyway, what's up?' he asked then.

'I know this is a bad time,' Dean said apologetically. 'But we've got some news that you're both going to want to hear.'

31

Skye had been drifting in and out of consciousness for two days before she came round properly, and she felt sick when she began to surface. But the nausea was instantly replaced by fear when she peeled her eyes open and gazed groggily around the unfamiliar room. Sure that she was in prison, a tiny squeak of terror escaped her dry lips.

'It's all right, sweetheart – I'm here.'

Her heart lurched at the sound of the voice and, when she turned her head in the direction it had come from and saw Jeff sitting in a chair by the window, her eyes flooded with tears.

'Daddy?'

'Hello, baby,' Jeff whispered, his own eyes glistening as he got up and came to sit on the bed beside her and hold her hand. 'Sshhh,' he crooned, stroking her hair as she clung to him. 'It's all over now. You're safe.'

'Where am I?' she asked. 'Is this prison?'

'No, you're in hospital,' Jeff told her, holding her close. Then, softly, because he knew it would be a shock, he said, 'I'm so sorry, love, but you lost the baby.'

'*What*?' Skye pulled herself free and gazed up at him in confusion.

'You lost a lot of blood and went into shock, that's why you're here,' Jeff explained. 'And it was already dead, so there was nothing they could do. I'm so sorry, love.'

'But – but Tom said I wasn't pregnant,' Skye gasped, gazing down at her stomach in disbelief. 'I couldn't have been.'

Jeff's eyes glinted with anger at the mention of that name. But he gritted his teeth and kept his voice even as he said, 'There is no Tom, love.'

'Yes, there is,' Skye insisted, crying again as the pain of realising that she had just lost the baby she hadn't known she was carrying settled over her. 'He loves me, and he would have loved our baby, so *he* should be here, not you. You're just trying to keep him away because he kept me safe when you and Mum wanted me dead.'

'Don't say that,' Jeff murmured, shocked that she would think such a thing. 'We'd *never* wish you dead. We love you, and it nearly destroyed us when we thought we'd lost you.'

'Liar!' Skye cried, wrenching her hand free. 'Tom told me everything. You blamed me for stabbing you when you knew it was Mum, and then told everyone I'd been murdered so you could bury me and forget about me.'

'Sweetheart, that's just not true,' Jeff insisted, feeling help-less now because he didn't know where this was coming from. 'I don't know what you've been told, but I swear we never blamed you. Is that why you ran away?' he asked then. 'Because you thought you were going to get into trouble?'

'You said it on the news,' Skye reminded him. 'You said I'd tried to kill you both, and you wished I'd never been born. Don't *lie*!' she screeched when Jeff shook his head. 'Tom *told* me. And how would he know it was you unless he'd seen you?'

'His name isn't Tom, it's Jamie,' Jeff told her. 'And he's a murderer.'

'You're lying.' Skye glared at him through her tears.

'No, he's not, love.'

Skye jerked her head round at the sound of the voice, and shrank back against her pillow when she saw PC Jones standing in the doorway.

Val Dunn stepped into the room behind Jones and, guessing from the look in Skye's eyes that she had seen the uniform and assumed the worst, said, 'Don't be scared – we just need to talk to you.'

'What's *she* doing here?' Skye asked Jeff, her voice little more than a whisper as her fear intensified.

'We're here to help,' Jones told her.

'No, you're not,' Skye whimpered. 'You're going to arrest me, aren't you?' Then, swallowing loudly when something else occurred to her, she said, 'Did I really lose the baby, or have you taken it away and given it to *her* 'cos you think I'm bad?'

Val placed her hand on Jeff's shoulder when he opened his mouth to explain, and gave a surreptitious shake of her head. They were aware from some of the things that Skye had said to the first officer she'd spoken with at the house before losing consciousness and being rushed to hospital that Jamie Thornton – or Tom, as Skye had known him – had done a pretty thorough job of grooming her during the time he'd held her. It was going to take time and careful handling to change her romantic view of him and make her accept that she had been his victim and not his consensual lover. They had held a meeting to discuss how best to handle the situation when Skye came round, and it had been agreed that they wouldn't tell her about the explicit sex videos that Thornton had uploaded onto his website, featuring not only her but also Chloe Lester – whose remarkable likeness to Skye had caused both the police and Jeff to think that she was actually Skye when her body had been found. They had also decided not to tell her just yet about Hayley having passed away, because they thought that it would upset her too much. But they needed her to understand that Jamie Thornton was not who he had claimed to be, in order to persuade her to tell them the truth of what she had endured at his hands.

'Why don't you go and see if Andrea's finished speaking with the doctor while we explain things to Skye?' Val suggested.

Jeff was reluctant to let this woman talk to Skye when he still blamed her for Skye having gone missing in the first place, but he had to admit that he wasn't doing too good a job of it himself so far. So, conceding defeat, he stood up and backed towards the door, telling Skye, 'I'll be right outside if you need me.'

Val sat down when he'd left the room, and shuffled the chair a little closer to the bed as Jones took a seat on the other side.

'We know you don't want to hear this,' she started gently, 'but the man you knew as Tom was not a good man, and whatever he told you about your parents was a lie. He just wanted to make you think that he was the only one you could trust so he could control you. It's called grooming.'

'No.' Skye shook her head. 'He loves me. We're going to get married. Look.' She held up her hand, and frowned when she saw that her finger was bare. 'Where's my ring?'

'It's been taken for evidence,' Jones told her.

'But it's mine,' Skye protested. 'Tom bought it for me.'

'No, my love, he didn't,' Val informed her. 'It belonged to the lady who owned the house, and he stole it from her after he murdered her. And then he moved into her house so that he could lure young girls like yourself there.'

'You don't even know him,' Skye muttered defensively. 'He's not like that – he wouldn't hurt anyone.'

'The old lady's body was found in a freezer in the shed,' Jones told her. 'And he's already confessed to killing her,' he added, trying to conceal his disgust at the memory of the almost gloating way in which Jamie Thornton had spoken about his crimes when they had collared him after removing Skye from the house. It seemed as if he had decided that, if he was going down for a long one, he might as well do it in a blaze of notoriety and admit to being a serial killer. Yet, strangely, despite having admitted to killing three people, Thornton had adamantly refused to accept that there had been anything inappropriate about his relationships with the girls – despite his first victim having been just thirteen years old, and the fact that he had drugged them all in order to render them helpless as he videoed himself abusing them. In his mind, they had all wanted it as much as he had.

A shadowy memory of Bernie trying desperately to get into the shed the first time she let him out had just flitted through Skye's mind. But she quickly shook it away, convinced that they were making it all up.

'He also murdered two young girls,' Jones went on. 'Their names were Sarah and Chloe, and they were both a little younger than you.'

'Chloe?' Skye repeated numbly.

'Did you know her?' Val asked, guessing from her reaction that she had.

Skye nodded, and croaked, 'She stayed with us for a few weeks, but then Tom took her home.'

'He didn't,' said Jones. 'He murdered her and dumped her body by the canal. She was wearing a necklace when she was found,' he went on gently. 'And it has since been identified as a necklace that was given to you.'

'My angel?' Skye peered up at him with agony in her eyes. 'Hayley gave it to me for my birthday.'

Conscious of their decision to avoid the subject of Hayley, Jones said, 'You look tired, so I think we'll leave it at that for today. We'll talk to you again when you're feeling a little stronger.'

'Are you going to send me to prison?' Skye asked.

'Of course not,' Val assured her. 'You've done nothing wrong, and you are *not* in trouble. The police just need to know what happened while you were staying at that house, so they can put their case together properly.'

'Are you going to take me away again?'

Val saw the dread in Skye's eyes and shook her head. 'No, you'll be allowed to go home when you leave here,' she promised. 'But I'll still be involved, because you've been through a traumatic experience and I'll need to monitor your progress and make sure you're settling back into normal life.'

Skye stared at her after she said this, and chewed on her lip. Then, her voice tiny, she asked, 'Did I really lose the baby, or have you given it to someone who can look after it better than me?'

'I'm really sorry, but you *did* lose it,' Val told her gently, omitting to add what all the adults who were involved in this case were thinking: that it was a blessing the baby hadn't survived. Skye might believe that she would have wanted it now, but her feelings would undoubtedly have changed once she'd faced up to the reality of the situation, and she might well have subconsciously transferred the blame for its father's actions onto its head at some point – which would have been terrible both for her *and* the baby.

Skye's face crumpled as the realisation that she hadn't just lost her baby but had actually *killed* it settled over her. Her dad had said that it was already dead when it was born, and that must have been because she'd been punching it. And it didn't matter that she hadn't known it was in there, or that she'd had no control over her actions. She had killed her baby, and she would never forgive herself for that.

'I want Tom,' she sobbed as fresh tears began to cascade down her cheeks.

Val asked Jones to go and fetch Skye's parents. Then, gazing down at Skye when he'd gone, she said, 'I know this is hard for you to understand right now, my love, but you have got to try and forget about Tom. We'll all do our very best to help you to get through this, so you never need to feel as though you're on your own. And if there's ever anything you feel uncomfortable discussing with your parents, I hope you know that you can always talk to me.'

Skye rolled onto her side without answering and sobbed into her pillow. She was the guilty one, not Tom, and she wished they would stop saying terrible things about him, because they didn't know him like she did. He was the only one who had ever really loved her, and she didn't believe that he had hurt those people. They were just trying to make her hate him so that she would have no one to protect her when they locked her up.

Jeff and Andrea had been sitting in silence in the corridor while Jones and the social worker spoke with Skye. They hadn't talked much since hearing that Skye had been found, and had been taking it in turns to sit beside her bed over the last two days while they waited for her to come round. And, now that she was back with them, they were both deep in thought about the future.

After hearing about the horrors that her child had suffered

at the hands of that depraved man, Andrea had realised that she had to stop thinking about herself and Jeff, and concentrate on Skye. In the weeks since they had buried that poor child who they had mistakenly thought was Skye, she had gone through agony: not only grieving for her daughter, but also for the loss of her marriage. She had been well for weeks, but had pretended not to be in order to keep Jeff from leaving. But it hadn't worked, and he had been on the verge of walking out when the news had come that Skye had been found. He hadn't left yet, but Andrea had realised that there was no point hanging onto him if his heart was no longer in it. It wouldn't be easy, because he was the only man she had ever truly loved – and she still did. But he was a good man and he deserved to be happy and, if that meant being away from her, then she was ready to let him go.

Determined that Skye should stay with her, she had already spoken to the housing officer about the urgency of them finding her somewhere to live; and she'd also spoken to her case worker about getting help to buy beds and furniture. Jeff would probably say that she wasn't ready to look after Skye on her own just yet, but she would do everything in her power to prove that she was.

Beside her, Jeff was also thinking about Skye. He hadn't really understood what Jones and Dean had meant when they had tried to warn him that Skye might be in denial about the man who had effectively abducted her, but he totally got it now. The evil bastard had fed her a pack of lies, and it broke Jeff's heart to think that Skye believed that he and Andrea hated her so much that they would try to pin the stabbing on her. But what really killed him was the thought of the physical abuse that his innocent child had endured at the hands of that beast, and the guilt that he hadn't been able to save her was already eating away at him. And, worse, it appeared that the grooming had started way before the stabbing, when, hidden behind the innocuous screen-name QTPye, this monster had gained his daughter's trust and got her to confide her inner thoughts by posing as a girl of the same age who understood how she felt.

This had all come to light after the police's IT experts had hacked into Skye's chat-room account and read the intimate conversations that she'd unwittingly had with the man. Jeff was ashamed to think that it had been going on right under his nose, and that he had never once realised how unhappy Skye was. More than that, he was ashamed to have been the cause of that misery. He'd thought she was unaffected by his and Andrea's fighting, but he couldn't have been more wrong. Skye had obviously been deeply hurt by the rift in her family, but with her parents too preoccupied with each other to notice her, and her only real-life friend often too ill to talk to, what choice had she had but to turn to a stranger for comfort?

'Jeff, Andrea . . . you can go in now.'

Jeff pushed his guilty thoughts to the back of his mind at the sound of Jones's voice. He stood up and thanked the man, and then turned to Andrea. She hadn't moved and, when he saw the fear in her eyes, he guessed that she was scared to face Skye because she felt every bit as guilty as he did.

'Come on, love,' he said softly, holding out his hand. 'I know it's hard, but she needs us.'

EPILOGUE

Shirley slowed the car down, and then came to a stop when she spotted the number of the aisle they were looking for.

'Is that Skye?' she asked when she gazed out through the window and saw a young girl kneeling beside a grave halfway along the row.

Jeff glanced out and said, 'Yeah, I think so,' as he reached over to the back seat for the flowers they had bought. 'Are you ready?' he asked then, unbuckling his seat belt.

'I think I'd better stay in the car,' Shirley said. 'There's a time and a place, and this isn't it,' she added, smiling to let him know that it was okay for him to go without her. 'I'll find the car park and wait for you there.'

Jeff nodded, and leaned over to kiss her. 'Won't be long.'

'Take as long as you need,' Shirley urged, stroking her swollen stomach. 'This little one will keep me occupied. I swear he must have smuggled a football in there while I wasn't looking.'

Jeff winked at her, and then climbed out of the car. The baby hadn't been planned, but he couldn't have been more delighted when Shirley had told him that she was pregnant. He'd told Skye and Andrea about it straight away, in order to save them from having to hear it from someone else. But he hadn't mentioned it since, because he hadn't wanted them to think he was rubbing their noses in his new-found happiness.

He and Andrea had been civil to each other since their split, but he knew it hadn't been easy for her and it was out of respect for her that he hadn't yet introduced Skye to Shirley. It would have to happen eventually, because she would soon have a little brother or sister. But Shirley was right: this was neither the time nor the place.

Skye hadn't heard the car, but she did hear the footsteps. A look of surprise came over her face when she glanced up and saw her dad walking towards her.

'What are you doing here?' she asked, wiping her hands on her jeans as she stood up to greet him.

'It's her anniversary,' said Jeff, nodding towards the other grave a little further down, in which he and Andrea had thought they'd been burying Skye at this time last year. 'I brought flowers.' He held up the bunches he was carrying. 'One for Chloe, and one for Hayley. Although I'm not sure she needs them,' he said, smiling as he gazed at the flowers already festooning Hayley's grave.

'She'd be touched that you bothered,' Skye told him, taking one of the bunches from his hand and squatting down to place them alongside the ones that she herself had brought. 'Where's Shirley?' she asked then, glancing round when she had straightened up.

'She's waiting in the car,' Jeff told her. 'She saw you down here, and didn't want you to think she was intruding.'

Skye sighed and gave him a mock-stern look. 'Dad, this is daft. I wish you'd all stop walking on eggshells around me.'

'It's not just you I'm thinking about – it's your mum as well,' Jeff reminded her.

'You've been separated for ages, and she's fine about it,' Skye assured him. 'Anyway,' she went on, a sly little smile coming onto her lips, 'she's got her eye on someone else, so she's not that bothered about you any more.'

'Really?' Jeff raised an eyebrow. 'Who's the lucky man?'

'That copper mate of yours,' Skye told him. 'Although I don't think he's realised yet.'

'Who, Jones?'

'Which one's he? The tall blond one, or the nice-looking dark-haired one.'

'The second.'

'Him, then.'

'Dean?' Jeff's eyebrow crept up a bit more. 'Wow. I'm surprised.'

'I don't see why.' Skye laughed. 'He's nice, and he looks a bit like you. I think he kind of likes her, as well,' she said then. ''Cos he's always calling round to see if we're okay. He makes out like it's just 'cos of what happened, but I can tell it's really her he's come to see. Doubt he'll ever say anything to her, though, 'cos he probably thinks he'll be treading on your toes.'

Jeff gazed at his daughter in wonderment. It had taken months for her to come to terms with her ordeal, and there had been times when he had thought that she would be scarred for ever. But with her mum's help, and the support of the police and Social Services, she had gradually accepted the truth of the situation and had been going from strength to strength ever since.

The final piece of the puzzle had fallen into place for her at Jamie Thornton's trial four months ago. It had dragged on for a couple of weeks, and Skye had bravely insisted on facing her abuser in court rather than give her evidence via a video link. She already knew by then that everything he had told her was a lie, but Jeff knew it had shocked her to learn that the man she had considered her saviour had been contemplating cutting his losses and disposing of her when she became pregnant, and only hadn't gone through with it because he hadn't been able to find a suitable replacement. It had also hurt her deeply to learn that *he* was the one who had been beating her stomach as she slept, in an effort to make her miscarry when the various medicines he'd been forcing her to take for her sickness had failed to do it.

But as shocked as she had been about all that, and as mortified as she had felt to face the court knowing that they had all seen extracts from the videos of herself and Chloe being raped and abused, Skye had held her head high after giving her evidence and had gone back to court every day afterwards to see out the rest of the trial. She had stared Jamie Thornton in the eye right up until the jury had delivered their verdicts of guilty on all counts, at which point she had calmly got up and walked out, letting her abuser know that she didn't give a damn how long a sentence the judge gave him.

Now, as Jeff looked at her, he saw no trace of the frightened, confused little girl she had been back then. Still not yet seventeen years of age, she had blossomed into the most beautiful self-assured young lady, and Jeff couldn't have been any more proud of her than he was right now.

'So, when am I going to meet her?' Skye asked, breaking into his thoughts. ''Cos there can't be long left, can there?'

'A couple of months,' Jeff told her. 'But you know where we are, and you're welcome to come round any time you like.'

'I'll give you a ring when I've finished my placement, so we can set something up,' Skye promised.

'How's that going?' Jeff asked. 'Still enjoying it?'

'It's great,' Skye said, smiling as she linked her arm through his and set off towards the other grave. 'I love being at the salon, and can't wait till I'm qualified and I can get a full-time job there. But I'll have to get my exams out of the way first and I'm dreading them.'

'You'll be fine,' Jeff assured her. 'I've got every confidence in you.'

'Let's see if you're still saying that when I want to cut *your* hair,' Skye teased. 'You're going to be my first victim after I qualify,' she warned him. 'You've had it like that for as long as I can remember, and I'm dying to drag you out of the 1980s.'

'Don't be so cheeky,' Jeff scolded, grinning. Then, 'So how's your mum getting on with Bernie? Is she used to him yet?'

'Not really.' Skye laughed. 'She says she likes him, but I think she's a bit scared of him.'

'Why? He's not vicious, is he?'

'Is he 'eck,' Skye scoffed. 'He's as soft as anything. I'm glad the police let me keep him 'cos it would have killed me if they'd put him down, poor thing.'

'Well, as long as you're happy,' said Jeff, putting his hand over hers and squeezing. 'That's all that matters.'

'I am,' Skye told him, gazing into his eyes as they walked. 'And you are, too, aren't you?'

'Yes, love, I am,' Jeff admitted. 'I'm sorry it didn't work out with your mum, but Shirley's a lovely woman.'

'I'm sure she is,' said Skye, a twinkle coming into her eye as she added, 'And your copper mate seems like a lovely man, too. So if you just give him a little nudge in the right direction next time you see him, we'll all be happy, won't we?'

'I guess so.' Jeff grinned. 'I'll see what I can do.'

They had reached Chloe's grave by now, and a feeling of

sadness settled over them both as they gazed down at it. In stark contrast to Hayley's well-tended, often-visited resting place, the only flowers adorning this one were the same ones that had been placed there in Skye's honour on the day of the funeral, and they were all long dead and shrivelled.

'God, it's such a shame,' Skye murmured wistfully. 'I can't believe he killed her like that. She was only a kid. And some of the stuff she told me about what her dad did to her . . .' She trailed off and shivered, before saying, 'She didn't deserve any of it.'

Jeff put his arm around her shoulder, and said, 'I know I shouldn't say it, but I'm just glad it wasn't you. It broke my heart when I had to leave you here that day.'

'Do you think she's at peace now?' Skye asked, resting her head on his chest.

'Definitely,' said Jeff. 'And she's got Hayley to look after her, hasn't she?'

'Yeah.' Skye reached up and touched her angel necklace. Then, sniffing back the tears that were stinging her eyes, she said, 'Let's go, Dad. It's time to move on.'

Jeff nodded and, taking her hand in his, strolled back along the path with her.